Advance praise for *Little Bones*

"If *Little Bones* were made into a movie, the ideal title song might be Leonard Cohen's haunting 'You Want It Darker,' for both works spin acerbic, grim, but ultimately affirming narratives from the shadows that dwell in the human heart and populate the cosmos at large. David Baillie's ingeniously plotted and gorgeously written chronicle of urban nomads living on the edge deserves comparison with the best of Peter Straub, Stephen King, and China Miéville.
—James Morrow, award-winning author of *Galápagos Regained*

"David Baillie writes about the marginalized, the forgotten, and the darkest of human conditions with compassion. He presents them with eloquence and magic. I aspire to be this good."
—Lauren B. Davis, author of *The Grimoire of Kensington Market, The Empty Room*, and *Our Daily Bread*

"*Little Bones* is an exceptional book—dark, sometimes brutally so, but also beautifully written and sometimes transcendent. The ending gave me goosebumps. David Baillie is a literary treasure."
—Elizabeth Hand, author of *Curious Toys and Generation Loss*

"*Little Bones* is written with heart. This is a richly descriptive book full of mystery, hope and survival with social commentary throughout. It's a riveting story written like punk rock poetry."
—Johnny Blitz, drummer for The Dead Boys

LITTLE BONES

ChiZine Publications

Distributed in Canada by
Fitzhenry & Whiteside Limited
195 Allstate Parkway
Markham, Ontario L3R 4T8
Phone: (905) 477-9700
e-mail: bookinfo@fitzhenry.ca

Distributed in the U.S. by
Consortium Book Sales & Distribution
34 Thirteenth Avenue, NE, Suite 101
Minneapolis, MN 55413
Phone: (612) 746-2600
e-mail: sales.orders@cbsd.com

Library and Archives Canada Cataloguing in Publication

Title: Little Bones / David Baillie.
Names: Baillie, David 1969- author.
Identifiers: Canadiana (print) 20190107367 | Canadiana (ebook) 20190107375 | ISBN 9781771485081
   (softcover) | ISBN 9781771485357 (hardcover) | ISBN 9781771485098 (PDF)
Classification: LCC PS8603.A44386 L58 2019 | DDC C813/.6—dc23

CHIZINE PUBLICATIONS
Peterborough, Canada
www.chizinepub.com
info@chizinepub.com

Edited by Sandra Kasturi
Copyedited and proofread by Leigh Teetzel

Canada Council   Conseil des arts
for the Arts   du Canada

We acknowledge the support of the Canada Council for the Arts which last year invested $20.1 million in writing and publishing throughout Canada.

ONTARIO ARTS COUNCIL
CONSEIL DES ARTS DE L'ONTARIO
an Ontario government agency
un organisme du gouvernement de l'Ontario

Published with the generous assistance of the Ontario Arts Council.

Printed in Canada

LITTLE
BONES

DAVID BAILLIE

For Grey, who overcame silence;
for Loch, who refused to be silent in the first place;

and

for Darcy, who knows—really knows—how to listen to me.

PROLOGUE

ANOTHER BOTTLE OF MILK.

After all, it had been his fault it fell off the table and smashed. The entire quart. It was only right that he should walk the six blocks to the dairy to buy another one. He had a quarter in his little fist, biting into his skin as he squeezed.

And Thomas, you make sure you bring me back the change, do you hear me?

That's what Mother had said as he left the house, his backside still stinging from the wallop he'd just received. Five sharp spanks that, strangely, kept time with Sinatra's newest song—*Young at Heart*—as it drifted effortlessly out of the radio cabinet. Father had not interfered, watching from the kitchen doorway and shaking his head sadly. But Thomas had a child's stiff endurance for unfair treatment, and he bore his lot in stoic silence.

Small and sullen, he avenged himself on sidewalk ants. On a wayward wildflower at the base of a streetlamp. On maple keys that had fluttered their unfortunate way into his path. All ground underfoot.

He made his way down the sidewalk, little feet stomping their vindictive way through the dusk that gathered in shop doorways, in between buildings, under the occasional tree. But the shadows reminded him that the dairy would close soon, and there was no milk delivery on Sunday.

He began to run, contemplated shortcuts, chose one.

IN THE NARROW COURTYARD behind the tenement, the coalman's horse and wagon waited in the gathering gloom. The swayback nag, broken-down old beast with the crisscross scars of its master's heavy lash along its rump, snorted as the child stopped short. The children in this part of the city avoided the coalman—intuition, maybe. There was just something about him: about his crook-backed posture and dry, dead voice; about the mechanical way he shoveled coal into the chutes; about the way he sometimes leered at them.

The grownups pretended sympathy, the way grownups did. The coalman was in his fifties and, thirty-odd years ago, had seen and done things in the Great War, the sorts of things that crawled into a man's soul like an infection. Incurable, mind-numbing. Some of the fathers, their own recent war experiences in Europe still haunting them, spoke authoritatively of this. They forgave the coalman his odd demeanor without the inconvenience of asking him anything directly. A man had a right, they said, to tend to pain in his own way.

No one but the children considered the possibility that the coalman was just plain broken, a husk hiding needs that consumed him: impotently recorded in a litany of vicious scars on the hide of an unfortunate horse—like a language, a warning.

The horse snorted again.

A bottle of milk, the boy thought, and turned to retrace his steps.

But the coalman was already upon him.

WHEN THE COALMAN WAS finished, there were limited options. At his feet lay the broken corpse of a child, naked and bloody from the waist down. The horse stood nearby, indifferent, a spectator to one more act of violence.

The coalman still panted, sweat gathering in droplets at the clumped ends of his straw-like hair before running in rivulets down his grimy neck. He gathered up the little bundle almost tenderly, lifting it from the alley shadows that gathered beneath the cart and in the corners where bricks met asphalt.

Hush, he whispered. *Shhh.*

He carried it toward the coal chute, a crude "X" chalked on its steel door. Marked to be sealed tomorrow, the bowels of this building (and soon all of them) already converted to oil. They had bricked up the other end some time ago. The monsters interred below could no longer eat; they now felt only perpetual thirst.

The coalman pulled open the steel mouth of the chute. A filthy finger pushed wayward hair from the child's forehead.

Shhh.

He gently traced his way across the little bridge of the nose, along the ocular bone, and then across the child's open sightless eye.

The finger went rigid, jagged nail catching above the iris.

Then it pushed.

AUGUST, 1987

SCOTTY

1

SUMMER RAINCLOUDS HANG OVER the city, swollen and languid jellyfish trailing their tendrils of drizzle across storefronts and streets, along the tar slabs of flat-roofed strip malls, in between the pungent narrows separating dumpster backs from alley walls. They ride the lazy current, pushed or dragged across the western tip of one Great Lake to skim the northern shore of the next one. The city's harbour, a grey and mottled mirror, wears the somber clouds like a bruise.

The city itself mostly ignores the rain, or its denizens momentarily note droplets making their shaky way down the outside of a bus window. Or how a sullen, greasy-coated dog pauses to shake before returning to nudge and nose some invisible street stain. Senses dulled to these minor shifts in the circuitry, people slip effortlessly back into their own tiny worlds.

But the senses, Scotty knows, process a reality that sometimes isn't real.

When it rains like this, Scotty's apartment smells like wet dog. His widowed neighbour smells like hot-dog water and old broccoli—not just when it rains but all the time. The girl he likes on the third floor smells good, like lemongrass some days and on others like peach yogurt. But her cramped flat smells of her boyfriend's stale clothes and recently extinguished scented candles, waxy and saccharine.

Tribal, when he comes over, smells of leather and weed and occasionally of violence. His brother Sirius smells of nothing. Sometimes regret, but Scotty knows this is imaginary.

How can regret have a smell?

Then again, Scotty doesn't own a dog.

IN THE RUNDOWN BREAKFAST counter down the street from Scotty's apartment building lingers the heavy and predictable scent of bacon, that smoky aroma that creeps across the roof of the mouth and into the nose from behind. It's from the kitchen, this Scotty knows, but the coffee tastes of it, too. Salt and grease and rind, comforting and constant.

When it rains, all street smells are suppressed, replaced by an acidic overtone that pervades everything. This is how Scotty imagines the clouds must smell, brooding above this industrial sprawl, absorbing the exhaust of the steel mills and the diesel fumes from trains, from tankers, from trucks.

Down by the harbour, the slate grey water always smells a little of diesel, or maybe of newly poured asphalt, but also of dead fish and of something else.

Escape, he thinks, on the empty afternoons he sometimes spends on one of the wharfs, or even on the abandoned public beach. The sand, lead-heavy and grey like the water, is littered with bits of discarded trash and the occasional bloated carp, black flies swarming about the soggy mush where an eye used to be. Scotty finds comfort in these random beach corpses, stopping to watch the frantic dance of busy insects as they buzz about, reckless and random, on and above and around the decay.

He thinks *Escape*, but not because of the dead fish; it is because of the vastness of the water. No morbid and clichéd melodrama for Scotty, fish just an occasional sideshow act and nothing more.

But the fish, living or dead, are like him: utterly silent.

EXCEPT FOR SCOTTY'S SOCIAL worker, Simon, Tribal visits more than anyone else, content to sit in comfortable silence as Scotty works on one of his baffling projects. Scotty is an artist of no particular faith—no degree, that is; everything he's learned has come from silent observation, careful listening, tortured contemplation. Sirius takes more of an interest in

Scotty's apartment assemblages and alley installations, but he doesn't say much about what he's thinking.

Today Tribal is restless. He leans on the arm of a battered and rain-damaged faux leather chair, a street find that arrived one night with Sirius.

"You gonna eat that? Hey, Scotty!"

Scotty looks up at Tribal from between his hands, cassette in one and scissors in the other. Not at Tribal's face, though; just at the hand that gestures at the last few inches of a sub.

"You gonna eat that?"

No, head turning toward the far wall.

"You mind?" Tribal is already reaching for it.

Whatever. Slight movement of the shoulders. Maybe a shrug.

"Cheers."

Tribal's cassette is damaged, caught in the tape heads and stretched. Scotty has a surgeon's reputation for tape splicing, though, a skill of which he is modestly proud. He coaxes the damaged piece of the ribbon out and examines it under the lamp. Careful pair of snips, a little scotch tape, good as new. Minus the damaged song, of course. This piece, this small audio hernia, he rolls carefully into a tight coil and slips into a matchbox he retrieves from a drawer. It has fifteen or twenty neighbours already, crinkled coils of industry standard, but a few lengths of type II chromium dioxide; even a strip of metal type IV—although that one isn't damaged at all. *A future transplant*, Scotty thinks, careful and knowing smile in place.

Tribal is finished eating, wiping his mouth carelessly with the back of his hand and catching his lip on one of the sharp outcroppings of a pewter ring.

"Fuck!"

He pulls the ring off and drops it with a sneer on the table. Then he notices the proffered cassette, Scotty holding it out, eyes blankly staring at the floor. Tribal reaches out and takes it, slips it into a pocket.

"Hey, cheers, man—appreciated."

Scotty's hands burrow into his pockets. *No problem.*

Tribal rises, shrugs his leather into place, and hands Scotty a gritty plastic bag containing two pieces of filthy cardboard. Scotty takes the offering and adds it to the pile of others he has accumulated. As Tribal reaches the door, though—back turned to Scotty, fist paused on the doorknob—he stops.

"Scotty?"

Tribal lets the sound hang there in the silence for eight or ten heartbeats.

9

"No? Oh well—worth a shot, eh? Later, brother."

Then he's gone.

⸻

IT'S THAT SCOTTY CAN'T.

Talk, that is—so simple and automatic for everyone else, it seems; Scotty watches in wonder as it pours out of mouths at cafés, in stores, on the streets. A torrent of words, sounds that wash over everything the way smells just can't.

But as soon as a noise—a voice—targets him, the claws tighten and the pounding begins. It starts deep in his chest, lungs and heart conspiring together to constrict even the shallowest of breaths. Scotty folds in on himself, like an origami box.

Simple and automatic.

Or maybe it's more like being underwater, submerged there by force, air just out of reach. Because there is distortion involved as well—this Scotty contemplates as he submerges himself in the dirty zinc tub in his coffin of a washroom. Head below the surface, he stares up at the ceiling through the film of water. He knows that the paint above him is peeling away from the old and water-stained plaster, but through the shimmering liquid lens it looks beautiful, a mosaic of vague and undulating shapes, indiscernible geometry at play. He attempts to make sense of it, searching for a familiar pattern, forcing himself to stay under just a little too long, lungs protesting in the tight vacuum of his thin chest—but it's a sensation he's used to.

He stays under just a little longer.

⸻

SCOTTY WAS FIVE WHEN his father left them—there was no traumatic fight, no smashing of dishes or throwing of glasses, of ashtrays, of those things you heard other people doing in that cavernous collection of squalid apartments. Just some tears, angry and quiet, his mother hunched on the broken kitchen chair (her favourite) with arms crossed and his father already a ghost as he swept through their small flat, collecting his things. He didn't take much—a battered suitcase half-full of clothes, some records, his toolbox.

Scotty watched in awe, knowing something was changing but not sure what it was. His dad walked around him and out the door. Didn't even look at him to say goodbye.

It was some time before his mother moved from the chair. When she finally did, it was to cross to the small and cluttered counter to dig through her purse for a cigarette. She glared down at Scotty, squatting barefoot on the filthy linoleum and playing with a three-wheeled car he'd found on the street a while ago.

"He left because of you—because of *you!*" She lit the cigarette with a shaking hand. And then, venomous, "Why don't you *talk* anymore?"

But now—so many years later and living alone—Scotty remembers words, the sound of his small voice. *I remember* so long ago, just vague snippets of memory really, *I remember speaking to kids—to Mom, maybe even to Dad—I remember* but he dreams about it, too, and it's hard to sort out one from the other. Dreams from memories, that is.

In his head, his words are high-pitched and enthusiastic, or high-pitched and whiny—a tiny child's repertoire, range limited to what little heap of sounds could be collected from the immediate surroundings. Food and feelings, words for the things at eye level and below, nothing much above that.

Scotty remembers.

It was in a place swarming with other children, that's where it happened. He can't recall the exact moment or precise place—schoolyard, maybe, or it might have been in the classroom—the place where he simply and irrevocably shut down. Stopped talking.

The other children were the first to notice, of course. Some coaxed, others teased, most just ignored. When the teacher finally realized something was different, she refused to let it go. At first, just amused little enquiries as if they were playing a game. Soon, though, her patience wore thin and she became insistent, demanding.

Then threatening.

"Scotty? Scott Campbell! *Look* at me when I am speaking!"

She spoke in a voice Scotty had never heard before, in front of everyone (in front of *everyone*), and he learned in that moment that necessity was one of the world's secret sources of magic; he saw, behind the inexplicable terror that rose immediately and unbidden within his small frame, that there was a retreat deep within him. A place of solace, of refuge. The road, however, was long—a complicated path that twisted back on itself so many times that he was soon lost in the depths of his own sojourn.

That piece of him still near the surface crumpled and folded under the weight of interrogation, but the real Scotty—he learned then and there how to disappear while in plain sight, as if his mind were a secret diving bell.

Without thinking, he began holding his breath anytime someone spoke to him. *At* him, really. Conserving air. There was only so much in the bubble.

Practice. Necessity. Scotty hardened himself to the outside world, his tiny surface repelling gentle inquiries, angry demands, concern, or ridicule like so much inclement weather—drizzle, hail. Scotty had to begin the sequence quickly; if he reacted too slowly, he would lose his breath. And once lost, it was almost impossible to find again. His breath and he would play a game, one hiding, the other frantically searching for that small parcel of air before it was too late.

But the sequence, when he began it in time, was simple: with breath trapped in his small lungs, there was no place for it to run, to hide. Then, his breath and he would climb into the bubble, seal the door, and descend below the tiled floors of doctor's offices, beneath the feet of social workers, in between the cracks of sidewalks, under the game-worn grass and sun-burnt dirt of playgrounds—Scotty and his breath companion tucked into an earth-borne bathysphere, safe from sight and sound.

When he was alone, left behind in the cramped apartment with no more words of assurance than one might afford a cat, Scotty often shared his loneliness with the plastic clock that hung crookedly on the cracked plaster of the kitchen wall.

Their time together went like this: the child holds his breath until the second hand ticks its steady pace almost all the way around, jumping with precision from one black mark to another. Jump, stop, jump, stop—a game. He had filled his small lungs just before the slender jumping stick leapt onto the middle of the 3; he gasps for air just after it passes the 2.

And it was a game, one he played often. But not when his mother was around; she was fiercely opposed to this type of play. But, then again, she took issue with just about everything he did. She became his echo, as silent to him as he was to her. Occasionally she would lash out at him with words, sharp and succinct and equivocal.

Speak! Goddamn you, stop this! Just fucking talk!

But mostly he existed in the cramped flat as if he were little more than a small and ragged ghost.

Like his missing father's tiny shadow.

⸝

HIS MOTHER TALKED TO others, though—talked in long, endless tumbling sentences, words spilling out of her until she had to pause for breath, sucking in as much air as possible to fuel the mechanism.

"Darlene? Darlene, it's me—yeah, me again, you won't believe it but that Radcliffe woman just did it again, right in plain sight of everybody! I mean, what kind of woman does that in front of—what? Radcliffe, Nancy Radcliffe in 516 with that asshole of a husband if it even is her husband, who's to say because—"

She talked mostly on the phone this way, but rarely she got hold of a neighbour in the elevator or the lobby or someone on the street.

Scotty became aware this way of body language, his mother's listener (they rarely spoke back) always with a shoulder turned, always in a polite suspension of movement. Or just looking back as they walked away, smiling and nodding, simulating (he realized later) urgency.

Or not. Some few, those who had recently migrated to this rundown corner of the city or those too steeped in their own cares to bother with propriety, just ignored her. Or told her to shut the hell up. She reacted badly to this. Compiled a mental list of enemies.

Scotty knows the list—his mother recited it over and over, a mantra of hate, under her breath and sometimes louder when she was alone (Scotty didn't count as company). It was an unconscious sort of thing, name followed by apartment number when known, invented appellation where necessary, fluctuating volume but always the same order: *Susan McCoy 205 Nancy Radcliffe 516 Ted Radcliffe 516 that smutty bitch in 1101 Moira Hepburn 211 John the asshole Calum MacLeod 908 that Polack on the sixth floor* and so on. It is a list without sequence, unless chronology of when the offence occurred counts.

And then she, too, fell silent. Stopped eating, sleeping, even smoking. She simply lost interest in her daily routine, as if the accumulated weight of words and glances and sneers and offences had finally reached a critical mass and the bridge that connected her to the outside world gave way, collapsed.

Collapsed seemed closest, Scotty pondering this as he thinks back on those last months of his mother's feeble existence. She had died in her bed, shriveled up inside her frail husk until nothing was left. He discovered her—or what was left behind, at least—just a skinny nine-year-old. Ghost-silent, he too bone-thin and alarmingly pale.

LIKE HIS MISSING MOTHER'S tiny shadow.

2

AFTER TRIBAL LEAVES, SCOTTY rummages through the meagre offerings in the long, narrow cupboard beside the fridge. A bag of rice, three cans of brown beans, a tin of Spam, and a small can of sliced black olives that was there when he first arrived. On the lowest shelf is a box of macaroni, but it has been shredded and chewed, its contents spilling out like desiccated pieces of miniature intestines. Tiny black droppings litter the area around the box. He sighs, reaches for the rice—the bag is still intact; they haven't made it that far yet.

Rice it is.

Scotty reaches for his sketchbook on top of the fridge. He flips through the pages until he gets to the picture of boiled rice, cut out from a magazine and taped in place. Below it, he has drawn a cup with oblong grains in it; beside it are two more cups with ripple lines near the brim.

The sketchbook is worn, its covers tattered. It has been with him for years, filled with pictures of simple foods and drawings of how to prepare them. Hot dogs, baked beans, rice, pasta, even grilled cheese—a collection of foster home staples he surreptitiously observed being prepared by a motley assortment of would-be mothers. An occasional man.

SCOTTY STARTED THE COLLECTION when he was fourteen. Sitting awkwardly at the kitchen table in a tiny north-end home, he'd watched as this newest guardian—a kind woman, heavy-set and old, sad-eyed and quiet—pulled two slices of bread from the bag, buttered them both, and laid one butter-side-down on the dented skillet. The sharp scent of burning butter accompanied the angry hiss; muttering, the wrinkled hand fumbled with the burner's dial.

He had only arrived the night before, rescued from people he had only lived with for three weeks. Scotty does not think of it this way, though. Memory is mercurial, fickle.

One of them, the woman who came for me, used that word—rescued. It was more like being pulled out of a bad sleep, a nightmare. And pushed into another kind of sleep . . . a different sleep.

"Rescued" was accurate, though: Scotty had been taken from his group home and delivered to a little house, welcomed by a young woman who reeked of cigarette smoke and something else, something sweet. But just days after arriving, the woman had pushed him into the back of a strange car and driven him to a wretched hovel to be left with someone. A relative, maybe.

Scotty didn't hear the knock on the night the social workers came to retrieve him, just the storm of angry voices as his keeper tried to push her surprise visitors back out the door. A lanky middle-aged man and a stocky woman had walked into his tiny room, materializing in the doorway in the wake of a cacophony of shouting.

"You gotta be kidding me," the man had said, wincing at the stench.

Because Scotty, already too thin and small for his age, sat listlessly on the stained, bare mattress, back against a wall black with mildew. Shirtless, his frail ribs hovered over the hollow of his stomach like a protective roof. A network of spidery blue veins snaked their way beneath his translucent skin. Against the other wall, an arm's-length away, were three litter boxes, heavy and dark with cat urine, studded with black feces that spilled out and across the sticky floor.

Nothing else was in the room. Not even a window. The stench of ammonia, sharp and pungent, crawled along the floor and walls like a vengeful ghost—it haunted everything in the room and beyond it. And there was something else, something cloying. The woman gagged, disappeared from the doorway.

16

The man lifted a camera to his face and snapped a picture. Another one. And another. Scotty stared ahead as if unaware, eyes locked on the corner of the room. Finished with the camera, the man took latex gloves out of his pocket and put them on. He stepped carefully toward Scotty, avoiding the trails of litter and lumps of cat droppings as best as he could.

"Hey," he said gently. "Scott, right? C'mon, Scott—we're getting you out of here. We have a nice place for you, I promise. Scott?"

But Scotty had slipped away already, down into the floor and below the sad foundations of this latest cell. Scotty and his breath, companions on this sojourn.

The man reached out a hand to shake him lightly, and then he noticed what Scotty had been watching, the place where the other smell emanated from.

The cat's carcass crawled with maggots.

SCOTTY TESTS THE RICE with a spoon, stirring it to see how gluey it is. *Seems done*, he thinks and he turns off the burner.

He adds three heaping spoons of brown beans and some cubed Spam, burying it all under the hot rice. He can't remember if he saw someone do this or if he made it up himself. *Doesn't matter*, he figures, although memory vaguely connects this recipe (such as it is) to a shabby mobile home he stayed in for a while. Maybe a couple of months, but he can't be sure. It was quiet, though—mostly retired folks in the trailer park, with little flower gardens kept behind white plastic picket fences. *Because of the rabbits*, he remembers. *I remember seeing rabbits hopping around, and the people muttering about them.*

Scotty spoons up some of the mess right out of the pot and tests it gingerly with his lips. He winces; still searing hot. *Rice and oatmeal. And hard-boiled eggs. Why do they all stay hot for so long?*

Scotty had been—twelve? thirteen?—something like that, and the old couple in that trailer had been kind to him. Bewildered by him, too, unable to comprehend Scotty's profound silence and his tendency to be at once sitting in front of them and absent at the same time, as if that chair were occupied by someone a light year away.

"He certainly is a *shy* boy," the old man would say. Not cruelly, not impatiently. His wife, however, would set her quivering, palsied hand gently on Scotty's shoulder. Scotty remembers its frail weight, its plethora of purplish-grey liver spots.

"Poor child," she'd say. "He's been through so much."

It's all Scotty could remember her saying. Or maybe it was the last thing she said to him, because Scotty recalls the panic, the wailing siren, the clump and clatter of heavy boots as the paramedics stormed in early one morning. They left with the old woman on a stretcher, her panicked husband holding her hand tightly in his own, as if she might die immediately without his touch. Even in his terror the old man remembered Scotty, calling to a neighbour to look in on the boy even as he climbed into the back of the ambulance.

Scotty spent that quiet day inside, drawing in his sketchpad. A social worker arrived just before suppertime, a narrow-shouldered man in a short-sleeved dress shirt and stained knitted tie. Scotty watched him get out of the car, walk toward the trailer. He didn't recognize him. The neighbour, a nervous woman with huge pink curlers in her thin hair, let him in.

"Good evening," he said. "I'm here to pick up the boy."

"How's Ethel?" the woman asked.

"Not well, I'm afraid. Scott?" The social worker turned to look at him. Or at his shell, at least. The man pointed at the back of Scotty's thin hand, covered in grey blotches.

"What's all over his skin?" he asked the woman.

"He drew on himself. What's wrong with Ethel? Do you know?"

"I'm sorry, I don't. I just know that the Kowalskis can't take care of Scott any longer and I have to take him with me. Scott?"

"He don't speak," she said. "Don't you know *nothing* more?"

"I'd tell you if I knew. I got a call and here I am. When did he draw on himself?"

"I dunno. Today sometime."

The social worker took out a notepad and a nubby pencil.

"You ever see him do this before?"

The woman picked incessantly at a scab on her own hand while she paced in what little space she had. "Nah," she finally offered. "Ethel would know, eh? Ethel would know."

THEN WHERE? *HOSPITAL*, SCOTTY thinks, because so often that was the intermediary step. But this might not be true. He recalls being placed in the car, though, the man's hand gently holding his wrist as he inspected the small marks left behind by the grey marker. Not for long, but for long enough to anchor itself in memory.

Ethel, Scotty thinks. *I'm gonna call this "Ethel's recipe."*

He takes the sketchbook into the front room, digs through the pile of odds and ends on the scarred table—wire, paper, cardboard, glue, paint. He finds a felt marker, but it's yellow. That won't do. Piece of a pencil next. Then another marker, this one grey. Scotty uncaps it, places the sketchbook on the slice of exposed table, and writes:

EtLs rspE

There, he thinks. *Now I won't forget. She was nice.*

She used to hum. He'd forgotten about that. She'd hum to herself, simple songs but melodic and in perfect tune. "We have a radio," she'd said once. "But the reception—well."

Scotty smiles at the memory, then he begins to replace the cap. But his hand, pen lid pinched between two fingers, suddenly freezes—he stares at the back of it.

What—when did I . . .

Because three small grey spots stare back at him, the ink still wet.

3

HER HANDS, TOO, SCOTTY thinks as he scrubs away at the grey ink under the kitchen faucet. It is stubborn, though. *Momma—her hands and arms. They were covered in spots like that.*

Or maybe something different. Sores rather than liver spots, it's hard to recall. Scotty remembers, though—that moment he realized that his mother was no more than a dry shell wrapped in sheets that stunk of old urine and worse.

He remembers.

IT TOOK HIM ALL morning. Scrawny and ragged and small for his age, Scotty exhausted himself pulling and tugging the bundle across the filth and flotsam of the warren-like flat, beyond the threshold and into the corridor, and then along that hideous carpet (threadbare in places, a cacophony of once-bright geometric shapes on a deep blue background, like demented clown confetti vomit after some midnight carnival). The elevator—when it worked—was down the hall and to the right. It stunk like a basement bingo hall, stale smoke and unwashed flesh, an old person smell, but it was preferable to the rank stench of urine in the concrete stairwell.

Scotty met no one. He didn't even have to wait long for the elevator, the old, sad door sliding open and Scotty once again tugging at the burden until its length was safely within the sagging confines of the car itself.

Then he pressed "> <" and "B" and waited for the slow, squeaky descent to begin.

The poured concrete floor of the basement was a dingy, uneven grey. Scotty's blanket-wrapped bundle, as light as it was, resisted his feeble tugs by snagging on the rough surface every few feet. By the time he had pulled it around the first corner, he was gulping at the fetid air. He slid down, thin back scraping against the rough mortar, needing to rest until the burning sensation in his stick-like legs subsided.

At some point, the crumbling brick walls of the basement had been white-washed. Now, though, the shoddy surfaces were yellowed from decades of cigarette smoke, or discoloured by ashy grime, black mildew, countless incidental and equivocal abuses. Paint peeled away from the rusty clutter that gathered like bulbous tumours around their joints; asbestos insulation sagged on others, like loose skin on ancient bone. Tied around many of the pipes were the frayed remains of rope—not long ago, when many of the apartment building's current tenants first arrived in a squalling, chaotic mass (*refugees*, the older folks had said), they had run clotheslines from the basement pipes. His neighbours complained, disdainful and superior, but Scotty loved the web-like network of lines. He snuck down to the basement corridors whenever he could, a tiny and lonely child invisible to the foreign women that gathered daily in the labyrinthine basement with their own running, laughing, crying, whining, sleeping, playing offspring.

It was the colours of the hanging clothes, so bright even under the weak glow of the bare light bulbs. Like a shabby carnival, a bohemian riot of colourful cloth still ripe with the odours that could somehow never be washed out: food smells, stale smells, pipe smoke, the echo of a hundred grandfathers. These things remained.

Scotty would drift through this underworld of clinging reds and earthy browns, of olive and tangerine and eggplant, of bustling women and the occasional old man. To all of them he was invisible.

But not to their children—to them, he was a new plaything, a natural phenomenon native to this new and foreign landscape. The little ones began to follow him around. Then the bigger ones. They spoke at him, too, but in a tongue he could not understand.

"Hei, copile! Cum te cheamă?"

"Cine ești tu?"

"Unde locuiești?"

Scotty marvelled at their words, syllables so raw and strange that even his breath didn't flee, as if it, too, were mildly curious about these creatures from another world. But they soon lost interest in him and went back to their own games.

"Poate el ieste o nălucă," said one. The others laughed.

Then they simply ignored him.

At some point, the super put an end to the makeshift laundromat—fire hazard, he'd bellowed above the angry protests of the soft-hipped matrons, knife in hand, slashing away at the ropes until nothing but frayed tatters remained around the larger pipes. They raised their arms and shook their cracked hands in frustration, loose, doughy flesh from armpits to elbows swinging back and forth, keeping rhythm with their fury. But they didn't argue for long or re-spin their webs; these were people who were used to having things taken away.

Scotty didn't dwell on these things—he simply remembered in passing the time of sagging ropes and damp cloth and alien smells, the way a child might recall a pleasant taste when he came across a torn and filthy candy wrapper caught against a chain link fence. Instead, Scotty stood up.

He entangled his cramped fingers into the stale and tattered quilt, making tight fists in the fabric. Then he pulled.

At the end of the dim corridor was a metal door, bumpy with rust beneath an old layer of reddish-brown paint. Corrosion had once again found its way to the surface, though, a persistent tumour that slowly ate away at the edges.

The door was never locked; even at nine years old, Scotty knew that the super was a lazy, swag-bellied braggart who rarely left his own bolt-hole of an apartment. In short, quick tugs, Scotty pulled the heavy door open enough for the two of them, him and his bundle. And with sweat matting down his unkempt hair and stinging his eyes, he dragged his burden into the cloying blackness before groping about for the lights, a stiff and spring-heavy switch (he knew this) at the bottom of a circuit panel. With a hollow click, a single bare bulb awakened and cast its dim glow into the cavernous darkness.

The furnace was a monstrous thing, a squat-bellied dragon held captive by a confusing tangle of pipes, wires, and cords. It was fitful and thirsty, drinking greedily from the equally monstrous black tanks along the far wall. Scotty could see the fire burning sullenly within, orangey light glimmering through narrow slats in the heavy iron door.

Like a giant's oven, Scotty thought, not for the first time. The oven door was small, though, barely big enough to fit a child. He peered into the shadows above the immense boiler, wide eyes searching for movement between the torso-thick pipes and the clutter of smaller iron hoses that wove their way across the ceiling before disappearing upward, carrying their own mysterious burdens clunking and banging to the rusty radiators high above.

Where are you? I need you! Tears slipping down his sallow cheeks now, leaving rivulets in the dirt and neglect. Scotty scoured the shadows for him—he who hid there sometimes, playful among the pipes. Or perhaps he was under the massive boiler itself, the space so narrow and thick with dust and rubbish that it would be impossible if it were anyone but him.

The Furnace Boy.

Elusive, mischievous, unpredictable—but lonely, too. Scotty knew about loneliness.

I don't know what to do. Please—come out!

Maybe he was hiding on Scotty. He liked that game; he made no noise at all, unless the whisper of cobwebs counted, for they would sometimes stir when he slipped by them.

Or maybe he's not here at all.

Scotty sat down beside his bundle, all skinny legs and arms—a ragged little spider alone in the dark. Beside him, a stick-thin hand lay on the concrete. It must have fallen out of the cocoon-like quilt some time ago, dragged along unnoticed, for the underside was black with filth. He took the withered thing, so pallid and cold, and slipped it back into the bundle. Tucked it in.

He wept then, silently at first. Then in rending sobs.

⸺

SCOTTY CAN'T REMEMBER WHERE his elusive and quiet friend came from, his fellow ragged dweller-in-shadows.

Two or three times per week, Scotty would find himself in the basement corridors of the tenement, slipping silently from one dark corner to another—avoiding the suspicious eyes of old women labouring under loads of dull laundry or even the careworn eyes of young immigrant mothers still too shell-shocked with change to pay him much mind.

This was how Scotty would make his furtive way to the heavy steel door and into the bowels of the building. Just to look, of course. And sometimes he'd be there, perched lightly on a pipe or peeking playfully out from beneath the oil tank as if waiting for Scotty. On these days they would play, Scotty chasing him around and around the discarded asbestos piles or the dust and rubbish the super had half-heartedly pushed into a heap near one wall. Or under the rusty stairs, or even through the maze of bone-white pipes that sprung from the monstrous boiler like the skeletal wings of some great prehistoric bird.

Scotty would sometimes laugh as they played, a small sound echoing in this immense dry cave. But his mischievous friend—he never made a single sound, not even as he ran lightly along the pipes or leaped over the machinery.

The Furnace Boy was utterly silent.

It was Scotty's mother who first told him of the elusive shadow that dwelt within the building's bowels, a story meant to frighten him into staying away from the basement.

"The super told me," she'd said one afternoon, after catching Scotty in the stairwell, "that the basement is *haunted*—so you keep away from there!"

She'd taken him by the thin wrist, talking as much to herself as to him as they returned to their hovel of an apartment.

"He told me that when they'd switched over from coal to oil years and years ago, back in the fifties, they'd sealed up the old coal chute. Then they had to change something on that wall last week and the men opened up the coal chute again. Do you know what they found?"

Scotty had shaken his head, a barely perceptible movement.

"They found little bones in the coal dust, a *child's* skeleton. Those bones been there for almost *a quarter century*."

She then did something she rarely did—she looked him in the eye.

"So you keep well away, you hear me? That child's ghost lives down there in that furnace room!"

But Scotty wasn't frightened at all. Intrigued, rather. He had already suspected he wasn't alone down there, and now he seemed to have found purpose: to scour the basement for this little lost ghost that emerged from the coal-black bones of a forgotten child.

And, as if anticipating this, the Furnace Boy was waiting for him. A good friend to have in the darkness.

IT WAS THE AUTUMN of '74 when the contractors, hired to reroute a pipe, opened up the sealed coal chute and discovered the child's makeshift tomb. Scotty recalls the reporters, the police, the coroner, but in a vague and muddled way—after all, he'd been seven-and-a-half when that minor mystery became news for a brief time.

Sometimes Scotty tries to recall the details of the old building's exterior, or landmarks that might lead him back to it. *Brown*, he believes. *I think it had a lot of brown. The balconies and the painted parts of the concrete. Or maybe it was just brown brick.*

The autumn day of that shocking discovery is not a date in Scotty's mind; it is a light show. He remembers the red flashing of police lights—of a hook-and-ladder rig, of other obscure vehicles. Men in uniforms gathered in the lobby; the entrance to the basement stairs had yellow tape across it, but the door was propped open. It seemed a strange arrangement to the child as his impatient mother tugged him across the dingy room. She was angry with him because of the marker all over his left forearm.

"Why," she hissed, "would you draw all over yourself? You're strange *enough* without that!"

She had collected him from school, waiting amongst the other women for the children to be filed out in a long line. Scotty hated this ritual, enduring the terrible weight of each stranger's stare. They all knew about him—his strangeness, his otherness. Even at seven he found their misplaced pity unbearable.

The mothers called out to their offspring, another ritual Scotty hated. *Like dogs at the park*, Scotty thinks now. Not then, though; then, he had simply endured the curious stares and cruel whispering. Like his inability to speak meant that he also lived in an invisible, soundproof bubble. His mother, haunted look about her dark-ringed eyes, had darted forward and snatched him by the arm. But she'd paused to stare at the oblong patch of brown drawn all over her son's left forearm. One of the other mothers had noticed it, too.

"Maybe they ran outa paper again," she'd offered. But his mother could only smile weakly as she pulled him away.

Because she found their misplaced pity unbearable, too.

The school itself was a shabby flat-roofed rectangle with perpetually filthy windows and floors of scarred linoleum. The cafeteria was Scotty's least favourite room—not because of the jostling crowd and persistent cacophony, but because the floor upon which he kept his eyes glued was so repulsive. It, too, was covered in linoleum, but the trails of the janitor's mop could be seen in the dried residue of filth, sludge soaked daily and then pushed about into new patterns. Scotty could smell the mop bucket water when he lined up for lunch; his place in line always anchored him right beside the janitor's closet. Within that cramped grotto, the murky stench collected like a sullen spirit—the next day, he would see its remnants upon the cafeteria floor, a silent and secret language, a quiet keening. And the sour odour—even Scotty's carelessly made sandwich would taste of it.

Once, the single slice of bologna slipped out from between the two pieces of bread and landed flat on the floor beneath his table. It was still there the next week, shellacked to the tile by a coat of grime.

The janitor himself was much like his mop bucket—dirty and sour, strangely useless. He went about his daily chores mechanically only when other adults were close by; beyond that, he went through the motions in a way that struck even a seven-year-old as utterly absurd. Like hanging streamers on a dumpster.

And he was always near. He leered at Scotty, sometimes from his stool in the back of the cramped and dark custodial closet when Scotty lined up in the corridor, sometimes from the steel slab of a door that led from some inaccessible and secret part of the sad building to a corner of the equally sad playground. A man of no particular age—grey-skinned and dark-haired—he seemed to make a religion of watching Scotty.

AS FOR THE MARKER on his skinny forearm? That was the sand table's fault.

The classroom had a sand table, but only one. On indoor recess days it was available, and the children clamoured for turns, elbowing and shoving each other. Six boys had it now, friends who lived on the same narrow street. They almost looked like brothers—light-haired and freckled and all but one with blue eyes. They also stood in line together because all their names started with O. O'Casey, O'Connor, O'Daly, O'Dea, O'Dugan, O'Dwyer.

Scotty sat alone on the floor with some felt markers, drawing. Other children played with wooden blocks or with toys out of the bins, gathered in pairs or in groups. Except Vishnu Patel, who, like Scotty, played by himself. He was the only brown-skinned child in the classroom, small and skinny and careful to hide his lunch. Anywhere but in his own cubby—Scotty knew this. Earlier that year, Tammy Kincaid *(Girard, Henderson, Jackson, Johnson, Kincaid)* had pulled Vishnu's Speed Buggy lunchbox out of his cubby and dumped its contents onto the play mat for all to see. "It stinks!" she'd declared, "and it looks like baby poo!"

"Baby poo!" the others had gleefully shouted. Vishnu had just stood there, staring at the mess. Miss Tracy, the teacher, had intervened.

"Everyone line up, right now! Who did this?"

Silence.

"Alright, Vishnu. Clean up your mess. Hurry up!"

"Baby pooooo!" someone shouted. The children laughed.

But Vishnu had started to cry. Scotty watched as Miss Tracy sighed and rolled her eyes in slow exaggeration. Tammy Kincaid copied her and giggled. Then all the girls did it and some of the boys.

"Vishnu," Miss Tracy said, "there is no need to cry. Crying is for babies. It's just an accident. Clean it up. *Now.*"

Miss Tracy had attempted to make Scotty and Vishnu play together on several occasions, the one perpetually silent, the other perpetually sad. But at Vishnu's tentative whispers and gestures Scotty could only shrink into himself, and Vishnu would eventually drift away like a small and aimless satellite. Scotty, fixed to the floor as if rooted there, would watch him go from the corner of his eye, ears roaring with the wind and shrill screaming that always accompanied these moments.

Like today. Vishnu had been deposited beside Scotty and handed a marker, but he only watched Scotty draw what he always drew: a boy in a red shirt holding hands with a black figure. The boy was always smiling. Vishnu let his own marker slip out of his fingers, then he got up and listlessly wandered away. Too close to the sand table, though; one of the O's saw him approach.

"You can't play, Baby Poo!"

"Yeah, Baby Poo!"

"Baby Poo!"

Vishnu walked away toward the cloakroom. Miss Tracy's voice rose over the ridicule, but Scotty couldn't hear what she said clearly. She had a friend visiting today, another woman who looked a lot like her.

Scotty, the wind in his ears an inaudible roar, chose a brown marker. Carefully, he added a third figure to his drawing. Like the smiling boy in the red shirt, this figure held the black shape's hand. They stood in a row, happy.

Then Scotty coloured the pale skin of his forearm with long deliberate strokes of the brown marker until it wouldn't draw anymore.

ANOTHER MEMORY, JUST A snippet, a piece of a phone conversation he overheard because he was under the kitchen table when his mother dialled the number.

"Did you *hear*? I can't even believe it . . . I *know*! Right there in the class-room—strangest thing, so *disgusting*!"

Scotty pushed a stiff piece of cold French fry through the dust, making a circle in the filth. She may have known he was there. Maybe not.

"*Yes!* His poor mother, eh? She had to come straight away from work to get him. . . . No, no, course not—they won't let him come back no more at *all*. Expelled from grade three! What? Yeah, but who knows how them types live at home, eh? There isn't any in *our* building, anyways."

Because eventually Vishnu had endured enough. Scotty was there, of course, when it all came to light. One last public humiliation, one last pas-sive dismissal by Miss Tracy, one last trip to the cloakroom. Where, among wet boots and soggy mittens and thirty little coats, he defecated in Tammy Kincaid's lunch pail.

Then he wiped his small behind with Sean O'Daly's tuna fish sandwich.

4

THESE ARE THE DULL mechanics of Scotty's days, a small and insignificant clockwork man clinging precariously to the illusory safety of the familiar. Not that there is a set schedule; there isn't. But his is a world defined by the narrow confines of what is familiar, immediate. Beyond that, the city and its surroundings might as well belong to another place. Or another planet.

His dreams, however, like his waking memories—they belong to a different time. As timid as he is in this life, he faces his own past with the reckless and relentless abandon of a salmon swimming against the torrent.

Struggling to reach something. An almost suicidal obsession with the obscure.

TRIBAL'S VISIT THIS MORNING was strange. Not because he doesn't visit often—he does—but because he had arrived so early. Scotty heard a pair of knuckle raps, Tribal's knock, and stared dumbly at the door.

Hasn't been home yet, Scotty thought immediately upon opening the door. Tribal had that weary look, and trailing him were the smells of night haunts and hidden places. They clung to Tribal like jealous lovers. He'd held out the damaged cassette almost immediately.

"Hey, man. You mind fixing this?" And then he'd walked over to the balcony slider and stared out at the pale morning.

Scotty had fixed the cassette as Tribal paced, wolfing down the last bit of the sub that someone had left. Tribal had paid—two good cardboard signs—and left. But when Scotty's social worker, Simon, arrived almost an hour later, Tribal showed up again. It felt festive, in a small way—*it's like I'm having a party*, Scotty mused—and he smiled behind the ragged curtain of stringy brown hair.

Or maybe a party I'm not actually at, he'd reconsidered while watching Tribal greet Simon. Surreptitiously, of course—just peripheral glances.

Scotty watched Simon's darker hand clutch Tribal's pale one. They talked about things that were as mysterious to Scotty as an alien tongue, a casual exchange of unrecognizable images that pawed at the raw edges of the mute's panic.

Like watching strangers speaking in another language through a window. In a language like . . . like . . . but he couldn't think of another language to name, that too a concept utterly alien to him.

Simon fulfilled his court-sanctioned obligation—handing over meds and watching Scotty take them—and then said his goodbyes, but not before consulting his battered journal. Sometimes Simon would arrange outings for that afternoon. Or the next day. Nothing on the agenda, though: Scotty was a free agent until next week.

Simon and Tribal left at the same time.

NOW, THOUGH. THE EMPTINESS of the lonely afternoon awaits him with arms open—a welcome embrace. Tribal's unexpected early morning visit, followed by Simon's expected one, has left Scotty exhausted and on edge.

A walk. *I need it. Maybe find some stuff, too.* For his art, he means. People bring him odds and ends, but much of what he uses is scrounged on his travels. Scotty's sculptures appear unexpectedly in parks or in alleys, sometimes on bus seats or at the end of a wharf. For most people, the source of these objects is a minor mystery—but momentary, somehow forgotten as soon as the discovery is out of sight. Like Scotty himself.

A walk. He picks up the small sculpture he has made since his morning visitors left—a foot-long fish made from chicken wire. Inside the fish's hollow body, a small, fetal figure dangles from a piece of cassette tape. It, too, is made of wire, but tightly twisted and painted black. He also picks up two more identical sculptures, although smaller. They will travel with him today.

It's unseasonably cool for late summer and raining, so he picks up his light jacket with the hood and heads toward the door.

Except something creeps along just behind him.

He turns, startled, and drops the sculptures—eyes wide and hands up in front of his face as if to fend off a blow. But nothing is there—a trick of the light, a cloud's playful game with the daylight that finds its way in through the balcony door.

Nothing, he concludes. *Just shadows from outside. But it's raining—no sun right now.* He stares harder down the meagre length of his apartment. The darkness near his bedroom door seems to shift. Ripple.

Scotty turns quickly and leaves.

Down Rebecca and then right on Catharine Street past the bus terminal. He doesn't make it much farther, though—already his lungs seem incapable of pulling in the wet air while his numbers swirl about him like startled bats. His mind grasps blindly into the swarm, hoping to catch a starting point. A quick swerve into the depot's parking lot—he takes shelter beneath a scraggly tree on the narrow island of soggy grass that segregates buses from cars. The tree helps, the dripping canopy of leaves like a leaking roof above him. Still, it lends him security. He leans heavily into the thin trunk until it hurts and he closes his eyes.

One, two, three, four—the numbers come easily now; breath returns and he traps it quickly. Sliding down the trunk onto his haunches, he finishes the sequence. At sixty, he exhales and breathes deeply. His head swims, but he feels in control again.

A STRONG STONE'S THROW from where Scotty still squats, a lone figure stands as rigid and still as a sign post, watching—a rag and bone assemblage clutching a filthy canvas bag to his chest. The few pedestrians who share the pavement with him alter course, swerving around him. Shadows crawl about the deep crevasses in his weathered face, in the hollows of his eye sockets, under the craggy angle of his bony chin.

Scotty slowly stands up, taking account of his immediate surroundings in darting glances. His eyes catch sight of the ragged scarecrow of a man, but the homeless wreck has already turned away, shuffling away along John Street toward King. Scotty has seen him before, and often. More so than the other members of that shiftless tribe to which he (unknowingly) is a government signature away from joining.

Always there, he contemplates. *And always walking away.* Then he notices the man's shadow, somehow too dark for this daylight chance meeting. *Like ravens in the sidewalk.* But that, too, might just be a trick of the light. Especially since it's raining.

Still, there's something familiar about him.

Scotty walks at a casual pace in the other direction. Walking in the rain is good—no one wants to be out in it. He considers walking all the way down to the lake.

And why not?

TRIBAL

5

THE ELEVATORS ARE JUST around the corner from Scotty's apartment, but Tribal won't use them. Too tight, too unreliable, and no options—he'd learned that the hard way from the System's second concerted attempt at forcing him into a foster home. That was three years ago; he'd been fourteen at the time. Nothing to do with the family itself, but the elevator in that building was the new haunt of an old hand, a semi-homeless addict who preyed on the elderly and children.

Instead, Tribal shoulders his way through the heavy door to the stairwell. The concrete stairs echo with the heavy fall of his steel-toed boots, like drum beats, which makes him think of his brother—or, more specifically, his brother's rhythmic way of pounding on doors.

By the time Tribal crosses the lobby and exits the building, however, his mind is focused on the immediate, steeled for the downtown sojourn through enemy territory to safer turf. Not that this end of Rebecca Street is all that dangerous.

Still, no need to be stupid. Hamilton, affectionately called "The Hammer," is well named. His brother got jumped by a pair of Nazi skinheads two months ago not too far from Scotty's, just up Catharine Street near King William.

A peaceful portage, though, still too early for most of the street tribes to be stirring. And there's the rain, of course. Tribal makes his way down Rebecca and hooks a left onto Mary Street. Then a right onto King, where he falls into step with the flow of foot traffic. He is neither tall nor imposing in stature, but his long hair, scarred leather jacket, and heavy Doc Martens lend him a fierceness that he wears like a second skin. Half-feral he seems, stalking wolf-like down King Street as if hunting for something specific. Fellow pedestrians politely give way, avoid eye contact.

King Street is crowded, despite the rain. Traffic makes its fitful way west, sudden stops and starts determined by the whim of traffic lights. Tribal smiles, just a humourless and predatory curl of the lips, as a traffic light turns green and the front runners bolt forward.

"PATTERNS," JIMMY HAD SAID to Tribal a few days ago as they made their way west themselves, trudging along the broad sidewalk at a determined pace. "Everything we do is determined by patterns." Jimmy smiled bitterly at the thought.

"Patterns of what?" Tribal asked.

Jimmy gestured vaguely to the cars lurching forward at the turn of the light. "Look at them—they're racing to the next intersection. They know there's a timer involved, and that if they hit just the right speed at just the right time, it's clear sailing from the Delta to the 403."

"So?"

But Jimmy had just shrugged and Tribal watched a sort of sadness creep into his companion's eyes, unbidden and unwelcome. It happened every so often, these black moods—as unfathomable as just about everything else about him.

Technically, Jimmy is Tribal's brother's friend. They met when they were fourteen, a few months before all three of them left home for good—Jimmy to escape the dangerous unpredictability of his alcoholic and violent father, Sirius and Tribal to escape the pathetic predictability of their alcoholic whore of a mother. That was four years ago. And while Sirius found his place among the boots, bull's eyes, and braces of hard mods, Jamaican rudeboys, and Trojan skinheads, Jimmy swam the main roads and side streets, byways and alleys, moving from tribe to tribe—sly catfish in the murky periphery. He dealt in everything from old-school LSD to information, and over time, he cultivated a reputation for fulfilling almost any vice. Even in the droughts.

Now, at seventeen and eighteen, Tribal and his brother are bitter and hale, skilled at weathering the storms of their kind: squat house politics, street ethics, hunger, poverty—the traps of their steel city youth. But Jimmy seems as old as stone, an entropic street mystic who defies every attempt to define him. Even then, as the two of them made their way down King Street in broad daylight, Jimmy seemed to exist simultaneously in the past and present. And it wasn't because of the ratty nest of dreads or the Lennon shirt or the retro bellbottoms, either; it was something else.

Jimmy reached into his dirty beadwork leather satchel to retrieve his pack of smokes. They walked on in silence for a while, and when they finally passed an older woman squatting beside her collection of tattered plastic bags in the alcove of one of the buildings, Jimmy wordlessly dropped the entire pack into her lap.

She didn't react—not a word or even a smile, as if Jimmy were invisible and had offered as he passed nothing more substantial than laughter or a breeze. She just stared woodenly at something on the pavement a hand span or two in front of her feet.

Tribal had sneered, unimpressed. He turned to Jimmy, shrapnel and venom gathered up in his mouth—but he swallowed it before anything escaped. Gone was the sadness of minutes before; in its place was that strange look of cosmic fulfilment that came over Jimmy in moments following one of his esoteric street rituals. They had all learned to take them in stride.

TRIBAL CROSSES JAMES STREET and heads into Jackson Square, the underground mall. It's too early yet, and he doesn't much feel like standing in the rain to wait.

For the others, that is: he has an appointment to keep. Another one of Tribal's overly complicated hustles requires volunteers, and every so often they actually work. "Nothing ventured, etc.," he's fond of saying.

But when Tribal, some two hours later, reaches the agreed-upon spot at the edge of Victoria Park on the Strathcona side, an unwelcome surprise awaits.

Seamus, Drew, and Matt are already there, avoiding the ancient homeless lunatic rooted like a dead and wind-blasted tree on the sidewalk close by. Avoiding him because, once he opens that wreckage of a mouth, one or two will stop to listen—amused at first, but then.

Ah, then.

Jimmy calls him Cottonmouth.

A street preacher, but a potent weaver of words, silk-soft and hypnotic. No screeching, no rabid and wild spittle accompanies his unwritten gospel. He stands in rigid outrage on a corner, stick arms thrown wide like a crucified scarecrow, or he shuffles as if shackled along James Street between King and York. Never straying beyond his own self-imposed points of A and B, and always on the west side of the street, weathered shoulder scraping along the bricks where possible.

Cottonmouth, because the gentle bite of his words (often merely whispers) seem laced with venomous intent—they seep and sink into every hidden fold, creases in the mind. They have all listened, Jimmy and the others, at first with detached interest or with bored indifference.

But Cottonmouth's words live in their heads, they dream them. Spiders nest in the hollow beneath his tongue, or centipedes ready to scuttle thought-quick across the space (that cosmic chasm) dividing the preacher from his unwitting flock. Those strands, silk-strong and cast across that rift with deft and subtle skill, snag them quietly.

Shrug them off, they might say, *just the raving words of another madman*.

And yet, when sleep finally finds them after an evening's mischief, they always dream the same dream: *I am trapped I am snared I cannot run or move or crawl I cannot breathe and what* (that small part of them asks) *lurks behind me above me below me?*

They know this. It is unspoken, though, and the four of them keep their distance from the old man as if assumed indifference were an insurmountable wall. But they are also part of that fierce and independent tribe, violent and proud and reckless sons of the Hammer, boot culture street denizens: they take their small victories and narrow defeats in stride; they shrug and laugh when luck is with them and shrug and shoulder adversity when it is not. They do not whine. They do not wonder at the unfairness of things.

But Jimmy privately notes how many of them have an aversion to spiders.

The preacher sees the small gathering, wall or no, his vision (or maybe Vision) too acute to miss the four friends talking and smoking and laughing and consciously ignoring him.

Cottonmouth has been waiting for one of them, after all.

"You!" he hisses, sharp and insistent, pointing a withered claw at Tribal.

The four turn as one to see whom the ancient finger has singled out, and wait. *Maybe because Tribal's not one of us*, the others think.

All four wear heavy and street-scuffed boots—black-laced Doc Martens—but only Tribal's hair hangs loosely past his shoulders and down his scarred leather jacket. The others are skinheads—bomber jackets and braces, tight jeans, and tools of the trade tucked away. Only Seamus's ugly length of chain is in sight, slung around his thick neck like a yoke.

Maybe because Tribal's not one of us. They think this, but would never say it, having borne the crushing weight of brotherhood that comes with their steel city existence.

"You!"

Cottonmouth points and glares, filmy eyed, and Tribal hesitates. Then thinks better of it maybe, and takes a step toward him, belligerent, swaggering. Though for show; his guts recoil at his own footfall.

"What the fuck do you want, old man?"

The street preacher's lower lip quivers, a palsy that disturbs the thick spit caught like silken cocoons in both corners of his mouth. He smiles, knowing and hard.

"I been told to tell ya!"

"Yeah? Tell me what?"

Cottonmouth stares, eyes pale and watery along the sagging red rims. Creases of loose skin black with grime create a delicate network, like the thin lines of a map.

"Reckonin's coming soon," he hisses. "Reckonin' for the wicked! I been told to tell ya." The words wheeze as if forced out by leaky lungs, but Tribal is trapped now, his hard, youthful eyes caught between the preacher's glare and the glob-like cocoons that mark the parameters of that ruined mouth.

And maybe it's the remnants of the acid he's still coming down from, but there is movement in those white viscous globes. It can't be, though; it must be a last lysergic trick of the light.

Tribal's eyes, though. They are caught in the illusion. Cottonmouth smiles now, a hard and humourless line that flattens the spittle.

"She seen it, boy," he hisses. "You seen it, too—you can't hide from it neither."

But then the old man flinches, looks up wild eyed at a sudden opening in the cloud cover's slow progress before glaring hard at Tribal once more.

"You been takin' from the lonely, the lost! She *told* me. Stealin' our tongues when we sleepin'! Reckonin's comin', boy."

Then he turns, frail and ragged and impossibly ancient, and shuffles eastward down King Street.

BY THE TIME COTTONMOUTH reaches Gore Park, the clouds are nothing more than wind-torn remnants. Dappled sunlight dances its way across puddles and bus windows; the summer wind shakes loose the last of rainfall's droplets from the branches of trees, the bottom of hydro wires.

Even the others avoid him, the fully initiated members of that ragged tribe—resting in the park, letting the sun's warmth caress joints stiffened after a night spent on cardboard in an alley or on a park bench, or even on a lumpy cot at a shelter. And, for his part, Cottonmouth ignores them, too.

He makes his way over to the west end of Gore Park, toward the statue of Queen Victoria. She stands, imperious and perennial, upon a great stone column with a lion crouching below her. She is unconcerned, unmoved by the comings and goings of the city. Cottonmouth shambles along the path until he is fully immersed in Her shadow, enveloped by the soothing coolness. Manoeuvring so that his invisible shadow matches Hers, he shuffles and worries over the proportions, the geometry—precision is crucial, he knows this. He cannot be certain, his own tattered shadow consumed by Hers, and that imperial shadow as ruthless as that of a sundial's. When he has matched Her, his head inside Her own, he waits for the voice.

Patience is important.

6

AND IT GNAWS AT Tribal as the day drifts on—Cottonmouth's words, in his head now, just like Jimmy warned. Hunger gnawing, too, it being some time since he'd come across anything to eat. The tail end of a sub this morning at Scotty's didn't go far. He decides to collect the necessary tribute and make his way back to Scotty's; at least there, Tribal can sort out his thoughts in peace—Scotty won't offer a word. Never has. Besides, the mute always has something edible, remnants of some other visit.

Tribal finds what he needs right on King Street itself. He doesn't make a big deal of it, taking the limp and filthy piece of cardboard from under the head of a catatonic sidewalk sleeper. He is curled up, fetal position, back to the street—about as close to the brick wall as he can get—wrapped in a ratty housecoat the colour of rust and rank with the stale and cloying odour of unwashed flesh. Usually, Tribal would leave something—a couple of smokes, a handful of coins—but he is in a sullen and petty mood now.

Another side effect of Cottonmouth's words: the poison ripples outward, passed along from one to another in small acts of cruelty.

He considers phoning Jimmy before heading over to Scotty's flat—Jimmy, that street shaman who, with medicine man logic, might dispel Cottonmouth's curse; but Tribal knows the price exacted for a witch-doctor house call, especially during daylight, Jimmy being a mostly nocturnal spirit—it used to be just a pack of smokes, but not recently: now, a rare cassette, old prog rock, like The Soft Machine or Gong (Jimmy refuses to recognize the difference on principle), a stolen smoke alarm or a smoke shop crucifix. (Also interchangeable. Same principle.)

Instead, Tribal runs into his brother.

Despite the wetness left behind by the recent rain, Sirius lounges indolently on the sidewalk outside the public library, back against the bricks. His guitar case is open, but the instrument itself is propped up against the wall beside him. He's reading, seemingly oblivious to the occasional pedestrian who tosses a few coins into the case.

Tribal laughs.

"You reinventing busking?"

Sirius looks up at his brother and smiles.

"Like it? Getting paid to sit here and read."

Tribal glances in the case, assesses.

"Wow," he drawls. "You might have, like, a bone thirty-five there, eh?"

"Hey, that's enough for a coffee for reading some Silko, so go fuck yourself."

"Who?"

"*Ceremony*, by Leslie—never mind. Simon gave it to me. Saw him up at Scotty's last week." Then Sirius notices the scraps of cardboard, the clumsy scrawl. "Which is where you're heading, I assume."

Tribal glances down York, east toward James Street. A pigeon with a broken wing struggles to keep its balance on a trash barrel. It fails and falls.

"Yeah. Was there this morning, too."

"You alright?"

"Yeah," but this too quickly. Sirius raises an eyebrow, closes the book. Waits.

Tribal sighs and squats down beside him. He hands his brother a cigarette and takes one himself.

"Fucking Cottonmouth—said some shit to me a while ago, eh? You know how that goes."

Sirius exhales, shakes his head.

"He's a crazy old fuck. Naught but shite comes out of that mouth of his, eh? Ignore it, brother." But Sirius doesn't sound all that convincing. Maybe he knows it because he adds, "How 'bout talking to Jimmy?"

Tribal sneers. "Sometimes Jimmy's just as bad. All I need is somewhere quiet to think."

"Well," Sirius laughs, "you'll definitely find that at Scotty's."

They finish smoking in silence, small and comforting respite from their own thoughts, both of them now idly watching the pigeon as it flounders about on the pavement.

Until the line of sight is suddenly cut off.

"You boys have a licence?"

The beat cop is thirtyish, wiry. A runner, Sirius thinks. Tribal's eyes drift to the man's knuckles, though, laced with silver scars, old and fading. A fighter in younger years, he knows.

And they don't even look at each other now, Tribal and Sirius, having navigated this weary river so many times that they already know every snag and hazard, shoal and eddy. Listlessly, they toy with the depths out of habit, bored and resigned.

"Licence for what, constable? Reading?" Sirius holds up the book.

The cop's not amused, though.

"Don't be a smartass. Show me a busking licence or move on."

But Sirius takes the guitar by the neck and places it carefully in its case. Tribal, still squatting beside his brother, gives the lid a nudge and it falls shut.

"There you go—no more confusion for the good pedestrians of Hamilton. Now, if you don't mind . . ." Sirius displays the book again.

The cop glares now, digging in. Tribal sees it, this one new to the job and afraid of backing down. He senses the buildup and attempts to diffuse.

"Alright, alright. That's cool, man. You want us to shog, we'll shog."

Sirius misses the cue, though.

"We will?"

"Yeah—come over to Scotty's with me."

And Tribal's out of character enough so that Sirius finally takes the hint. He reluctantly gathers his things and gets up.

But Scotty isn't home.

"Where the hell could he be?" Tribal grumbles. "Not like he's got a shit-ton of people to see and places to go, eh?"

Sirius leans his guitar against the wall and shrugs. "Maybe Simon took him to an appointment or something."

"Nah, I was here this morning when Simon showed. Told Scotty he got the day free."

"Guess he fucked off somewhere, eh?" Sirius offers.

Inane observation, though; Tribal doesn't respond. Instead, he slips the battered piece of cardboard he's still carrying under the door and heads for the stairwell.

THE BROTHERS UNKNOWINGLY WALK in Scotty's wake, aiming for the bus depot.

"Where's this gig of yours tonight?" Tribal asks.

"Lion's Head. Coming?"

"Yeah. Tight place—not much dosh from cover charges there. Surprised you guys even bother, eh?"

Sirius shrugs. "Jimmy owes a favour. Plus, it's actually my favourite pub to play."

"Why, for fuck's sake?"

"Dunno. Good karma, maybe."

Tribal shoots his brother a sideways glance. "Christ—you're starting to *sound* like Jimmy."

"That's my bus," Sirius says, pointing. "Sure you're good?"

"Yeah. I guess." Tribal looks down the rest of Rebecca Street.

"See you 'round ten, eh?"

"Yeah. Later, brother."

Tribal heads out toward James Street. Although warm, the air is heavy again with the scent of impending rain. He spares the late afternoon sky a cursory glance. Ominous clouds crawl along indolently, bloated from their slow journey across Lake Ontario. The low rumble of thunder to the northeast is just audible enough to assure him that it will pour within the hour.

He comes to the end of Rebecca and turns right onto James Street North, skimming the outside of Irving's, the clothing shop housed in the ancient-looking grey building that occupies that corner. Sometimes the owner, friendly and well-loved, is outside watching the foot traffic, but not today.

In the next storefront's alcove doorway, an old woman is curled up and asleep on what appears to be a stained scrap of salvaged carpet. *Like a welcome mat*, Tribal thinks absently. *Her own invitation to any door.*

"Christ," he snarls out loud. "Now *I'm* starting to sound like Jimmy."

She is old, but Tribal knows that age is deceptive, the street exacting a heavy tithe for hard living. Still, the dirt trapped in the wrinkles and folds of her face make a bold map—deep rivers and countless tributaries. A topography of sorrows.

There's an old piece of plastic folded up by her head and a makeshift bouquet of dried-up flowers on the pavement by her feet. Tribal considers rolling her over carefully with his boot. Just to search for a cardboard sign, something to bring to Scotty's on a future visit, although no one seems to know what the mute wants with the things.

But something moves above them both and Tribal looks up to discover that Scotty has already been here: dangling from the alcove's light fixture is a small wire fish sculpture with a little human-like figure hanging inside it.

"How the fuck did you tie it up there?" he mumbles. He doesn't know. But he does know that if the woman had a sign, then Scotty has it now.

Tribal recalls Jimmy's observation, made one night in a dark parking lot over a shared joint. Scotty's fish are hard to find—unless you know where the homeless sleep. Because Scotty, that gentle urban scavenger, won't take without leaving. A thin-limbed and unobtrusive street ghost, slipping away with others' words and replacing them with his obscure version of a thank you—a sigil for a sign.

Or maybe the fish are like receipts.

Thunder accompanied by a few tentative plops of rain shake him out of his reverie. Tribal begins to cross the street, but then changes his mind. Instead, he retrieves the old sheet of plastic, unfolds it, drapes it over the comatose form, and heads up James Street.

Just around the corner from the Armoury—that immense heap of red bricks and heavy grey blocks that commands almost an entire city block— is a nameless underground record shop. Or nameless officially. Tribal's lot know it as Mallet Sally's.

He reaches the end of the Armoury just as the rain starts in earnest, hooks a right on Robert Street, then crosses to an unassuming alley to weave through overstuffed trash cans and a rusted heap that once served as a dumpster. He stops in front of a gunmetal grey door covered in religious pamphlets and graffiti. *"SALVATION! SALVATION FOR THE DAMNED!"* the largest placard promises. Tribal knocks on the steel slab four times slowly.

After a few moments the door creaks open an inch or two, accompanied by the rattle of a security chain.

"Whatcha want?" a soft voice asks from within.

"Salvation," Tribal answers.

The door closes momentarily as the chain is removed, and then it swings out like a vertical mouth to swallow him.

Tribal passes the emaciated goth girl who unlocked the first door. The heel-gnawed wooden stairs down are dimly lit by a single naked bulb dangling from a cord. On the wall at the bottom of the stairwell is a massive piece of graffiti art depicting a pig-tailed girl's head—straw-blonde, fiercely mono-browed, grinning maniacally at those navigating the descent. Her left eye is a brass-rimmed porthole, currently open. Tribal stands in front of the small window impatiently until the steel door to his left opens.

Tribal pushes through, shooting the heavyset punk doorman an irritated look.

"It's fuckin' four in the afternoon, eh? Paranoid idiots."

"Hey, rules is rules," the punk says. His neon red hair rises in dozens of tendrils from his thick round head, like an obscene sea anemone growing on a blunt stone.

The record shop itself occupies a tight, low-ceilinged subterranean hollow tucked between the heavy foundation of a 1920s three-storey James Street shop-and-tenement combination, and a shabby cinderblock wall meant to divide Mallet Sally's from the basement next door. Tribal makes his way through the tables of milk crates holding LPs toward the concrete wall, aiming for the lone floor-to-ceiling bookshelf stacked with used cassettes and low-end porn.

He looks over his shoulder at the small, green-haired punk girl by the cash box.

She shakes her head. "Too early, Tribal. Not ready."

"C'mon, Leah—just want a couple beers, eh?"

"Fuck off. Come back later—Rabid Defiance plays tonight. Craig's band. Around two. Cover is ten bones, but you get a beer at the door with it."

"Craig don't like me too much."

Leah nods sympathetically. "That's true. None of us do, though, so don't take it personal. That's punk for ya."

"Yeah . . . that's also kinda why I'm here now. Beer I like. Punk not so much."

Leah, without breaking eye contact with Tribal, reaches to her left and presses "play" on the boom box. Cockney Rejects' "Headbanger" blasts through the speakers rigged throughout the long, narrow room.

Tribal sighs and turns back to look longingly at the bookshelf. Or at what he knows is behind it, in any case. Because, when unlocked, the shelf unit swings open to reveal a hole in that wall, roughly rectangular and framed by a pair of steel Lally columns and a thick wooden lintel.

But then he notices what has been in plain sight on the shelf the whole time, resting on a disorganized heap of Teenage Head cassettes: a wire sculpture of a fish with a tiny black fetal figure dangling inside. Like the one out on James Street.

"Leah!" he bellows over the Rejects. "Where'd this come from?"

"Wha?" she bellows back.

Tribal snags the fish and weaves his way through the tables.

"Where'd this come from?"

Leah gives it a cursory glance. Shrugs. She picks at the torn and gluey remnants of a sticker on the side of the bass amp she uses as a seat.

"C'mon—tell me."

She pokes the sculpture with a long black nail so that the little figure inside swings like a pendulum. "Inbred subhuman filth," she says.

"What?"

"Go get it—it's a song on my Rabid Defiance cassette. Oh, and The Cramps. *Psychedelic Jungle*." And she points at a crate on the table behind Tribal.

He sweeps his straggly hair out of his face and turns savagely on the crate, rummaging through the cassettes and LPs.

"Nothing's in order! Don't you guys got a system?" He finds the album, though, between an empty Dead Kennedys sleeve and the Sex Pistols' *Never Mind the Bollocks*. The cassette juts out of the top of the sleeve for *We Have Come for Your Children*, by the Dead Boys. He pulls it out and hands both items over.

Leah stows the cassette and removes the vinyl with a gentle shake. "System's up here." She taps a long black nail on the side of her head between a pair of her neon green liberty spikes, then points at different groups of crates around the room. "That's shit I love and won't sell. That's shit I love and *will* sell. That's shit I hate and wanna sell. And that's shit I hate and won't sell. Unless I hate you. Then I'll sell." She smiles sweetly, white teeth like a secret behind black lipstick. "Wanna guess your section?"

"Seriously, Leah—where'd the fish come from?"

She looks at it again, uninterested. "Sally found it somewhere. Brought it in this afternoon."

"Where'd he find it?"

Leah bristles. "*She* didn't say."

The anemone opens the door to admit two punks, who head immediately to the "shit-I-love-but-won't-sell" section. The anorexic goth girl follows them in and something like recognition creeps into her glazed eyes when she sees Tribal.

"Hey," she drawls as she wanders over.

Tribal smirks at Leah. "She's a little old for glue-huffing, ain't she?"

Leah gives him the finger and turns to the goth. "You gotta stay at street level, Rem."

"I know but I'm gonna but Sally she said that artist kid he don't she need to talk to like one of them." Then she points vaguely at Tribal.

"Not a fucking word, Tribal," Leah snaps. Tribal, still smirking, just shrugs.

Leah turns Rem around and gives her a gentle push toward the anemone. Tribal points after her. "What the f—"

"Are you fucking *deaf*? Not a word!" She hands Tribal a key and points at the bookshelf. "Go. Sally wants to see Jimmy, but you'll have to do."

"Is he downstairs?"

"*She* is setting up for tonight. Go get your fucking beer."

BEYOND THE OPENING IS a trashed concrete room, spray-painted from floor to ceiling with graffiti art and rife with empty or smashed beer bottles, cigarette butts, discarded clothing—like a post-apocalyptic art gallery. In the far corner, a gaping hole drops away into blackness. No one knows what it was meant for—a well, maybe, or an access shaft for a deep sub-basement. The murk within is bone-chillingly cold. Painted onto the crumbling concrete in front of it is a neatly lettered sign:

VIP Entrance for Nazi Punks

To the left of the makeshift opening behind the shelves is the stairwell leading down to an old and spacious sub-basement—the *real* Mallet Sally's, a booze can that specializes in underground punk. Literally. The beer isn't all that cold and it's expensive, but it's available when everywhere else is closed. Like Toronto, Hamilton has its fair share of booze cans. And like others of its kind, Mallet Sally's is an illegal fiefdom with its own policies.

Tribal makes his way down the stairs and into the clammy recesses of the strange grotto below the record shop. Like the room above, graffiti covers every possible surface; even the thick bundle of extension cords carrying in pirated electricity has been painted to look like a reticulated python.

The first part of the illegal club is a long brick and mortar barrel vault that regulars have dubbed "the Sewer." Tables and chairs scrounged from the ruins of a restaurant fire have been arranged against the curved walls, leaving a narrow corridor down the middle so that denizens can reach the main part of the venue.

Tribal makes his way down the barrel vault. Without its mosh pit swarm of drunken hooligans, deafening live music, chromatic floodlights, and obligatory haze of smoke, the club seems more like a Medieval charnel house. Or a secret dungeon.

Beyond the Sewer is a wide, low rectangular room held up by concrete block pillars. Most of the club is swathed in impenetrable shadows; the garish spotlights and strobes have been temporarily substituted for quiet clusters of flickering candles that illuminate select portions of the room, lending it an atmosphere not unlike the Baroque vision of a debtors' prison.

One corner has additional steel Lally columns arranged under a cracked beam of ancient wood, and protecting the steel posts from drunken mistakes is the bar itself, constructed of three wooden doors arranged in an "L" and nailed down to saw horses. Diagonally from the bar is the stage, such as it is: eight wood pallets arranged in two rows and surfaced in plywood. Depending upon the strength and direction of those who use the wooden edge to propel themselves into the mosh, the stage itself has been known to drift like a ligneous continental plate.

An opportunist by nature, Tribal drifts quietly toward the bar. Nonchalant, seemingly bored, eyes scanning the shadows for signs of company. Maybe Leah was wrong about Sally being down here; he moves toward the opening to where the coolers are stacked.

"Tsk tsk, darling," a deep voice admonishes. Sally emerges from behind the stack speakers, armed with a pair of pliers and a coil of wire.

Even in the black leather bustier, matching crinoline skirt, and spider web stockings—or maybe because of them—Sally is an imposing sight. Some years ago, Sally was named Dimitris. Or, more infamously, "The Corinthian Constrictor," a wrestler on the semi-professional circuit who specialized in turnbuckle antics, low blows featuring a supposedly authentic ancient bronze vase, and a submission hold called (predictably perhaps) the "python's grip."

Now, Sally looks like a terrifying cross between Elvira, Mistress of the Dark, and a Russian circus bear. In six-inch stiletto heels. The punks and goths of Hamilton either love her or hold their peace; few cross her—or, at least, cross her twice. That dented and tarnished vase sits prominently on the bar beside a plastic cup of broken teeth and dried blood.

Tribal leans against the edge of the bar and taps absently at an antique door knob that rises from the gouged surface like a bloated patina toadstool. "Leah said to come down and have a beer," he offers quickly.

"*Did* she?" Sally now looms over Tribal, close enough so that cloying perfume and body odour compete for dominance. Rivulets of sweat run down her thick, stubbly neck before disappearing into the forest of hair that covers the ample flesh above the bustier. Chest, shoulders, and back are covered—like a shaggy stole. Her makeup, however—from foundation to the deep purple eye shadow that sweeps dramatically up to her temples—is absolutely perfect. Like a brilliantly constructed mask.

"Well," Tribal concedes, "not in so many words." He shifts, uncomfortable in Sally's company even when he's with others. "She said you wanted Jimmy."

Sally raises a thick eyebrow.

"To *talk* to Jimmy," Tribal amends.

Sally manoeuvres around her nervous guest, treating him to a sly and bitter smile. Behind the bar, she retrieves a bottle from the top cooler.

"Ooh, Molson Brador. The Golden Arm. You're a lucky boy—we've had nothing but Steeler for weeks."

"I like Steeler."

"You little tramps like anything." She pops the cap off on the edge of the bar with practiced ease and hands him the bottle.

"Uh, cheers," Tribal says. "You got a message for Jimmy? I'm gonna see him in a few hours, eh?"

Sally delicately flicks grit from her calf-thick forearm with a long, glossy red nail. An old tattoo of a serpent wraps around the entire limb, its fanged head adorning the side of her powerful shoulder.

"Do I make you nervous, darling?"

"Look, I'm fuckin' here, right?"

Sally looks away, a long gaze at the stack of speakers she hasn't finished rigging together.

"It's alright." Her voice is husky. "We all fear the unknown." Then she turns to look full into Tribal's guarded eyes with her own deep belladonna gaze. "I *understand* you, darling. But I just don't give a shit."

Tribal takes a swig of warm beer. "Message?" he says.

Sally reaches under one of the sawhorses to retrieve her purse, a glossy red leather bag bristling on one side with drywall screws. She rummages around until she finds her cigarettes, and then waits patiently until Tribal takes the hint.

When he doesn't, she clears her throat.

Sneering, he pulls one of the flickering pillar candles loose from its waxy mooring and holds it out for her.

Smoke curls out of the edge of her mouth, and crawls up her face and into the blackness above them. "I don't know *what* Jimmy sees in *any* of you." Then she exhales the rest of the drag and clutches Tribal's wrist in her delicately manicured bear trap of a hand.

"What the fuck!"

"*Relax*, darling—you aren't that attractive. Let me see your palm."

He doesn't have much of a choice. Beyond using the half empty beer bottle in his other fist, that is, but Jimmy's serene face flashes through his mind. He sighs and complies.

Jimmy's face—because this is the cavernous lair of the guru's Guru, the wellspring (Jimmy says) of ebb and flow street magic. Sally has an Old World psychic's reputation for sortilege, this techno grotto her own punk cabaret fortune teller's tent. But there is nothing itinerant about her, no trace of anything nomadic.

She is immutable. A taproot.

Tribal, caught in her spell, follows a long red fingernail as it traces its way across the lines on his palm.

"Well, well," she says softly. "What *have* we been up to, darling? Taking things that aren't ours?"

"Who doesn't?" Tribal snarls.

"But from—oh, sweetie, the *homeless*?"

Tribal pales visibly. "How the fuck can you—"

But Sally laughs, sultry and indulgent. "I'm just playing, darling. A little bird told me that tidbit. That's not how palm reading works."

"Yeah, well . . . I don't believe in that shit anyway."

"What 'shit' would that be?"

"Fate and all that bullshit."

But in response, Sally looks deeply into Tribal's hand. Her thick brows come together as she concentrates. "Cup your hand for me, just a little."

She touches the fleshy mound that rises at the base of his index finger, then coaxes his hand flat again and traces a long line that runs in a sweeping arc from his wrist to the base of his middle finger. She releases him and smiles.

"What?" Tribal asks.

"Nothing, darling. You don't believe in 'fate and all that bullshit.' However . . ."

"Yeah?"

"Well," Sally says with narrowing eyes, "for someone who claims not to believe in fate, you have a pretty prominent fate line. And one that indicates that—wait: what brought you here in the first place?"

Tribal shrugs. "Rain. And beer."

"Water," she mumbles. "But I see fire. I see . . ." She closes her eyes a moment, then opens them to look into Tribal's. "Alright—rain and beer. Maybe. But I mean what brought you down here? To me?"

"Uh, I guess that scrawny goth chick you got up at the alley door."

Sally raises a sculpted eyebrow. "You mean *Rem*?"

Tribal takes a long swig, draining the bottle. "Yeah. The real stoned one."

"She's not *stoned*, darling," Sally whispers, as if to herself. And then she takes a step toward Tribal, looming over him like a giant perfumed, corpulent vampire. "*She* said that I wanted to see you?"

Unable to retreat, Tribal bristles as logic and instinct claw for purchase. "I don't—I don't know, eh? She said a bunch of fuckin' words I didn't catch! Didn't make sense, all tangled up." His eyes shift from side to side, agitated and caged and claustrophobic. Then he remembers. "Leah—yeah, she knew what the goth meant. I was asking her about that fish of Scotty's. Then she told me to come down here."

Sally considers. "*She* told you to come down. Leah or Rem?"

"Both of 'em, I suppose."

"That fish . . . Oh, darling," Sally says, stroking his cheek with her soft paw, "that is what we in the Business call 'portentous.'" She releases Tribal and walks with heavy clicks of her spiked heels into the shadowed recesses between bar and stage, returning a moment later with a card about the width and length of Tribal's open hand. It is weathered, its antique edges curling in on themselves like a dying leaf's. Upon its surface is the picture of a slender young man in a robe, belted by a serpent biting its own tail; he holds a raised wand in one hand and points down with the other. Above his head is a horizontal figure eight.

"Give this to Jimmy for me," Sally says sadly.

Tribal takes the card. "That's *it*? What's it supposed to mean?"

"He'll know, darling. He'll know."

7

THE LION'S HEAD IS usually packed, but that isn't saying much—it's the smallest venue on the circuit. Many of Hamilton's musicians started on its tiny corner stage, and some of the city's heavy-hitting bands occasionally find themselves crammed into the tight space between the unusable dart cabinets and the plate glass front window, wondering afterwards in bemused frustration why free beer and sixty dollars collected at the door seemed like a fair trade for a Friday night. Or any night.

Nostalgia's gravitational pull, they conclude, and move on.

Not that Tribal's brother plays in a band of that magnitude—circuit regulars, yes; top earners, not so much. Tonight's crowd is a motley and eclectic collection of pub rats, friends of the band, and the small but loyal following of late-night denizens that find meaning in the migration from gig to gig, listening to the same set list for eight or ten or twelve shows before drifting into the wake of another circuit band.

Rumours of a house party up on the Escarpment are reliable enough to follow up on, taking place (supposedly) in one of the newer neighbourhoods. And even though it's after 1:00 a.m. before the last of the equipment is loaded into the van, Sirius and the others drive off to investigate.

"Why not you, too?" This from Jimmy who stands with Tribal outside the Lion's Head. They share a sizable joint, protected from light drizzle and casual observation by standing a metre down the narrow, covered alley to the right of the pub. It's little more than a steep concrete ramp leading up to a postage stamp parking lot, but it's one of Jimmy's favourite means of slipping away from John Street. "Chance for you to terrify some middle-class suburban kids, man—thought that was high on the priority list for you." Jimmy smirks and passes the joint.

Tribal smiles, but mouth only. His eyes are elsewhere, wandering—like a pair of restless and sullen ghosts. He takes a moment to inspect the joint, then licks his finger and wets the faster burning side. "This shit," he snarls, "is half seeds and stems. Where'd you get this, the hay-weed section of the fuckin' Bulk Barn?"

Jimmy reaches for the joint. "It was a gift," he says, a touch haughtily. "Ah."

"Anyway," Jimmy continues, "you didn't answer my question. Why aren't you with your brother and the rest?"

"Why aren't you, eh?" An apt question. Their lot rarely find their way into a middle-class high school party, and Jimmy—Hamilton's own mobile urban shaman and distributor of temporary visions of the lysergic variety—can sell his entire stock in a matter of about thirty minutes and then leave. Which is a good thing, since cops show up uninvited more often than not, and Jimmy is hardly inconspicuous in his retro-'70s drug rug and dreads.

Jimmy takes a heavy toke and glances down the alley toward the gloomy parking lot. "As long as you're—here, take this—as long as you're here, you might as well tell me."

Tribal follows Jimmy's glance. "Tell you what?"

"C'mon, man. My bass, my amp, and my second favourite patch cord went to a party that's likely being busted as we speak. Heavy price to pay to hear what Sally said."

"What the *fuck*, Jimmy!" Tribal snarls. "Alright. Screw it—I'll bite. How the hell'd you find out I saw Sally, eh? You were on *stage* for most of the night."

A raccoon wanders into the alley from the parking lot end, but stops suddenly to contemplate the pair blocking the exit to the street. Tribal takes a last toke and flicks the roach at the newcomer, which bounces once and comes to a stop a boot's length from the raccoon's front paws. After a heartbeat, the raccoon snags the ragged nub and turns, waddling back at that leisurely and entitled pace of urban scavengers.

Jimmy laughs. "I swear to Hendrix, man, that little trash panda's been stalking me for, like, two weeks."

Tribal, though. "Seriously—how'd you know? That fuckin' raccoon tell you?"

But Jimmy smirks and shrugs.

"Whatever," Tribal says. "He told me to give you this." And he pulls out the weathered placard.

"*She*," Jimmy mumbles, taking the card. He glances at it and frowns. "Mind telling me how you ended up in the depths of Mallet Sally's at four in the afternoon?"

"Ask the raccoon."

"It's actually important. You and your brother," Jimmy says, rolling his eyes. "Everything's a confrontation."

"It's our stellar upbringing. Anyway, it ain't the same thing: Sirius actually *believes* half the shit you tell him."

Jimmy smiles slyly. "In truth, Tribal, I think you secretly believe the other half. C'mon—give."

A small group of loud drunk girls escorted by two nervous-looking guys tumbles by the alley opening, heading north on John Street. Tribal watches them pass with a cruel grin as he reaches into his leather to retrieve his pack of smokes.

"That's Opportunity, brother," he says wistfully.

Jimmy helps himself to a cigarette. "Let the night have them. Seriously, Tribal—I'm trying to piece something together. I don't need details, man. Just the gist."

Another look, at once plaintive and predatory, crosses Tribal's face as intoxicated laughter echoes down John Street. Then he sighs, resigned.

"Alright, Jimmy. But there ain't much to tell, eh? Wanted a beer or two and didn't feel like walking in the rain. Mallet Sally's was closest."

"Closest to what?"

"Scotty's. Me and Sirius, we headed up there around three or four, but he wasn't home."

Jimmy signals Tribal to follow him deeper into the alley. A moment later, a cruiser rolls by.

"Sometimes," Tribal says, "I actually think you *are* psychic."

"Strata, man—just gotta know what to listen for. The streets, they take care of their own. Send out warnings. You know that."

Tribal takes a last drag before knocking the heater off the end of his cigarette, storing what's left back in the pack.

"So," Jimmy coaxes, "Scotty wasn't home and you shogged it to Sally's?"

"Yeah," Tribal nods. "But Leah wouldn't let me downstairs. Then I started asking her about one of Scotty's fish I found on the bookcase—you know, the door thing—and that fucked-up goth girl said a bunch of shit that didn't make no sense."

"Rem, you mean?" Jimmy asks.

"Yeah—the stoned goth chick."

"She's not stoned, man."

Tribal scoffs. "That's what Sally said, too."

"She's right," Jimmy says softly. "That's brain damage from Rem's violent-as-shit rapist stepfather. He's serving a pretty extensive sentence, and Rem's mom overdosed a year ago. Sally took her in."

"Oh," Tribal says. "I'm a dick."

"You have your moments. Continue."

"So, I guess Sally told Rem h—*she* needed to talk to you, and that's why Leah let me in—kinda like your . . . Whatchacallit?"

"Avatar?"

"Yeah, that. I told Sally I saw the fish sculpture upstairs, and she said it was . . . important? Nah, that ain't it." Tribal digs around for the word. "Por-something. Dunno—I ain't Sirius. He'd know the word."

"Doesn't matter," Jimmy says. "Then she gave you this?" He holds up the placard.

"Yeah—said you'd know what it means."

Jimmy furrows his brow and nods slowly, as if in response to some quiet conversation beyond the liminal threshold. Tribal has accompanied Jimmy to Sally's grotto before. He knows that Jimmy—transient street mystic hovering ghost-like on the periphery of every urban tribe there is—sees Sally as more divine than diva.

The guru's goddess.

And so Tribal waits, watching the shadows and wondering whether his brother and the others made out alright. Jimmy's face, half hidden by the darkness, toys with the mechanics of this new information. Finally, he exhales heavily.

"Well?" Tribal asks.

"This," Jimmy says, holding up the antique card, "is the Magician. A few nights ago, I asked Sally a couple questions—something didn't feel right downtown. Hasn't for a while. This card is . . . well, that's not important. The fish you found is the real sign—gotta find him."

"You mean Scotty?"

"No—Scotty's lifeline, the miracle worker. The magician. Gotta find Simon."

"That's easy—he's at Scotty's pretty much every morning."

"I know," Jimmy says, heading toward the far end of the alley. "But we need to bring him something. And I'm going to need your help to get it."

"Tonight?"

Jimmy pauses and considers. "No. Not tonight. Need to put some pieces together. Probably soon, though. Sometime next week."

"Why's Simon so important?" Tribal asks.

Jimmy shrugs. "Because Sally says so."

SIMON

8

His is a story of rage and loss. Then of drowning. And finally of rage and redemption.

Or a redemption of sorts.

On a muggy summer night some years ago, Simon Ten-Bones side-armed a lit M-80 through the open window of a cruiser. Already speeding, the street way too narrow and dark and populated, and the cop not even with his roof rack lit up in warning. That M-80 soared arrow-straight and must have bounced around inside for a few seconds before it exploded, because the cruiser swerved a bit and then the lights went on and the siren gave a short and rising wail, like an enquiry, as the car leapt the curb and glanced off the telephone pole at the corner of the Beer Store parking lot.

Simon laughed—he laughed a lot—and jumped on his motorcycle, roaring off in the opposite direction.

Simon Ten-Bones was just what his white friends called him.

"Sounds way more Indian," they laughed. "More Indian than Simon Johnson," they meant, which was his real name. Simon didn't seem to mind, though, laughing in their ignorant white faces through strong teeth and week-old, patchy stubble.

"Whatever, palefaces," he'd say. "So long's your beer's cold and you got a couch to sleep on when I need it."

There were a couple of houses on the street occupied by Mohawks, but they were grim-faced and reticent, not wanting anything to do with the squat-house full of lazy white transients midway down the road. Not Simon, though; on weekends, he drifted across the city on that bike of his from crowd to crowd, staying with one group of friends until he got bored or felt that he'd stayed long enough. Then he'd migrate to the next. As they watched the taillight of his bike disappear around the corner, they knew it would be at least three or four weeks before he'd show up again.

But the time between weekend visits stretched out until he became more memory than maniac—and then, eventually, the visits stopped altogether. Unbeknownst to any of them, his weekdays had been spent in classes at McMaster University, and his weeknights in the university library.

Once he had his degree, Simon Ten-Bones left his appellation behind—or, more accurately, he locked it away inside where it occasionally tugged playfully on his skeleton or rattled the cage in boredom—and he became Simon Johnson. Collage in place and newly employed, he would make his rounds, driving in a rust-and-pale-blue Chevy Celebrity from one sad situation to the next.

Social worker: thankless pilgrimage from one halfway house to another, or from clinic to clinic, tenement to tenement, receiving a pittance (poverty-level pay) to administer meds, make observations, taxi human wreckage to and from court-sanctioned appointments, and deliver prosaic clichés about life choices.

Simon's mom was proud, though. It was a financial struggle to keep him in school, a mother's heavy burden. No loans or handouts—it was a matter of pride.

"I wish your father could see you," she'd said after Simon had climbed the stairs and been handed his degree. This was at the modest reception afterward. "He would have been so proud." Then she'd reached out to touch the wooden turtle pendant that hung around Simon's neck.

The accompanying tears had worried Simon—his mom was strong; she never cried. At least not since Simon's father had died just after Simon's tenth birthday. It had been a rapid and wasting illness. The family felt robbed, outraged when the gentle and soft-spoken man suddenly disappeared under the crushing weight of the disease.

He died alone in his hospital bed in the early morning hours with nothing but a high-pitched bleeping machine for company. It wailed, though, when the drumbeat of his heart finally stumbled to a halt. A mourning cry that was eventually silenced by the nurse on duty.

LATE MONDAY MORNING. SIMON considers his options; an emergency room visit with a client had cost Simon his regular morning rounds, and now it's after eleven, his usual time for lunch.

"Scotty," he says to himself. "As good a start as any. At least he'll be up."

It is a quick call, and easy. The mute is as reliable as a clock—up around daybreak, always sober, always compliant, nearly always home. Just silent. Simon knows that his visits used to distress Scotty on some level, the enigmatic artist standing awkwardly in polite apprehension as Simon fulfilled his obligations to a doctor's court-sanctioned recommendation. Or a court-sanctioned best guess.

Now, though, enough time has passed so that the prescribed course of action—in this case, a small handful of antidepressants delivered daily—has become the Right Path to recovery.

Woefully out of date, Simon is sure, but he is obliged to follow the instructions on the printout: *Deliver meds. a.m. Watch patient swallow all pills.* Doesn't matter; Scotty is barely on anyone's radar, a small and utterly silent wheel in the squeaking, wheezing grind of an immensely complicated and indifferent machine.

And then there's the small detail that Scotty aged out of assistance on his eighteenth birthday, almost two years ago. However, Simon's supervisor has some pull at the Ministry—how or why Simon doesn't know. An exception, "under review," they called it. It won't last, though.

Simon parks on a side street and walks to the dreary apartment building. It is a woefully unattractive structure, an ugly green and beige and sadly out of touch with its surroundings. As if it were forgotten, somehow.

The lobby, a pathetic assortment of motley drabs, is empty. Simon has a key to get in: the super grew tired of his incessant buzzing, since Scotty's speaker is broken and it seemed less trouble to hand out an extra key than to fix the intercom of a mute.

"At least the elevator works," he mumbles to himself.

~

SCOTTY KNOWS BY THE knock.

Simon's is four quick raps—not hard or insistent, not an official-sounding knock, even though his reason for coming is. And, of course, only Simon comes by before noon. Sometimes Sirius does, too (like today), but his is a strange knock: two thumps with his palm, as if doors were primitive drums.

Knockknockknockknock.

Sirius looks up from where he sits on the floor, back against the wall. He's restringing his Fender acoustic.

"Want me to get that?"

But Scotty is already on his feet, moving toward the door. He exhales, inhales deeply, and turns the handle.

"Hey, man." Simon steps into the cramped flat. Then he sees Sirius.

"Oh, hey—didn't think Scotty'd have company at 11:00 a.m., but I'm glad you're here—got something for you in my car."

"Yeah?" says Sirius as he stands up to shake Simon's hand. "What is it?"

"Novel called *Love Medicine*. By Louise Erdrrich—I want you to read it."

Sirius looks puzzled. "Who?"

"Louise Erd—never mind, just read it. It's good."

"Sure, brother—you know me, eh?"

And Simon does. Sirius reads more than anyone he knows, and Simon himself is pretty prolific.

Scotty has gone back to his habitual place, an old chair rescued from the street. Simon rummages through a canvas satchel, pulls out the bag of meds with the right name on it. He retrieves a glass of water from the cramped galley kitchen and hands the meds and glass to Scotty.

"Alright. Here you go, man."

Scotty takes the glass and the meds without looking up, places the small handful of pills in his mouth and takes a drink. Automatic. Compliant.

Simon takes the glass. "Remember, Scotty—it's Monday. Gotta pick you up this afternoon for Group."

Scotty stares intently at the floor between his two visitors, the one packing up his guitar and the other writing something down in a black journal.

"Okay? Group at 4:00 p.m. Meet me out front at 3:30." Then Simon leaves, followed by Sirius.

Group. Scotty hates this, dreads it. A dreary room in a rundown clinic, circle of ten or twelve chairs, a "share session" they call it.

As for the pick-up time, well.

Scotty smiles.

You didn't say "Simon says."

9

THE BUILDING THAT HOUSES the Children's Aid Society in Hamilton is not attractive. Like the CAS itself, it is utilitarian—a frontline response to ugly necessity. Simon loves it, though, from its unadorned brick exterior to the scuffed and chipped linoleum floor of the dingy break room.

Still idealistic, still young. That's what some of the veterans tell him with a condescending shoulder pat or a weary smile. *To hell with that,* Simon thinks, watching instead his supervisor, Frank, as he paces back and forth as far as the stretched-out coils of his old phone cord will allow. As he talks, Frank waves his free hand around like he's fending off hornets; his thinning hair, always unmoored by midmorning, waves about in wild wisps, blissfully unaware of gravity. Frank's tone is insistent, urgent, sincere. He's talking to an overwhelmed foster parent or a despairing youth worker. Or his son, maybe. Fifty years old, twenty-six years' service under his belt and the man is indefatigable. Unbreakable. The harder the case, the harder Frank struggles to make things work. Not that they always do, of course, but his belief in the system is absolute—faith and pragmatism in equal parts. Like a blind man who, without hesitation, tackles and subdues a runaway chainsaw in a daycare. Madness with method.

Simon digs through files for the notes of his predecessors. There had been many. Still, there wasn't much written down—or, at least, not much that said anything differently. It isn't his first time digging through the disorganized heap, but between his heavy caseload and the infuriating fact that much of Scotty's information had been misfiled in a different cabinet altogether, he hasn't given the records the attention they deserve. It was a co-worker who actually discovered the mistake, and only because she was searching for fossils of her own in the drawer marked "G-H-I."

As Simon is stacking his findings, Frank appears from around the corner with a Styrofoam cup of coffee in one hand and a honey cruller in the other. He glimpses down at the top folder. "Campbell again, eh?"

Simon straightens the stack. "Yeah. He's been different lately."

"Different how?"

"Oh, more emotional. More moody, I guess. Unpredictable, too—he's restless. If I could figure out the source—"

Frank tapped the top of the stack. "I have a meeting next month, you know."

"I know, Frank."

"They'll probably say no."

"I know."

"The Ministry is not inclined to make exceptions. To be honest, I still can't believe we got the first extension after Campbell aged out—and for *two* years. I can't pull that trick again."

"Frank, I just—"

"Hey," the older man says, poking Simon in the chest with the doughnut. "I never said give up on him, did I? You know me better than that. Just . . . you know. Just have what you need from those files before next month."

Which means Frank knows that Simon will continue to work with Scotty with or without the Ministry's permission. After all, it's what Frank would do. *Has* done, in fact.

After the older man leaves, Simon sits in his broken office chair and starts flipping through the folders, at first in no particular order. Then chronologically. Then backwards, *as if I were an archaeologist at a dig*, he thinks, sifting through strata, one miniscule layer of injustice at a time. How many workers before him had reached this stage before giving up? Scotty's case is perplexing, frustrating—even aggravating.

"Just shit luck," Simon mumbles. So many had simply walked away from him, foster families *and* workers. The catatonic silence was too much, the absence too alien. Or there were the standard, tired reasons—job burnout, change in family stability, people moved away. Simon reads through each prosaic report.

Eventually, Frank reappears with two cups of coffee and puts one on Simon's disaster of a desk. "You've been at it for a solid two hours. What else do you think you'll find?"

Simon just shakes his head. "I don't know. Nothing, probably. Only half of these notes ever got typed up. Then there's stuff like this." He holds up a handful of faded instamatic pictures and a dozen scraps of paper with barely legible scrawl across them.

"Looks like abstract art, eh?" Frank says.

"Which, the photos or the notes?"

Frank chuckles. "Both, I guess. One month, Johnson." Friendly shoulder squeeze and he's gone again.

The photos are odd—no context and clustered together in one of the oldest files. A "'76" is on the back corner of one, just fading blue ink.

"1976," Simon mumbles. Eleven years ago—Scotty would have been nine.

One picture shows what appears to be a cluster of grey dots on something pale, but the whole thing is overexposed. Another picture is of an angry and jagged red X—*Not razor*, he decides. *Too jagged.* On an arm? Leg? The damned picture is too close to the wound to tell. Then there are the pictures of odds and ends—a wing nut, a red Christmas tree bulb, a handful of acorns. Other things, some by themselves and some in little collections.

"None of this makes any sense," he grumbles aloud, frustrated. The notes are just as cryptic—catalogues of small household items. Like a grocery list for a housewife in a hardware store.

In the oldest folder, tucked in amongst leaves of smudged writing on yellow foolscap, is a lone photograph. It depicts a child's pale left hand with one black finger—painted, perhaps. The little hand had been placed, palm down, on a flat surface and documented. Simon flips the photo over and finds a word, something in hasty cursive. The first letter, capitalized, is either a narrow "G" or a boxy "S"; the rest of the short word is little more than a jittery line. He frowns, puts the picture aside.

The yellow papers are just as cryptic—most of the notes are in smeared pencil, documenting observations in sparse spurts.

10-13 SG unresponsive. Blackened index finger left hand. Acorns (10), also black.

10-17 SG still same, but foster p. reports compliance with house rules. No conflicts so far with other children in household.

10-28 SG. Placement uncertain—foster p. complained of G's behavior. Removed all cabinet knobs in kitchen and bathroom during quiet hours. Painted them black.

Simon drops the small collection of notes onto his desk and rubs his temples. *"Behavior,"* he thinks. *Well, that explains the month-day dates. First worker must have been American.* Still, why the SG, or the lone G? He gets up, stretches, picks up the sheaf, and heads for Frank's office.

"You got a minute?"

Frank looks up at Simon over the top of his bifocals. "Sure. Did you make any sense of that mess?"

"Actually, I got a question. Do you remember an American working here ten or eleven years ago?"

Frank takes off his glasses and squints at the drop ceiling tiles. Simon smirks—it's Frank's signature deep-in-professional-thought gesture, as if all lore was actually stored secretly above the asbestos tiles of the second-floor ceiling.

"We've had a couple Americans pass through," Frank mumbles. "Why do you ask?"

Simon leans against the doorframe. "Pretty sure Scotty's first worker was American. Kinda hoping you remember who it was. I need to know if he's still in the area—his notes are . . . problematic."

"How so?"

"Well, to start, they read like, I dunno . . . telegrams, I guess. But I'm mostly confused by the initials he uses—SG or just G." Simon rummages through the notes until he finds the strange picture of the small hand with the black index finger. He turns it over and hands it to Frank. "See? Just a letter—S or G—then something illegible."

Frank's brows knit together as he stares at the word. "Leave this with me, eh? I'll phone a couple people—I think I might be able to find something out for you."

"Thanks, Frank."

"Now, if you could maybe pay a little attention today to a couple clients who *haven't* aged out—"

Simon smiles. "Okay, boss."

THE HOSPITAL IS ON the way from the CAS to Scotty's, and the mute isn't expecting Simon until their 3:30 p.m. rendezvous in the lobby. There's still enough time for Simon to check on the client he drove to the E.R. this morning.

Simon hates emergency rooms. Fresh vomit lurks between the cloying scent of rancid coffee and the heavy fug of stale clothes on unwashed flesh; on bad days, the rotten meat stink of infected abscesses accompanies the invasive stench of feces. The clingy presence of antiseptic tiptoes from person to person like a half-hearted apology.

And then there are the waiting-room parishioners who watch the nurse at the check-in desk with furtive glances. Some lose their cool—they rant or beg or threaten. It makes little difference to the duty nurse.

But Simon takes the smells and emotional climate in stride; after all, his job requires him to peer into dark corners daily. These aren't the reasons.

It's the art.

The paintings themselves are different from hospital to hospital, but they're all the same starving-artist-Bob-Ross-disciple-type dreck nonetheless. Supposedly serene nature scenes, mostly, palette-knifed onto the canvas in a way that utterly defies naturalism itself. Hermetically sealed generic Canadian wilderness.

As a boy, he'd spent hours at a stretch in a waiting room. Waiting, he realized eventually, for his dad to die. Simon's mother fretted away the time before visiting hours started, knitting mittens that never got finished, or sewing quilt squares that ended up in a ragged and forgotten heap at home. She sat in silence with her dying husband when it was permitted, holding his wasted hand—his brittle and delicate bones caught between her thin strong ones. Simon could only stand so much, and the waiting room was really the only place he could go.

Just Simon and the paintings. He'd try to picture a boy navigating those toxic landscapes—a savagely pink sunset; a forest of dagger-sharp conifers; blackish-grey mountains of uniform angles, all wearing stark white smears.

EVEN NOW, YEARS LATER, Simon studiously ignores the framed painting or print or whatever it is to the right of the check-in desk. The clock above the picture says 2:47 p.m. The nurse on duty glances up at him.

"Hi, Simon."

"Hey, Jan." Most of the day-shift nurses know him by sight and often by name, but Jan knew Simon in his wilder days, when he roared in and out of cliques and crowds on his father's beat up motorcycle, bartering his way into sleeping on couches and occasionally in beds with packs of smokes he never touched himself. He shared one of those beds with Jan's little sister on occasion, an arrangement that confused him because neither she nor Jan seemed to think anything of it at all.

"You're here for the kid you brought in this morning, right?"

"Yeah," Simon nods. "How's he doing?"

"I'm pretty sure he's—just a sec." Jan digs through papers on the desk until she locates the right one. "Yeah, he's gonna stay. Doctor's orders."

"Figured as much. I'll check back later."

SIMON RETURNS TO SCOTTY'S for their 3:30 p.m. rendezvous, but his quiet client doesn't materialize in the lobby. Sometimes Scotty forgets—or pretends to forget—but Simon can't blame him: Group seems like a useless exercise for an introverted mute.

Ten minutes later, four rapid knocks and no answer.

"C'mon, Scotty!" Simon shouts at the door. "I know you're there—we got Group!"

"Group, eh? *That* should work," says a voice behind him.

Simon jumps and spins around. "Holy *shit*, Jimmy! You trying to give me a heart attack? Where the hell did you come from?"

"Third floor. Alise's. I came up the stairs and saw you getting out of the elevator."

"For a smoker, you climb a lot of stairs."

Jimmy smiles faintly. "I don't do elevators."

"Neither does Tribal, I've noticed."

"Or his brother. Or a lot of us. The System sometimes gives you an education you'd rather not have. You'd be surprised how often elevators work their way into that."

Now Simon smiles, but sadly. "As an official *of* the System, I'm well aware of it. Now, if you don't mind, I got an appointment to keep." And he reaches out to knock again.

"Hold on—allow me," Jimmy says, stepping up to the door.

Simon shrugs and stands back, but Jimmy doesn't do anything at all. He just stands there silently and lets the seconds slip past. After half a minute, Simon's perplexity gives way to impatience.

"Jimmy, I—"

But then the lock springs and the door slips open.

OF THAT ENTIRE STREET tribe drifting in and out of Simon's periphery, he's known Jimmy the longest. And between them has always been an unspoken agreement: Simon, despite his position, never took the steps necessary to bring Jimmy into the System. The same applied to the select few Jimmy marked as "beyond reach." It's an arrangement that only needs to be observed for another seven or eight months; then the last of Jimmy's circle will have aged out.

It isn't goodwill, though—not exactly. It's because of a prank.

Simon had been nineteen at the time, a fierce advocate for Indigenous rights and pursuing a degree in social work. His friends at school—mostly white—were in mild awe of his passion, unsure of how to support his efforts without seeming like bandwagon wannabes. Anti-Apartheid activism was easier for the white conscience: it had all the trappings of responsible social concern and none of the inconvenience of face-to-face controversy.

Simon's friends outside of university—also mostly white—were impressed with his wild spirit: he was like a motorized urban warrior, migrating from crowd to crowd on the beaten-up motorcycle that had belonged to his father, doing crazy stunts that put him (more often than not) at legal risk of life and limb. "Crazy Horse," one drunken white friend named him. "Crazy Horse-*Power*, you mean!" someone else countered as Simon roared off after flinging that M-80 through the open window of a police cruiser.

THURSDAY, 1ST APRIL, 1982.

White man's April Fools' Day, and two days before Simon's twentieth birthday. Simon and three other friends—all born and raised on the Six Nations of the Grand River Reservation—took it upon themselves to avenge a ridiculous indignity: a white developer's legal bid to annex yet one more piece of ancestral land for a white man's pastime: golf.

Simon had done his research, at least. The developer—a privileged, third-generation trust fund product named Weston Peterson—had a sprawling estate out in Ancaster. Daddy, Grandpa, and most of the extended family were buried in a cemetery not five kilometres away from the family home. The university library microfiche had confirmed it.

The four friends hopped the low iron cemetery fence at about 11:00 p.m., dressed in the darkest clothes they owned. Earlier that day, Simon and his cousin Thomas had surreptitiously planted stakes in the ground, marking out a rectangle roughly one hundred and ten yards by sixty yards. Within that rectangle were other stakes, measured out to the best of their ability.

Thomas threw a coil of string to Simon. "Okay, Cousin. Tie it and run the line down to the far corner. John, you do the other side—it'll go faster. Me and Logan'll string the insides." The four separated, working quickly—four hearts pounding with the immensity of what they were doing.

They met again at the same corner. Thomas pulled three of the four spray paint cans out of his backpack, handing them out in silence.

"Hey," Simon hissed. "Try not to hit any of the grave stones. Just the grass."

"Shit, Cousin—why not? Fuck these assholes and their dead relatives!"

"No," Simon snapped. "This is a statement, not a declaration of war. Just the grass."

Thomas mumbled something under his breath and stalked off into the night with his can. John and Logan, shaking theirs in unison, grinned viciously and slipped off to do their part. Simon sighed, shook his own can, uncapped it, and began the long walk between stakes, spraying the grass with a straight line of white paint.

All told, it took just over an hour. By a little after midnight, Logan and Thomas were each carrying a makeshift goal of sticks and old fishing net to opposite ends of their handiwork: a roughly marked out playing field.

For an Indigenous pastime: lacrosse.

Logan came back after Thomas, still wearing that cruel grin. "Hey," he hissed, "you ain't gonna believe this—follow me!" And off he went toward the net he'd set up, followed by the others.

It was perfect: blocking half the net was the gravestone of one John Oliver Peterson—Grandpa himself. They stared and then laughed.

"Holy shit!" Thomas said. "In the fuckin' crease! That's interference—we should give him thirty years for that!"

"Or at least hang a red card on the stone," added John.

"Nah," Simon sneered. "Something more . . . obvious." He shook his can, stepped away from the tombstone, and sprayed onto the grass one word: INTERFERENCE. And then he added an arrow from the word to the base of the stone.

Thomas nodded his approval, and the other two laughed. Simon wasn't sure if they got it the way Thomas did, though.

"Let's go," Thomas said, heading back toward the fence and his beat-up car.

But Simon stayed behind. "I'll catch up. My bike's on the other end anyway. Save me a beer!"

"Not fuckin' likely!" Logan laughed over his shoulder, and the three made their way through the stones and over the fence. Alone, Simon started his own trek back to where he'd hidden his bike.

That's when he saw the kid. Young, scrawny punk wrapped in an oversized motorcycle jacket. A white kid with a full mohawk sitting on one of the bigger tombstones. In the bright moonlight, he looked like a semi-comical gargoyle on his granite perch.

"Nice night," the kid said, casually.

"Yeah," Simon managed. "How long you been here?"

"Up here? Not long. Here on Earth? Not much longer. Fourteen years, more or less."

Simon, hands in his pockets, approached the kid. "How about here in the cemetery?"

"Oh. Well, long enough."

But Simon, Consequence hovering over him like a threatening foreign angel, needed assurances. *A fucking treaty*, he thought—a bitter aftertaste to this small, sweet victory. "Look, man, we just—"

"I'm Jimmy. And you could dig up a grave and dance around with a skull for all I care. Don't have to explain it to me, man—not my gig. My karma's mine, yours is yours."

Simon smiled in spite of himself. "I'm Simon. You don't talk like you're fourteen."

"Yeah," Jimmy said, slipping forward off the stone and landing on his feet. "Everybody says that. But I am and that's how I talk, so they gotta be wrong, eh?"

"I guess," Simon laughed. "So, now what?"

"You told your friend that you had to get your bike—I could use a ride."

Simon nodded. "Yeah, sure. But I only got one helmet."

Jimmy's teeth flashed in the moonlight. "*Helmet?* You know how long it took to get these spikes just right?"

"Where you wanna go?"

Jimmy watched a thin cloud slip across the moon as he answered. "That's, uh, kinda the other thing. I could use a place to crash tonight."

"Oh." Simon thought for a bit. "Look," he finally said, "I can get you a couch at a friend's place in Hamilton, but it'll cost ten bucks. It's kinda like a hotel under the radar."

"Ten bones for a couch," Jimmy pondered.

"And something to eat, if you want."

"So," Jimmy said slowly, "there's this other thing I need. . . ."

"Lemme guess: ten bucks."

Jimmy grinned foolishly, nodding.

"Yeah, alright. C'mon."

And later that night, on a squat house couch among strangers brought together by fate (or Fate), Simon's new appellation was summoned into being—Simon Ten-Bones. He wasn't there, unaware of his own rebirth. "Ten-Bones" stuck, though. It fit—much to Simon's eventual chagrin.

For the most part, the four vigilantes' handiwork was condemned as vandalism. But one intrepid journalist wrote a scathing article that captured (so to speak) the spirit of the act, condemning Peterson's attempt at a quasi-legal land grab. The article, reprinted nationally, gathered under its wings enough stormy turmoil to send the developer elsewhere. A clever title, too:

VISITING TEAM: 5,000,000
HOME TEAM: 1

Simon secretly wished he'd thought of it and painted that, too, on a scoreboard that cool April night.

Although instead of "Visiting" he would have written "Invading."

JIMMY

10

SCOTTY'S CURRENT PLACE OF residence, the high rise on Rebecca Street, is a cluster of tight little warrens. Government assistance cases like Scotty live in many of the apartments, but not in all. Some residents are young and of modest means, or old and living on pension scraps.

He did not choose this building—sixteen floors of ugly concrete and shabby carpets and parquet floors and yellowing drop-ceiling tiles—but he has never had a choice in where he lives. Scotty believes that Simon, as his court-assigned social worker, found this apartment for him. Whether this is true or not matters little to the mute; Simon was the one who drove him here, handed him the key. Shifted like inanimate jetsam from one type of institution to another. Or maybe just tucked away out of sight, like a lonesome cellar plant that requires minimal attention.

Not that Scotty dwells often on such things, self-pity being out of character. But he watches the world as if he were somehow slightly out of step, or perhaps as if he were always one step behind. Sometimes he rides the bus for this reason, for there—in that strange terrarium of endless stops and starts—the world and he are separated by the dirty glass and all travellers keep to themselves. No one talks, no one invades his little aura of space. No one even looks at him.

Simon introduced him to Hamilton's public transit system. Not that Scotty was unaware of it, but he hadn't been on a city bus since childhood.

Back then, pulled along by his mother and struggling with everything he had to keep himself from flying apart, the bus rides to and from grocery stores and appointments and job interviews and the welfare office were terrifying episodes. Adults ignored each other on the bus, but children— *everyone* talked to him, clawed away at his frayed nerves until the screaming in his head deafened him to numbness.

But Simon figured out pretty quickly how to talk to Scotty. Within a week of bringing him to this apartment, in fact. Simon didn't confront Scotty or search for eye contact or even play the twenty questions game ("You can at least *nod*, can't you?" said more than one frustrated therapist or nurse or doctor or foster parent. *No*, Scotty would hear a distant part of him say. *It doesn't work like that*).

Instead, Simon simply spoke his thoughts out loud, addressed the dingy linoleum floor or a bare wall or the cheap wood cabinets in the tiny galley kitchen. A voice that would never rise too far above a murmur, really, the way someone might talk to an ailing plant, coaxing it slowly back to health.

Or out of its closed seed buried in the black loam.

IT WAS THIS WAY, maybe a year ago:

Scotty stood awkwardly, angled toward the corner of the room, head bowed, eyes caught in the predictable pattern of the vertical radiator slats. Simon stood on Scotty's left, back turned to him and maybe two metres away.

". . . bsstp . . . bout tmnts wlk . . . not far."

Just a mumble, someone thinking absently enough so that partial sounds slipped out unnoticed.

Again.

". . . bsstp . . . bout tmnts wlk . . . not far."

Then Simon stretched, yawned, and walked out. When Scotty finally turned around, there was a bus pass on the counter. He pondered, *bsstp . . . bout tmnts wlk . . . not far*, working the sounds over. A game. Simon left him with something to ponder, to play.

bsstp

bsstp

Bus stop.

Scotty smiled shyly. He picked up the plastic card.

ABOUT TWO MINUTES' WALK, not far, was a bus stop. Furtively, he lingered behind a trash bin and watched as two old women and a young man got on the bus. They all wore identical grim expressions. Bus faces, Scotty learned soon after, were welcome masks from behind which no one emerges. Unless there are children, but Scotty is far beyond that designation.

The two old women fiddled about with coins, but the man had a plastic pass. Scotty watched, learned. It was easy—no words were exchanged, not even looks. When the next bus came, Scotty did not hesitate.

He selected a seat not too far back, right by the window. The bus made its way along its prescribed route, oddly smooth, gliding in a way that cars just can't. People got on or off or both in twos and threes. Sometimes more. Scotty took small glances about, noticed the bus faces—not just the set mouths (*as if*, he thought, *those mouths were made to never speak*), but the glazed over eyes. Eyes that looked without seeing, without prying.

Did Simon know? Was it possible that this newest social worker (there had been so many) knew that there on the bus Scotty would feel (*what? What is this, am I*) free?

But it was an illusion—or, at least, a state of mind that needed occasional preemptive action in order to preserve anonymity. And autonomy. Scotty learned, for instance, that bus routes have ends and drivers have shifts.

The bus stopped and the doors opened.

"End of the line," the driver said over his shoulder. Scotty looked up, confused. There were only two other passengers still on the bus, teenagers, and they stood up and exited. Scotty followed suit.

The bus drove away empty. Scotty, marooned on a north-end corner across from a Salvation Army thrift store, watched as the two friends pointed at something in the display window and laughed.

"Holy fuck," said the one in dreads and an old woolen drug rug. "Look at that."

Scotty followed their line of sight, but found nothing out of the ordinary. Leafs jersey on a mannequin, a framed poster leaning against it, a threadbare coat.

The other one, close-cropped hair and heavy steel-toed Docs, shook his head in disbelief. *Private joke?* Scotty wondered. *Must be.* And then, *This one is my opposite—everything about him is meant to draw attention, there's even a bull's-eye on the back of his army coat.*

The pair crossed the street, walking with purpose. They had a place to go. Scotty watched them, unsure of what to do, glaringly out of place and still holding his bus pass in one hand.

Then the gentle-looking one in dreads stopped, looked back, called to his companion.

"Sirius! Hold up."

Eye contact but inadvertent—Scotty looked away immediately. Awkward, frozen in a half step, still as a photograph. But Scotty saw in peripherals by necessity, watched in alarm as the woolen poncho and bellbottom jeans and sandals sauntered toward him.

Breathe. Count. I am not here I am beneath us now.

"Hey, man." The voice was soothing, kind. "You lost, brother? You look lost."

"Jimmy!" This from across the street where the un-gentle one still stood. "What the fuck?"

But Jimmy—*this one's name is Jimmy*—ignored his companion.

"You need some help, man?"

Scotty had slipped far enough away to endure this, he watched as from a distance. But across the street, the one that carried himself like a bulldog grew impatient.

"Jimmy, shit! We're gonna be here a while if we don't shog and make that next bus, eh?"

Again, that soothing voice. "Okay, brother, I get it. You're here and you're not here."

How? Scotty's head jerked, just a slight twitch.

"Because I know." Jimmy lit a smoke, took a long slow drag, faded out himself for a moment. As if he, too, were there and not there. But he returned a moment later, glanced back at Impatience.

"Him and me, we're headed for a bus stop. Catching the last ride downtown for a while."

Then he turned and walked back to his friend. Not so much as another glance back. Scotty watched them, torn. Then he followed the receding pair before they slipped out of sight.

↗

"JIMMY—REALLY?"

This from the one called Sirius. Scotty heard this as he made his way to where the pair waited, Jimmy studying (it seemed) the lifeless terminus of the lamppost under which he stood, Sirius sprawled out indolently on the bench.

Jimmy looked at his friend, confused.

"What's wrong?"

"Buddy came with. You're the fucking Pied Piper of the misbegotten, man." He jerked a thumb in Scotty's direction.

Jimmy glanced at Scotty who had stopped, body turned left shoulder toward them, slightly hunched as if against storm wind or hail. Stringy brown hair hung like a veil across his face.

"What the—" but Jimmy stopped Sirius mid-sentence.

"Leave him be, brother. He's just here for the bus, like us."

Sirius shrugged, then looked directly at him. Scotty saw this through the veil.

"Hey, brother, you got a name?"

Seven, eight, nine

"Oi! Brother, name?"

thirteen, fourteen, fifteen

But Jimmy stepped between them, back turned to Scotty.

"Enough, man. Just let him be. He doesn't speak."

Sirius rose, strode straight at Scotty, Jimmy notwithstanding. He clutched Scotty's wrist and turned it so that he could read the plastic card Scotty still held.

"Scott Campbell. Lives on Rebecca in one of the high rises." Scotty's body shook then, an involuntary quiver barely perceptible. His breathing, too, quickened. Sirius let go of his wrist, stepped back, gave Scotty space, looked at him as if for the first time. "Don't worry, brother," Sirius said, gently. "We'll get you back where you started."

"Bus is here," Jimmy said in a quiet voice. Scotty looked up quickly enough to catch the look on Jimmy's face as he watched Sirius—contemplative, wise, knowing.

↗

IT WAS CROWDED, SO the three of them had to stand. Scotty mimicked Jimmy, reaching up for one of the loops that dangled like nooses from the dull bars stretching from post to post. When he was a child and on the bus with his mother, he was enthralled with the hanging loops and the myriad hands that clung to them. Scotty recalled this as the bus lurched its way down Barton. When the bus was that crowded—crowded enough so that the corridor was packed with stony-eyed passengers, that is—Scotty could come up for air; no one would speak to him, put his mother in that awkward and embarrassing position between him and the world to apologize for or laugh away his behaviour. Or his utter lack of it. She could join that impassive mob, clutching her own loop in a white knuckled fist.

Like a leash, Scotty thought, *for a dog*. Because that's how it was, Scotty's mother dragging Hope behind her, that unwilling beast, until the stony silence of that road broke it to pieces. *She tried*. Scotty squeezed the stiff loop tighter in his thin hand. *She held on for as long as she could.* Jaw clenched tight against memory then, he felt the enigmatic eyes of Jimmy studying him in furtive glances.

Sirius, though. Hands in his pockets, he stared out the window indifferently. He leaned on one of the dull silver posts and watched the buildings drift by like river jetsam. Even in the middle of a bus corridor he looked like a fighter between matches, hangdog haunted look of being slightly out of place without an opponent in plain sight. Scotty watched Sirius' feet, heavy steel-toe boots planted firmly against the unsteady sway, that unpredictable rhythm of bus language.

And then familiar sights, storefronts and street signs. Jimmy pulled the cord (Scotty had forgotten about the cord) and the bus decelerated in a protest of undercarriage screeches and squeals before drifting in beside a bus shelter.

Downtown was busy. The three of them stood momentarily on the sidewalk like mooring posts in a brisk river. Sirius spoke first.

"I'll be in the music shop, man. Need strings."

If Jimmy heard him, he gave no sign. Instead, he stared curiously at the image on Scotty's black tee, hidden until then by a ratty flannel shirt.

"I've seen that before," he said, though mostly to himself.

It was a fish, twisting upward, fins stretched and mouth agape. Skillfully hand-painted in sinuous white lines.

But Scotty turned abruptly, as if summoned, and walked away.

11

Hydrogen, gravity, and time.

These are the only necessary components for the formation of a star. Hydrogen, pulled in and condensed by the sort of crushing gravitational forces that swirl, vortex-like, in the depths of the galactic span, will compress—eventually—into a self-sustaining fuel source. An energy so hot that atoms fuse and energy pulses in vast columns from the epicentre, columns of searing brightness that stretch light years away from the forming star's core.

Sirius contemplates this, having found the information by flipping through a magazine that had been left on a park bench. Jimmy is beside him, smoking quietly and watching a black squirrel dig through a nearby trashcan.

"Hey, Jimmy."

"Yeah?"

"Why 'Sirius'?"

Jimmy had bestowed the name upon him, a bong-water baptism, just as he had renamed Sirius's brother Tribal and a dozen others across the city at one point or another.

But Jimmy just smiles in that knowing and ageless way of his kind.

"Because there are two of you, man."

Jimmy watches as the squirrel scrambles up and out of the receptacle one last time, hidden prize stuffed conspicuously in its bulging pouch of a cheek. Then, in its jerky stop-motion animation sort of way, it finds its way down and across the grass to a nearby maple.

Sirius watches it, too.

"Whatcha say, Jimmy, you wanna come back as one of those next round?"

"Me? No. Better to come back as whatever it is it's carrying."

"Not me, man, I—"

But Jimmy stops Sirius with a raised hand, his eyes in the tree branches because he's followed the squirrel's ascent. He points and Sirius looks, too. It isn't one of the larger ones, but it's definitely one of Scotty's—the wire fish dangles from a branch maybe three metres up, spinning in a lazy circle.

"Weird," Sirius says.

"Yeah," Jimmy mumbles. "I gotta go—something's not right."

"Don't be so fucking dramatic."

"Yeah," Jimmy mumbles again. "Later, brother."

Not too far away, Jimmy finds another one, this time under a bench. More accurately, under an occupied bench. He saunters by, simulating a nonchalance he doesn't feel. When he's close enough, he takes a glance at the sleeping figure buried under the shredded remains of a tarp.

"Hey," Jimmy says gently, "Marta—you awake?"

The prone figure shifts and snarls something. She doesn't emerge from her makeshift tent, though.

Jimmy moves on. Three more fish hang from tree branches, another one impaled on the wrought iron fence by the garden. One of the bigger sculptures has been crammed between the fence and the back of the bus shelter.

It isn't the fish themselves that disturb Jimmy—it's the fact that they're all empty. Each sculpture has had its occupant removed, the little fetal figure that dangles within the belly of the fish. Without its curled-up cargo, each fish looks incomplete, abandoned. Like a haunted house whose ghost has been evicted.

JIMMY RECALLS SIMON'S PARTING words to Scotty earlier that afternoon. *I don't know if I'm any help to you at all. Wish I knew what's going on in that head of yours.* They had stung. Simon didn't see it, leaving those words in his wake on his way out the door, but Jimmy had. Scotty's head had slumped a little and his cheeks flushed. Even through the curtain of stringy hair, Jimmy could see the change.

"He doesn't mean it," Jimmy had said to Scotty after Simon left. "He just doesn't listen to you all the time's all. Too much else weighing him down."

But he knew that was true of Scotty as well—his cramped apartment was fast becoming one of the more eclectically bizarre corners of Hamilton, its single silent occupant steadily burying himself under the weight of odds and ends salvaged from a thousand other corners. Just the cardboard signs themselves, scavenged from their indigent authors, were enough of a burden on the mute.

Not that he can't handle the weight, Jimmy had thought. Scotty had collected most of the signs into an untidy heap, a recent development. Jimmy had interpreted that as a sign, too.

JIMMY FINDS CALICO JUST outside the small park, offering advertisement flyers to passersby officially, but asking for handouts unofficially when they ignore his initial spiel. Calico, so named because his mangy orange hair is strewn with patches of stark white, doesn't like Jimmy. He also isn't overly shy about expressing his feelings, so Jimmy makes sure he isn't seen before he reaches his volatile destination.

To be fair, Calico doesn't like anybody. His claim to fame is that he is a direct descendent of Rocco Perri, the so-called "King of the Bootleggers," one of Hamilton's most infamous Prohibition-era gangsters. It's as absurd as it is implausible, but humouring Calico is the only way to coax him into conversation. And, truth be told, the foul-tempered misanthrope doesn't miss much that happens between Catharine and Bay Streets North.

"Hey!" Jimmy starts, stopping just out of foul-tempered fist swing range. "How's Hamilton's favourite gangster's grandson today?"

Calico spares him a moody glance. "Fuck off. I'm working."

Encouraging, though: despite his words, Calico holds his head up a touch higher at Jimmy's greeting, as befits a man of illustrious lineage who must endure the indignities of a Fallen Family.

"I was just down on Bay Street, eh?" Jimmy lies. "They should put up a plaque or something." Rocco's home and base of operations was at 166 Bay Street South, one of Calico's pet pieces of trivia.

Jimmy watches the struggle in Calico's rheumy eyes—he recognizes Jimmy's insincerity, but so few afford him the opportunity to recount his criminal ancestry that he swallows down his distaste.

"First fuckin' thing you ever said that makes sense," Calico offers begrudgingly.

"Yeah, man—or they should put a statue where your grandfather was shot by the Mob."

"Wasn't him got shot, idiot!" Calico snaps. "It was his wife, Bessie. Bessie Starkman. Mob hit in a parking garage."

"Oh," Jimmy says. "Sorry, didn't know. Where was that?"

"Ain't there no more." Calico's intonations begin to lean slightly toward a generic Chicago gangster-ese. "Centre Mall's there now, on Barton. They tore down the garage to build the mall, but *they* know it was Mob money made that deal happen. Cover the evidence."

Jimmy doesn't ask who *they* might be. Nor does he point out that a couple of the old timers he sells painkillers to told him that the Centre Mall was built in the '50s on the former site of the Jockey Club racetrack. One used to mind the stables; the other was an avid gambler.

"So, Bessie—that was your grandmother, eh?"

"Fuck, no! My grandmother was one of Rocco's working girls." Calico squats down against the low wall on this side of the Park and drops the stack of flyers. "Nobody don't know shit."

"Doing my best, Cal," Jimmy says, squatting down beside him. "Once you tell me, though, I won't forget. I never do."

Calico gives him a suspicious sideways look. "Whatcha want? *You* don't give a shit what I got to say. Nobody does."

"Won't lie—I need your help. But if you give, you get, man. I'll take in your whole history, like your chronicler."

"My *what*?"

"Like your historian—I got ways of making it real."

Calico bristles. "It *is* fuckin' real!"

"Yeah," Jimmy says, soothing the circuitry, "but I mean I can make it real to other people—they'll look at you different, man. Living legend status."

"Really?" Incredulity hovers over this sad street installment, an ominous angel with garbage bag wings casting shadows of Doubt over his entire petty existence. Jimmy watches as it floats there, smug and immovable. *Enough*, he says, suddenly irritated. *You've done enough damage.*

"Really." And Jimmy is sincere. "You'll see, man—imagine some cat offering you dosh to tell them history. *Your* history," he adds.

Calico shifts himself into a more comfortable position. "That'll be the fucking day," he snarls. But then he looks at the pile of flyers and back to Jimmy. "A'right—whatcha wanna know?"

"It's the fish. The ones around here—the sculptures."

"Yeah? What about 'em?"

But Jimmy suddenly scoops up the flyers and hands half of them to Calico. He holds one out silently to a Monday downtown shopper, but she hobbles past as if they're both invisible. Not two breaths behind her are a pair of beat cops, sauntering into Calico's periphery just a touch too late.

"Afternoon," Jimmy says to the pair, holding out a flyer. "Support local economy?"

They ignore the flyer, though, and move on. They aren't fools, but the illusion of employment is good enough for them.

Calico, however, stares at Jimmy in disbelief. "Are you fucking *nuts*?"

"What's wrong, man? They moved on without a word."

"Look at the fucking flyer," he hisses through clenched teeth.

Jimmy glances at the front of the folded paper he still holds in his outstretched hand, taking in the marijuana leaf around which naked people frolic in a circle. Then he laughs. "Church of the Universe, eh? *Love* these guys."

Calico snatches the flyer out of Jimmy's hand and then grabs at the rest of them, tucking them away. "Cops *don't*!"

"Alright, alright—disaster averted. Back to the fish, eh?"

"Fine," Calico snaps. "What?"

"Simple question, man: who's fucking with them? Stealing that inside part?"

"Simple answer," Calico says. "It's that street preacher hangs around the statue. The one all the others is scared of."

"Cottonmouth," Jimmy mumbles.

"You, too? Ha!"

"And you, Cal," Jimmy says. "Just good sense to be. Anything else?"

"Nah. Well, he moves 'em around, too. Seen 'em on the stairs going up the Mountain." Calico means the hundred-metre-high Niagara Escarpment that separates Hamilton into the lower and upper cities.

"Which stairs? There's, like, six or seven Mountain accesses."

Calico turns to look Jimmy in the eyes. *"All* of 'em."

Jimmy pulls at his straggly goatee and sucks at his teeth for a moment. "Know what he does with the stuff he removes from the fish?"

"Nope," Calico says.

Sally's cryptic plaque crosses Jimmy's mind.

"Alright, Cal," Jimmy says, settling in. "A deal's a deal. Gimme the whole story. And don't skimp on the details."

Calico nods solemnly. He begins.

12

Of all the things Simon made Scotty do, Group was by far the worst. Scotty considers Simon's parting words of earlier that afternoon, when he'd returned after Scotty didn't show up at 3:30 p.m. in the lobby. His social worker didn't linger, though; one foot out the door, Simon had seemed on edge.

"I don't know, Scotty," he'd said as he left. "I don't know if I'm any help to you at all. Wish I knew what's going on in that head of yours." Then he'd closed the door quietly. Simon never talked like that. Something was gnawing at him, that much was clear.

Later that evening and beneath the surface, submerged within the cramped confines of the old tub, Scotty's thoughts drift, as aimless as jellyfish. So much of his childhood—and especially the events after he was discovered with his mother's corpse wrapped in a patchwork pall in that tenement furnace room—is fragmented. Lost puzzle pieces scattered along the way.

Maybe that's what Simon's supposed to do, Scotty thinks. *Maybe that's his job. Putting me back together.* The tepid water cannot embrace all of him; pale and bony knees jut out, the tip of his flaccid penis bobs playfully on the surface as well. Above him, through the hand's width of water that separates eyes from air, he watches the stains on the narrow ceiling.

The stains and patches undulate as always, subtle shifts of position, but it is a restless modulation of silent geometry. Scotty watches—concerned because he can usually draw them into patterns.

Tonight, though.

Deep in his thin chest, Scotty's lungs register a small complaint. He ignores it.

How could he put me back together? Too much is lost. Too much is scattered across this city. How many foster homes? How many tired and routine check-ups in cold emergency rooms?

Again, his lungs.

This time, they throb in protest. A dull burning sensation creeps into the bottom of his chest, slipping in beneath his ribs. Above him, though, the shapes finally settle into something recognizable—an oblong dark patch, like a tree trunk. Then limbs, a pair of them separate, unfold in graceful and sinuous dignity. They open wide, as if to embrace him.

But the nagging need for air—

Scotty ignores his enraged lungs, his sluggish blood, because the shape above shifts again, a flat oval emerges as if cut from black paper or painted tin.

A head.

It tilts to the side, curious or playful. But it is hard to see now, the shape obscured by the starbursts of light.

Beautiful lights.

Variegated. Translucent.

Air!

But his limbs, limp as kelp.

Am I drowning?

Am I?

And then a voice: *YES.*

Scotty slips deeper now, the constellations behind his eyes follow him into the depths. Lantern fish, roaming sea stars, they are beautiful. *I will drown.*

Again, the voice: *YOU WILL NOT.*

A pair of sinuous shadows slip beneath the water, cradle Scotty's head, lift. *YOU MUST FIND ME.*

Air!

And then his thin face breaches the surface—Scotty inhales greedily, thrashing madly as life returns to his numb limbs, fingers clutching for purchase on the tub's slippery rim. He breathes and breathes and breathes in rending gasps. Life, too, returns to his eyes. He scans frantically for the shadow.

But it is gone.

You must find me.

But where to start?

It had to be him, that elusive playmate of Scotty's forlorn and lonesome childhood. Who else *could* it be? Scotty gulps in air, clings weakly to the side of the tub. His foot absently touches the rubber stopper and he clutches at the protruding ring with his toes, pulling it free. He feels the minute tug of suction on his ankle as the water drains, and then a sudden stillness in the current as the stopper is sucked back into place. He pries it up again, deposits it on the edge.

He is weak. *Maybe some tea*, he thinks. *I wish I wasn't so*—but he stops himself, confused. *I wish I wasn't so*—again, he stops short.

Scotty pulls on his grey sweatpants and goes into the kitchen. He turns on the burner and rummages through a drawer for a tea bag. He has to pry at the drawer to open it, though; he removed the plain white knob a while ago.

You must find me, it said, but where to start?

Mug in hand, Scotty makes his way into the tight front room of his tiny apartment. Not tight because the walls are only eleven feet apart, but because Scotty has been busy.

Now at his small table, Scotty collects what he needs: pliers, snips, screwdriver. His work gloves are under the table. They are both righthanded, pulled from an old garbage bag of mouldering clothes he came across in an alley some months ago. It occurred to Scotty later that the bag might have belonged to one of the homeless men who often rummaged through that

90

area, but he didn't want to return them. The gloves are essential to his work, and he only needs to wear one upside down on his left hand.

Also under the table is a roll of chicken wire, a gift from Alise. She lives on the third floor, a bassist in an all-girl punk band. But she is also an artist like Scotty. Alise spends time with Scotty when she can spare it. And sometimes when she can't.

He sits on the floor and unrolls what he needs from the wire. *Just a regular one*, he decides, stopping at about a metre and snipping through the thin steel. Then he begins to shape the wire, forming a cylinder. Carefully, he tapers the ends, rounding off one and bringing the other to a spear-like point. Next, he pushes in the sides so that the form takes on height while losing width.

Another bout with the snips and he has more bits to work with. He adds a flat, gracefully triangular piece to the sharply tapered end, and a series of flattened protrusions to the top and sides.

A fish.

Scotty reaches up onto the table and gropes about for a smaller sculpture he made earlier—this one human-shaped and fetal, with a drawer knob for a head. It is black, meticulously painted. A single strand of cassette tape has been tied to its torso.

A few snips along the fish's belly and Scotty has enough space to insert the figure. Scotty worries over the string of tape, drawing it out and passing it through the wire that serves simultaneously as the fish's spine and anchor for the dorsal fin. Using the needle nose pliers in one hand and the deft fingers of the other, he ties a knot. It is ready.

Above the table, I guess. It's really one of the only open spaces left in the front room, so he stands on the chair and pushes a screw into the skim coat of the ceiling drywall. A few turns of the screwdriver and it's ready to take the slight weight of the wire fish and its quiet human cargo. He ties it in place, steps down off the chair, and admires his work. It rotates lazily for a while before settling on a direction.

THE FOLLOWING MORNING, SCOTTY walks with purpose down John Street North, stringy hair pulled down over his face like a ragged veil, baggy flannel shirt swallowing his skinny frame. A high-rise looms in the distance, toward the Lake. It's a start. He'll start there.

I have to start somewhere.

It was the dream that determined this course of action, cause and effect. Not the vision of the previous evening—at least, not directly. After all, it isn't the first time that the shadowy figure has sought him out, although it is the first time he ever spoke to Scotty. Such as it was.

No—the dream: he is in the cavernous furnace room of the building, squatting in the dark. Beside him are his mother's remains, wrapped tightly in linens once white but now filthy with dirt, with dust. One bare bulb sheds a weak and inconstant light, dangling from the murk above by a string. The bulb, surrounded by a wire cage, slowly turns and turns, as if unsure of where it is.

Above them, mother and son, looms the humming furnace. It hovers over them like a monstrous metallic scorpion, pipes and vents spread from its bulky centre like segmented legs, claws, a threatening tail, it reeks of oil and something else. *Rot,* Scotty says. *It is rotting—like old meat left out too long.* The furnace itself does not hum—it is the incessant and angry buzzing of tens of thousands of flies. They gather on the furnace in glistening swarms, the dim light flickering across their tiny bluish-green carapaces. They crawl and leap over each other, or burst forth in furious flight only to gather again on the same surface. Scotty is caught in their hypnotic patterns, their fits of starts and undulating seizures.

And then, a voice—soft, weak, distant.

"Please—I need you."

Scotty turns around. He is no longer beside the bundled corpse; it is across the gloom, almost invisible. Beside it is a child, a ragged little boy hunched against the darkness. "Please!" the little boy says. "Come out!"

Scotty stands up, but the distance . . . He can't seem to move. When he tries to take a step the flies swarm and buffet him, push him back. Scotty swings angrily at them, but they elude his feeble flailing.

The child notices, though—he stares hard in Scotty's direction, eyes wide against the blackness. "Are you there?" he shouts.

Behind the little boy, something disturbs the shrouded corpse. It jerks a little, cat-pawed by the darkness.

Scotty had awoken badly that morning, tangled up in his damp and clammy sweat-soaked sheet, throbbing headache because of clenching his jaw, grinding his teeth. In pain, alarmed, but determined: he would find his childhood home. Breakfast (peanut butter sandwich), bus pass, chalk, and John Street North to start.

But as he tries to cross Cannon, a girl approaches him, heading in the opposite direction toward downtown.

"Hey, you got a dollar? Can I have a dollar, man?"

Scotty can only see the red combat boots, white-laced, and the fishnets stretched over her thin legs. Then he feels a finger against his chest—not hard, but enough to stop him.

"C'mon, man, just gimme a dollar. You got some dosh, gimme some."

Then he can't see anything at all, panic toying with his lungs and obscuring sight. He dodges the girl and tries to cross the street.

"Asshole!" she yells. Then a sharp stab of pain as she lashes out with the boot, catching him on the back of his leg just above the knee. Scotty gasps and stumbles. Breath dodges him, he tries desperately to catch it, can't. He falls.

Another voice now, deeper and male. It comes from high above the pair of huge and heavy combat boots in front of Scotty's face, black and scarred and also white-laced like the girl's.

"Shoulda given her some dosh, eh?" Then a short laugh. Scotty shakes visibly, mouth working in quick gasps, trying to catch the elusive air. A pair of strong hands wrap around his arms and he is lifted, effortlessly it seems, out of the road and onto the sidewalk.

"What the fuck ya doing?" yells the girl from somewhere else.

"Can't leave him in the *road*," answers the male voice.

"Why the fuck *not*?"

"How come you're always such a fuckin' bitch?" he answers. She responds, but too far away now. Scotty finds the strength to pull his knees up into his chest and closes his eyes, concentrates now.

twelve, thirteen, fourteen

He counts to sixty, then starts again.

A SKUNKY SCENT CREEPS into Scotty's mouth and curls stubbornly around his tongue. He opens his eyes, scans the pavement he's lying on. Close by, a beer bottle lies on its side, the dregs stagnating within. A raindrop hits his cheek. Then another. He pulls himself into a sitting position and wraps his arms around his knees.

I can breathe I can breathe—he holds on to that thought and looks around. Brick, pavement, cars flying through the intersection while others wait impatiently. A prickly weed tickles the small of his back. He scratches and absently tucks the back of his T-shirt into his jeans. Then he touches the spot where he was kicked, prodding gently. It hurts, but not as badly as he expected. Just across Cannon a pair of tenements looms, but under the slate sky they look ominous. Angry.

Home, he decides. *It's just too much right now.* He rises and begins the journey back. Eyes skim along the ground just ahead of him, a world reduced to the shoes and shins of those within his immediate vicinity. Soon things become familiar. He knows this route, following it by way of familiar landmarks—frost heave shaped like a Y, bottom step with three missing tiles, manhole cover with one splotch of yellow paint, green iron fence, fire hydrant with black arrow at the base.

Chalk fish on a wet sidewalk slab. Scotty redraws it every so often—in the warmer, dryer weather, at least—his marker for home. Today, a friendly little cartoon spider perches upon the fish's head, drawn there in black marker. Scotty smiles. *She's back.*

Alise, that is.

She lives on the third floor of his building, friendly and helpful without being overly intrusive. Alise's band plays regularly, but that's mostly just on weekends. In the weekday evenings, and often into the wee hours of morning, Alise engages in after-hours art—graffiti, mostly, but some rogue installments as well.

Scotty remembers the day they met, if that's the right term for it. About a year ago. *She must have watched me redraw the chalk fish*, he thinks, *and then followed me.* But he has no recollection of anyone else in the elevator. *Maybe she stood in the lobby, watched the light until it stopped.*

Certainly that was a possibility. It was, after all, how Scotty figured out where Alise lived.

AND THEN THERE SHE is, standing outside his apartment door.

Alise smiles, duffle bag slung over one shoulder and holding something spherical and cloth-covered in her cupped hands.

"Hey," she says. "I'm back, *finally*. Long couple of weeks. Haven't even been to my own apartment yet." Her neon pink Mohawk is perfect, rising majestically from the black velvet that covers the rest of her scalp.

Scotty fumbles with the key, turns the knob, enters the dingy and cluttered little space. He leaves the door open behind him. She follows him in, but stops short just beyond the threshold.

"Wow."

Because before Alise had left, she'd given Scotty's place a reasonably thorough cleaning. She hadn't touched his art materials—the cardboard, the wire hangers, the milk crates of odds and ends—but she'd scoured the kitchen and washroom, picked up what she could in the cramped living space and tiny bedroom. She'd even made Scotty carry a heap of dirty clothes down to the laundry in the basement and oversaw that process.

But it isn't the fact that the tiny apartment is once again a disaster—piles of sagging cardboard, a heap of wire coat hangers, snippets of newspaper all over the floor, dirty clothes. These things do not shock Alise.

It's the fish.

Dozens upon dozens of them—each a clever fabrication of wire—hang from the ceiling. Most are modest in scale, maybe the size of sunfish or small carp; others are larger, like heavy trout or pike; the largest of the lot is a monster, easily the length of Scotty himself. It rests on the floor against the sliding door of the tiny concrete balcony he never uses.

And inside each and every hanging fish is a smaller human figure, also made of wire. Crude—each head just a walnut or an acorn or even a drawer knob, a discarded film canister, a spool, a June bug—and the body a simple skeleton of bent wires twisted into a fetal curl. Each passenger meticulously painted black. The figures dangle from threads of cassette tape inside their hosts, floating there as if suspended in vitro.

"You've been busy," Alise says quietly, as if to herself. She makes her way along a narrow tunnel to the tiny kitchenette, fish dangling above and around her, and places her little bundle on the cluttered counter. "I mean, there were, what, five or six of these when I left? Just—wow."

Like all of the building's one-bedroom apartments, Scotty's home is a cramped cinder block rectangle thirty-five feet deep by eleven feet wide.

The living room and bedroom are on opposite ends, separated by a narrow strip of linoleum that passes between a galley kitchen to the left and a tiny washroom to the right.

Most of the fish dangle from the living room ceiling, which is riddled with thumbtacks and screws, but a small school of them has made its way into the space between the galley kitchen and the washroom door.

Alise surveys the damage—the dirty dishes, the empty boxes, and residue of clumsily made meals.

"I see you've managed to undo my work in the two weeks I was gone. You used these, though!" She holds up one of two hardened amorphous white blobs, remains of the scented candles she brought over just before she left. "Vanilla. Took me a while to figure that out, didn't it?"

Scotty stands at that awkward angle, three-quarter profile and looking down. Like he's listening for something below the shabby linoleum floor. But he stands closer to Alise than he stands to others.

Alise smells the lumpy wax and places it down on the counter beside the other one. She unslings her satchel, opens it up, and reaches in. Out come a handful of black walnuts.

"I have no idea whether you're still collecting these. I picked them up at the corner. You know, that tree by the Women's Centre? Anyway," she lets the nuts roll onto the crowded countertop, "here you go."

Scotty waits a moment. Then he picks up the walnuts, one at a time, and stows them away in his pockets.

She laughs. "You're like a squirrel! You should stuff them in your cheeks."

Scotty smiles, too, furtively behind his curtain of stringy brown hair.

"Oh yeah! I brought you this, too." She lifts the bit of cloth off the object she had placed on the counter, revealing her gift: a small glass bowl of water holding a single black fish. "It's called a beta. They really don't like other fish, so it has to be alone."

Scotty smiles, openly this time. Then, an urgent reminder from his breath and he folds inward again.

But not all the way. Not even close.

"Gotta go." Alise shoulders the duffle bag and heads back toward the door, mohawk weaving carefully between the schools of wire fish like a fierce pink shark fin. "Troy doesn't even know I'm back—I thought we'd be gone another two days, but the last gig fell through. Later!"

THE NEXT MORNING, THOUGH.

"Hey," Simon exclaims from the galley kitchen, "where'd the fish come from? The *real* one, I mean?" He emerges with a glass of water for Scotty's meds, shaking his head. "Now, why the hell didn't I think of that?"

Scotty works on another tiny sculpture for one of the smaller wire fish. Hunched over his work, the mute does not see at first that Simon has placed pills and glass on the table.

"Scotty? Time to take these, man."

Suddenly aware of Simon's closeness, Scotty hunches inward. Involuntary, as if something within him could pull his being into itself. Simon steps back, begins a casual stroll through the fish. There is now only one tight and meandering path in the living room through the myriad sculptures where he can walk without ducking and dodging—it connects Scotty's workstation table to the balcony door to the torn and stained recliner to the kitchen. Simon follows the route, strolling as if in a garden, until he arrives back at the little fishbowl on the counter. Beyond the kitchen, Scotty's bedroom door is closed. *A new behaviour*, Simon notes. *Like the multiplying wire fish and their strange cargo.*

Then Simon notices that all the cardboard signs are gone, too. There were scores of them—greasy, dirty, many of them damp, all of them street signs scavenged by Scotty or by the few who use Scotty's apartment. That's how Simon thinks of it—they use the apartment. Use Scotty, really.

NOT MANY, BUT ENOUGH so that Simon felt obliged to mention it to the super. This was before he got to know the handful of people who, against all reasonable odds, found their way into the mute's hidden Hamilton corner. Simon mentioned the intrusion, but just in passing, figuring the super would take the hint. But he didn't, a gentle old guy who mostly worried over the elevators and the basement laundry facilities.

"That boy?" he'd said. "Good for him to have a couple friends."

"Yeah," Simon had countered, "but I'm not convinced that they're entirely welcome."

"Well, he could tell 'em to leave, or ask me to see 'em out."

Simon had smirked at the thought. "I don't think that's likely."

But the super had picked up his canvas bag of tools, heading for the basement stairway. Then he had paused and looked back at Simon.

"Son, you got nothing to worry about. Alise'd tell me if there was a problem."

And Simon had stood there for a moment, staring at the door as it slowly closed.

"Who the hell is Alise?" he'd mumbled.

But Simon met Alise later that same week when she answered Scotty's door. He was late that day because another client had an early morning court date; Simon's habit of starting his rounds with Scotty meant that he only saw the residue of Scotty's supposed guests—fast food wrappers, cigarette butts in makeshift beer bottle ashtrays, and the cardboard signs. Always the signs, never the signifier.

It had been close to 11:00 a.m. by the time Simon had gotten to Scotty's. He knocked, already apologizing when the door began to open moments later.

"Sorry, Scotty! Really busy morn—uh, hi . . ." Because Alise—bright pink mohawk devoid of gel and limp on the side of a stubbly scalp and dressed in a ratty grey sweatshirt covered in dried paint, like a fabric palette—was stunning. *Not beautiful*, Simon thought at the time, *stunning*. Her eyes, maybe. They were a strange bluish-grey, like a sullen bruise.

"Hi," she said. "You looking for Scotty?" Casual tone, but her portal guardian body language was clear enough. As she shifted, her large grey sweatshirt hugged the swell of her frame, heavy for her height, which was just over five feet.

His initial assessment was that she wore baggy clothing because she was self-conscious. He found out later that she didn't give much of a damn what anyone thought.

"Yeah," Simon answered. "I'm his social worker. Gotta see him." Then, hand jutting out quickly, "I'm Simon. Simon Johnson."

She took the proffered hand, the back of her own tattooed with a spider. "Alise. I'm a friend from downstairs. He didn't mention me?"

"Uh, Scotty? No—I mean, he—"

"I'm kidding! I know. C'mon in."

"Gotta be Alise," Simon mumbles, watching the beta as it manoeuvres beneath a sheltering leaf of the single plastic plant in the small bowl. "Or maybe Jimmy." Beside the bowl are a small, bright yellow tube of beta pellets and a piece of dull orange construction paper. Simon picks up the paper, looks at the drawings—simple yet skillfully rendered pictures of when to feed the fish and how much arranged around a clock. Simon smiles. The clock, right down to the cartoonish vegetable medley on its face (eggplant, radish, carrot, lettuce), captures perfectly the real thing on Scotty's wall. A friendly spider serves as a signature.

"Alise," Simon confirms, putting the instructions back. He turns toward the worktable, but Scotty is no longer there. Instead, the mute stands at the balcony slider, staring out at the city.

"I'm gonna head, Scotty. Grocery shopping at 3:00 p.m., okay? Today, you're gonna hand the money to the cashier." Simon notes the shift in posture—Scotty's shoulders sliding forward, head sinking—and sighs. "C'mon, man. You did it last week. You can do it again. See you at three."

13

SCOTTY HEARS THE DOOR close, feels that comforting emptiness of being alone again. But he remains at the balcony slider, staring off into the city. Not that it's much of a view: Wilson Street down below lined with its tight clusters of brick houses, Ferguson North stretching off toward the Lake. He knows that the ominous heap of orange-brown bricks on Ferguson just beyond Barton Street is the detention centre—he can just make it out from his apartment. Tribal once mentioned a friend caged up in there, which is how he came to learn of the complex's purpose.

It was a happy coincidence. Before he knew what the building was, Scotty had discovered art—or what he took for art—on the stretch of road that passed it. On that occasion, it had only been letters chalked onto the street, but there was also a heart and Scotty thought it was nice.

Now that Scotty knows that the hastily scrawled words speak to those trapped inside, he visits once or twice per month, riding the bus to Barton and walking from there. Street graffiti occasionally appears beside the messages, some of it stretching the entire width of the southbound lane. Standing on the gravelly stretch of scraggly grass with his back to the prison, Scotty likes to work out some of the words. Or do his best. Sometimes he copies them down faithfully in his journal to ponder later.

And no one can speak back to those words, thinking now of the black slots that serve as windows or the giant silver coil of wire that sits playfully on top of the outer wall. As if the words themselves are too big to fit through the narrow jail windows, or they get caught on the sharp edges of that span of razor wire. Like ragged scraps of colourful ribbon waving meaninglessly in the breeze.

Or maybe the words can't speak at all. Like the words on my cardboard signs. Or like the words trapped on the stowed coils of spliced cassette tapes, a small part of him adds—ragged scraps of ribbon hidden meaninglessly in a matchbox. For now.

For now, that same small part of him says. *I'm not ready for that yet.*

Scotty's sharp eyes follow Ferguson until it slips under the clutter of cityscape. Then he scans the city's edge to the north, hunting for fragments of the grey lake between buildings and smokestacks. But his balcony isn't high enough for that; instead, he turns and moves with purpose toward the door, snatching up his jacket on the way because it looks like it might rain.

FORTY MINUTES LATER, SCOTTY squats on his thin haunches, canvas sneakers sinking into the leaden sand as he watches the seagulls wheel above the choppy steel waters of Lake Ontario. An unforgiving lake—a collector of mariners' secrets, of husks of ships hidden away in her silent depths like jealous memories.

A single gull dips suddenly away from the lazy gyre of birds above, hurls itself greedily at some water-borne tidbit, only to drop it again inches into its ascent. Shredded plastic, Scotty decides. Half a dozen birds do the same, compelled by the undulating shape and oblivious to memory. Perhaps it is the same bird again and again.

Scotty rises, skinny knees lodging a mild protest to movement after sustained compression. He moves along the beach, just far enough back so that the uninviting tongues of water lapping at the sand can't soak his canvas sneakers. Before long, he comes across a fish carcass half submerged in wet sand, its dull silver scales barely catching the weak light of the sun that makes its way across the overcast August sky.

Not far away is a black stick, waterlogged and half interred in sand. Like the fish. Scotty pulls it up and returns to his bloated beach find, gently pushes on its swollen gut—no aggression, no purpose, just dull curiosity.

Sometimes a stick will insert itself easily, tip buried in soggy flesh. Not today, though; the white belly gives, but only so much.

The eye, though—it tilts with each gentle prod, sightless readjustment. Then, without much ceremony, a small brown spider exits the fish's mouth at a brisk spider sprint.

Scotty, delighted, laughs—until the firm tightening in his chest, his throat, chokes away the sound; he looks around, self-conscious, but he is alone. As long as the gulls don't count. Then at least his smile returns at the reappearance of the spider, darting across the heavy sand and straight into its fish cave. *A fish secret*, he thinks, *like a memory*.

And then Scotty thinks *Spider*, which is what he has named the beta. He didn't feed it this morning. He heads home immediately. He has become an old hand at navigating the complexities of bus routes—and many of the drivers know him now by sight.

It isn't just the anonymity that bus travel provides, but the smell that seems to linger in each of the city's vessels of public transportation. Scotty likes it. He can't place it, though; it isn't like anything else he's ever encountered.

Maybe it's part of how they're built, he considers.

The city slips by, a moving picture show of bricks and alleys and lamp posts, of bus shelters and parks and people. Trash has gathered in the corners, the way trash does—along the edge of curbs where sidewalks meet the road. Or along fences, where colourful bits of rubbish entangle themselves in weeds or seem to climb up the chain link barriers. Some of the smaller pieces have made it through, dancing playfully in the wind or making their way with purpose across old asphalt yards split by frost heaves and neglect. Only Scotty seems to notice.

Then the bus jolts and heaves its way to a stop, hissing loudly like an old steam radiator as the doors open and people shuffle their way on and off. That's when Scotty sees him, standing as if in rigid outrage against the tide of King Street shoppers—a fierce and stubborn vessel firmly anchored against the rush of that indifferent river.

He is ragged and old, wrapped in a grubby patchwork quilt and with a dirty canvas sack slung over one of his bony shoulders. He clutches a filthy garbage bag up against his chest, as if at any moment someone might make a serious attempt to deprive him of it. And like many of the other downtown vagrants, he has a greasy cardboard sign—but this one hangs around his neck on an old piece of twine. Only the brown corners of the sign are visible, the rest concealed by the dirty black plastic bag and the jealous hands.

Scotty watches him in idle curiosity as the old man stares intently down at his own shadow, nodding in grim agreement with something.

Or someone, Scotty considers. Then it strikes him, like a scent recalled. *I know him! Or I think I do . . . Why do I—*

But Scotty's breath suddenly toys with him, hiding for moments here and there on the bus. In its place, his breath leaves the tattered remnants of memory—a fetid and invasive stink, sour and stale—a haunt that clings stubbornly to the back of his throat.

And then he knows it: a mop bucket smell.

Because the shabby harlequin suddenly raises his head, weathered skin and stubble stretched too fiercely across that skull; he leers at Scotty, still nodding, and drops his hands.

There are no words on the sign, but Scotty reads it anyway. Breath utterly abandons him, as if the bus were suddenly a vacuum chamber. His head swims and he lurches back into the hard plastic edge of the next seat as the bus pulls forward. The old vagabond is gone now, out of sight, but Scotty struggles to recall numbers, to find the beginning of the sequence.

Something grabs his arm and a face floats briefly into view, mouth moving and kind eyes concerned. But Scotty dismisses the intrusion, hide-and-seek with his breath his only priority.

Shouting now, others gather around him, clutch at him.

Scotty cannot recall the numerical incantation—he gasps desperately, drowning right in front of them all, the bus now writhing with staring eyes and grabbing hands and a cacophony of voices. As he slips under into the waiting darkness, the wall of bus people fades, replaced by one final vision, that ancient head—still nodding, vehement eyes gloating at him.

And the sign.

For secured to the sagging cardboard hanging around that creature's neck was a child's crayon picture: a smiling boy in a red shirt holding hands with a stark black shadow.

14

By the time Simon arrives, I.D. in one hand and case file in the other, Scotty breathes in a slow, steady rhythm, slumped like a drunk in one of the waiting room chairs. *Not even in one of the beds*, he thinks. At least they put him within sight of the nurses' station.

Hypnotics—Simon wonders how high a dosage they gave him; he sees a thin line of anxiolytic drool stretch down from chin to chest. He wipes it away with his bare hand and then goes over to fill out the paperwork. The nurse, Julie, already holds it out.

"Hi, Simon."

"Hey, Julie. How bad?"

She shrugs. "I'd tell you I've seen him worse, but I'd be lying."

"You said that last time."

"Last time," she says, handing over her pen, "he didn't have to be carried in here."

Simon sighs. "What'd they give him? Benzodiazepine cocktail?"

"With a chaser."

"Great. Just great." Simon finishes filling in the release, then hands form and pen back to Julie.

"You can't save them all, you know."

Simon smiles wearily. "Can't even save *one* of them. Thanks for calling me."

"Anytime."

Simon walks across the room and takes a seat beside Scotty. "Come on, man," he says. "Let's get you home." Simon throws the mute's thin arm over his shoulder, but he winces at the smell. "And maybe a shower and a clean shirt, eh? You're pretty ripe."

Simon stands, dragging Scotty to his feet. His ward complies, not as out of it as he seems. Together, they shuffle out of the clinic and toward the parking lot.

SURPRISINGLY, JIMMY WAITS OUTSIDE Scotty's building, smoking a cigarette and contemplating (it seems) a small patch of pavement. Simon glances downward as he and Scotty reach the lobby door; wind and time have deposited a strange collection of things on the sidewalk slab—scraps of weather-worn gum wrappers, the soggy shell of a cigarette pack, an oak leaf, seven or eight tiny balls of tinfoil, a brown feather, and a playing card face down.

Simon readjusts Scotty's arm, which is over his shoulder once again. "Hey," he says.

"Hi," Jimmy returns, eyes still glued to the pavement.

"You doing anything in particular? Looks like you're reading the street version of tea leaves."

"Sorta," Jimmy mumbles. "Trying to figure out what that card might be."

"How 'bout a hand, eh?" Simon fumbles awkwardly for his keys and holds them out. "It's the—"

"I know which one," Jimmy says, taking them. "I was actually waiting here for you. Well, for both of you."

"You *knew* about this?" Simon asks, gesturing at Scotty with his head. "How?"

"Seamus—he was on the bus when Scotty collapsed. You know him?"

Simon navigates Scotty through the open door and into the lobby. "Yeah—well, *of* him. Skinhead. Hangs out with Sirius. Look, man—Scotty ain't getting any lighter. Mind helping me get him up to his apartment?"

"How 'bout to the elevator?" Jimmy says, handing the keys back to Simon. "I wanna ask Seamus what happened."

"Now?"

"Before he finds a bottle, yeah. Anyway, Tribal will help you. He's up there already."

"Weird. Why?"

Jimmy shrugs. "Because he is, man."

JIMMY IS RIGHT: TRIBAL waits outside Scotty's apartment.

"They let him go like that?" he says by way of a hello while rummaging through Scotty's pockets for his door key.

"Yep," Simon confirms. "It ain't exactly a perfect system."

"No shit." Key in hand, he unlocks Scotty's door. Together, Simon and Tribal guide Scotty toward his closet of a bedroom, dodging the wire fish that dangle everywhere. When they reach the bedroom door, however, Scotty stiffens. Gently, the mute shrugs them off and waits, one hand on the doorknob.

Simon steps back. "I think he's alright on his own."

Tribal steps back as well. Together, they turn and head back toward the front room. Behind them, Scotty's door opens and then quickly closes.

"Any idea what he's got squirrelled away in there?" Simon asks quietly.

Tribal shakes his head. "Nah. I don't see none of those cardboard signs, though. And Sirius said he heard, like, music or something coming outa that room. Or voices, I think he said."

"*Voices?*"

"Yeah. Something like that—I don't remember so good. Where's Jimmy? He said I should wait up here in case you needed me."

Simon turns to look at Tribal. "How the hell did he find out about Scotty *and* get you to wait here? I just found out about this myself!"

Tribal shrugs. "Who the fuck knows, eh? It's Jimmy. But it's the streets, man—news has a way of getting places pretty quick. Where'd you say he was?"

"Jimmy? Said he wanted to talk to that skinhead buddy of your brother's and took off."

"Derek?"

Simon shakes his head. "No—Seamus."

"Oh. Yeah, he saw some shit, I guess."

"That's what Jimmy said."

Tribal picks up one of the wire people from Scotty's worktable and pokes at something inside it, something small and hard and black. "You should probably talk to Seamus yourself, eh? Might find out something."

Simon scoffs. "You want me to talk to a *skinhead*? I'm not much of a fighter, Tribal."

But Tribal shoots Simon a quizzical look. "Whatdya mean? Just 'cause he's a skin don't mean he'll scrap anyone who *talks* to him."

"Anyone white, you mean."

Tribal laughs. "He's a SHARP, brother."

Simon shrugs.

"As in 'Skinhead Against Racial Prejudice.' That's Sirius's crowd. Thought you worked with street kids—how the fuck you don't know this shit?"

"I guess I never really took an interest. None of my clients are stomping around in those war boots you all love so much."

"Guess that makes sense," Tribal admits. "Just pay attention to boot laces. Red or white—racist assholes. Black laces, *not* racist assholes. Simple."

"That a hard and fast rule?"

Tribal smirks. "Not exactly. But if you gotta roll the dice, it's a good starting point."

Simon looks around the muggy confines of the cramped and narrow front room. Milk crates of odds and ends, scraps of wood—mostly from hurricane fences—and tattered plastic bags of Salvation Army cast-offs, tin cans and salvaged beer caps, paint cans and brushes, felt-tip markers of every description. But no cardboard.

"Or cassettes," Simon notes.

"What?" Tribal asks, looking up from the small wire sculpture he still holds.

"You said the cardboard signs are missing. So are all the tapes. And that boom box."

But Tribal shakes his shaggy brown hair out of his face and reaches for his leather. "You still need me, man? Gotta see what Sirius is up to."

Simon shakes his head. "I'm good. Thanks for the hand getting him in here. Oh, but if you see Jimmy, could you ask him to find me?"

"Yeah. Be good to see if he dug anything up, eh? Later, brother." Then he's gone.

TRIBAL IS GOOD TO his word: Jimmy reappears that evening at Scotty's.

"Holy shit—you're still here!" Jimmy says, grinning, as Simon opens the door.

Simon shrugs. "Couldn't bring myself to leave. Tribal helped me get him in here, then he disappeared for a couple hours into his room." He relays this information at a whisper. "He's out now—working at his table."

"Well. Let's have a look at the patient." Jimmy drifts in, glancing around with a practiced eye. "You clean up while he was, you know, out of it?"

Simon shakes his head.

"Huh. Seem to be some things missing."

"Tribal noticed, too."

Jimmy nods, pulling thoughtfully at his goatee. Then he reaches into his weathered satchel, pulls out a Walkman, places it on the table in front of Scotty, and weaves his way back through the hanging fish until he's on the far side of the tight room.

Scotty presses the eject button on the Walkman, pulls the cassette out, and inspects the clear plastic case. He holds it with both hands by the bottom two corners, pinches the case tightly, returns it to the machine, and presses play. A barely audible squeak mingles with the chorus of "This Ain't Hollywood" that drifts quietly out of the headphones that dangle off the side of the table. Scotty frowns.

Jimmy, standing by the immense chicken-wire fish by the balcony slider, frowns, too. "I hope it can be salvaged, man. Forgotten Rebels live recording *that* good is like currency." He retrieves his pack of smokes from beneath the wool poncho he still wears despite the heat that remains trapped in Scotty's murky apartment. "You can even hear the *thwack!* between songs when this cat crowned this other cat with a beer bottle."

"I thought you didn't condone violence," calls Simon from the kitchenette. He emerges into the surreal aquarium of Scotty's front room with two mugs of coffee.

Jimmy smiles. "I don't—I just hope Karma had a hand, 'cuz if it did, then that tape has a genuine example of it."

"A genuine example of what?"

"The voice itself, brother! The Universe speaks and we rarely ever stop to listen. That's the only *real* source of tragedy, Ten-Bones."

Simon sighs. "Jimmy—"

"I know, I know. You don't dig nicknames. But don't blame me, man. I just gave sound to the name assigned to you." Then Jimmy grins. "I'm an avatar, man, willing servant of Consequence. And," he adds with a smirk, "in all fairness, I just pointed out the obvious."

Scotty, head partially turned toward them, has grown still. Jimmy notices first—the sudden paleness of the mute's cheeks, the hands that place the cassette gently on the table before him and then, reverently it seems, spread out into a display of ten thin fingers. Palms up, a supplication. Simon watches, too, now.

But Scotty returns to the task at hand as quickly as he stopped it moments before, fingers busy now as he removes the small screw with a miniature screwdriver and lifts the top of the shell off the cassette.

Scotty gets up and ducks under a small school of fish that hang as if they were swimming in a graceful arc. He reaches into an old milk crate, rummaging around for a spare cassette.

A donor. That's what Vince called the one he moved the tape into, a donor. Stupid rollers are just plastic pegs, he thinks. He has the right oil, but sometimes it gets on the magnetic tape itself and ruins it.

Scotty pulls a cassette out from beneath the tangled strips of motley cloth that also occupy the crate. He looks at the thing briefly—factory welded; no good. He tosses it aside, and tries again. This time his hand emerges with a semi-transparent cassette with five screws holding the halves together.

Scotty gives it a small sage nod. *V-I-N-C-E,* he recites, touching each screw. *"V" means "five." I remember.*

⸻

VINCE AND DONNA STECHEY. In Stoney Creek. *Miller Road? Millen? Something like that.* The details are difficult. He stayed with them over the winter when he was sixteen, a kind and friendly foster family without kids of their own. Vince repaired hospital equipment, but his basement make-shift home recording studio was incredible. Scotty would sit with him in the evenings and watch as he worked the mixing board. Friends' recordings, mostly. Sometimes his own stuff.

"This junk?" Vince would say, holding up a cheap plastic cassette. "Sonic weld. You can use a knife, pry it apart like a shellfish, but I like the vice. Pop that open for me, eh?"

Scotty would take the cassette, uninhibited because Vince was never really there—headphones on, he'd be on an audio journey to far and foreign lands, adjusting knobs and levels, alive inside the music. Scotty knew how to place the shell into the vice and gently squeeze it until it popped, then turn it 90 degrees and do it again.

Vince's finger would suddenly appear, wagging in time to whatever he was listening to. He would point at the safety glasses.

"Brittle plastic!" he'd yell because of the headphones. "Gotta mind those eyes, eh!"

Scotty learned. Sonic weld versus screws. Corner wheels versus plain pegs. How to re-spool. How to splice. How to transplant. Deft fingers and single-minded concentration made him good at all of it.

Of course, it didn't last, this small refuge. Vince's basement studio and workshop, the small and comfortable bedroom with a lockable door (Scotty never felt the need), Vince's wife Donna's small kindnesses—watching to see if Scotty preferred soft cookies to hard, or apple juice to grape. Or her way of moving from the kitchen chair that she knew Scotty preferred.

Vince had been the one to tell him, eyes staring at the soundboard as his fingers fiddled nervously with the equalizers. He tried for businesslike, but he couldn't maintain it for long—it just wasn't who he was. He gave up, stopped fiddling, looked at Scotty. "Man, I wish it could be, you know, different, eh? But Donna—she got this offer and we *gotta* move. We gotta. Edmonton—it's . . . She's gotta leave next week. Me, I can get a job fixing stuff anywhere, but opportunities like she got offered, you just can't say no."

Scotty had carried those words—forlorn and ragged, this hand-me-down excuse—into his bubble and down, down. The wind rush ringing then in his ears, and he huddled resolutely against the storm. *It's how everything ends*, Scotty had thought. Not with anger or vitriol, though—it just wasn't in him. *No one wants to keep me. Why would they? I'm no good for anybody. I wish I wasn't so . . .*

Scotty sighs.

V is for "five." I remember. He carries the cassette back to his worktable and begins to remove the screws. Simon and Jimmy drink coffee and talk about music, watching the grey city through the dirty glass of the slider.

Scotty's jaw tightens, his thin fingers tremble. *I hope they're doing well*, he thinks. *Maybe they have a kid now. I think they really wanted one. Of their own.*

A tear—just one—slips out and down across his hollow cheek and then pauses on his jaw as if frightened of the fall. He sweeps it away with a flick and returns to the task of coaxing each tiny screw out of its miniscule socket.

Lifting off the top half of the case, Scotty dumps the two spools of tape out onto the table. It's blank, no sound at all has been captured on its magnetized surface. He carefully transplants Jimmy's tape into the empty shell and replaces the top, the screws. Then, after a pause, he brings down an angry fist on the discarded pile of tape. He pushes it off the table, gets up, and goes into his bedroom. Slam.

Across the room, Jimmy and Simon watch the door in silence. After a moment, Jimmy retrieves the repaired cassette and his Walkman.

"Gotta go," he says to Simon on the way by. "Something I need to do."

15

MOONLIGHT ROUSES THE OLD man from the shabby corners of sleep, like the rough shake of a cold hand. Pulled suddenly from the ragged path he was walking in his dream, he struggles to recall the direction, the surroundings. He remembers trees and light, though not sunlight—fluorescent light somewhere above a tree-lined asphalt path, that incessant buzzing of electricity, droning hum without pause. Then nothing.

He opens his eyes, blurry with age and exhaustion, and is startled by the sharpness of the moonlight as it stabs through the clouds above. The pale glow sweeps across the park, creeping into hollows and slipping effortlessly through holes in the foliage to caress the grey grass below.

Stiffly, he pushes himself upright on the bench; folded newspapers, arranged like overlapping shingles along the length of the painted wood, do little to soften this makeshift pallet. His coat, so matted and begrimed with age and use that some of the other street denizens call it his rat-skin, slips from his bony shoulder. It is damp; arthritic fingers gather the rotten material and pull it quickly away from the newspapers—each one identical to its neighbour.

"Who's there?" he calls out, tremulously. Because something just flickered across the old man's peripheral vision. And again. He struggles to his feet, ignoring the numbness in his heels, the cramps in his toes, the dull savage ache in his left hip—the betrayals of biology and Sister Circumstance.

There it is again—just a flicker of darkness to his right, a shadow darker than those around it.

"I done what I could!" he yells, his forlorn, despondent voice quavering into the empty night. And then, in barely more than a whisper, "I tried. I couldn't." He sinks down again onto the bench, buries his wasted face into withered hands and sobs bitterly.

FROM BENEATH THE CONCEALING blackness of an ancient oak, a single figure watches the old man in his misery until he lies down again on his carefully arranged newspapers. Then quietly, just sandals on soft grass, he slips away and out of the park. Once under the hazy glare of a street lamp, he pauses, tugging absently at one of his dreads. Above him, the heavy drone of electric heat has attracted its nocturnal parishioners, a swarm of moths and other insects, each consumed with its own frantic ecstasy of lamp worship. A secret religion.

"And why not?" he whispers to the post. Above him, the insects swirl and billow like smoke—no pattern, no unity or murmuration. But purpose—that much is present. "And why not?" the watcher repeats.

He shrugs his wool poncho a little forward on his shoulders so that the opening isn't against his throat, then saunters along the sidewalk toward a bus shelter a half-dozen lampposts away. Inside the shelter, another figure waits, lounging indolently against the scarred and filthy plexiglass, a silhouette in heavy street boots and long hair, hands shoved into his pockets.

The ponchoed walker stops at the shelter opening. "Tribal," he says.

"Jimmy. About fuckin' time. Find what you were looking for?"

"Maybe. I, uh, need you to do something for me."

Tribal sighs. "What sort of 'something'?"

"I need you to get me one of the newspapers on a bench about a stone's throw into the park."

"Shit, Jimmy, why not just grab the thing yourself?"

Jimmy tugs at his goatee and looks back the way he came. "It's kinda under Cottonmouth right now."

"Fuck off! I ain't going near that goddamn vampire!"

"C'mon, Tribal—this is for Scotty."

"You mean for Simon. Or for Alise—and they can fuck off, too."

But Jimmy smiles vaguely and looks up at the buzzing light above them, this one a strange orangey-pink. Like the first street lamp, this one has its frantic mob. One, a wide winged brown moth, detaches from the swarm and drifts downward on the still night air, dead. Jimmy and Tribal watch its descent until it lands without so much as a whisper on the street.

Jimmy frowns, tugging his goatee again. Tribal, though—he walks over to the tiny corpse, picks it up out of the road, and lays it against the base of the lamppost.

"I never thought of you as superstitious, man," Jimmy says. "Correction: I never thought of you as sharing *my* superstitions."

"Just saving you the trouble."

A late-night driver drifts by on the far side of the road, speed under control but not so much the weaving. The two friends watch until the car makes an uncertain right turn onto a side street.

Tribal looks back toward the park and sighs. "How heavy you figure he sleeps?"

FROM WHERE TRIBAL STANDS some five or six metres away, the old man looks dead—a frail, dry husk wrapped in a ratty pall. Avoiding the gravel path, Tribal treads as softly as he can on the wet grass. But the air is cool and damp—a clammy night for late August. His scarred leather jacket creaks like the stiff hinges of an old vessel, a coffer lid in a dark closet.

A sudden shudder in that husk's withered frame pins Tribal to the spot, but it is only a night tremor—the old man does not move again. Tribal stands for long moments three or four good strides away, still as stone. It is some time before he realizes that he's holding his breath, too. Then, patience exhausted and true to the reckless way of his blood, he makes a decision.

"Fuck this," he whispers, closing the distance quickly—he snags the first folded paper he can reach, turns, and returns to the blackness of the park's wooded border. He does not run.

From the bench, the old man watches with one open eye as the street kid with long hair and leather strides away. Grey lips peel back from rotten teeth in some semblance of a leering grin.

"'Bout time, boy," he rasps quietly. "'Bout time."

SEVEN HOURS LATER, SIMON stops in the worn lobby of Scotty's building, surprised. Even in the dimness, his eyes not yet adjusted to the gloom, he recognizes Jimmy. Today, along with his trademark vintage sandals and a T-shirt with a fading Tibetan prayer flag on it, Jimmy wears ludicrous bell-bottoms. The jeans have been slit at the outer seams and a massive triangle of '70s paisley upholstery has been sewn in.

"8:00 a.m., Jimmy—little early for you, isn't it?" Then he gestures at the jeans. "Nice. New?"

Jimmy smiles and lights a smoke. "Got a friend who makes 'em—Hodge. Wanna pair? All you need are jeans and a good eye for fabric. He's got a heap of it from Ottawa Street."

Simon smirks and shakes his head. "Too confusing. I think that whole hippie movement was really half about white folks trying to be Indigenous. At least on some level. Cultural appropriation, Jimmy—we got some hang-ups."

"Hey, man, I just dig the groovy flare." Then, more seriously, "I got something you and Alise should probably see. Let's head up."

"Scotty's apartment first. He'll get anxious if I'm late."

"Alright," Jimmy says. "I'll wait for you outside Alise's."

ALISE ANSWERS THE DOOR, groggy and reluctant. Her mohawk flops across one half of her head like a bedraggled, neon pink spider plant. She still wears shredded black jeans and a red flannel shirt, heavy makeup sleep-smeared into a bandit's mask of green and black.

"This better be a goddamn emergency," she snarls.

"Sorry," Simon offers. "Gig last night?"

Alise responds in what sounds like a negative, just a throaty growl, and heads through the debris—dirty clothes, crumpled papers, boots, books, guitars—toward the tiny kitchen and its grimy little coffee maker. Simon follows Alise; Jimmy makes it as far as a Peavey bass half-concealed by an avalanche of gutted sheet music books and a roll of raw canvas. He pauses to excavate.

"Shit," Alise mumbles as she opens the top of the coffee maker. Even from where Simon stands, he can see the pale blurry fuzz of prolific mold as she jerks the filter out. Alise knocks the rotten grounds loose on a burnt pot jutting out of the plethora of dirty dishes that occupies the sink. She gives it a cursory rinse. "You want coffee?" she asks Simon over her shoulder.

"Oh, uh— No."

"Yeah," she says. "Me, neither." She throws the filter viciously toward a stack of empty pasta boxes leaning against a dead potted plant. "This is too much. Assholes."

Simon takes in the army of beer bottles on the counter, the ashtrays heaped with dozens of butts, the stale pizza crusts scattered over the floor, the single Chuck Taylor high top lying under the tiny café table. Like much of the clothing in the other room, it is clearly male in origin.

And although Simon keeps his peace, Alise feels obliged to offer an explanation. "I let my boyfriend stay here while I was gigging down in London and Windsor. He fucking *promised* me he wouldn't have people over. I got back yesterday and haven't seen him yet, so who the hell knows where that asshole is?" Alise's shoulders fall and she pokes at half a cigarette sticking out of the ashes. "Probably ran outa shit to trash here and went to one of his asshole friend's squats. Fuck him."

"Sorry things didn't work out," Simon mumbles at her back, reaching out for that defeated shoulder. Before he makes contact, though, he drops his hand down to his side.

A whisper, as of loose papers sliding along the ground, causes Simon to look behind him. In the entrance to the kitchenette stands Jimmy, his face unreadable. After a moment, though, he gestures for Simon to follow and heads toward the front door.

Simon looks again at Alise, still facing the back wall of the cramped kitchenette. Her head is slightly bowed, as if praying, but her shoulders quiver and her breaths are quietly ragged. Reluctantly, he turns and follows Jimmy.

In the corridor outside Alise's apartment, Jimmy reaches under his drug rug and pulls out a yellowy folded newspaper, weatherworn and old. He hands it to Simon, points to the front page, nods a farewell, and walks away.

Simon watches the enigmatic figure until he drifts around the corner and out of sight before finally looking at the front of the paper. He reads the headline once, then again, confused. He checks the date.

"What the hell is this supposed to mean?" he mumbles, starting after Jimmy. "Hey, Jimmy! Wait up!"

But Jimmy, that ragged and enigmatic street ghost, is gone. Simon shakes his head in disbelief and turns back toward Alise's apartment. *Where the hell did he get a newspaper from October of 1974?* he wonders.

"Child's Remains Incomplete!" the headline shouts. Simon skims through the article—victim still unidentified, remains of a nine- or ten-year-old boy, entombed probably for twenty years, damage to skull points to foul play, pieces of skeleton missing—ten of the smaller bones: fingers, a knuckle, some vertebrae.

But Simon folds the paper after a moment—there's no time for one of Jimmy's recondite cosmic scavenger hunts. He'll figure it out later. Right now, Alise could use a friend. He heads back to her trashed apartment.

ALISE

16

FROM THE VERY BEGINNING, there were spiders. Her mother's boyfriend saw to that.

"Keep your fuckin' legs closed! You want spiders to get in there?" Half a case of beers down and still going strong—Paul was a keeper. That's what Alise's mother said, anyway. "You're fuckin' what, eight? Nine? Jesus fuck! What the shit did your idiot mother teach ya, eh?"

A keeper. That's what she called him. Paul had a full-time job at Procter & Gamble, a considerable step up from Alise's father, a bassist still playing the band circuit in Kingston, Ontario.

Kingston. Alise's birthplace and the city her mother felt she had escaped from. The woman left the city in the middle of the day, pulling Alise from her first-grade classroom early and thrusting her into the back of a car crammed with the sad residue of a failed life. Alise never got the chance to say goodbye to the world she was torn from. The birthday party invitation she'd received that morning—her very first ever—lay in her school cubby for weeks before it was finally thrown away.

Paul was the latest manifestation of would-be father figures in Alise's young life. He was a heavy drinker and boorish when drunk, but he never touched Alise. Ever. Not so much as a friendly hand on the shoulder or a kind stroke of her hair. Not like the one before him, but Alise left that door closed.

Alise, eight years old and already defiant, felt the blood rush to her cheeks as she clamped her bony knees together. It wasn't embarrassment, though; it was fury. Rage dwelt in that tiny frame like a restless spirit—a small wight in the bone house, bent on vengeance. Not the petty, prepubescent reprisals of playground imagination, conceived under the slide or while mashing ants to paste on the asphalt edges of the school grounds, but retribution conceived in a mind unburdened as of yet by the significance of consequence.

Spiders, he said. Paul hated spiders. *Hated* them. She would show him. She would show them all.

HAMILTON WAS AN ALIEN world to Alise. Its very geography was a mystery—her earliest memory of the city was standing on the strip of grass that separated Concession Street from the sheer drop off the Niagara Escarpment, looking down at the sprawl of houses and streets, the cluster of high rises and office buildings, the monstrous expanse of steel mills, the immensity of the bridge that leapt across the harbour, and—beyond it all—the endless stretch of Lake Ontario.

"Well, what do you think?" her mother had asked her.

"When will I see Daddy?" is all she'd replied.

Alise missed her father more than anything else she'd left behind. She missed his middle-of-the-night stories, home late from a gig and reeking of cigarettes and sweat and something else—weed, she'd later figure out. He'd sneak into her little room and wake her up to tell her wild tales of fairies and dragons, of unicorns and princesses. He'd pass out on her bed some nights, halfway through a convoluted tale. On those nights, Alise would snuggle up next to him and pretend he was a friendly giant. Sometimes she'd use him to make a blanket fort on her bed, their secret cave.

By second grade, those memories were painful—bittersweet remnants of another world. In Hamilton, Alise felt like an intruder in her own home. Her mother and she lived in a modest apartment on the escarpment, but it was the "roommate," the man who shared a bedroom with her mother. To help with the rent. Paul just appeared on the threadbare couch one day in the summer—he commandeered the small television and the coffee table, chose Alise's seat at the table during meals, and made off with most of her mother's time and attention, like a thief.

"Or a disease," Alise decided years later, thinking back upon her mother's situation in those early years—not unsympathetically. Alise was no fool; she knew that her father wasn't the type of man to support a family back then. And Paul, for all his faults, at least went to work every morning. Still, she could not forgive the coldness, the petty cruelties with which he greeted her. Even now, years later.

But second grade. They'd changed apartments in August and Alise had to go to a new school after only spending a few months in the first one. That was a stroke of luck, though, because she was placed in Miss Emily Steiger's class. Miss Steiger knew loneliness when she saw it—insightful, young, edgy; she wore the sorts of outfits that skirted the boundaries of proper attire, and her hair was boyish, dyed black, and spiky. She let Alise touch it once when they were alone. Alise, with that infallible instinct of childhood, sensed an ally, a kindred spirit.

On a cold October morning during recess, Alise saw her opportunity.

"Miss Steiger?"

"Hi, Alise. What do you need?"

Alise shifted from one small foot to the other and looked around, just a quick survey of the playground. They were as alone as they could be. "Could you . . . could you tell me how to write a letter?"

"A letter, eh? To whom? Santa?" A kind smile, a wink.

Alise mumbled something into the collar of her coat.

"I'm sorry, I can't hear you," Miss Steiger said. Then she crouched down so that she was at eye level. Her face became serious, attentive. "To whom?" she asked again.

"To my daddy."

"Oh, I see. Where is he? Away?"

"He lives in a different city."

Miss Steiger smiled then, but sadly—a smile that crept into her eyes like a secret, like a conspirator. Alise, falling into those eyes, smiled too, shyly.

◢

"So, she actually *did* it?" Simon sits at the tiny table in Alise's kitchenette. They share the one remaining beer they found in the back of the fridge beneath a lumpy mound of Kraft Dinner, small reward for the herculean effort they put into cleaning the disaster Alise's boyfriend and buddies left in their drunken wake.

Alise takes a swig and passes the bottle back to Simon. "Yeah. I never figured out how she got his name or address, but I'm sure it was through the music scene."

"Unless musicians share some kind of hive mind, I still don't see how she knew to look in Kingston—kind of a haul from Hamilton, eh?"

"You underestimate us," she replies with a hint of a smile.

"C'mon. She must have dug through your records."

"Yeah, probably. Don't matter—she did it is the point."

"She still teaching up there?"

Alise scoffed. "Miss Emily Steiger? Nah. She barely made it the year. The other staff had it in for her—you know the type, wool skirts below their knees and horn-rimmed schoolmarm uniform glasses. Emily had this portable record player in her classroom—she used to play us Kinks albums when we were painting and drawing. She always wanted us to 'draw what we heard.' Cool shit like that."

Simon took a drink from the bottle. "Too bad—sounds like she was pretty great."

"She still is!"

"You're in contact with her, after all this time?"

Alise openly grins for the first time that day. "Well, yeah—she's married to my dad now."

Simon takes a moment to process. "That's incredible!"

"Karma, baby. Karma."

"You sound like Jimmy," Simon grins.

Alise takes one more small sip and signals Simon to finish the beer. "My dad got the letter, wrote back through Emily, and eventually moved here to be near me. As it turned out, the scene in the Hammer was *way* better for him—good energy, lots of people who liked his style. He cleaned himself up. They own a music store on Upper Ottawa now, but Emily's also an artist."

Simon shakes his head. "And you end up an artist *and* a musician. A bassist, even."

"Well, kinda by design. Em taught me the one, my dad taught me the other. We're pretty close still, all three of us."

"Huh. So, what about—Paul, was it?"

Alise sneers and rolls her eyes. "He's still around, too. My mom and him, they live on Bayfield Avenue. You know it?"

Simon nods. "Yeah. North End."

"That's me—a North End girl. Well, sorta. Anyway, Paul's kind of the reason behind the spider thing I got going. The more he hated them, the more I loved them. I used to catch them as a kid and put them in the cereal box—right in the bag with the Fruit Loops." Alise's eyes drift, afloat in the memory. "I must have caught a mother with an egg sack at some point because one morning he opened the box, unrolled the bag, and poured— then he squealed. I mean, *squealed*! About two hundred of those little fuckers swarmed out of that red, yellow, and orange heap."

Simon laughs. He reaches for the empty bottle, but Alise's hand is there first. For a moment, their fingers touch. And linger.

"We should—" Simon starts.

"—get going on the front room, yeah. Hey, look, I really appreciate you sticking around to help, eh?"

"No problem. You definitely need it." Simon gets up, but the old newspaper he'd tossed on the counter before they started cleaning up the kitchen catches his eye. "Shit! Sorry—I totally forgot as soon as I came back in. Jimmy gave me this in the corridor as he was leaving." He grabs the paper and hands it to Alise.

She scans the front-page headline, frowns, and reads the first few paragraphs of the article before looking up at Simon. "What's this supposed to—"

"Look at the date."

She stares at it, clearly perplexed. "October, 1974? Why the fuck would Jimmy give you a paper that's, what . . . almost thirteen years old?"

"That's what I said at first, too. But read it through. Jimmy thinks it's got to do with Scotty. It's the missing bones that creep me out."

"The missing *bones*?"

"Read it!"

Alise takes her time now, perusing the article carefully; Simon walks around and behind her, pressed close to read it over her shoulder. It was published three days after the initial discovery, but there is scant substance amidst the sensationalist framework: emotional quotes from the men who opened up the wall with sledgehammers lend the article a humanizing quality; eerie descriptions of the coal-dust-coated bones removed by careful coroner's hands are reminiscent of late-night horror flicks. The remains of an unidentified child meekly returning to the light of day one piece at a time. As if shy of the attention.

"Three days," Simon mumbles.

"Three days what?"

Simon points to a line in the article. "This was written three days after they discovered the skeleton. Says the kid's body must have been in that old coal chute for twenty years. You'd think they'd have at least made some guesses on who it was. Instead, it says 'the victim's identity is still a mystery.' There's nothing in here about kids who went missing in, what, the fifties? Pretty basic journalism, digging up things like that."

Alise puts the paper down on the table and leans back into Simon. "Jimmy gave this to you?"

Simon pauses, feeling Alise's softness against his own wiry frame. "Huh? Uh, yeah . . . Yeah. Jimmy. Downstairs—said we need to look at it."

She plays with the corner of the paper on the table. "He's so goddamn cryptic."

"I don't think he means to be," Simon counters. "Just the way he's wired."

"Yeah, maybe."

They don't move for another half-a-minute, but then Alise sighs.

"Front room?"

Simon smiles. "Yeah. Let's get to it."

17

HE IS DETERMINED. A brown building. Somewhere out in that sprawl of concrete and asphalt and smog and noise that fill the flat land between lake and ledge—between the wharf-heavy shore of the seemingly endless water and the hundred-metre-high Niagara Escarpment. Somewhere in that urban grid is the unassuming building of his childhood.

Brown. Or maybe just the balconies? Scotty can't be sure—its image is buried under the burden of foster homes in shabby tenements, or in yard-less narrow brick houses crammed together in claustrophobic madness. Or under the terror of doctors' offices, emergency rooms, strangers' cars.

"That's chloroform you're smelling," one stranger told him once while he was crammed in the back of a hot sedan. Scotty recalls avoiding the seatbelt buckle because it burned. He doesn't recall who the stranger was or where he was taking him; he only remembers the voice. Not cruel, not kind. "That's chloroform," the voice said again. It came from a cardboard box of clinking jars.

Chloro. Scotty thinks as he packs for an excursion. *Chloro-form. I remember that word. It has a bad smell.*

He feeds Spider as per Alise's instructions, and heads out. He will go east this time, in as straight a line as he can. East, because the man—the mop bucket man—is in the other direction.

I've seen him before—he's always been around! Why didn't I know?

That he is a creature from his childhood, he means, the strange monster in the broom closet. *And why,* he agonizes further, *does he have one of my old drawings?*

Fear, now. A tingling sensation that toys with the nape of his neck. But Scotty forces it down.

That man can't make me hide, he thinks fiercely. *"Find me!" That's what Furnace Boy said. It was him—I know it! He saved me. Now I need to—*

But Scotty isn't quite sure what he's meant to do. Find him, yes; that much is clear.

But why?

At the corner of Rebecca and Wellington, Scotty looks to the right as a heavy truck rumbles its way by. His eyes drift from the back of the truck to the top of a pale apartment building a couple blocks away. It is white, or maybe grey. Definitely not brown.

Still.

If I could get on top of one of those, I could see far!

It's much taller than his own building, the roof of which proved inadequate when he finally tried it. And it's occupied by different groups of teenagers from time to time, which discourages him from further sojourns up there.

Then he looks beyond the high rise—the Escarpment looms above everything.

So stupid I'm so stupid so stupid so He turns onto Wellington and follows the traffic south toward the cliff.

HE IS INVISIBLE. YEARS of practice have taught him how to occupy the least amount of physical space, all but completely unnoticed by his fellow pedestrians. He floats along Hamilton's streets and side roads like an unassuming stick in the torrent.

But even Scotty is conspicuous, standing awkwardly at the end of Wellington, neck craned in a futile attempt to see over a tall concrete barrier that separates him from the last two hundred metres. Like a root-bound weed, or a ragged little sunflower.

A fellow pedestrian takes notice, anticipates the dilemma.

"If you're looking for a way up," says the friendly voice, "the closest is the Wentworth stairs." Then he points east. "That way."

Scotty catches the gesture out of the corner of his eye, but he cannot move otherwise. His breath dances around him, playful fluctuating shadow in the sunlight. He counts.

"You alright, buddy?"

At fourteen Scotty has it—disobedient breath trapped at last in the tight confines of his chest. He clings to it like a miser and begins to walk, grateful for the help. *Thank you*, he offers.

"Geez, you're welcome, buddy! Don't mention it, eh? Dick."

But Scotty is accustomed to this kind of disdain.

He weaves his way through the labyrinth of right angles until he comes to a low chain-link fence separating the dead end of a road from a strip of scraggly woods. Beyond the trees is a rail line that runs parallel to the bottom of the Escarpment. He clambers over.

A three-minute walk along rusty tracks and he sees the base of the stairs on the other side of a wide street that begins its hairpin ascent up the cliff face. The stairs themselves climb their steep way through the heavily wooded base of the Escarpment, disappearing into the cool green shadows. A welcome relief from the summer morning sun—Scotty slips into the shade and begins the arduous climb.

Not too far up, though, he stops short: dangling from a low branch by a piece of dirty twine is one of his wire fish.

A copy? He clings to the possibility; he has never been here before. But it isn't—he recognizes its swell and curve. It's the fish he hung in Gore Park, on the tree closest to the statue of Queen Victoria. Two weeks ago. It was gone when he passed back through the park an hour later, but that wasn't surprising: street art has a lifespan of a couple days at most.

He hung it there because an old woman was beneath that tree, asleep. Or passed out. She was rank with her own tangy stench, a dumpster smell. A small bouquet of wild flowers was pinned under her hand, as if they might sneak away while she slept. Scotty hung the fish on a branch above her head, as if she were dreaming it.

But now.

The small black figure inside is missing—in its place is a crumpled-up ball of paper. Scotty, heart thumping out its own secret warning, reaches for the wire and separates it at the seam. Quivering fingers clutch the yellowed paper, pull it out. He breathes—in, out.

In.

Out.

In.

Slowly he opens the paper ball, but it is old and damp, yielding reluctantly to his careful fingers. Words appear. The first one has a "C" and an "h"—*That says "ch." I know that one.* Then an "ild's" follows. Then an "R" in front of "emains." The "R," "m," and "s" register, but the other letters are too amorphous. He tries to unravel them anyway, his mind grateful for the distraction.

But as he works at the creases and folds, he finds that a second piece of paper has been crumpled into the first, this one silk-smooth and grey. He exhales and his breath, before he can draw it back in, leaps up and away into the branches.

I need you! Come back, I—I need

Air.

It gathers in the shadows above him, or behind the trunks of trees. Even under the treads of the stairs. Scotty reels, lurching forward and into the steel edges of the steps. Searing pain explodes in his bony right shin, and the world flashes white.

But the shock—he inhales sharply, tears welling up as throbbing waves wash over his senses, a steady heartbeat of agony in his thin leg. A whimper escapes him, just one. The sound of it hangs about the branches, bewildered. Then it dissipates.

Scotty tries to focus. He smells loam, redolent of fresh grass or alfalfa sprouts or maybe just clay—wet and heavy here in the shadows. The earthy scent cloaks the more aggressive smells of earlier: hot asphalt, tar, exhaust. He closes his eyes, tries to separate them.

His left palm, too, he now notices. Just skinned. With a sigh, Scotty opens his eyes and stares at the second piece of paper that emerged from the newsprint.

It is one of his childhood drawings, torn in half. Just the black figure. Alone.

"CHILD'S REMAINS INCOMPLETE!"

It was a sensationalist headline, but true: there were bones missing. The police had cordoned off the basement of Scotty's apartment building, giving the coroner time to assess. Foul play was assumed from the beginning. Elevator and stairwell: the police had these access points well in hand.

The original stairs, though.

Scotty slipped away from his mother in the chaos of reporters and police, tenants and visitors, making his quiet way to the end of the lobby.

Then down a fetid corridor that smelled strongly of cabbage and that pungent, musty fug that haunts secondhand clothing stores. The narrow corridor ended in a heavy door with words on it, but Scotty didn't have the means to decipher them. They were on a real sign, though: large black, blocky letters on a white rectangle. Someone had written something else on the sign in black marker, hastily scribbled below the official words. There was an "O"—that letter he knew; it was one of the five or six he could recall. To Scotty, it looked like a mouth that shouted nothing. A silent void. In the cracked mirror of their little apartment's dingy bathroom, he would sometimes watch himself make his mouth that shape.

Low on the wall to the right of that sealed and forbidden door was an old vent covered in a thin metal grill. Not long ago, Scotty had discovered it in his wanderings, found that—with a little urging—the plate came off. Old, rotten wood couldn't even stop a seven-year-old from prying the metal away, screws stripped completely. It wasn't a large opening by any means—but for Scotty, small for his age, it was perfect.

He had explored this forgotten secret several times already in the past month or so, returning to the squalid apartment upstairs to be berated by his distraught mother for the cobwebs and filth and soot he had thoroughly ground into his clothes.

"*Look* at you!" she'd hiss. "What'll people *think* when you go out in those clothes? Those are your *only pants!*"

She never yelled at him for the grime on his skin or in his hair; it was like she didn't really see it. And that was his responsibility anyway—cleaning himself up, which he did with a child's definition of acceptable.

Scotty pulled the plate away, set it against the wall, and slipped into the old vent shaft. He knew where the tunnel divided, where each branch led. He chose the nearest branch, squeezed through, and lowered himself down, right onto the old stairs behind the door with the sign. Stairs down to the furnace room.

Which was lit up with portable spotlights on tripods, extension cords snaking away and out the big metal door that had been flung wide open by the police. Men milled about, most in a uniform of some sort—four policemen, two men in white coats, a firefighter. By the door on the other side of the cavernous room, a tall man in a jacket and tie was asking the super a lot of questions and scribbling away on a little pad of paper every time the buffoon spoke. That's what many of the neighbours called the super: "the buffoon." Scotty supposed it was his title.

The men in white coats were leaning into a new hole in the cinder blocks, busy with their hands and talking to each other in strange words. They stopped often, took a picture with a large camera and a blinding flashbulb, and then went back to work. Digging, it sounded like.

Scotty squatted down behind the pipes that led to and from the huge oil burner. It was hot, and sweat soon rolled down his face and neck, leaving runnels in the filth. But he was entranced by the men's interest in the very new hole in a very old wall.

Eventually, the super was dismissed and the man in the tie barked an order. The others made their way out of the furnace room, and others came in with a stretcher. From where Scotty hid, he could see the men in white coats carefully laying things on the stretcher—a large round black stone, many other objects that looked like black sticks, and then many smaller black stones—some so small that they disappeared as they rolled under the sticks.

Finally, one of the men retrieved something that looked like a bird's cage, it too black and ominous. He placed it carefully among the other things, then waited for his friend to emerge from the dark aperture in the wall.

When he did, he too was holding something wonderful—a rigid, black sculpture that looked like a pair of butterfly's wings. He placed it between the bird's cage and the stone. Then they covered the stretcher with a sheet, picked it up between them, and carefully left the furnace room.

A policeman stepped into the cavernous chamber briefly. He looked around and, apparently satisfied by what he saw, closed the heavy steel door with a resounding bang.

WITHOUT REALIZING IT, SCOTTY found himself counting. Or counting in a manner of speaking. Breath trapped securely inside, he drummed a skinny finger against the old, crusty asbestos-covered pipe. Tap tap tap tap until the policeman was gone.

Scotty emerged from shadowy concealment like a little ghost, unaware that he would soon meet another down here in the gloom—a friend, a playmate. His first and only companion.

For the moment, though.

He crept toward the hole, starkly black because of the fierce glare of the spotlights that painted this side of the wall a pale, luminescent white, like blocks of bone. Broken concrete, tossed aside hastily, lay in a heap below the rough opening. He climbed it and peered inside.

The tallest spotlight shone directly onto the floor of the tight chamber, and Scotty had to move his head aside so that his shadow didn't obliterate vision. Lumps of dull black rocks covered the bottom of the cramped space, gathered into small mounds or moved aside to form hollows. Scotty let his small fingers drift across that bumpy topography, black dust gathering thickly on his fingertips.

Until he touched something else, a shift in texture.

He pried it out of the black rocks, a small object—thin and cylindrical, lumpy at both ends. Then another one, a touch shorter.

Scotty gently moved the dusty black rocks aside, one at a time, until he had found another eight foreign pieces. They were small, oddly shaped, and when he scraped one with his nail, he exposed a little white line just below the black dust that coated it.

Intrigued, he stowed away the ten treasures in his pockets and retraced his steps.

The lobby was still bustling with morbidly curious gawkers too stubborn to give up until the last official was gone. A police officer blocking the stair-well to the basement listened stoically to a shabby, angry old woman with a full laundry basket propped on her hip; the elevator was temporarily out of service.

Did they stop the skinny little boy covered in coal dust with the bulging pockets? Did anyone—even the rubberneckers—see the little phantom as he slipped through the lobby toward the access stairwell that led only up?

No.

But, of course, Scotty was accustomed to being invisible.

⌐

BUT SCOTTY'S CHILDHOOD WAS haunted by a number of reticent ghosts.

The weakest ghost belonged to his father, for whom Scotty had only the tenuous shreds of fading memory. That bedraggled phantom, hugging his gig-bag tight to his chest, visited only on rare occasions, and then only at the ragged ends of other dreams. Timidly. He had no definitive face or costume, that gig-bag the only constant. A sporadic visitor and unreliable because all he did was glance about uncertainly, just short of apology, and then dissipate.

The Furnace Boy, though—he was the wide-awake ghost of lonely after-noons, waiting impatiently in the basement for Scotty to visit, restless for play. Or sometimes he wasn't there, but Scotty didn't know where else the boy's shadow went. Still, the Furnace Boy never went away for long; for that little ghost, home was the sooty humming playground of giant pipes and shadowy machines.

Scotty's mother, however. She was a ghost before she even died, just a fading spirit—she haunted the small corners of their tiny apartment, and then just her bedroom, cloaked in the brume of cigarette smoke, like an attendant apparition—someone to talk to. Or at least to listen to her.

Until, of course, she fell silent, too. That's how she died, in pieces: her voice died first, and the rest of her quietly followed suit. Once dead, Scotty's mother seemed to climb onto his small back and wrap her limbs around him, determined never to let go again.

And then there was the janitor.

Scotty first remembers him from school, where he lurked in the dank miasma of the custodial closet or watched him furtively from doorways. But memory is fickle—he may have always been around in some form or another.

The Creep. That's what Miss Tracy called the janitor, Scotty overhearing this almost daily when he was seven. Like Scotty's own mother, Miss Tracy eventually just treated Scotty as if he were a mildly inconvenient room accessory—occasionally underfoot because he moved about, like sentient furniture, but safe to speak her mind around because (she assumed) he could neither understand nor report what she said. A small fish in a fishbowl. Keeping her fishbowl secrets.

She was partially right, but Scotty recalls words—fragments of barbed phrases. Some caught.

For instance.

"And yesterday," Miss Tracy said quietly to her visiting friend, a woman who seemed connected somehow to one of the O's, "the Creep was in *here*! Over there, by the art wall." She gestured at the dingy little bulletin board where she sometimes tacked up student drawings and paintings, or the occasional craft. "I mean, the room was locked and the lights were off—I opened the door and almost *screamed*!"

"He was just there? In the *dark*?" said the friend. "Doing what?"

"Who knows? *Creep* things. He just looked at me real hard, then left."

Scotty knew, though—without having to look, he knew that his little drawing would be missing. Sometimes Scotty brought them home, folded up and tucked away in pockets or in his flimsy lunch pail. But when Miss Tracy pinned them up, they'd disappear. She never noticed.

And now he knew who had been taking them, his pictures of the smiling boy in a red shirt holding hands with the black shape. At seven, though, he did not question why: it just seemed to be another part of their secret relationship.

It was a simple arrangement, seemingly determined by whatever forces dictated such things. Scotty didn't think to object—not because he was too small or because he really didn't have the means, but because there was a pattern to all of it that made it bearable. Scotty clung to patterns, to predictability.

A simple arrangement: at morning line-up, the janitor would be in the custodial closet on his stool, watching him. At recess, he would be at the ugly metal door that led to the out-of-bounds places, watching. At lunch, he would watch Scotty from the trash bin in the corner, where he adjusted and readjusted the black garbage bag over and over again, as if he were a finicky tailor dressing an uncooperative mannequin. And at afternoon dismissal line-up, he was once again in the closet. Watching.

He spoke directly to Scotty only once, during dismissal line-up—a strange and disjointed memory. From the shadowy corner of the custodial closet, the weathered face broke into a leering sort of grimace; in his thin hand was one of Scotty's drawings, which he shook at the boy as if to dislodge the crude pair of figures drawn there.

"Boy!" he'd hissed. "You seen him, ain'tcha? Boy!"

And Scotty, unprepared, had lost his breath almost immediately—there was no place to hide; instead, he'd gasped at what air he could get.

"Boy!" the janitor had persisted, relentless. "I need t'know! Tell me!"

But the line surged forward, carrying Scotty in its wake.

AFTER THAT, THEIR RELATIONSHIP changed. Or, at least, it did for Scotty. Not the routine of actions—the watching, the waiting—but in how Scotty perceived him. Older, Scotty might have considered the mechanics behind this. *Maybe I believed that only I could see him*, he might have thought. After all, he'd never known the man to speak. In fact, Scotty just assumed that he couldn't, like himself. But a threshold had been crossed, and from then on Scotty saw the mad eyed custodian as a vague threat—just one more rocky shoal to navigate around during the stormy ebb and swell of his day.

When a picture that he'd drawn some time ago inexplicably reappeared in his lunch box, Scotty gasped for air as if he had just broken the surface of a deep and dark lake. This was in the cafeteria. The children around him watched in dull curiosity, as if it were a performance meant to break up the monotony of rigid routine.

The teacher on lunch duty, however, panicked. She bounded across the crowded room, deftly weaving between the squalling masses on their aluminum benches, and landed a heavy palm in the middle of Scotty's thin back. The thud could be heard four tables away. And although Scotty wasn't choking, as she believed, her well-meaning gesture had the desired effect—he was so surprised by her that he stopped gasping.

A ragged cheer went up, the other children excited by the unexpected dramatics. Some of the older boys started pounding on their friends' backs and laughing. The few teachers staffing this circus descended upon the mob to cut short the worst of the rough housing before it rippled outward.

Scotty, abandoned by his would-be saviour, saw only one thing, as if through a tunnel: the janitor ogling him from his waste bin station, mocking grin stretched across his grey face, exposing the grimy nubs of his rotten teeth. He lifted a single bony hand and pointed straight at Scotty, barking out in vicious coughs that might well have been laughter.

And just as quickly as his breath had returned, he lost it again. Scotty froze, little fingers at first still clutching the drawing of a happy child in a red shirt holding hands with a black bipedal shape, but his fingers loosened as the air within was stripped down to nothing—just empty filler in his tight lungs. The room began to spin. Shapes, myriad fragments, leapt playfully about him, a riotous swarm of colours. The stale reek of the filthy floor rose up like an angry tide, bodies on either side jostled him roughly, a small hand landed sharply on his back and laughter overwhelmed him. Through all of it, the janitor. Gleefully hacking away and nodding seemingly in rhythm to his wild laughter—one more secret for them to share.

Scotty reeled, off kilter as the bench itself lurched violently beneath him. He fell.

As for the janitor, he too fell—dramatically, from the good graces and threadbare pity of the school's administration. His exit, the following week, was also dramatic. In custody, as a matter of fact. At seven-and-a-half, Scotty only registered the visceral details—the police, towering above everyone and wearing massive belts weighed down with a dozen different mysteries; the brief scuffle (heard, not seen) in the custodial closet; the curses and oaths of the man as they hauled him out by his wiry arms (*Goddamn sons o' Satan, this is God's work you're stopping, sons o' bitches!*); the fetid and mephitic stench of the greyish-brown water from the upset mop pail that rushed across the floor in his wake as he was manhandled out of the closet. Following him, it seemed.

But why was he taken? Scotty had no idea. He only knew it had something to do with him. His mother picked him up early that day, emerging from the principal's office wide-eyed and pale, as if she'd just been told that she actually lived in a different city—or that this one was just a cleverly illusive construct. The principal himself stuck his turtle-like head out into the corridor briefly, catching Scotty's eye before the child could look away. He said something to Scotty's mother, parting words kindly offered, then disappeared.

The bewildered woman, staring off in the distance strangely, felt around for Scotty's hand. She found it and grasped it tightly.

"I just—I wish you wasn't so—"

But she never finished her sentence.

Still clutching his little hand, she moved with purpose toward the front door.

18

ALISE SMILES AT SIMON. "I can't believe you actually stayed through this shit storm."

She throws herself on the couch, the last thing they excavated. Simon hauls the final trash bag to the pile near the door and then joins her.

"I could *definitely* use a shower," she says.

"Yeah—me, too."

The air conditioner, a bulky unit from the mid-'70s, squats in the window like a giant black toad. With emphysema. At best it pushes the humid air around like a half-hearted bully.

Simon frowns. "Hey—what time is it?"

"Thursday."

"Seriously, I need to finish my rounds. It's a light day for me, but I got a couple clients who need meds."

Alise wrinkles her nose. At some point, she has wrestled her failing pink mohawk into a veil that lays obediently down one side of her head. Makeup, too, Simon notices suddenly—not the stage paint of late-night gigs, but subtle. Pretty.

"They can't do without for one day?" she asks. "I should try to feed you, at least!"

"Sorry—can't skip. And I've seen the inside of your fridge. All of it, in fact: we threw everything out. Except for that bottle of mustard."

Alise smiles. "Well, come back tonight. I owe you dinner."

Simon nods. "Cool—what time?"

"Tonight," she repeats. "What's with you and time?" Then she pokes him in the ribs.

3:14 P.M. LATE, BUT not completely unreasonable. Simon drives to a group home just off of Ottawa Street South, logs his visit, and leaves. But as he's crossing Dunsmure, he spots Jimmy entering the giant Tim Horton's that occupies that corner.

He hunts around for a parking spot.

"Jimmy—the paper. Where'd you get it?" Simon isn't even close to Jimmy's corner of the coffee shop when he asks. The Tim's isn't too crowded, so his voice hangs heavy in the space between them.

An old woman shushes at Simon as he closes the gap between the door and Jimmy. Simon ignores her, but Jimmy grins as Simon falls into the chair across from him.

"Geez, Simon—keep it down. This is a religious institution, man."

"It's a Tim Horton's," he says flatly.

But Jimmy raises an eyebrow. "It's coffee *Mecca*, man—the first Tim's ever. They got a manger upstairs where Canadian Everyman identity was born."

But Simon is impatient. "Seriously, Jimmy—where'd you get the paper?"

"Hey, did you ever notice?" Jimmy leans in—a conspiracy, a secret. "Did you ever notice that when you sit across from someone smoking in a Tim Horton's that the smoke never reaches you?"

"Uh, I—"

"Seriously! I exhale toward you, but the smoke goes upward about midway across the table." Jimmy points up without breaking eye contact with Simon. "As if there are fans or something in the ceiling. But there *aren't*."

"Jimmy—"

"It's like sacrificial smoke, brother—but no fat and, what . . . thigh bones, right? Just plain tobacco. Still, the gods need their fix, too, eh?" Jimmy smiles now and leans back in his chair. "Hard times, Ten-Bones, hard times. The gods gotta take what they can get."

Simon sighs. He knows that Jimmy works on his own cryptic frequency. "You have a point, I assume?"

"Yeah—hard times. Thirteen years ago, couple of those Canadian every-man types found something under this city that probably haunted them for years. Maybe it still does. Rerouting a pipe and finding a child's coal-black-ened bones instead? Hard times."

"Worse for the boy's family," Simon offers. "Although the article was written a couple days after the discovery. Never says who the boy was."

"And no follow-up," Jimmy adds. "I must've gone through a hundred feet of microfiche at the library."

This surprises Simon. "You did? When?"

"Earlier today."

"Can't envision you digging through microfiche."

"Well," Jimmy says, "it wasn't me *exactly*. One of the volunteers happens to like a certain type of acid, and I—"

"Got it."

"Anyway," Jimmy continues, "it's too bad. I was hoping she'd find some-thing. I asked Sirius first—he's squirrelled away in some corner of that library almost every day—but he's . . . not himself lately. Girl trouble on the horizon, I'd wager."

Simon leans back and looks up at the ceiling tiles, sweeping a long strand of black hair from his face. "Good idea, though."

"You want coffee?" Jimmy asks suddenly.

"I guess."

"You *guess*? They *invented* coffee here, man! Best coffee in the world!"

Simon smiles and sighs. "Sorry. Of course, you're right—I'd love a coffee."

"Yeah, man, me too. Thanks for offering. Large double-double."

Simon rolls his eyes and gets up to order the coffees at the counter. By the time he returns, Jimmy's half way through another smoke. Placing the coffees on the table, he sits back down.

"Cheers," Jimmy says, opening the tab on the lid. Then, more quietly, "So—the article claims that the child's skeleton was incomplete. You remember how many pieces were missing?"

Simon's eyes narrow. "Yeah, ten. Small pieces, like parts of fingers and a wrist. Piece of the spine, too."

Jimmy nods. "Ten bones," he says simply. "When I called you 'Ten-Bones' in front of Scotty last night—"

"He reacted! I remember. Made that strange gesture with his hands."

"Right. Now Scotty, he's been going for long walks lately. I asked around. People have seen him snooping around high rises down on Barton and beyond. Know where he was seen this morning?"

"No—where?"

"On top of the Escarpment, staring out at the city below."

"Lots of people do that," Simon offers.

"I got two gifts, man. First, I know when I've been somewhere for too long. Starting to get that tingling right now, actually." Jimmy gets up with his coffee and he heads toward the door.

But Simon, still seated, calls after him. "What's the second?"

Jimmy pauses, then turns to face him. "Addictions, brother. I got a nose for people's addictions. He's looking for a building. You got an address now— take him."

And then he's gone.

BUT IT ISN'T ENOUGH for Simon. Not that he doubts Jimmy's instincts: Scotty's surreptitious wanderings point toward a search for something. However, driving him into the North End to confront whatever exists at that address—if anything at all—seems reckless. Maybe he missed something in the records.

Simon contemplates this on the way back to Alise's, armed now with a bottle of wine and the element of surprise. He has a key to the building, after all—no need to have Alise buzz him in.

But when he gets there, he thinks better of it and presses the button anyway.

A deep hum, as if an amplifier were just turned on, resonates from the speaker. "C'mon up," says Alise's voice. Then the sharp buzz.

Simon enters the elevator and absently presses the button for Scotty's floor.

"Damn it," he mumbles, noticing his mistake just as the car passes the third floor. He fumbles with the buttons, gets off on the fifth floor, and heads for the stairwell.

He's had time to get home and change, overdressing just enough to pique his mom's curiosity. She hadn't been coy about it.

"Hey—where you off to?"

"Back into the city," he said.

"Like that? You better stop somewhere for flowers."

Simon winced—he knew where this was headed. And, true to form, his mom pressed.

"So this girl in the city, does she have a name?"

"Alise," Simon offered. "Ma, I gotta—"

"'Alise.' Is that an Oneida name? Onondaga?"

Simon sighed. "If you're asking if she's white, then the answer is yes."

"I won at bingo this afternoon."

"You hate bingo."

Mom smiled vaguely. "I like it when I win. I won $450."

Simon whistled. "That's great, ma! We could use it."

"Not as much as Eunice Hill could. Her boy—Shaun, the younger one—he ran away again. Pawned all that china she collects for drug money."

"Look," Simon countered, knowing this tactic well, "she's just a friend and we're having dinner. I promise not to marry her and move to Toronto tonight, okay?"

His mom, still with that vague smile, raised her hands. "Hey, just giving you the local news. Speaking of which, Aunt Arleen told me that there might be an opening in Ohswé:ken, at Children's Aid. That new guy, he isn't working out."

Simon paused. "You sure about that?"

"It's Aunt Arleen—she wouldn't have said it if she hadn't done some groundwork."

"Aright, good to know. Gotta go—love you."

19

Simon knocks and Alise yells from somewhere inside.

"It's open!"

She'd been busy since he was last here. Together, they had sorted through the disaster her ex and his friends had left behind, but the front room is now so welcoming in a quirky way that it seems out of place in this shabby building: a shag area rug, its oranges and reds accentuated by candlelight, covers much of the chipped and worn parquet floor; a long string of tiny soft white Christmas lights, tacked up like luminous crown moulding, runs the entire periphery of the front room; two place settings have been put out on the low coffee table in front of the beaten sectional. Music—fast-paced and heavy— drifts quietly from the speakers of the Sony stack stereo nestled between Alise's bass amplifier, her P.A. system (disassembled), and three electric bass guitars. The walls are covered in posters—some framed, others just tacked up—advertising a menagerie of punk bands. The Clash, the Dead Boys, Sex Pistols, the Adverts, Bad Brains, Minor Threat. Interspersed between the posters are smaller flyers advertising local shows—the Wet Spots, the Dik Van Dykes, Teenage Head, Forgotten Rebels, Problem Children—and painted on the middle of the wall above the couch is a massive rendition of a black spider. Its legs and abdomen bristle with hairs made from pieces of guitar strings.

"Hope you like spaghetti!" she says from the kitchen.

"Uh, sure! Need help?"

"Nope. This is a thank you for all the help you already gave. Sit down."

Instead, Simon leans against the wall to the narrow corridor. "At least let me open the wine I brought."

"*Wine*, eh? You also wearing a tie?"

"No tie. Didn't think you'd mind."

Alise steps out of the narrow kitchenette and looks him up and down. "Hate them. I'm not wearing one, either."

True. Alise wears a short houndstooth dress that hugs her full figure. Pink hair falls softly down one side of her head still, almost touching her shoulder.

"You're wearing a dress!"

"Wow," she says. "You *nailed* it!"

Simon grins. "C'mon—I've never seen you in a dress before."

"Got a few. I was briefly into the mod scene."

"Mods," Simon repeats, trying his best to keep his eyes from drifting below her chin. "They're the ones in the army jackets, right? Bull's eyes and patches all over them?"

Alise laughs. "Kind of—you really don't know your scenes, eh?" Then she takes the bottle from him and goes back into the kitchenette. Simon follows her in.

"I guess not," he says. "Do I need to?"

"You're asking the bassist of an all-girl punk band."

Simon watches Alise open a drawer to rummage around fruitlessly for a bottle opener. He pulls out a foldable silver corkscrew from his pocket, walks up behind her, and reaches around her waist to place it in the drawer.

"Will this do?" he asks.

Alise elbows him gently. "Smart ass."

"I didn't see one this morning when we put everything away."

"How'd you remember a little thing like that?" she says, surprised.

Simon shrugs. "Noticing little things is kind of useful in my occupation."

"That makes sense," she concedes, opening the bottle and placing it on the tiny countertop. "Now for wine cups. Unless, of course, you have a pair of those in your jeans, too."

Simon, at a loss for a decent comeback, grins foolishly instead.

Alise's eyes flash playfully. "Ha! Not so smooth now, are you?"

"How's that spaghetti doing?"

Alise looks in alarm at the pot on the stove, then moves in to rescue her pasta. She pulls it off the burner and fishes out a strand to test.

"Fuck. It's a little soft—sorry."

"That's okay," he says. "I like soft."

She spares him a sly glance while she moves the pot to the sink. "You flirting with me?"

"Maybe."

Alise turns to face him in mock defiance. "This is spaghetti. It's kinda time sensitive."

"What's with you and time?" Then he pokes her in the ribs.

THE DARKNESS HELPS.

Neither of them witness the vulnerable uncertainty, the intimate fear that crouches like runners in their eyes. Poised to bolt. But inhibitions slip away, too, like their clothing—and as they stand in the gloom and wrap themselves up in each other, they come dangerously close to tripping on the tangle of material gathered in a confused heap at their feet.

Alise giggles as Simon stumbles, quick readjustment to compensate. Until he realizes that one hand is buried in the soft flesh of her heavy breast. Alise giggles again, playfully, and moves his hand down the swell of her belly and into a languid softness that receives him willingly.

Then she pulls him down onto the bed.

"WHAT TIME IS IT?" Simon asks sleepily. His watch is somewhere, either lost in the tangle of sheets or on the floor under discarded clothes.

Alise, lying against him on her side, arm thrown across his chest and thigh across his stomach, gives the semblance of a shrug. "Dunno. Eleven, maybe." Rib poke.

"Hey!" he laughs. "That was a legitimate question—I got work in the morning."

"Call in sick," she suggests.

"I would," he says, "but I got a kid in the psych ward I need to see."

But Simon notices a sudden stillness in Alise.

"Hey, if you gotta go—"

"Actually," he says quickly, "I was hoping you wouldn't mind if I stayed. If I'm not driving in from Ohswegen, I'll have time to make us breakfast."

"Oh." She relaxes again, and Simon absently runs his fingers up and down the rose and thorns tattoo on her thigh.

"Is that a yes 'oh,' or a no 'oh'?"

Alise props herself up on her elbow and studies his face in the gloom. At some point the bedroom door has swung open, admitting the soft glow of the few candles that are still lit in the other room. "You can stay if you want," she says softly.

"Cool. Wait—where you going?"

Because Alise sits up and starts to dress. "It's Thursday—I got a gig tonight. Gotta turn on a light to find jewelry."

Black Dead Kennedys T-shirt, shredded jean shorts over fishnets, and neon paint-spattered eight-hole Doc Martens—she digs through a shoebox for accessories, grabs a handful of rings from the top of a tiny table.

"Dig that turtle pendant you wear—can I borrow it?"

Simon touches it absently. "Sorry—it never comes off. It was my dad's."

"Oh. What's it mean?"

"It's Mohawk. Turtle Clan."

Alise nods, eyes drifting to the tattoo on Simon's chest—the Haudenosaunee symbol, a sharply pointed tree flanked on each side by a rectangle and then a square. She begins to say something, but changes her mind, heading instead for the door.

"Hair and makeup time. Want the light off?"

"Hold up—where's this gig of yours?"

Alise gives him a bemused look. "I doubt you've heard of the place."

Simon sits up and crosses his arms. "Try me," he says.

"Aright—it's called The Asylum."

"The *Asyl*—I'm there all the time! Great beer selection!"

Alise laughs. "You have no idea, do you?"

"Nope! I like the name. What kind of place is it?"

"Booze can. In the basement of a machine shop on Barton East." Then she gives him a sly look. "You wouldn't want to tag along, would you?"

Simon looks over at his button-down shirt draped over a chair. "I don't think I'd fit in all that well—left my fishnets and punk band tee T-shirts back home."

"We could always improvise," she says, walking over to the scarred and battered four-drawer bureau shoved up in the corner of the room like an afterthought. She yanks open the bottom drawer and pulls out a small pile of clothes. "These belonged to a former roommate. *Not* the recent former roommate," she adds. "Just a friend. Drummer."

Simon digs through the derelict collection: combats, a few T-shirts, some flannel. A little big, but doable.

"Alright. I'll go."

Alise smiles. "Really? That's fuckin' cool—it's a great crowd! You'll have a good time, I promise." She heads out to the washroom to get ready, but looks back at him from the bedroom door. "You're sure, right? We won't be out of there until probably sunrise."

"Yeah—I wasn't always a working stiff with a day job. I know how the all-nighter works."

Alise nods and leaves Simon to go through his options. Combats, a studded belt, and the flannel are easy choices, but the tees seem like a commitment because he doesn't recognize any of the bands. He grabs them, walks down the short hall, and calls to Alise through the washroom door.

"I'll feel like a total poser," Simon admits. "I don't recognize any of these names." He feels like he's confessing this to Siouxsie and the Banshees because a band poster hangs on the washroom door.

"You mean the shirts?" Alise calls back. "Which ones you got?"

"Let's see. 'Dresden War Crimes,' 'Proles,' 'Young Charlatans,' and 'Ron Rude.'"

The door opens and a cloud of industrial strength hair spray billows into the tight corridor. Alise, hair half done into sharp pink spikes, looks at the shirts sadly. "Those were Paul's favourites. I forgot that those were the ones I still had."

"Why'd he leave them behind?" Simon asks.

"He OD'd two years ago," she says quietly. "He was twenty."

"Oh. Sorry."

"Thanks. He was a good friend. Sweet, you know? Just . . . out of control." She touches the shirts, one at a time, smiling wistfully. "Paul was an Aussie.

These are all bands from the Melbourne punk scene—no one's gonna know any of them, so you might get questions. Or not, depends. Any other shirts?"

"Just some shredded remains and something made of mesh. That one ain't happening.

There's one with a giant gorilla fist on it, too. That one—"

"Can't wear that one. That was Paul's band, Fur Hammer. It still hurts to see that shirt. Quick rundown on the others: Young Charlatans sound like a cross between The Kinks and The Pogues. Dresden War Crimes are a Jim Morrison singing Joy Division sorta thing. Don't know much about the Proles, and the only thing I remember about Ron Rude is that he got air time by threatening to drown himself in a bucket unless a radio station played some tracks."

"Charlatans it is."

Alise nods. "Good choice. Dig around in the box by the stereo—there's a cassette in there you could listen to if you want. I'll be ready in about thirty minutes."

JUST AFTER MIDNIGHT, ALISE and Simon—along with her equipment—wait outside the building for their ride. Alise has added to her ensemble a jean jacket so heavily decorated that the denim is hardly more than sinuous lines between metal studs, band patches, and buttons. On the back of her jacket, "The Plasmatics" has been carefully hand-painted in giant white letters on a black background.

"I think we could get this stuff into my car," Simon offers.

"Nah, but thanks—we got a system down. Here they come." She points down the street.

Simon follows Alise's finger to a boxy, retro RV rolling toward them at a somewhat cavalier speed. It's hard to tell because of the artificial glare of streetlamps, but it looks like it's been painted a garish lime green. Along its length in spray paint is the band's name: Mary Mayhem.

"Wow—that's your . . ."

"Band wagon, so to speak. Yeah—1972 Winnebago Brave. Cool, eh?"

"Uh, sure—it looks like something deranged, transient clowns sell ice cream out of."

Alise elbows him. "Whatever, Nine-to-Five. We love it."

The VW comes to a jolting stop in front of the building and the only visible door on the vehicle, a narrow rectangle behind the front passenger seat, flies open. Two of the three women inside tumble out to help load Alise's gear.

"We're late," says a tall, thin punk—her liberty spikes match the green of the VW.

The second one, electric blue hair in a wild tangle of tendrils, zeroes in on Simon. "Who's your friend?" she asks.

"This is Simon. He's coming with. Simon, this is Joanie and Mel." She points to Green and then Blue. "Louisa's driving."

"Hey," Simon nods. Between the hair, the costumes, and the heavy dark mask-like eye makeup, they look like intergalactic bank robbers.

"Let's go, eh?" Joanie says, hauling Alise's amp through the door and up the step. Mel grabs one of the P.A.s, rolls her eyes in Joanie's direction, and follows her in.

Alise shakes her head, picks up the other P.A. speaker, and looks at Simon. "Grab my bass, will you?"

THE ASYLUM IS A bigger venue than Simon expected, having seen it first from the outside. Louisa, whose jet-black hair would fall into a sort of New Wave sensibility if it weren't for three inches of it dyed blood red, guesses at Simon's confusion.

"The building's footprint," she says with a slightly English accent or affect, "was way bigger, some years ago. We're in the original structure's basement." She carries a mike stand in one hand and cradles a milk crate of gear under the opposite arm. Louisa is the singer.

The long space's low ceiling is held aloft by a forest of steel posts, although most of them are wrapped in heavy foam held in place with duct tape. A sizeable crowd of punks, goths, and metal heads stand in beer swilling groups, yelling at each other to compete with the DJ who fills in between live sets. There is a scattering of others who seem out of place—clean-cut kids, twenty-something cubicle dwellers—and a small contingent of skinheads, three of whom are black.

"That's, like, the entire SHARP population of Hamilton," Alise says. "Kind of pathetic, but that's the Hammer for you. Those three are Trojan skins from Jamaica. Nice guys."

"At least this place is pretty diverse," Louisa adds on her way by.

Simon scans the late-night denizens: with the exception of the three Jamaicans and Simon, the entire crowd is white.

But that isn't exactly true, as Simon learns from an overly friendly bartender to whom he confides that this is his first visit. The bartender is also clearly hopped up on speed.

"Asylum," he explains after giving Simon an overpriced plastic cup of luke-warm beer, "is named after the Napa State Mental Hospital in California. Lucas—you know Lucas?"

Simon shakes his head.

"Lucas fuckin' Gonzalez? He's the owner, eh! He's a poet, man! A *poet*! He was an inmate at the hospital for five or six years—then, in '78, the Cramps played a gig there for nothin'. He was fuckin' *cured*, man! Had, like, a fuckin' *revelation* or some shit. They discharged him the *next fuckin' day!*"

"Wow," Simon manages, looking around for Alise.

"Hey—what band is that? Don't know those guys." Speed jabs him in the chest over the makeshift two-by-ten that serves as the bar.

"Oh, uh, Young Charlatans? Australian. They broke up a while ago, though."

"Fuckin' cool! You want a couple?" He holds out a handful of pills. "Black beauties—you in?"

Simon sighs. "Nah—thanks, man. Not my scene."

"Whatever—I been up for fuckin' thirty hours, eh! Goin' for a fuckin' *record!*"

A heavy hand falls on Simon's shoulder and Tribal's voice booms over the DJ's speakers.

"That's fuckin' great, Tony—you should take that whole handful. Simon, what the fuck you doin' here?"

Simon turns to look at Tribal in the dim half-light of the booze can. Heavy leather despite the summer heat covers an Iron Maiden tee; his long brown hair tumbles over his shoulders and down his back.

"Holy shit!" Simon exclaims, genuinely pleased to see a familiar face. "How long have you been here?"

"Came in with Jimmy—booze cans are good places to deal. I get a cut for minding his back. You?"

"Came in with Alise. Actually, with her and her band."

Tribal smirks at him. "That don't sound like it adds up quite right—something you wanna tell me?"

Before Simon can respond, though, the Asylum erupts into a cacophony of trebly guitar and cymbal smashing, and Alise emerges from the mob carrying her bass. She smiles at Simon, points him toward Jimmy, then grabs Tribal by the shoulder, signalling him to follow her toward one of the dark alcoves that leads to a labyrinth of smaller subterranean rooms.

In the comparative shelter of what was once a storeroom for automotive paint, Alise looks for a place to lean her bass. Frowning, she instead throws the strap over her head and slings the instrument across her back.

"What gives?" Tribal asks. "I'm supposed to be minding Jimmy."

"Jimmy's why I need to talk to you—anyway, he's fine down here. Know that hundred bones and change you owe me? I need it."

"*Now?*"

"Now would be good, yeah."

A month ago, Tribal's girlfriend and her sister had acquired a pair of fifty-three seventy-fives—the standard fine for drinking in public—and Alise had lent him the money to lend to his girlfriend. She'd happily taken the money, paid off the fines, and then dumped Tribal a week later for cheating on her. With her sister.

"Bit short notice," he tries. "Why the sudden demand?"

"Because I fucking *need* it, Tribal, and you *owe* me." Alise, bass guitar still slung across her back, punctuates her words by stabbing Tribal in the chest with a pewter ring-clad finger; her mohawk—rigid and sharp, like the blade of a giant pink battle axe—comes dangerously close to his right eye.

"Woah! Watch it with that thing, eh? I'll get your dosh, don't worry."

"When?" She has to shout now because the band on stage keep adjusting its amps. The opening act is a ridiculous collection of hardcore wannabes called the Passion Flaps; like many opening bands, they live under the illusion that excessive volume cleverly disguises lack of talent.

"Soon! Tomorrow, maybe!" Tribal bellows. "Don't you got a gig to play?"

"How're you gonna get it?"

"Don't worry, little sister." Tribal flashes her a wolfish smile through his curtain of long brown hair. "I got an idea."

20

TRIBAL NEVER ASKS *WHY* Jimmy is the catalyst for Alise's late night reckoning of an old debt, although in an indirect way it was Tribal's own fault: he's the one who stole a cardboard sign from a catatonic drunk on the way to the Asylum. He stashed it behind a rusting fender lying forgotten against the side of the building, and then caught up to Jimmy as he descended.

"You know that Scotty has a method of getting those things for himself, right?" Jimmy has always disapproved of Tribal's cavalier approach. "He *pays* for those things, man."

"Weird wire fish don't really count as dosh."

"Willful ignorance, Tribal," Jimmy said. "Ignorance of Cosmic Currency is no excuse."

"Gimme a fuckin' break, Jimmy. What the fuck's he gonna *do* with that heap of shit, anyway?"

Jimmy entered the Asylum contemplating Tribal's offhand insensitivity, traded tabs for a ten with a skid standing just inside the door, and then spotted Alise.

He headed straight for her.

"Got a question for you," he said by way of a greeting.

"Hey, Jimmy. What?"

"Your mom—she still working at the art gallery?"

"My m— Oh, you mean Emily. She doesn't work there. She's got some stuff in a group show right now, if that's what you mean."

"Yeah! Yeah, that's cool."

"Why?" she asked, suspicious.

Jimmy furrowed his brow, choosing his next words carefully. "You ever show anything there?"

"Me?" Alise said. "No—of course not. I just dabble in a little innocent vandalism. You know, street art."

Jimmy nodded. "What about Scotty? Think he just 'dabbles,' or do you think he's got something to say?"

Before she'd left with her band to tour, Alise had found Scotty standing outside the Art Gallery of Hamilton one late afternoon. She'd gotten them both in for free because the person on duty at the desk recognized her as Emily's stepdaughter. Their visit had been brief, but Alise had found it strange that Scotty paid the closest attention to the little placards reminding patrons about the rules regarding photography. Or gallery etiquette. He had also marvelled at the vast open spaces of several bare walls. She had relayed this to Jimmy that same night following a show at Mallet Sally's.

"You're thinking about that story I told you a few weeks ago?" she asked him. "Scotty's Scotty—he does weird stuff all the time."

"He's an artist," Jimmy replied simply. "Just ask him if he wants to get in and then find him a way if he says yes."

"But how the hell—"

"You'll know. He'll tell you, in his own way. And," Jimmy added, "*don't* tell Simon."

Alise bit her lip. "Dunno, Jimmy. Seems like a lot of risk for nothing."

But Jimmy raised his eyebrows. "This might be the most punk thing you ever do. Think about it that way. Now," he said, pulling a clear plastic bag of neatly cut paper squares from beneath his drug rug, "I have some customers eager for a little retro acid of yesteryear. Want one? Hundred micrograms per hit—you'll explode into colours mid-set!"

"I don't do drugs, Jimmy. You know that."

"That's cool—but offering communion to the non-believer is a religious obligation. Hendrix be with you! Later."

TWELVE HOURS LATER, SIRIUS sits down on the park bench beside his brother, facing the busy street. Behind them is Woodlands Park, a somewhat lofty appellation for the sunburnt patch of dirt and grass that stretches between Empire Steel's monstrous facility and Barton Street East. Tribal nods a greeting, but his eyes don't leave the corner across the intersection where the heavy brick Catholic Church stands, peaked and stain glass façade flanked by a pair of squat crenellated towers.

It isn't the church he's interested in, though; it's the short middle-aged man in the Expos cap and tasseled loafers. Tribal smiles, a toothy grin that Sirius knows well.

"Okay, what you got planned at 2:00 p.m. on a fucking Friday afternoon, eh? Why the phone call?"

Tribal exhales, looking at his brother. "Alright—see that cat over there? He's been walking up and down Sanford for twenty minutes. From his car to the corner, then back again. Lots of looking around and hat pulling, like he ain't big on being seen."

"So, he's a fucking part-time junkie or something. Shoulda phoned Jimmy, eh?"

"Nah," Tribal says. "Buddy's looking for a girl and he don't know where to start. So I'm gonna help."

"Uh, okay. And by 'help' you mean—"

Tribal reaches into his pocket and pulls out a key attached to a flat red plastic oval. He hands it to Sirius. On one side of the plastic tag are the numbers "218."

"Tribal, what the fuck is this?"

"It's a motel room key," he grins.

"Where'd you get it?" Sirius asks.

"I made it!" Tribal says, taking it back. "Know that ring of keys we found two weeks ago? I got these cheap fuckin' key chain tags from Canadian Tire and wrote some numbers on them." He looks at it in his palm, clearly proud. "This grift needs believable props. Now, come up when I signal and play along."

"And do fuckin' *what*?" Sirius asks.

But Tribal smiles. "Improvise, man! Shit, don't be such a square fuckin' cube, eh!" Then Tribal saunters to the corner, waits for the light, and crosses. Sirius follows at a distance.

Tribal doesn't waste any time.

"Hey, man—you look a little lost. You, uh, looking for something in particular?" The would-be john turns, startled. But Tribal carries on, oily and at ease. "Because you've come to the right neighbourhood if you wanna stay below the radar. How'd you like me to introduce you to a girl?"

The man, nervous and clearly out of his element, glances back at his car before answering. "What—what kind of girl?"

Tribal smiles and lights a smoke. "You tell me, brother. Unless you like surprises." He throws the man a smile, winks.

"I dunno," he says, hands thrust into the pockets of his flannel trousers. But then he looks at Tribal, just a furtive glance. "Aren't you a little young to be, uh—"

"Pimping?" Tribal answers. "Not out here, brother. I'm just the middleman, though. Here's what we'll do: I'm gonna give you this motel room key and an address. All's you gotta do is go there and wait. You from outa town?"

"I'm here on business," the man answers automatically.

"Ah," says Tribal. "Then directions would be better. Go down this road—this is Barton—until you get to Sherman. Then hook a right. Not too far up the street there's a motel on your left. Easy. No need to check in—just go to room 218. Use the stairs on the right side, otherwise you gotta walk the length of the balcony. Got it?"

"Yeah. Yes. Right on Sherman, hotel on the left," he repeats this, detached it seems, as if this were all too surreal.

"*Motel*, not a hotel. Right-hand staircase. Oh, and you pay me, not her—hundred bones. Safer that way. Here's the key. Don't lose it and *remember* to leave it behind, eh? They're expensive to replace and I'm responsible for it."

Dazed, the man pulls out a small wad of bills and peels off five twenties. Then he pauses. "Is the girl already there?"

"Nah," Tribal laughs disarmingly. "My partner's gonna pick her up for you." He turns to Sirius. "Who's available right now?"

Sirius stumbles a bit, repeating the question. "Available? Now?"

"Yeah, man," Tribal says. "Now."

"Uh, well, how about—Sue?" Sirius manages.

"No way," Tribal says. "Too tall. Wait—" and here he turns to the john "—you like tall girls?"

"Well, I, um—"

"That's a no," says Tribal. "Who else?"

"How about Rachel?" Sirius says.

"Perfect!" Tribal smiles, turning once more to the john. "Rachel—you're gonna *love* her. Unless . . . Okay—she's twenty. Now, I can't get anyone older, but younger—younger I can do. It's gonna be fifty bucks extra for every year underage, though."

The john's eyes dart around, but just from point to point on the slab of concrete he's standing on, calculating something darker than currency it seems. His breathing is ragged. Sirius takes a subtle step back, removes both hands from his pockets.

Then, calculations seemingly complete, the stranger pulls out the wad and quickly peels off another two hundred and fifty dollars. "Make her young," he says in a dead voice, eyes just flat and glazed now.

Sirius watches. Even Tribal, a street eel by nature, is a bit shaken; he recovers quickly though.

"You got it, man. Her name's Sam, as in Samantha. Down Barton, right on Sherman. Give us fifteen minutes because I gotta make the call. And *please* remember to leave the key, eh? They're expensive to replace."

The john nods and heads back toward his car, and the brothers cross Sanford to head west on Barton. The van Sirius borrowed is parked half a block away.

"That was clever," says Sirius when they reach the van. "Overcomplicated, fuckin' creepy, but clever."

"Gotta have fun with it, brother. Otherwise, what's the point?"

"I can name about three hundred and fifty points right now."

Tribal smiles and struts, proud. "A hundred of this is claimed—that's all I was after. The rest is ours."

"Who gave you the idea?"

"Hey, fuck you!" Tribal lights another smoke, offers one to his brother. "Fine. Derek came up with it—but the 'fifty bones per year' thing was my on-the-spot adjustment. Wait 'til I tell Derek it fuckin' worked!"

"Hey," Sirius grins, "You told him to make a right on Sherman. That's a one-way."

Tribal nods. "I know. It'll keep that fuckin' pervert distracted as he looks for a way around. Wait 'til he gets to his destination."

"Where'd you send him?"

Tribal's teeth flash. "Right up that piece of shit's alley: a Catholic elementary school."

21

THE NORTHERN TERMINUS OF Route 20 crosses the Queen Elizabeth Way and then turns on itself, inserting lanes into that main artery, emptying the contents of the North End into the guileless streams of traffic that make their way across the Skyway Bridge immediately to the northwest, or toward Niagara forty minutes to the east. Service roads also coil themselves around this junction, like sinuous fingers wrapped around an unassuming throat.

Simon, unsure of the area, navigates the confusing knot with difficulty, but he finds what he's looking for on his first pass: the quiet, almost furtive road known as Beach Boulevard. It runs parallel to the QEW, like its small shadow, until the highway's many lanes sweep dramatically upward and across the twin steel monstrosities that take traffic up and over the industry ship entrance to the Harbour.

Taking Beach Boulevard is like time travel, in a way, for it leads to an all but forgotten strip of land that still holds the old and still operational lift bridge, and small houses that haven't changed much since the city brought the hammer down (so to speak) on the last of the shabby carnival rides in 1978, thus ending well over a century of shady amusements—dance halls and drinking establishments tucked away between carousels, the funhouse, a small roller coaster, and a Ferris wheel. And then there was the lightless strip of beach bordering the seemingly endless expanse of Lake Ontario itself.

Simon absently contemplates this area's colourful history as he makes his way past the little side streets. Arden, Lagoon, Clare, Granville—they even sound like names from a threadbare yesteryear. He drives a little farther and finds the road he wants. He makes a left.

*

"MY PARENTS," FRANK TOLD Simon earlier that day, "saw Duke Ellington at the Pier Ballroom down there! Or maybe it was at the Forum."

"No kidding," Simon managed in return.

"Oh, c'mon—you can do better than that! Duke Ellington! February 8, 1954. That was my father's birthday."

Simon smiled. "Would you like a vacant stare of amazement, or more of a 'Geez, I wish I'd been there, too' kinda vibe?"

"You don't know who he was, do you?"

"No."

Frank sighed. "Oh well. I was seventeen, it was a school night, and I was left in charge of my four younger siblings. Missed my big chance to see a legend. My folks came home pretty tight. Speaking of which, you look a little hung over yourself!"

"Late night. So, the Beach, eh? Are you sure he's still here?"

Frank looked at the paper he'd handed Simon when he'd come in the office. On it was a name—"Doug M"—followed by an address. Former employee ("of sorts," Frank had said). An American who served as Scotty's first youth worker while refusing to serve his own country; Doug was a draft dodger who went into hiding and never came out.

"He's there," Frank said simply. "Took me some time to convince him that you're alright, though."

"Pretty paranoid, huh? How long has he been here, hiding? The Vietnam War ended in, what, '73?"

"'75."

"Okay," Simon conceded. "So that's twelve years ago. American government can't still care, can they?"

"Officially, no. Carter issued some sort of pardon in the late '70s. But Doug . . . Well, he's kind of—he's a different kind of guy. You'll see."

Simon folded up the address and slipped it into his pocket. "Thanks for hunting him down for me."

"That's okay, kid. Just—" Frank paused, looked up at those ceiling tiles of his, brow furrowed slightly. "Just don't push too hard. He only agreed to meet with you because you're . . ."

"Because I'm what?"

"Well, because you're Ind—First Nations," Frank said.

Simon tensed. "Ah," he said.

"You know, he feels like he gets it—the oppression," Frank added.

Simon, however, had turned. "Okay," he said over his shoulder. This was Frank—he would let this one go.

But Frank seemed compelled to explain. "Doug and me, we've been friends for a long time—I vouched for you, but he was real hesitant. Still, once I said you were from the First Nations, he said, 'Give him my address.' Just like that! He really understands what it's like to be treated like a second-class citizen, honest."

And it took Simon a lifetime of incidental encounters, four years of university, and his hard-won two years in the field to swallow back the words that sprang urgently and angrily upward—fury's clenched fists shaking violently on his skeleton like a prisoner in a cage, pushing even now against the inside of clenched teeth. Instead, with magnanimity and patience that befit a far older man, he waved a non-committal hand over one shoulder and aimed for the stairwell.

AND NOW.

Simon pulls up in front of an unassuming bungalow. Beside it is a weathered cottage with a newer-looking second floor, but both are painted an identical shade of pale green with white trim. They also share an eight-foot-tall grey wooden fence, like a palisade. It seems to wrap around both properties and continues back toward other lots behind them. The only reason Simon can see any of this is that the gates to the driveway, also eight-foot panels of pressure-treated fencing, are open. A shirtless older man with long, stringy, iron-grey hair kneels on the gravel. He has an ancient screwdriver in one hand and a can of WD-40 in the other. He is perfectly bald on the top of his head, as if a splotchy egg were rising out of drab kelp. His soft, sun-browned flesh sways as he stabs away at one of the hinges.

He looks up at the soft bang of Simon's closing car door. "Private property, son. Whatever it is, we ain't buying." Not unfriendly, but with a dismissive finality.

"That's okay—I ain't selling," Simon responds casually. "I'm looking for Doug. He's expecting me."

"Oh," the older man says with a nod. "You must be the Indian. Nice hair—mine was that long once. Not as black, though. More brownish."

"Yeah . . . that's great. And it's Indigenous, by the way."

"What?"

"Nothing. Is Doug inside?"

"Nah. He's around back—beans."

"Sorry, what?"

He points with the screwdriver. "Around back. Picking beans."

AS HE TURNS THE corner behind the bungalow, Simon realizes that he's in a compound. The palisade continues until it wraps around two more houses behind the bungalow and cottage; they must face another road parallel to the one he just turned down. The yards of all four properties have been combined into a small farm—gnarled apple trees grow along the entire inside border of the fence; the broad, heavy foliage of potato plants carpets the ground immediately to his left; melons, tomato vines, and a score of vegetable plots flourish in this strange little world. A dozen people bend over various patches of garden, weeding or harvesting. Behind the cottage, picking beans off vine-covered latticework, is a man in dirty jeans, a black tee, and a flannel shirt. Simon shakes his head. *Just like Scotty*, he thinks.

Simon navigates around a raised garden bursting with peppers at one end and cucumbers at the other, then down a narrow path between two patches of barely controlled raspberry bushes. The man works methodically, dropping his harvest by the handful into a wooden basket between his bare feet. Behind him is an ancient wheelbarrow with cardboard boxes from the LCBO containing eggplants, beets, and onions.

"Hey," Simon starts. "You must be Doug. I'm Simon. Frank sent me."

Doug's jaw clenches visibly under days of stubble and sun browned skin. The beans seem to consume his attention. His salt-and-pepper hair is neatly cut, strangely at odds with the rest of him—dirt has gathered in the creases of his skin; his bristly arm hair is a trap for wood chips; he smells of sweat and loam. With that hangdog look and his large, watery blue eyes, he looks to Simon like a farmer who, upon returning home from the town barber, found himself evicted and homeless.

The silence becomes awkward. "If now's a bad time," Simon finally adds, "I can come back later."

Expert fingers fly quickly along the vines, pinching off and dropping beans in a steady rhythm.

"A'right," Simon shrugs. "Maybe we can talk about Scotty some other time. Sorry for bothering you."

The fingers stop, as if the machinery has seized up. Doug turns to look at Simon, seems to pull at him with those watery eyes, dog-tired and bloodshot, swollen pinkish-grey sacs below them. He lowers his hands from the beans and looks down at the basket at his feet. "No," he says, voice raspy and tired. "No, that's okay. We can talk now."

"CAIN," THEY CALL IT, this furtive garden otherworld between cities.

Four contiguous properties, purchased by an anonymous benefactor in the early seventies, house a small community of twenty-nine off-grid semi-urban hippies. The commune is almost completely self-sufficient, growing enough food for its own needs on its two-and-a-half acres and selling the considerable surplus at the Farmers' Market downtown. By-laws make chickens impossible because of the racket, but two of Cain's women ("Cain's Daughters," Doug calls them) tend a flock of Muscovy ducks—a virtually silent breed that lay good eggs and provide a little meat for the few members of Cain who partake.

One garage serves as a woodshop where furniture is made—or old furniture is refurbished; another is an art studio, including two potter's wheels and a small kiln powered by a gas generator; a third is a space for making clothes or even the occasional quilt, although in the winter it also doubles as a shelter for the commune's beehives; and the fourth is their common meeting hall.

"We have a five-person governing body," Doug explains, "but everyone— even the children—gets a vote on important stuff. We sell enough honey, fruits, and vegetables to cover some expenses, but the pottery and fur- niture—it really helps." He is more at ease now, sipping away at a mug of pungent tea. Another one, barely touched, sits on the table in front of Simon.

They sit on a makeshift bench—a heavy silvery plank propped up on each end by wooden stepladders under the shade of the apple trees. The table, an old "For Sale" sign, rests on the handles of the wheelbarrow still full of vegetables.

"It's impressive," Simon admits. And it is; he's curious in spite of himself. "What about utilities? Water, hydro—"

"So you wanna talk about Scotty," Doug says. "He aged out, didn't he? Rules change?"

Simon is well versed enough to pretend to be distracted. "More like an exception to the rule was made. But I'm running out of time. He's changed lately. Something happened."

Doug scoffs gently. "There's an understatement. Poor kid." From the pocket of his flannel shirt, he retrieves a joint. Then he smiles sadly at Simon. "What do you want from me, man?"

"Just—just anything, really. I got Scotty's case in the summer of '85, right after I started working for the CAS. One of my first, you know? He'd already turned eighteen, but Frank arranged for an extension and assist- ance. Still, eighteen in a group home—he needed to move out, so I found him an apartment."

"So, now Scotty's twenty. . . ." Doug's face became a complex mechanism, working its way through the chasm of missing years. "Wow, man. I feel so old. You can't be too much older than him yourself."

Simon absently pets a mangy dog that has padded up to them. "Not by much. I'm twenty-four. Got the job right after graduation." The dog realizes that neither of them have food and meanders off.

Doug takes a contemplative puff or two and offers the joint to Simon. "No thanks."

The older man shrugs, takes a deeper haul, and exhales a question. "He still quiet?"

Simon watches the cloud of lazy pot smoke as it dissipates in the still August air. *He's like that smoke*, he thinks. Then, "Yeah. Not a word. He's an artist—a sculptor. Mostly he makes—"

"Fish?"

"Yeah. Yeah! Hey—how'd you know?"

Doug looks above them, squints as if concentrating, and then reaches up to a low, twisted branch to retrieve a small red apple. He hands it to Simon and picks another one for himself.

"After his mom died, I packed up Scotty's stuff. Should have seen that place—what a dump. You know what I mean."

"Yeah," Simon mumbles. "I've seen some beauties."

Another sad smile and Doug continues: "His 'bed,' if you could call it that, was this stained cot of rotten canvas. Something secondhand or salvaged maybe. There was only one tiny bedroom, so Scotty's cot was set up in the corner of the front room behind a couch that looked like it probably came with the apartment."

Doug finishes his joint and pinches off the fading heater. He shreds the nubby remains and spreads them out below the tree like mulch.

"There wasn't much to pack. Drawings, mostly. But he had these little clay lumps, too. Probably took them from school. He made fish out of them. There were a couple dozen of them back there, most of them under a pretty thick carpet of dust and filth. Like the rest of the apartment."

"Where are they now?" Simon asks.

"Oh, probably still in the box. I mean, if you guys haven't given it to him yet."

"Box?"

Doug looks at Simon like he misunderstood the word. "Yeah, man—Scotty's stuff. I packed it myself. I labelled it and then put it in storage."

"I looked all through everything—there's no box labelled 'Campbell' or even just 'Scott' down there. Maybe it got thrown out?"

Doug opens his mouth as if to speak, but stands up instead. "Grab those mugs for me, will ya?" He removes the "For Sale" sign and leans it up against the tree. "C'mon," he says, picking up the wheelbarrow handles and pushing it toward the bungalow.

Simon follows. The sons and daughters of Cain now move toward the farthest building, compelled it seems by some silent call.

Doug parks his load beside the raised garden of peppers and cucumbers, looks at Simon, and sighs. "Gagnon," he says finally.

"Gagnon?" Simon repeats. "Is that another case worker I need to—"

"No—Gagnon. That's Scotty's last name. His mother's. 'Campbell' was just . . . Well, doesn't matter now." He turns and begins to walk toward the far building like the others. "Get him that box," he says over his shoulder. "His mom's in there."

22

AND THERE IT IS, in plain sight. *Gagnon, Denise.* On a shelf in the file storage room.

The name is the only legibly written thing on the sturdy storage box. The rest of the information is little more than a black smudge, obliterated by a spill of some kind. Water, Simon thinks at first, but there is a vague brownish outline, as if an antiquated topographer had outlined a continent. Tea, maybe. Or coffee. He pulls it down and heads back upstairs with it, but then changes his mind when he reaches the landing. *Not here*, he thinks. He heads for the exit into the parking lot.

Simon sets the box in the back of his car, amid empty coffee cups and the other accumulated trash of passengers. Then he drives his rounds, steadfastly ignoring the silent box full of ghosts behind him until his obligations to Friday's client list has been satisfied. A little after 4:00 p.m., he drives to Scotty's building.

But he and the box only make it to the third floor.

"BACK SO SOON?" ALISE jokes when she opens the door. "I figured that gig last night would give you second thoughts."

"I'm not easily discouraged," Simon replies. "We're a stubborn people."

"What's that?" she asks, pointing at the box. "Breakfast?"

"Hey," he counters, "the breakfast deal was null and void as soon as I agreed to come to your gig. Which I'm still deaf from, by the way."

"Punk's an acquired taste for some. Give it time. Wanna come in?"

"Yeah."

She's wearing a threadbare kimono and clearly not much else. Simon puts the box on the low coffee table, walks back over to her, and slides his hands along her full hips. She breathes in quickly at his touch.

"Look," she whispers, "no games. I can't—"

He kisses her.

"No games," he says. And then he kisses her again.

IT IS DIFFERENT THIS time. In the murky bedroom of late afternoon, there is none of the urgency of last night's fierceness. Nor any of the awkwardness of a first encounter.

Now they take their time, unveiling a complexity that neither of them had realized was there—his hands slip along her contours, and she exists only where he touches her. Everything else is timelessness and silence. Fingers of one hand hover moth-like over her breast, as if timid. They circle her nipple slowly as his other hand drifts—aimlessly it seems, as if daydreaming—until it slips between her open thighs. And then into her as the first hand's fingers tighten around her nipple. She needs a release, digging into his hard back with her strong fingers, arching into him and rolling him over. A quick shift of position and she bears down on him, trapping him inside her.

For him it is the song of bones—his skeleton hums at her lightest touch, but this heavy thrusting is a rhythm for a deeper dance. Why her? Why this reckless white girl with the sinuous tattoos across her ample flesh? Why this girl, fierce and wild and from a world so alien to his own? He marvels that they speak the same language. The shock of pink hair tickles his face as her hips move on top of him, surge and swell, as rhythmic as soft waves lapping at the stony shore.

Water is relentless. He loses himself in the depths.

SEVERAL FLOORS ABOVE THEM, Scotty clings by a thread to his capering breath as it leaps across the shadows of his cluttered walls. He feels its mirth, feels its reckless abandon that leaves him confused. Terrified.

He doesn't know why he feels this way. But that doesn't help him to stop the tears or the ragged sobs that fill the quiet corners of the little apartment.

TWO MUGS OF COFFEE on the low table. Curled into each other on the couch while twilight creeps in through the slider. Music at a low volume filling the comfortable silence between them. If it were something softer than The Stooges on the stereo, and if there weren't a monstrous black spider painted on the wall behind them, Simon might think of this as an old married couple moment.

"Do we open it?" Alise asks. The box has remained untouched for hours, waiting patiently for them on the table.

"I don't know." Simon contemplates it, this cardboard sarcophagus for Scotty's sad childhood. "He's twenty—there's no reason he shouldn't open it himself."

"Except he doesn't even know it exists. What if there's something in there that will give you a clue—you know, some insight into that quiet head of his?"

Simon reaches for his coffee. "Oh, I don't think it's very quiet inside that head of his."

"Not an answer."

He sighs. "I know, I know—you're right. For his own sake, I should open it."

Alise sits up and pulls the box to the edge of the table.

There are small things: dozens of crayon drawings of a smiling boy in a red shirt holding hands with a black silhouette; little fish made of modelling clay; bits of linty yarn and a handful of dry acorns in a cracked jar; a rusty red Matchbox car with only three wheels.

There are tragic things: the death certificate of Denise Marie Gagnon, aged thirty-four. And a plain white urn holding her meagre remains.

And then there is the small red metal lunch pail, dented and worn, decorated with faded and scratched Provincial crests. In it are a few odd objects—a drawer knob, six stones, three marbles—all painted black. But there's also a journal tucked carefully into the container. On top of it is something small and vaguely cylindrical wrapped in tissue. Simon brushes it aside and picks up the journal.

Why did Doug leave a journal in the box, buried all these years like a secret? It should have been in the file, along with his other notes and observations. Simon holds it carefully, turning the dry pages slowly. Unlike the official notes in Scotty's file, Doug's journal entries are personal, erratic. Even a cursory read through a few pages is enough: the hand that wrote the words was weighed down by many things, not the least of which were a terrible sense of responsibility and the crushing burden of consequence. But Simon knows these stones well—he, too, has carried them for a time. In some ways, you never put them down, not exactly; instead, they tumble along behind you on a tether, rumbling in your wake like terrible regrets.

For a social worker, Frank had said after Simon lost his first client to an overdose, *it is not a question of if or when you fail, but of how much failure you can bear. Blame and regret,* he'd added, *are not luxuries we can afford.*

But blame and regret—Simon carries them nonetheless. They all do. As for the journal, it becomes clear after selecting a random page that he and Doug have at least those burdens in common:

I can't do this. I can't face that silent mouth and those lost eyes and that way he has of not really being there. I'm no good for him. He needs someone equipped to handle whatever it is that weighs him down, holds him below the surface and away from the world. I had to hand the child his own mother in a jar, for Christ's sake. How am I supposed to act like life is normal? Like there's some kind of hope?

And now this. That psycho released on a technicality?! I can't protect the boy. Changing his name will only hide him for so long.

"Name change," Simon mumbles. "Who the hell was after him?"

"Sorry?" Alise asks. She is carefully unwrapping the small, tissue-wrapped object that rested on top of the journal in the tin pail.

"Scotty's name, it's Gagnon. I learned that this afternoon when I—doesn't matter. Long story. Anyway, the CAS or maybe just my boss and an old social worker changed Scotty's name from Gagnon to Campbell."

"Why?"

Simon holds up the battered little notebook. "According to this journal—it's Doug's, his first social worker; he packed this box—they had to change Scotty's name to protect him."

"Jesus," Alise says. "He was just a little kid. Protect him from what?"

"Don't know, yet."

Simon hunts through the journal for other references. Much of it consists of short laments, or small confessions of perceived failures. One or two pages hint at Doug's plan to fall completely off the grid. *He was in too long*, Simon thinks. *Or went in carrying too much of his own.* Whatever it was, Doug was clearly not built to bear this kind of weight.

But Simon understands.

At the shabby, ill-attended funeral of Simon's first client, the boy's mother had lashed out at him. Vicious and cruel accusations. Beneath the screams and raving, though, Simon could still hear that unspeakable tone of ultimate lament. He remembers focusing on it—that primal antecedent of all human loss, its deepest, cruelest taproot: a mother's keening for her dead child.

Frank had been there, too, wise hand on Simon's shoulder to steady him through the storm. *It's not you*, he'd whispered as she'd raged. *It's not you—she's screaming at Death, but only she can see Him. He's standing in front of you.* Simon's knees had almost failed him, though, and Frank had grabbed his arm. *Johnson!* Frank hissed, mouth merely a finger's width from his ear. *It's not you she blames!*

It had almost broken Simon. All the pedagogy, the case studies, the anecdotal stories of his professors—none of that had meant anything that day. It was then that he'd realized that *this* was how he'd really be educated—one unequivocally raw encounter at a time.

Later that night, lying in bed, he could hear his mother fussing over something in the kitchen. Making him a lunch, he suddenly realized, and it broke him. He wept. Bitterly. And it brought him no relief.

She must have heard him, but a mother understands grief like no one else—she didn't intrude on the sanctity of his anguish.

"You okay?"

Alise, hand on his arm, gives him a gentle shake.

"Yeah, sorry. I was just—"

"Lost. No, I get it." Alise leans over to glance at the journal. "Or I think I do—this is pretty weird for you, eh? Finding out all this stuff about Scotty after taking care of him for, what, two years?"

"Yeah," he says. "This job's pretty hard sometimes."

Alise puts the half-unwrapped bundle on the table and hugs him. "You probably just do it for the money and the chicks," she says.

Simon smiles. "Yeah. It's a pretty glamourous lifestyle. Society *really* takes us seriously, too."

"Well, we have that in common," Alise smiles.

"Of course, if I wanted to really get shit on by society—I mean, *really* take a government beating, I could work for my own Community. But I digress."

He flips to the first few pages of the journal, skimming each page. And then, six pages in, he finds it. Or a clue, at least.

"Hey, listen to this," he says, reading the passage aloud.

They finally arrested that creepy bastard today. Vice principal was on the ball, at least. He overheard him talking to one of Scotty's drawings, of all fucking things! Something about bones and murder and the tongue-less boy knowing too much. I interviewed the VP later after the cops left, but that's all the guy heard from outside the janitor's closet. He was pretty shaken up by it.

"Holy shit," Alise says. "That's some horror movie stuff right there."

"Yep. And according to a later entry, this guy was released."

"Figures. What's that?" she asks, flicking the corner of paper jutting out of the back of the journal.

Simon opens the back cover to reveal a wax paper-pressed maple leaf, a couple of illegible receipts, and a folded newspaper clipping. He carefully unfolds it.

"It's a headline and part of an article. *'Custodian in Custody!'* it says."

"Clever," Alise scoffs. "Better than 'Janitor in Jail' I guess."

Simon skims the truncated remains of the article. "Norman LeRoy, 53. Gives the YMCA as a home address. Says he was fired and refused to leave. Had to be forcibly removed from an elementary school, but doesn't say which one. No mention of a child at all. Or at least not in what we have here."

Alise takes the clipping and reads through it, too. "How old is this stuff?"

"Scotty was nine when his mom died, but some of these things are from before that happened. So eleven or twelve years ago. Maybe even a few years before. Hey—you mind if I leave this stuff with you? I need to get a couple things from my office."

"You coming back?"

"Yeah, if that's cool with you."

Alise shakes her head. "I can't believe I'm sleeping with a guy who says shit like 'I need a couple things from my office.'"

"Yeah, you're a real poser. I'm telling all my punk friends back home."

Alise brushes a strand of Simon's black hair out of his face, sweeping it behind his ear. "My 'office' is that milk crate full of gear. I guess it's not fair to dress you up like a band groupie and drag you to gigs, eh?"

"Well," he says, "if it makes me any cooler, I'm already in a band."

"Wait, what? I—oh. I get it." Because Simon points to his only tattoo, the Haudenosaunee symbol across his left pectoral. She gives him a shove and reaches for her mug, leaning over the table.

Then something catches her eye in the box. Alise moves some of the small, strange objects aside. From beneath the random collection, she pulls out a yellowed newspaper, opens it, and wordlessly turns it around so Simon can see it.

"What the hell?" Because it is identical to the paper Jimmy brought him yesterday: *Child's Remains Incomplete*. He takes it and leans back into the couch, shaking his head. He skims through the article again, but it's just as frustratingly vague as it was yesterday. "This box needs an archaeologist, not a social worker."

"Only if that archaeologist is, like, Indiana Jones-good," Alise says almost under her breath, holding up the object she's finally unwrapped from the tissue paper. It is black with soot and oddly shaped—cylindrical, rounded on one side, three-pronged on the other, and hollow in the middle. And small enough for Alise to cradle it in her palm.

A child's coal-black vertebra.

"Fuck," he says. "Now what?"

Alise stares, hypnotized by the hollow passage through the little bone, like the cyclopean eye socket of some sort of strange and fossilized deep sea fish. "What the fuck was this thing doing in there?" she whispers.

Simon touches it tentatively with his finger. "More a matter of *why* was it in there? Doug wrapped this—he must have known what it was."

"And he put in that newspaper. When was that from again?" Alise takes the paper in her free hand and looks at the date. "October, 1974."

"Scotty was seven. More like seven-and-a-half. Hey, any more of those things in there?"

She digs carefully through the rest of the objects. "None that I can see."

Simon spreads his hands out, palms up, extending his fingers slowly.

"What are you doing?" Alise asks.

Simon drops his hands back down. "Nothing. Just something I remember seeing Scotty do once. I *really* need to grab Scotty's files—something's missing."

"Yeah," Alise says. "A bunch of bones and a potential psycho named Doug."

"I don't think so," Simon mumbles, half to himself. "About Doug, I mean. He didn't know Scotty until '76, after *she* died." He taps the top of the simple urn. "Those pieces of bone weren't there when they unearthed the skeleton in '74. That's what the paper says."

"Then how the fuck did *this* get in here?" she asks again.

Simon frowns. "Keep this stuff safe, eh? I'll be back in a bit." He kisses her. "Later, punk girl."

"Whenever, Nine-to-Five."

✦

TWENTY MINUTES LATER, SOMEONE buzzes her apartment.

"Who is it?" she says into the intercom.

"Tribal," says the static.

She buzzes him in. "There's no fucking way," she mumbles to herself. "Not already."

But she's wrong: five minutes later, she opens her door to find Tribal with a lollipop stick jutting out of his mouth and cash in hand.

"Here you go," he announces, holding five twenties out to her.

Alise takes the money, pleasantly surprised. "That was fast!"

"Told you I'd get it. You got any tweezers? Got a stinger in my hand."

"Sure. C'mon in."

Alise finds some tweezers in her disaster of a medicine cabinet and hands them to Tribal. She snatches her purse from the top of her amplifier and shoves the money in it.

"Not that I don't love your company," she says on her way to the door, "but I gotta go out for a bit. If you're still here when Simon shows up, tell him to wait for me, eh?"

Tribal cocks his head, eyes narrowing. "You two together, or you just fucking him?"

Alise, smiling sweetly, walks back over to Tribal and backhands the red welt on his palm.

"Fuck!" he yells, cupping his hand. "That fuckin' hurt!"

"Any other questions?"

"Nah," he manages. "I'm good."

She returns to the door. "Ask him to stay if he shows up before you're done," she says over her shoulder on the way out.

She heads to the bus depot down the street. It's the closest place with payphones.

"Hi, Dad—is Em there? What? No, everything's good. Just had a question for her."

A stray dog, greasy and skinny and bleeding from scabs in its ears, pads up to Alise cautiously. She holds out her hand for a sniff and gives it an absent scratch on the head.

"Em, hi—got something weird I need your help with. Wanna meet me for coffee?"

THEY MEET AT A Tim Horton's on Upper James.

"Sorry," Alise says as she greets her stepmom with a hug. "Some construction on the bus route."

"I just got here myself," Emily says.

In the fourteen years Alise has known Emily—from that second-grade classroom onward—she has hardly changed at all. Still edgy, with an art-school-meets-CBGB fashion sense and a tendency to defy authority in minor ways. Mischief for mischief's sake.

Even now in her late thirties, she still looks twenty-five. It's her eyes, Alise believes: fiercely blue, challenging everything from condescending curators to traffic lights. Equally. Emily's hair is still raven-black, short and spiky, a stunning contrast with her pale complexion. She wears a vintage '60s dress that looks like a Mondrian painting, and patent leather go-go boots. The outfit clings perfectly to her tall, thin frame.

"You look great—going out?" Alise asks.

"Your dad and I are heading into Toronto. Jan's opening is tonight." Janice Weinrib, Emily's best friend, rarely comes to Hamilton. She's an installation artist with some clout in much bigger circles.

Alise nods. "Oh yeah—and *Dad's* going? Wow. Thought Friday was a gig night."

Emily smiles and rolls her eyes. "He's absolutely convinced that Geddy Lee is going to show up."

"*Geddy Lee!* Isn't Rush on tour or something?"

"Not until October. He checked."

Alise sighs. "Of *course* he did. And why exactly does he think this?"

"He 'has his sources,' as you know. There must be a secret and sacred order of bassists that I'm unaware of. You in it, too?"

"Hammer Chapter President, North End."

"Ah. He's envious that I saw Rush before they were famous—saw them in Toronto at the Victory Burlesque in 1970 or '71 when they opened for the New York Dolls."

"Holy shit!" Alise says.

"Yeah, they were—"

"You saw the New York Dolls?!"

Emily smiles and looks over at the counter. "Let's get coffee and I'll have a cigarette," she says, standing up. "Then you can tell me why we're here."

"You sure? You still have to get to Toronto."

"There's no point in showing up to Janice's shows before 10:00 p.m."

They attract attention, neither of them representative of the standard Friday evening patrons of an Upper James Street coffee shop. Alise doesn't like the Escarpment anyway; it lacks the cohesiveness of tight streets and history and grit that makes the city worth living in. From the base of the Escarpment to the shore of Lake Ontario: that's the Hammer. Up here? It's just Hamilton.

Over two coffees and a cigarette, Alise explains her idea as concisely as possible. She leaves Simon out of it, though. Jimmy's advice is just good street sense: you aren't culpable if you don't know. After all, Simon has the disadvantage of a job he'll lose if anything were to go wrong. Alise doesn't care about her own position; she skirts the edge of the dangerous world Jimmy and Tribal and the others live in, her meagre safety net just a bus-ride up the Escarpment away. Still, it's a safety net. Most of her friends and acquaintances live on luck or tenacity.

"So," Emily says quietly, "you want to sneak your friend into the AGH so he can do a rogue installation piece?"

"That's about it."

Emily plays absently with the lip of the cardboard coffee cup, rolling it up and then down. Her lips are pursed with a slow exhale, and her eyes squint just enough so that a slight crease forms across her otherwise perfect forehead.

"This is the part where you're supposed to get all parental," Alise offers wryly.

"We both know that's not likely. How *big* is this installation piece? That's going to make all the difference."

Alise gives her a wicked smile. "He's got different projects, but his fish sculptures seem to be what he's into right now."

"Fish sculptures? You don't mean those wire things that have been popping up around the city, do you?"

"Wait, you *know* them?"

Emily nods dramatically. "Oh yes—there's quite the buzz about them in certain circles. They've been found hanging at the bottom of every stairway up the Escarpment. When people steal them or destroy them, another one appears a few days later. And, of course," she adds, "they're all over downtown."

"Can it be done? Getting him in, I mean?"

"Ask him how many of those fish he was planning on sneaking in. One or two, sure. Twenty or thirty? That would take some work."

"Alright," Alise says. "I'll see what I can find out. I figured a little dosh to turn a key or switch off an alarm would be handy, too, so I got that set aside."

Emily gives a small, appreciative nod. "Good foresight. How much?"

"Hundred."

"Okay. I might have an idea or two. Get me particulars on the materials and I'll talk to a friend or two."

"Cool—don't mention anything to Dad, eh? You know how he worries." Alise gathers her things and gets up. "Have a good time tonight. Oh, and say hi to Geddy for me."

23

WHEN SIMON RETURNS JUST over an hour later, Alise isn't there; instead, he finds Tribal leaning against the kitchen counter, lollipop stick jutting out of his mouth like a movie gangster's toothpick. He has one hand palm-up toward the weak yellowy light; in his other hand are tweezers, with which he prods the swollen, angry red area at the base of his little finger.

"Where's Alise?"

"Had something to do," Tribal mumbles.

"Bee sting?" Simon asks.

"Nope. Scorpion."

"*Scorpion*? C'mon, Tribal." Simon navigates around him, reaching for a glass so he can get himself some water. "No scorpions in Ontario."

"There's at least one, man."

"Yeah?" Simon asks, filling the glass from the faucet's weak dribble. "And where's this scorpion now?"

"In my fucking mouth." Tribal drops the tweezers on the counter, grabs the stick, and pulls it out. There, encased in a misshapen lump of bright green candy, is a small black scorpion. Its tail, arched upward like a periscope, has been sheared off at the candy surface.

Simon can only stare. Tribal pops the thing back on top of his tongue and picks up the tweezers again, digging a bit more aggressively. "Before you ask," he says, "Derek left it under the one fuckin' mug where me and Sirius live. Big goddamn joke, eh? I trapped this little fucker under a bowl after it stung me. Then I took every sour apple Jolly Rancher outa my girlfriend's purse and melted them in a pot. When they were bubbling, I dumped the little asshole in and shoved him under the steaming goop with a fork."

"So, you killed it like a lobster—only in molten candy instead of boiling water."

"I guess," Tribal shrugged. "Threw the pot in the freezer for a few minutes—you know, to harden it a bit—then I shoved this lollipop stick up its ass." Tribal winces and pulls his injured hand away from the tweezers. "Ow—fuck! Need better light."

"What exactly you trying to do?"

"Get the fuckin' stinger out, whatcha think I'm doing?"

"Tribal, if it's a scorpion sting, then it's venom. There's no stinger to remove."

The tweezers pause, then drop to the counter with a clatter. "How the hell you know that? Some kinda First Nations thing?"

Annoyance flashes in Simon's eyes. "I think we'll chalk that one up to common sense," he says.

But Tribal flashes Simon a toothy grin. "Sorry, brother. Just fuckin' with you, eh?"

"You're a tool. Seriously—where'd Alise go?"

"Told ya. She had something to do. You two a thing, or just fucking? I asked her, but she just backhanded me right in the sting. Hurt like a motherfucker."

"Don't know." Simon looks over at the box, but it hasn't moved. "She say how long she'd be?"

Tribal sticks his hand under the faucet. "Didn't say. I came over to give her some dosh I owed her, and she took off, eh?" Then he looks up. "Oh yeah—now I remember: she said if you showed up, you should hang out until she gets back. Wanna partake?" He holds up a misshapen joint.

"Nah—never had any interest."

"Suit yourself, man. Alise ain't too big on drugs, either. I better do this on the balcony."

Simon drops down on the couch. "That's real goddamn courteous of you."

"Nope," Tribal grins. "Just good sense. That girl can scrap!"

WHEN ALISE GETS HOME, she finds Simon on the couch beside a small pile of files, reading. The box has not only been opened, but emptied: everything in it has been arranged on the coffee table.

"Hey," she says.

"Hi. Hope you don't mind." Simon gestures at the clutter. "But then, I suppose you've had enough of guys who make messes of your apartment, eh?"

"Night and day. Find anything?"

Simon closes the file and tosses it on top of the others, shaking his head.

"Was Tribal still here when you got back?" she asks.

"Yeah. He didn't stay long, though."

Alise walks over to the slider and pushes it the rest of the way closed. "Thought so," she says. "I can smell him."

"At least he went outside to smoke it," Simon offers.

"Could have been worse, I guess. His brother could have been with him." Alise walks around the table and plops down on the couch beside Simon.

"Not a fan of Sirius?"

"Not a fan of them together—they're like a pair of wolves. Unless Jimmy's there to keep them on leash, of course." She smiles ruefully. "Then they're more like, I dunno, alley dog and eel."

Simon laughs.

Alise picks up a stack of old Polaroids, flipping through them absently. Simon picks up one of the black chestnuts and puts it down. He opens up a file and pretends to read it for a while.

An awkward silence, unexpected and unwelcome, has settled over them. It is Tribal's question: it lurks in the quiet corners of the apartment, waiting patiently. Simon steels himself and gives it voice.

"So . . . we should probably talk, eh?"

Alise starts at the beginning of the instamatics again, going through them methodically. "Yeah," she says quietly.

Simon closes the file and puts it down. "Tribal, in his eloquent way—"

"Tribal can be an asshole," she says. "Also, he should mind his own fucking business."

"Accurate," Simon agrees. "But I'm a little curious, myself, to be honest."

Alise shrugs. "I guess that makes two of us."

"We make a pretty odd couple," he offers.

Alise looks away, staring out at the night glow beyond the balcony slider. "Yeah, well, no pressure. I just got out of a shit relationship anyway. Don't feel like you—"

"I meant," he says, reaching out for her hand, "that we make a pretty odd couple. Nothing wrong with odd, punk girl."

Alise looks at him now, eyes guarded. *Eggshell eyes*, Frank calls that look—simultaneously hard and fragile. "Yeah?" she asks.

"Yeah."

"A little early for me to know where my shit's at. You know that, right?"

Simon nods.

"Might have to be patient."

"Alise," he says expansively, "I'm Indigenous *and* a social worker. You need patience?" He reclines deep into the couch and clasps his hands behind his head. "Patience I got."

SIMON UNTANGLES HIMSELF FROM the sheets and contemplates slipping out of bed as quietly as he can. But when he slowly turns his head to look at her, she's not there. He gropes around for his clothes, but all he can find are his jeans.

Just shy of midnight, according to his watch, and all of her equipment is gone. Simon smiles sadly, wisely: eventually, he knows, their two worlds will clash. He can't play the part of the groupie; and as for imagining her sitting down with that haircut (of all haircuts) at the kitchen table with his Mohawk mother, well.

A bridge for another time, he thinks, and turns on the floor lamp by the couch. Doug's photos, stacked between three plasticine fish and a black acorn, seem to mock him. Alise has left one of the strangest pictures on top, the jagged red "X."

As for the most macabre of Scotty's totems, it once again lies within its pall of tissue paper. Simon picks it up and holds it in his hand, feeling the hardness beneath the give. No point in handing it over to cops—that could mean reopening a stone-cold case that would drag a number of people into some murky waters. Him, for one, but also Frank. And Doug, if they can find him.

And, of course, Scotty. He certainly couldn't allow that.

Simon wasn't lying when he told Alise he was patient. It frustrates his mother, he knows, but it's a trait he inherited from his father. Their infrequent arguments are mild, but also tainted with their shared sense of loss. Simon's father was a gentle and kind man—a loving dad. A loving husband. She never really got over his death.

Simon's wild side—his pranks, his recklessness, his weekend migrations from crowd to crowd—was tempered with a mischievous joy; he rarely got truly angry at anyone. But that was before he'd finished university. Once he had a degree in hand, Simon first searched for a position in the Six Nations Child and Family Services. Nothing was available.

"You could volunteer," his mom had suggested.

"Can't pay the bills like that," he'd said. "There's openings in Hamilton, at the CAS. They're looking for social workers."

"Of course they are," she'd said bitterly. "We need people *here*."

"I know."

"Then volunteer! I *got* a job—we've always got by."

Simon had looked out the screen door to where the fireflies blinked in and out, like fickle constellations. "I'm *sick* of how hard you work, Ma. I want to help."

"Help the Community."

"I want to do that, too, Ma. I will."

Within two months of signing on under Frank, though, Simon was completely overwhelmed by the enormity of what lay before him. There were manageable bits—simple visits, contented kids in stable foster homes, for instance. But watching them bury a fifteen-year-old addict while under a barrage of mindless rage from an inconsolable mother, witnessing unbelievable living conditions time and again, and struggling under a legal system absolutely paralyzed with useless theory in the glaring face of practice, Simon struggled with despair.

In a way, Frank assigning him to Scotty was therapeutic. The mute never seemed to be in distress, and figuring out a way to communicate with him was an intellectual endeavour, not an emotional one. Simon found himself looking forward to those morning visits.

Simon also knows that further exceptions will not be made for Scotty. Without the scant financial support of the Government, he will quickly slip under the surface of the streets and disappear.

In his palm, the small piece of bone has substance, weight. But it means nothing to him beyond its small part in a crime committed in the 1950s, a crime unearthed around a decade and a half after that, and as of yet unsolved. Worse, really: utterly forgotten.

Ten small bones missing.

Ten small bones missing, officially.

"Well, Doug," Simon whispers to the little bundle, "here's one. Where the hell are the rest?"

He carefully repacks the box—everything but the journal—and heads back to bed.

24

WHAT WAS THAT? SCOTTY wakes up, startled. The tail end of his dream slithers out from under him and beyond reach. In its wake it leaves remnants: a feeling of entanglement, of choking; thorny vines wrapped around limbs; a man's voice—"C'mon Scotty," it said. "Time to take these."

It's frustrating. Scotty's dreams are vivid and often keep him company throughout the morning. His memories of them, that is. When they evade him like this, he feels empty.

He weaves his way through the clutter that has gathered in his narrow closet of a bedroom—cardboard and cassettes and odds and ends. Cardboard has its own distinct smell, but many of the scavenged signs are rank with an array of accompanying odours. Mildew and dampness, mostly, but others as well: the salty, fetid reek of sweat; the pungent stink of fish; the high sweet trace of urine; vinegary wine or stale, skunky beer. One greasy sign even smells of a cloying perfume—heady and powerful, like rotting flowers. Scotty's senses are alive with it all.

He uses the washroom and then wanders into the front room. Dawn creeps slowly through the glass slider, but it is still a good hour until sunrise. It will be hours before Simon comes.

His journey up the Escarpment two days ago was also like waking up without remembering a dream—frustrating, hollow. He refused to be discouraged by the sudden discovery of one of his own sculptures hanging like a sentry above the access. Even its strange cargo could not dissuade him. He knew with certainty who had put it there—but why, after all these years, had the mop bucket man once again decided to haunt him?

At the lip of the Escarpment, there were more trees than he would have expected. Still, he found a good vantage point and stared out across the city that lay one hundred metres below him, lines of houses and trees and apartment buildings and factories—a compact landscape of grey and brown and red and green that filled the five kilometres between him and the Lake. Beyond the forest of steel-mill smokestacks that guarded the shore like a giant palisade, an immense steel arch spanned the gap that allowed the monstrous cargo ships into Hamilton Harbour. He knew what that was, though, from his many sojourns to the same lonely beach—the Skyway Bridge was like a gate to the vast loneliness of the unforgiving Lake beyond. But from his position at the top of the cliff, Scotty could also just make out Toronto's core some seventy kilometres away across the flat blue water. Its buildings piled up like a steel and concrete mountain, and from its centre stretched a pale tower that rose above it all, impossibly high.

So many buildings, Scotty thought, overwhelmed by what he saw. Then, a sudden fear gripped him. *What if my building is over there, across the water? What if my building isn't even here at all?* Panicking, his eyes swept the cityscape below him, singling out any high-rise with brown on it. But the farthest of Hamilton's buildings, those down in the North End, were obscured by the haze of the hot August afternoon—everything was the same colour.

Too much, he intoned. *Too much. I wish I wasn't so—*

"Hey!"

The shout came from a pale yellow car with a smashed-in fender. Someone in it was yelling at him.

"Hey! Scott, right? Scotty? You lost, man?"

Scotty folded in on himself, counting to catch his breath. It was hard to see that elusive shadow in the blinding sunlight, though. By the time he'd regained control, the car was gone.

Now, in the slow hours of early morning, Scotty faces a reality. *I can't go up there again*, he concludes. *I'll just—*

Just what? What else can he do but wander the grid, his breadcrumbs a sequence of surreptitiously drawn chalk fish that point the way back? The search, though; it gives him something he's never had before: purpose.

Keep looking. I'll just keep looking.

An early start on empty streets. That would be a good way to start the day, although it means that Simon would arrive to find an empty apartment. What would he do with the pills? What would he scribble in his little book? Scotty hadn't the faintest notion of any of it.

But what if he needs me to go somewhere? Not that Scotty looks forward to that possibility. The thought triggers a tug on his lungs, shadowy hand giving him a disdainful pull. He looks around, following his own shadow across the floor and up the wall. Within the pale darkness, he perceives another—an elfish shadow, skinny and standoffish, arms crossed and chin jutting out.

Simon's nice to me! Scotty argues. *He found me this place. He wants to help me.*

But it's gone again. Moments later, there's a soft knock on his door.

Alise's knock. Confused, Scotty crosses the front room and unlatches the lock, turning the knob so that the door is ajar.

"Wow," she says as she enters. "You're actually up! I knocked softly because I figured you'd still be asleep, eh? I know you get up early, but it's, like, 5:00 a.m.!"

Clearly Alise hasn't been home yet. She wears a torn and dirt-stained white blouse over a tank top, a red plaid mini skirt, and the cloying stench of cigarette smoke. Like her blouse, her fishnets are ripped. The sinuous tendrils of the tattoo on her thigh look like they're escaping from a chain link prison. Her eight-hole oxblood Doc Martens, like the left side of her body, are coated in dry mud.

"Like my new look? It's called 'Friday night cop evasion chic.' It's easy: you just dress normally and then spend the last hour of your night dodging cops by running through a graveyard. Hammer Pigs, man—no sense of decency. Busted up a perfectly good after-party."

Scotty can tell she's talking just to put him at ease, as if she knows that he likes the sound of her voice. She's savvy enough not to make eye contact, talking away as if to the fish still hanging from the ceiling. Or perhaps to the box of gutted cassettes under the table. Scotty doesn't care, so long as he can sink into the sound of her.

"I actually came up for a reason," she says. "I wanted to ask you something."

Scotty stands almost within reach of her, his eyes glued to the little plastic wheel of a cassette that lies on the floor about a metre in front of Alise.

"Look, if I could find you a way into the AGH—the art gallery, the one we visited together a while ago—would you be interested? I don't mean during the day. You'd be all alone in there. You could hang some art. Or make some."

His head half-swivels toward her and freezes. His breathing deepens audibly and his eyes widen.

"Jimmy was right," Alise mumbles. She makes her way over to where Spider floats alone in his little bowl. It is still exactly where she placed it on the narrow counter days ago. "If you want to bring anything in, like the rest of these fish, we'd have to find a way to get them into the gallery first. I'd need to take stuff with me."

Scotty moves now, a brisk awkward walk past her and toward his bedroom. He opens the door and closes it behind him.

For a while longer, Alise watches Spider as he bobs contentedly in his tiny world. Then she sighs and heads for the front door. *Or not*, she thinks. *Maybe I just scared the shit outa him.*

ALISE UNLOCKS HER OWN apartment door and closes it behind her quietly. She notices that the contents of the box have been packed away since she slipped out of the apartment around midnight.

Maybe Simon left. She forgot to tell him she had a gig to play, and he was already sound asleep when it finally occurred to her to let him know. But she spots his shirt in a crumpled heap under the table, undisturbed since she pulled it off him and threw it there last evening.

And there he is, sprawled out in her bed. She considers a shower, but she's exhausted. She unties the laces on her Docs and pulls them off. They're a mess—usually cops can't be bothered with a sustained chase without good reason, but Alise had the misfortune of attracting the attention of a younger cop in good shape, and she certainly wasn't going to outrun him.

Dumb luck saved her—that, and a stray beer bottle. She snatched it up, hurled it hard and high to her left, and then dodged right before it hit. Concealed behind a monument, she heard the cop pound by her toward the sound of broken glass. Instinct urged her to run while he was distracted, but street logic grounded her: her pursuer was chasing a shaky summary offence at best; once he lost her trail, chances were he'd shrug and return to the pack. She made herself wait another ten minutes before carefully making her way toward the street. That's when she hit the mud and slipped. Once on the pavement, she traded caution for casual and made her way home.

Damn it. Maybe I should. Shower, she means, the mud more extensive than she realized. She picks up the boots to carry them to the balcony, but a noise from the front room stops her mid-step.

Then it registers: a knock. Or a knock of sorts—more like the tentative scratching of a timid dog. She walks across the narrow room and looks out the peephole, but no one's there.

"What the shit," she growls. "Who's screwing around in the hall at five fucking thirty?" She yanks the door open, but the corridor is empty.

Except, that is, for the dozens of dirty cardboard signs stacked up against the walls flanking her door. She smiles, shaking her head.

"Fucking Jimmy. He was right."

The balcony, she decides. Because the signs carry with them a catalogue of odours, soiled with the litany of miseries and indignities their previous authors and owners endured. *And even if it rains later,* she thinks, *it's nothing they haven't sat through before. Anyway, I'll use a few garbage bags to protect them.*

This is what she comforts herself with, in any case, while she makes trip after trip between hall door and slider, carrying stacks of twenty or twenty-five signs at a time. She tucks them away in the corner on the balcony, wrapped in the heavy black plastic of leaf bags she retrieves from one of her milk crates. They come in handy when moving amplifiers and other equipment in the rain.

When she is finished, she stands in the small living room and gives the slider a cursory glance. Nothing looks out of the ordinary, anyway.

Meaning that Simon won't likely notice. Guilt nags her—a hiss behind her ear, a tug at her guts. Angrily, she tries to shake it, but she knows that will be impossible. Jimmy's words—*don't tell Simon*—hover over the cardboard signs like shadowy and ominous birds.

"Fucking Jimmy," she mumbles again. No smile this time, though.

Because she knows he's right about this, too.

A BIT BEFORE 7:00 a.m., showered and exhausted, she tries to slip into bed without waking Simon. But the mattress is shot—the springs protest in a chorus of squeaks, startling him.

"Sorry," she says. "I tried not to wake you."

"That's alright," he says, rolling onto his back. "Gotta be close to time, anyway."

Alise shifts so that she can rest her head where Simon's chest and shoulder meet, throwing an arm across his stomach. "You gotta work today? It's Saturday."

"I know, but lots of paperwork to catch up on. *Some*thing's been interrupting my routine lately."

"Aha," Alise says, closing her eyes and inching closer. "I'm an interruption, am I?"

"To put it mildly," he says, poking her.

"Well, it's all part of my anarchistic plan, Nine-to-Five. I'm toppling the System one pillar at a time."

Simon laughs. "I'm a 'pillar of the System,' am I?"

"Well, so to speak. Tax-paying contributor to the oppression machine."

But his sudden stillness doesn't feel right—Alise props herself up on an elbow. "Hey, what's wrong?"

"Huh? Oh—nothing. Gig was good?"

"Uh, yeah, but—"

"Cool. Get some sleep, punk girl. I gotta get this stuff done." He climbs out of bed to hunt for his clothes. "See you in a few hours?"

"You're not leaving yet," she says, pulling him back into bed.

But afterward, she doesn't sleep for long. Restless dreams haunt her, melding into a non sequitur string of impressions: on stage mid gig but with no patch cord; pushing Simon down a flight of stairs; hiding in a basement from Tribal who is dressed as a cop.

"Fuck it," she snarls, dragging herself from bed just after 9:00 a.m. She navigates the cramped space, careful not to upset the disorganized mountain that currently occupies the top of her bureau, and digs through the closet for clothes.

Already her apartment is muggy, and the dingy corridor leading to the elevators is even worse. Instead, Alise opts for the stairs.

Once out in the blinding sunlight, she heads north on Rebecca toward the bus depot payphones. Other pedestrians move sluggishly through the thick air—late Saturday morning commuters or just those driven out of their hidden corners by the heat. As she crosses Catharine Street, though, she looks north toward the Lake. Storm clouds gather there like an indecisive moot. Still, it's a promising sign; rain would at least break the humidity.

A small consolation: the payphones are in the shade. She punches in the number for her dad's music store and waits for one of them to pick up.

"Working Man Music."

"Sid, it's Alise. My dad or Em in yet?"

"You're kidding, right? It's not even 10:00 a.m."

"Stupid question."

"Your order came in, though—you gonna pick this stuff up?"

"Already? Wasn't expecting that shit 'til next month! I'll be up soon."

Like most of her friends and acquaintances, Alise must find ways to make ends meet. Gigs provide enough income to cover a week's worth of expenses, but everything else must be scrounged or earned. They all have something: Jimmy deals; Tribal does temp labour like his brother, but he also runs grifts; her bandmates work day jobs in shops; other musicians she knows work as mechanics, hair dressers, forklift operators, elevator repairmen, security, factory workers. Some few have the means to work toward a degree of some sort—one crazy bastard in a punk band has an actual PhD in history, but works on McMaster University's maintenance crew.

Alise, however, deals in rare vinyl—she has an eclectic client base, from embarrassingly elite Toronto avant-garde artists and dealers to misanthropic collectors who prowl the local record shops like rabid sex offenders.

It's the dirty, forgotten corners of punk they're after.

As fiercely proud as Hamilton is of its vibrant and eclectic music scene, most of it is rooted in a wholesome earth not worth digging into. Alise wants the toxic seeds of rare lo-fi and garage punk, and her two main suppliers—an old flame of Emily's who runs a pirate radio station out of a commune in California, and Alise's former drummer roommate's bohemian sister in Brisbane, Australia—know exactly what to send her when they find it. They split the profits, using the music store as a go-between.

Not that the '80s Hamilton punk scene isn't strong, but anyone can get their claws into a bootleg recording of Teenage Head or the Forgotten Rebels. Even Simply Saucer recordings aren't too rare. Try laying hands on Mike Rep and the Quotas' 1975 "Rocket to Nowhere," though—two hundred pressed, half of which have signed inserts. Alise has one of each.

As the bus lurches to a stop on Upper Ottawa Street, the rain begins in heavy drops. Fortunately, the music store is a short sprint from the bus stop and she doesn't have her hair up anyway, for which she's grateful. Glue in the eyes hurts.

Sid sits on a stool behind the counter sorting a cascading mound of guitar picks into five smaller piles. The wellspring of his labour, a plastic grocery bag bursting with yet-to-be-sorted nylon triangles, sits prominently on the counter where the business card holder ordinarily rests. Even from the door, Alise can hear the trebly guitar leaking out of the headphones of his Sony Discman.

"Sid!" Alise shouts from the door. Nothing—he's in the pick-sorting zone.

"Sid!" she tries again, a little closer. Absolute devotion to task, though.

She closes the distance. "SIDDHARTH!"

Startled, Sid almost falls off his perch. He gropes around for the pause button on the Discman while pushing his curtain of thick black hair out of his eyes.

"Shit, Alise—you scared the fuck outa me!"

"I coulda walked out with that fuckin' Fender bass amp next to the door and you wouldn't have even noticed, eh?"

But Sid points a spidery finger accusingly at the sack of picks nesting on top of the business cards. "Blame your dad! *Look* at this shit—where the hell does he find a bag of random picks? 'Sort 'em,' he says. Then he hocks 'em at a buck for, like, a fistful."

"Hey, it coulda been a bag of loose guitar strings."

"True," Sid concedes. "My one consolation is that the fall semester starts in a couple weeks—this'll be the next guy's problem. Want your stuff?"

"I'll get it," she says, squeezing behind the counter. The parcels, stiff with protective packaging, rest upright on a shelf between a bucket of drum sticks and a pile of sheet music weighted down by a shapeless lump of concrete that Alise's father swears is from *The Wall*'s dramatic penultimate explosion scene.

"What's the haul this month?" Sid, a devout parishioner of New Wave, endures with herculean resolve the long summer days of Rush, Yes, and Jethro Tull that Alise's father plays religiously through the store's speakers. Sometimes there is a week-long Zeppelin phase or some Guess Who, but to Sid that isn't a notable improvement. Alise's musical tastes simultaneously fascinate and horrify Sid, as if they were some sort of soundtrack equivalent of a carnival freak show of yesteryear.

Alise opens the first parcel carefully with the store's box cutter, slicing gently along the apex of the package and then down each side to reveal foam and a pair of protective wooden panels. She carefully removes five albums, each sleeve separated from the next by a layer of tissue paper, and sets them down carefully.

"Well?" Sid asks, but then he sees the sleeve in front. "Is that 7" EP by *Joy Division*?! Thought you were strictly punk!"

Alise, however, cannot answer. She inspects the sleeve and contents with a reverence befitting a relic.

"Alise?"

"Siddharth," she finally says, "this little four-track EP is one of the holy grails of punk—'Ideal for Living,' 1978. Still has the poster inside, which is *signed*, by the way. Only a thousand albums pressed." She places it carefully aside. "You're looking at my rent for a couple months. Already got a buyer in mind."

"Shit," Sid mumbles. "A summer's wages here cover the first two Engineering parties' worth of booze and that's about it. Shoulda taken you seriously when you offered to cut me in for a hundred, eh?"

"Next time," she says absently. The other albums—a sealed copy of the Stooges' "Raw Power," The Blazers' 1966 LP "On Fire," and a pair of singles by the Mo-Dettes—she sets down beside the remaining unopened parcels.

"Hey," Sid suddenly calls out toward the opening door, "you're early! Wasn't expecting you until 10:00 a.m.!"

Alise turns around to witness Emily's cautious entry; her eyes are concealed behind retro Jackie O. sunglasses with tortoiseshell rims, but her pale skin and slow-motion approach indicate a hangover of considerable magnitude.

"10:00 a.m. was an hour ago," Emily croaks.

"I know," Sid smirks, "but I meant 10:00 a.m. *tomorrow*."

"Good art opening last night?" Alise ventures.

"He was right," Emily manages softly.

"Sorry?"

"Your father—he was right. Geddy Lee actually showed up."

Sid rolls his eyes and heads for the back of the store to tune guitars. "Great," he says over his shoulder. "There's the topic of a very one-sided conversation until school starts."

Alise, however, shakes her head in disbelief.

"You're kidding."

"My vodka-to-coffee ratio is too out of balance for me to lie. Speaking of which . . ."

"On it," Alise says, reaching for the empty pot of the coffee maker tucked behind the sack of unsorted picks.

It only takes a pot of black coffee and an hour of puttering around the store before Alise settles the details with Emily. It would have taken longer, had Andy Warhol's iconic banana not come to the rescue.

Still intact, in fact: unpeeled and adorning the cover of the 1967 debut album of the Velvet Underground. It was the first album to emerge from the second parcel from California.

"I'm surprised Richie parted with that," Emily had said from her semi-prone post behind the front counter. She'd been pretending to mind the cash register since the coffee was ready. "Lou Reed was his personal god. Also one of the reasons we broke up. Well," she'd added, "that and the whole weird cult thing."

"I've seen a few around, but the stickers are always peeled."

Emily had nodded slowly. "It was a good gimmick. I don't think you'll get too much for it, though, unpeeled or not."

Alise had shrugged. "As long as we're on the topic of art . . ."

✎

ONE HUNDRED DOLLARS TO the right security guard and a trunkful of cardboard to be smuggled in via a willing artist's crated work. A little after noon, Emily drives Alise back downtown so that they can fetch the bags from the balcony.

"No fish?" Emily asks as she surveys the stacks of plastic-wrapped cardboard.

"Nope. Don't know what he has in mind, but it's just these."

Between the two of them, they manage to get the lot down to the car in one trip.

"Sunday night," Emily says out the driver's window. "Get your mystery artist to the AGH by 8:00 p.m. Look for a dark blue van on Summers Lane."

"Got it. Hey, thanks for helping him out, eh?"

Emily flashes her a tired smile and drives off with Scotty's enigmatic cargo.

Alise gives a grateful wave as Emily pulls onto Rebecca Street, and then heads back down to the payphones. She has at least eight or ten phone calls to make, after all, if she's going to secure buyers for some of the rarer records. It's an eclectic collection of albums this time, but some could be marketed as a set.

Then maybe I can crash for a few hours, she considers. *It's only around 1:00 p.m.* She wants to be awake for Simon when he gets off work, but there's a midnight gig at Mallet Sally's tonight, too.

But when she reaches the station, she walks right by the phones and toward the Barton Street bus.

"Fuck it," she says under her breath. "I gotta see this place for myself."

25

IT WASN'T A BAD way to spend a Saturday morning.

Simon considers this as he drives into Hamilton's East End for the second time today. Scotty accompanies him on this run, a ragged flannel phantom of no particular haunt quietly watching the living city drift by through a dirty window. Glancing furtively at his quiet companion, Simon sighs under his breath.

But it'll be a shit way to spend a Saturday afternoon.

ALISE'S POST-GIG SHOWER HAD woken her up enough to pull the sheets down and straddle him. And although she had pawed drowsily at him to remain with her, Simon knew he'd never slip back under himself.

"I'm still behind on paperwork," he'd said. "I'll be back in a couple hours."

When he slipped out of bed at 8:30 a.m., he first thought about heading up to Scotty's to deliver meds, but it's technically his day off. At twenty years old, Scotty is already in that undefined liminal zone—there is no real backup plan in place, and (of course) Scotty isn't going to lodge a complaint about it. Either Simon shows up or Scotty goes a day without.

Not that the meds make a bit of difference, he'd thought bitterly. *He'd be better off hording pills and selling them to Jimmy.* In fact, Jimmy has hinted at this—a primary motivation, Simon suddenly realized, for making sure Scotty swallows the things.

Simon had edged his way out of the tiny room, doing his best not to bump bed or bureau. The bed squeaks, especially near that one corner where the springs are shot, but the bureau is the real danger: it is topped by a mountain of precariously balanced clutter—cassettes, makeup, cans of hairspray, loose jewelry, panties, an impossibly tangled ball of bras and stockings, loose photos, coins, three shoes. A moth-eaten stuffed bear with a missing button eye is barely visible on one side of the slope, as if he has been trapped by an avalanche, while a lone leather boot rises above the mess on the other side, broken buckle dangling from the side. The boot currently plays the part of a vase, holding a bouquet of dried flowers. The axis mundi of the mess is an ornate lamp on top of a battered jewelry box.

Her bedroom and the washroom—they are the only places Alise tolerates (or, perhaps more accurately, cultivates) clutter. Simon smiled at this as he sifted through the strata on the floor in search of his other sock.

The building was crypt-quiet this morning. But instead of heading up to Scotty's, he made his way to the lobby and out to the parking lot. Once on Rebecca Street, Simon drove to the corner of James and makes a right toward Barton.

The East End—his destination was an address beyond Parkdale Avenue and south of the sprawl known as Industrial Sector G: 44 Faulman Glen Road.

According to an article written thirteen years ago, anyway.

Lying to Alise about having to do paperwork didn't feel right, but he knew he needed to do this alone. Impulsive and unpredictable, Alise may not have tolerated a simple drive-by.

Barton Street was quiet this morning. The arterial road is Hamilton's longest stretch at just over twenty kilometres, and although it provides access to a wide range of neighbourhoods, the street itself is trapped somewhere between the quaintly shabby decay of yesteryear's elegance and the spartan aesthetic of a bleak industrial present. Modest red brick houses from the early twentieth century soon give way to one and two-story flat roofed storefronts—billiard halls and beauty salons, taverns and thrift shops. After the immense General Hospital and its satellite medical supply businesses, low-rent housing and dumpy corner variety stores press up against the odd generations-old hardware store or small import business. Churches, soup kitchens, laundromats, a deli, sports bars, strip malls, empty lots, cheap rental banquet halls, a faith-based bookstore or two, the derelict summer shell of a district high school—Simon drifted by them all.

A block after the little utilitarian grassy patch known as Fairfield Park, however, Barton changes: the sprawling brick-and-mortar flea market and the Coca-Cola plant are interrupted by Mahoney Park's green and dirt-brown expanse, and then the city's support industries—truck and heavy equipment mechanics, distributor warehouses, a concrete factory—consume the landscape almost until the Red Hill Valley and its sewage-choked creek. Just west and across the street of where the cement mixers enter and exit the yard, Simon made a right onto Faulman Glen Road.

It's a one-way street heading *toward* Barton, but Simon knew it didn't matter: the short connector between Barton and Melvin may as well not even exist. As for its name, if there was once a glen in the area, it certainly isn't there now. Unless the name refers to one of the weed-ridden parking lots, of course. He turned onto the street and wove slowly around the pot-holes and refuse—a blown-out tire, a half-flattened garbage can, decaying upholstered heaps that used to be a pair of chairs. Garbage has collected in colourful drifts against the knee-high grass that flanks the road, or against the sagging stretches of chain link fence that still stand.

None of this was new to Simon; he knew this road well enough. At the far end, where Faulman Glen meets Melvin Avenue, an old tavern and dance hall from the '40s called the Le Palais Est still stands; it is a lofty appellation, even for when it was in its heyday. In the '60s, new owners renovated the three-storey building, adding close to fifty tiny apartments. The structure is often without heat, the plumbing is unreliable, the elevator is a death-trap, and cockroaches and bedbugs have the run of the place. Last autumn, Simon rescued a ten-year-old boy and his six-year-old half-sister from a nightmarish hovel on the second floor. After he and the police were done collecting up the salvageable belongings, he had gone behind the building and stripped off the jeans and flannel shirt he'd bought at a thrift shop beforehand, throwing the clothes away and changing into his own clothes which he'd brought with him in a tightly sealed plastic bag.

This morning, though—he parked in front of an eight-storey low-rise about one inspection away from being condemned, walked past the only business on the road—a bottle and can recycling depot—and stopped in front of 44 Faulman Glen Road.

The building, sixteen floors of crumbling concrete and flaking brown paint, waited patiently for an end to its long, sad existence. The ground floor was boarded up, "condemned" signs clearly visible, but most of its reachable surface was covered in graffiti; every window for the first four floors was smashed, and some rock-throwing enthusiasts had even managed to break windows as high as the seventh storey. Simon knew it was impossible, but the whole structure seemed to sag in on itself, desperate for the dignity of the wrecking ball.

Simon sighed and walked back to his car, leaving the building behind. *Coma*, he'd thought. *Like an old, old woman trapped in a coma. Waiting for someone to unplug the life support.*

He did not yet know that this would happen.

Nor did he know that he would soon play a role in the unplugging.

—

ALISE WAS GONE AGAIN when Simon returned to her apartment just shy of 10:45 a.m. He knew better than to feel hard done by, or to confront her. Or to ask her to leave a note or something. She was a free agent, and she expected him to be the same. Simon was good at reading the subtext between actions and reactions; he knew, for instance, that Alise was definitely in love with the chance encounter—*not* knowing each other's plans created a dynamic spontaneity that fuelled something deep in Alise's psyche.

Must remind her of how her dad was when she was little, those surprise midnight stories. Simon understood, but he would keep this to himself.

For a good minute, he stood in the doorway and stared at the box marked *Gagnon*. What else could he do for his enigmatic charge? The Palais or some other equally decrepit shithole was in Scotty's immediate future—this building's owners would start the eviction process within hours of losing their first government rent cheque.

"Or worse," he said softly. Than the Palais Est, he meant—it was more likely that Scotty would be forced into homelessness.

"Fuck it. He deserves his stuff."

Simon picked up the box and headed for Scotty's.

Simon greeted Scotty as the door opened.

"Hey, man. I know it's Saturday and I don't usually show, but we need to talk." He looked down at the box and smiled sadly. "Well, how 'bout *I* talk? I need you to hear what I'm saying, though."

Scotty walked back to his work table. Instead of sculptures, today he seemed to be unspooling tape from cassettes. A fair pile of it was on the table already, and the empty plastic shells gathered beneath his chair.

Walking over to the table, Simon placed the box on the scarred and stained surface. He pointed at the name on the side.

"'Gagnon,'" he said. "That's you, Scotty. That's your real last name—your mom's last name."

I know.

"I just found out. From your first worker—Doug. I went to see him and he told me."

Scotty's fingers grew still. He focused on the strange smell that often escaped a cassette—sometimes it was a sweet, cloying scent, others smelled a bit like paint. The BASF cassette in his hand then, though, smelled like crayons.

"This stuff is yours, Scotty. It came from your apartment—the one you lived in with your mom. She—she's in there, too." Simon placed a gentle hand on the lid of the box. "I'm gonna give you some time alone with this. I'll be back, though."

Simon walked to the door and let himself out, determined to shed at least some of the weight on his conscience. He headed for his office to catch up on some paperwork.

Gagnon. I know that's my name. Why did people start calling me Campbell?

No one ever took the time to explain it to him. Urgency, necessity: these things took priority over the sort of careful courtesy and patience it would take to explain the way of the world to a newly orphaned nine-year-old boy. After all, they had no idea of what the crazy old custodian was capable; all they knew was that he was obsessed with the child. The vice principal was publicly praised by the newspaper and privately grilled by the police. The administrator's recollection of what he overheard outside the janitor's closet—a madman in an earnest and terrifyingly disturbing conversation with a child's drawing—made for great journalism. It frustrated law enforcement, though. Institutionalizing him would only keep him off the streets for so long.

Doug chose the name and Frank did the paperwork, a pair of clandestine midwives overseeing the birth of a new child: Scott Campbell, *né* Gagnon. They buried the boy's old identity in a cardboard coffin and shoved it on a shelf.

The first time Scotty heard his new name, he was understandably confused. But he deduced that you must get a new name when your mother dies. He wondered how many other children in the group home also had new names forced upon them. He was also confused by what they did with his mother's remains. The police constable who gently but firmly guided him away from his mother's body and out of the boiler room did his best to block his view. With a child's penchant for the macabre, he imagined a number of horrifying scenarios, not the least of which was the remaining police stuffing her shell into the furnace.

He wasn't far off, because later Scotty learned that his mother was cremated. The word confused him, but it was explained to him in a practical, clinical way, by a kind-faced lady at the group home he had to live in. No details, of course: in the same way that a child might be told of photosynthesis or light refraction in rainbows.

"The body goes to a place that burns it," she said, "turns it to ash. Then you get an urn." Like it was a prize, an award. A sort of consolation.

Scotty wrestled with the concept—it was difficult, imagining his mother (wrapped in a dirty sheet, dust-covered with one black knuckled hand from where it dragged on the floor) placed in a receptacle and converted from one sad form to another. Fire eating up everything—the greasy, thinning hair; the loose skin that fell away from her frail bones; her yellowy cracked fingernails and chewed-upon cuticles; her perpetually sad eyes. Other things, too: her broken teeth, cracked from grinding on the husks of her bitter dreams; her anger and baffled frustration and the crushing weight of unfairness. All these things would burn to ash, too.

Nothing was explained to him at the time, though. Doug, his first social worker, brought him to the building where it had happened—an austere structure, grey with four ominous pillars holding up a dour looking triangle.

There were wide stairs leading up to a gaping black door—twenty-four of them, in fact. Scotty counted as he was led up by the hand.

"Time to say goodbye to your mother," Doug said. His voice was empty, hollow. Scotty could feel the hesitation in the big hand that held his own—he knew that feeling, one of forward momentum outside and back pulling inside. Scotty snuck a furtive glance at Doug's face—red and swollen-eyed, tired.

Defeated, he might have thought at the time, had he the capacity. But at nine, all he saw was sadness. *Did he know her?* he wondered. *Is this man sad because she's gone?* And then, more alarmingly, *Where am I? What is this place? Do I have to live here now?*

Scotty's breath quickened at the possibility. Doug stopped, took a deep breath himself.

"I'm sorry, pal. We gotta do this. Then you can go h—" Doug paused, clutching around blindly for something more. "Then we can go," he finally said.

At the top of the wide stairs, the huge door led into a room of polished stone. Scotty could see his own vague reflection in some of the surfaces, blurred. Like a colourful shadow.

Once inside, Doug guided Scotty over to a chair and sat him down. Then he spoke briefly to another person, a young man with a nervous tick that reminded Scotty of a clock. The clock man ticked a quick *yesyesyes* and disappeared through a door. A few moments later, he reappeared carrying a plain white container.

For a while, no one moved. The man with the container stood in front of the door he'd just emerged from, patiently. Scotty sat on the hard chair, confused. Doug, though—he fought against something palpable that even the child could recognize.

Necessity.

It was one of the two monsters that crept along with Scotty, a monster that hid around upcoming corners and behind unopened doors. No matter how hard he focused on his immediate future, it always managed to surprise him anyway.

The other monster was Dread. It lurked behind him, dogging his steps. Often, Scotty felt as though Dread were a corpse, a deadweight to be dragged along.

Necessity triggered in him a sort of horrid energy, a crushing anxiety that left him breathless. Dread just exhausted him.

Watching Doug stand there in awkward reluctance, Scotty realized with the sudden and intense clarity that horrific tragedy will sometimes provide (like another urn, another kind of consolation) that Necessity and Dread were the same monster—that the first filled him with the second. A nine-year-old vessel to be forever filled by this endless cycle.

Doug finally steeled himself and crossed the room to take the urn from the clock man. Then, together, the two men approached Scotty with the solemnity of a procession.

They showed him the urn. Then they took it away.

WHEN SIMON RETURNED TO Scotty's apartment a little over two hours later at 1:30 p.m., he found Scotty holding the urn of his mother's remains. Tear stains streaked the mute's face, although he was no longer crying. Other things—the small objects, the jar of acorns, the little car—were on the table; the little clay fish nestled in the tangle of gutted cassette tape like seaweed. The drawings were stacked neatly in his lap; the lunch pail and newspaper were still in the box.

Of the tissue-wrapped bundle there was no sign.

"I'm really sorry, Scotty." Simon didn't know what else to say—he had no idea if he'd opened a door or closed one. And then there was the harder conversation that lurked on the horizon, the lightless dawn of Scotty's bleak future, but that had to wait.

Now anger, sullen and ancient, crept up into Simon's bones. It was something he hadn't felt for two mind-numbing years. Or maybe this was different. He closed his eyes and suddenly saw those of his mother—dark, wise, patient, angry. *This fucking government*, he said to the darkness. To the eyes. *Genocide and theft with no more than a shrug for an apology. That's all we've ever been: an Indigenous afterthought, a fucking inconvenience standing in the way of so-called progress. But they do it to their own, too—what's Scotty to them? Just an inconvenience. Take his home and let him die.*

Simon reached into the box and pulled out the newspaper. *I will take him home—show him the building. What the hell else can I do?* He put the paper down in front of Scotty and pointed at the words that meant nothing to the mute.

"This paper told me where you grew up, Scotty. Want me to show you? To take you there?"

The chair slid backward as Scotty sprung to his feet, childhood drawings spilling across the filthy floor. Still holding the urn, the mute made his way toward the door. Simon had to scramble to keep up.

⟶

SIMON CHOOSES AS STRAIGHTFORWARD a route as possible: down Barton all the way to Parkdale. A right turn, a quick left on Melvin. Then another left on Faulman Glen.

"That's it, Scotty. That's where you lived."

But he cannot even look at it. *Not like this*, a small part of him says, *not like this*, numb to everything but the cool hard urn in his hands. He stares intently at the car radio, it seems, dazed and wide-eyed.

"You okay?" Simon asks. "Maybe this was a mistake. We'll go, eh?"

Scotty does not so much as blink, as if he has somehow slipped outside the flow of time. A circadian refugee.

"Alright." Simon shifts into drive and weaves his way through the obstacles to Barton. "At least you know where it is."

But as he turns the corner to begin the long drive back down Barton, he sees Alise walking toward them on the south side of the street a hundred metres away.

"Must have taken a bus down here," he says, driving up until almost parallel with her and then pulling over. He rolls down his window. "Alise!" he yells.

She turns and sees Simon, waving. But Scotty suddenly throws the door open and jumps out. He leaves the urn behind.

"Scotty! What the hell, man?"

Scotty doesn't even close the car door behind him, running as soon as his feet hit the pavement. He sprints across Barton at an angle, a blind dash into traffic, and disappears down Faulman Glen.

Simon scrambles to shut the passenger door and then pulls back into traffic to wait frantically for a chance to U-turn into the east-bound lanes.

Alise signals for him to catch up when he can and takes off in pursuit of Scotty.

He finds a parking spot on Barton about half a block east of Faulman; Alise meets him there, opening the passenger door.

"Did you see him?" Simon asks.

"Yeah," she says, getting in the car. "You already showed him the building?"

"He didn't even look at it—just sat where you are now holding *that*." He points to the urn at her feet. "Let's find him."

"Wait," Alise says, putting a hand on his shoulder. "Give him a few minutes, eh? Maybe he just needs to see it for himself. Process it, you know?"

Simon sighs. "Yeah—you're probably right. I just feel responsible because I brought him down here."

"I woulda done the same. Wanted to see it for myself, so I jumped the bus."

"Enough time?"

Alise shakes her head. "A few minutes," she repeats.

26

FOR A LONG TIME, he just stands in front of it, staring.

He can't tell whether or not it looks smaller, nor if there is something hauntingly familiar about it. But Scotty can't be held accountable for feeling numb—he's never had a homecoming before.

The shabby apartment building is profoundly sad; of this there is no doubt: sixteen stories of pitted concrete and cascading rust stains, almost every window within stone's throw is broken, and all means of egress on the ground floor have been boarded over and spray painted. The narrow strip of lawn between the weathered sidewalk and the building itself is a wild tangle of shin-high grass and weeds.

But of colour, too—purple heather has claimed the left side of the patch, and Queen Anne's lace rises like mist to half-conceal the trash that has gathered in the neglected grass.

There are other apartment buildings flanking this one, to the right and behind it. The abandoned husk of this building is the tallest structure on the road that connects Barton Street to Melvin, although Scotty can't pronounce the name on the sign. *F-A-U-L-M-A-N G-L-E-N.* Smaller buildings of drab cinder block or grey-red brick fill the remainder of the lane. Still occupied, signs of life sporadically visible: garments pinned to a short clothesline running the length of a balcony; a thin towel with a Leafs logo doubling as a curtain; an air conditioner rattling away in a window.

Not the building in front of him, though. It is a dead shell, a grotesque monument to the myriad nobodies of yesteryear—hundreds of strangers living beside and on top of and below one another in virtual isolation, occasionally in competition for the same scarce resources. An elevator, or maybe one of the coin operated dryers that worked. People really didn't have much interest in anything other than their own struggles—*it was like living in a giant crowded bus*, Scotty thinks. *No one really talked to anyone else.* Just people living their own hard lives with bitter resolve.

Except one, of course. Resolve abandoned her, dissipating like exhaled smoke. She died late one night in a small cinderblock room on the eleventh floor and was found the next morning by a frightened nine-year-old boy. Scotty counts balconies until he reaches the right floor, but he can't recall which side their apartment was on. *At least the windows aren't busted that high up.* It's a small comfort.

Scotty's own resolve begins to abandon him, too. It seems so improbable, finding a way into this piece of his past. This mausoleum of childhood. The building might as well be in a hidden corner of some distant city or as ethereal as memory, so unapproachable at this moment.

What was I thinking? he frets, nails digging into palms. A tear slides unnoticed down his wan cheek. Another. The looming structure blurs away into shimmering planes of drab shapes as the tears fall unchecked, breath just ragged intakes and sniffles. The shapes float as if unmoored, drifting playfully.

Until.

Scotty stands utterly still, suddenly and completely, breath held in mid gasp. He does not blink, allowing the tears to work their strange magic on his vision. The shards cease their playful undulations and begin to take shape—something familiar. A dark central patch, long and vertical. Now something else floats down from above, smaller. Oval. It settles on top of the first shape. Then another one, thin and impossibly long—it detaches from the first shape and crawls its way across the grey-brown blur of the building, as if gesturing urgently, restlessly.

But in his own urgency to make out the gesture, Scotty focuses too hard and the entire vision collapses into nonsense. He releases the little air still trapped in his thin chest and gulps in fresh air greedily, eyes still bound to the terminus of that sinuous final shape.

And then he bounds across the wild grass and broken concrete in a mad dash, unbelieving eyes fixed above the rotting lintel of the boarded-up doorway, upon the weatherworn concrete relief.

Of a fish.

SIMON AND ALISE ARRIVE too late. Scotty has already disappeared around the side of the building.

"Are you sure?" Simon asks, tense.

"I dunno," Alise says sharply. "Who the hell else would it be? He was standing there on the street and then he just bolted toward the building."

"Better'n what I got," he says. "Let's go."

Simon is only acquainted with isolated parts of this neighbourhood, and Alise doesn't know it at all. Both know by instinct that caution is necessary, though—Alise by way of street politics and Simon by way of common sense. And profession, this building having all the indicators of a squat house. Or worse.

Much worse, Alise first to point it out.

"Yeah, I see it," Simon confirms. The swastika superimposes all other graffiti, angular black on a white background. It is a recent and angry addition to the sad litany of sigils, signs, and symbols that decorate wood and walls. "Stay here. My client, my responsibility."

"Fuck you, Prince Charming! My *friend*, my choice." And she breaks into a jog, forcing Simon to run in order to catch up.

The side of the building is a solid cinderblock wall, broken only by one small opening that might have been a vent of some sort. There are windows higher up, but they are narrow and sparsely distributed. Stairwell and elevator shafts, Simon reckons.

They round the corner to the back of the building. A patch of asphalt, cracked and pitted by years of frost heaves and the tough roots of weeds, once served as a parking lot. There is only one vehicle there now, though: a dirty white utility van up on blocks. There are no tires, nor is there a hood to cover the rust-orange engine. There is, however, a massive red swastika on the side.

And the sound of harsh laughter from within. A trickle of smoke leaks out of the ill-fitting back doors, sweet and pungent.

"Shit," Alise whispers, stopping short and slipping back around the corner. "Nazi skins. How the hell did Scotty get by without them seeing him?"

Simon assesses, just a quick look. "They're hot-boxing that piece of shit van, so that helps. We could probably get by without them noticing."

"You realize what would happen if you're wrong, eh? Hamilton's big, but the scene's pretty tight. They'd know me by sight. And you? Well, they ain't known for being all that tolerant."

"Cops, then! Scotty's in way over his head. Us, too."

Alise throws him a quizzical look, as if just noticing his eyes are different colours. "*Cops?* Jimmy told me you were kind of a bad ass not too many years ago. 'Ten-Bones,' right? I need you to find *that* guy, Simon. Kinda *now*. We'll find another way in." And she turns back the way they came.

"Fuck," Simon grumbles. But inside, something toys with the locks. His bones begin to hum.

IT DOESN'T TAKE HIM long. The ancient air conditioner, lying in a broken, weed-choked heap on the ground below the opening, provides enough of a boost for Scotty to hoist himself up and in. He drops blindly into the dank space on the other side, a sagging room heavy with the stink of mildew. There, squatting behind the remains of an old desk, Scotty waits for his eyes to adjust.

He isn't the first to use this means of egress—as his eyes acclimate to the dimness, he sees evidence of recent passage: new footprints in the old filth; cigarette butts that haven't yet acquired that weathered, wilted look; greasy fast food wrappers still smeared with condiments—untouched as of yet by the rats. They, too, have left signs of their passage. Mostly droppings and trails like whispers through the accumulated sediment, but also the tell-tale ammonia reek of cat urine from the feral hunters that stalk them. Scotty knows this from alleys, where many of his art supplies are scavenged.

Probably a whole bunch in here somewhere, he thinks.

Across the small room are the remains of a door, still clinging to the frame. A rusty filing cabinet, its bottom drawer pulled all the way open, leans at an angle. The cabinet's front corner has begun to sink into the floor, but the drawer props it up. On top of the cabinet is something angular and grey, like a frayed rag covering a small pile of thin sticks. Then it takes shape, the sharp taper of a beak. A long-dead pigeon. Above it, a framed photograph still clings to the wall: six men in identical shirts; one holds a bowling ball. Even from across the room, Scotty sees the fool's grin of the super, swagger immortalized in this one remaining relic.

I remember! Scotty looks on and around the desk for more personal effects, but nothing is discernable in the rubbish. *I remember him—he was always mean. He hurt me that day that—that he . . .*

But even this memory, like all memories of his childhood, is vague and muddled, buried under the heap of legalities, inquiries, car rides, strange bedrooms, nameless faces—the brutal and merciless and cumulative sequence of terrifying experiences that followed when he was discovered in that dark and cavernous basement, a little traumatized heap beside a poorly wrapped corpse.

Because it was the super who found him, clad in that very bowling shirt, swaggering in with that air of self-importance and indignant at the unexpected discovery. Scotty was beyond reach, though, comatose for all intents and purposes. The oafish lout gave the child a hearty poke with one meaty finger as he unwrapped the cover with the other hand.

And then he staggered back as if the filthy bundle were filled with vipers.

Anger wells up in Scotty, indignant fury for the cold indifference and petty cruelty of an adult toward a helpless child. He picks up a broken piece of brick and takes aim at the photograph—then stops.

No. No, this is better, he considers. *This place is perfect for that picture.*

A shrine, he means, complete with sacrificial bird left arbitrarily on the tilting altar. A tiny temple to the Petty God of Failure. Scotty places the broken brick reverently on the desk and crosses the room.

It's time, he thinks. *Time to find him again.*

The Furnace Boy. A good friend to have in the darkness.

He chooses the stairwell closest to the super's office. Not just because he won't have to cross the ruined lobby, but because it's closer to the furnace room. The heavy steel door to the stairwell is half open already, held in place by a thick carpet of rotting trash. Scotty steps gingerly as he crosses it, afraid of stirring up a rats' nest, and begins his decent.

"GOTTA BE THERE," ALISE says, pointing at the opening two metres up the wall.

"Yeah," Simon agrees. "Can't see how else he would have gotten in."

"There's gotta be more ways—always are."

Simon gestures back toward the weed-choked graveyard of a parking lot. "This building could have a gilded five-star entrance with a doorman and complimentary beer, but I'm not walking by that van full of white power assholes to find out."

Alise nods. "Yeah—me neither. I think we should get to—FUCK!"

Because out of nowhere, Jimmy appears.

"Damn it, Jimmy!" Alise hisses. "You scared the living shit outa us!"

But Jimmy just nods sagely, as if confirming something profound and unspoken, and signals for them to follow.

"Seriously, Jimmy!" Simon manages in a quivering whisper. "What the hell are you doing here?"

"Been here for a while," he says. "Quite a while, actually. I know a couple people in the area—asked them to let me know if they saw your car."

"We both got here, like, ten or fifteen minutes ago!" Alise snaps. "How the fuck could you—"

"I drove down here earlier today," Simon admits. "On my way to my office," he adds lamely.

"Right. So I set up shop not too far away. Figured it was only a matter of time until you brought Scotty home. I got Tribal with me, too. He's waiting inside."

Alise and Simon look at each other, a silent exchange. But Jimmy hears it anyway.

"Squat house 1-0-1: every tribe has its own access point."

"Meaning?" Simon asks.

"Meaning that this place is big enough for more than just the white lace skins I'm sure you noticed on your way to this point." Jimmy saunters along the perimeter of the building, Simon and Alise now in tow. He turns the corner and walks into a niche maybe four or five metres wide and three metres deep. A collapsing commercial dumpster is the primary occupant of the space, although smashed brick and shattered glass compete for second place. Broken pieces of wood pallets have also been collected together in a pile, along with slats from hurricane fences, fallen tree branches, and scraps of construction lumber.

"Firewood," Jimmy explains.

"And this other entrance?" Alise asks.

"The dumpster," Jimmy says, pointing at the rusting heap. "There's a hole rusted right through on the back side. The dumpster hides an old access door of some sort, but it's long since been kicked in."

Simon considers the implications of the climb and crawl he can't quite believe he's about to do. "Who uses this way in?"

Jimmy grows still, brooding. Then he starts forward toward the stack of concrete blocks piled up to make the climb in easier. "You wouldn't know him," he says quietly over his shoulder.

True enough, there's Tribal. He's nervous, that much is clear: he stands in the gloom of a moldering corridor, blade out. At his feet is a pile of old rags and bony limbs.

Jimmy, startled, points down at the heap. "Tribal, what the fuck did you do?!"

"Nothing!" Tribal says, waspishly. "I mean, I barely clipped him."

"*Barely?* He's out cold!"

"I swear to fuckin' Thor, Jimmy—he came around that corner and scared the shit right outa me. All I did was clip him and he dropped."

"The *knife*?" Jimmy snaps, pointing to the blade.

"Afterthought. Figured better have it out, eh? Seriously, he took a right hook, that's all."

Jimmy turns back to Simon and Alise apologetically. "This is why we can't go anywhere nice," he explains.

Simon kneels down beside the wretched figure, as does Jimmy. Together, they gently roll him over.

"*Fugh!* He's pretty ripe," Simon gags.

"And not really all that unconscious," adds Jimmy. "But he *is* high as a kite. He's fine—let's move. Scotty's this way, I think."

They move cautiously down the sagging corridor and around a corner. The air, still and fetid and alive with mold, has them all breathing in shallow gasps within minutes. Of them all, Jimmy struggles the hardest, his smoker's lungs protesting against undue exertion even under the best of circumstances.

Tribal pushes his way up front. "I'm leading—Sirius'd never let me live it down if some fuckin' hopped-up hobo jacked you from a doorway, Jimmy."

"I'll go next," Simon offers.

"Yeah . . . no offence, man, but I'd rather have Alise up here."

Simon's protest is lost in the shuffle as Alise, armed with a piece of rebar she snagged from inside the dumpster, silently files in behind Tribal.

Jimmy lays a reassuring hand on Simon's shoulder and whispers, "It's a good move, Ten-Bones."

"But—"

"You ever see that girl scrap?"

"Well, no, but—"

Jimmy coughs violently, trying his best to suppress the worst of it. "Look, man," he finally manages, "she's a punk bassist playing illegal warehouse shows and booze-can gigs. She's pretty handy."

THE STAIRWELL STINKS OF rot and mildew, a heavy fug that embraces Scotty in its invisible arms. It is also inky black—not so much as a glimmer reaches the basement. He can only shuffle forward, careful and disoriented steps in this half-forgotten labyrinth.

I shouldn't do this, he scolds himself. *I need light! A candle or something.*

But he still pads forward through the blackness as if compelled, pulled. Or perhaps pushed. With no more choice in the matter than a lonely cloud has in the late summer sky.

It is a world of sounds: the rhythmic plopping of water and sharp squeaks of rats, occasional scuffling, a terrifying clatter when he kicks an invisible can into an invisible wall; and a world of scents: ammonia and that musky stink so particular to rodents creep along the walls like ghostly tendrils, a complex tapestry of decay accompanies these, rot and mildew and feces and the old stale taste of vomit.

And something else. What is that? Something close and familiar. His skin crawls with the memory of it.

Something greasy and warm and heavy pushes by his ankle and Scotty leaps forward, frightened by the contact. But there is nothing ahead, no footing—he flails, arms flung outward, blind eyes stretched wide as he falls into a void.

Mop bucket—

It comes to him as he hits the invisible icy water below.

TRIBAL MAKES HIS WAY to the edge of the gaping doorway, holding a warning hand out to the others. If it weren't for the fight going on somewhere in the gutted apartment, their progress up the corridor would have been obvious—every footfall results in a squeaking protest from the warped and rotting floor. It's like walking on stale sponge.

Tribal glances around the corner into the dark recesses, just a quick look before pulling back. Within, the four of them hear a violent altercation between at least two fighters, a rhythmic thump of fists and kicks and heavy grunts. A woman wails away, a forlorn melody to the vicious beat, but other voices—all male—drown out her protests with encouragement.

Jimmy reaches forward to touch Tribal's shoulder and signals to the corridor wall opposite the doorway. WHITE POWER has been spray painted prominently on the decaying surface, along with a surprisingly good rendition of a pair of Doc Marten Gladiators. Each oxblood boot has twenty pieces of actual white hockey lace stretching from eyelet to eyelet, pushed into holes in the wall's surface.

The four of them retreat down the hallway and around a corner.

"Creative bastards," Alise hisses.

Simon, however, is clearly upset. He grabs at Jimmy's arm. "Look," he whispers, "this is getting outa control. We need to back out, find a phone, and call the cops."

"No cops," his three companions whisper back simultaneously.

Simon points down the dark corridor in the direction of the artwork. "Don't really wanna end up in a nest of skinheads!" he says in a vicious whisper.

"They ain't real skinheads," Tribal mumbles. "Just think they are."

"*Seriously?* I don't care about the fucking *semantics*, Tribal! I just want to find Scotty!"

Tribal shrugs. "Then c'mon—cops can't help him, Ten-Bones. He's been in here way too long as is." And he starts forward again, followed by Jimmy.

Alise turns to face Simon, cupping the side of his head with her hand. She holds his frightened eyes in hers. "Tribal's right," she says. "I get it—this seems insane. But shitholes like this . . . We're running outa time and so is he."

"Someone's getting the living shit kicked out of him in there—what if it's Simon?"

"It isn't. Two fighters, and each one has money on him."

Simon cocks his head, unconvinced. "How do you *know*?"

"Look, Simon," Alise says calmly, "Scotty's no scrapper and I know a close fight when I hear one. Trust me. Now, let's go." And she slips around the corner after Tribal and Jimmy.

"Fuck," he mumbles to himself. "I'll get fired for sure for this stunt." An eruption of cheers and whistling explodes from the recesses of the occupied apartment just as he reaches the doorway. *Assuming*, he adds silently, *that I don't get killed first.*

But then Alise emerges from the darkness of the corridor ahead, grabs Simon by the shirt, and hauls him into the shadows beyond the opening. Jimmy and Tribal wait a couple of metres ahead.

"Which way?" Tribal whispers to Jimmy, and then he knocks over a small stack of empty beer bottles hidden in the darkest shadows—they fall with a clatter.

"What the fuck was that?" booms a voice from inside the apartment.

Jimmy waves his long-fingered hand like a maître d' toward the welcoming darkness. "That way, I'd suggest. And sharpish."

EVERYTHING IS INVISIBLE: THE water, the walls, the floating debris that teases his numb hands as he clutches at it blindly. Scotty can't swim.

Everything is silent: beneath the black surface of the water, his eyes, wide open, might as well be made of stone. His limbs, though—they thrash about madly, like bits of ragged ribbon in the wind. He sinks.

Everything is peaceful: *I will die here*, a part of him muses. *In the blackness. I will die because I went looking for a shadow.*

But then.

A light from above, beautiful and multifaceted. It cuts through the black water, like a lantern fish or the porthole of a descending bathysphere. With the last of his failing strength, he reaches for it.

And finds the powerful grip of a determined hand.

Scotty is hauled from the cold blackness and onto solid concrete. Above him bobs the light, an ancient flashlight held by an ancient hand.

"I got ya, boy," the flashlight owner rasps. "Prodigal son. Heh heh! I got ya."

Scotty, still in shock, looks up as the light catches the ruined mouth, the sallow skin, the yellowed eyes.

"Welcome home," Cottonmouth says with a hideous smile.

NO NEED FOR CAUTION now, just speed. And luck.

Tribal lets Jimmy take the lead, hoping that whatever psychedelic frequency guides him infallibly through life will tune him in here as well. *And,* Tribal adds silently, *I'm of more use in the back. If things come down to it.*

Close behind Jimmy are Alise and Simon, pounding recklessly down the half-rotten floor of the nearly lightless corridor. Door-less apartments or offices maybe allow just enough light in to avoid crashing headlong into a rusty shopping cart, wheels up in surrender, or into a thick sheet of dirty tattered plastic that drapes from the ceiling like a ghost ship's ruined sail. Dodge and weave.

Then a sharp turn, hurdling over a solid lump draped in rotten cloth stretched across the hallway. Simon catches the shape of a swollen foot jutting out of the lump's end, *A man!* he thinks and then he's over and gone.

Behind them, angry shouting and the thump of steel-toed boots on a sagging floor—at least four, probably more like six, Tribal reckons. For a brief moment he wishes his brother were with them, but then shakes the thought loose angrily. Wouldn't make a difference, not with these odds.

Tribal spins around the corner after the others and plants a heavy boot mid-lump, eliciting a surprised gasp from the prone figure. Up ahead, he sees the shadowy shapes of Simon and Alise disappear to the left; Jimmy appears in their place, gesturing to him wildly—a door? Another corridor?

A stairwell, but one with a serviceable fire door still intact. And a little light leaking in from a vent slot in the wall above them. In he goes and spins around to help Jimmy secure the door—a deadbolt, of all things! But why?

Jimmy is also at a loss to explain it.

Then there is a howl of agony from down the corridor, a cacophony of violent yelling, and more cries of pain.

"Guess they found that junkie," Tribal says.

"Shhh." Jimmy crouches by the bolted door, as if there were a porthole in it. He sweats with the effort it takes to suppress the coughing fit that struggles to escape, like an angry djinn from a bottle. Tribal stands his ground, knife in one hand, the other held out to silence Alise and Simon who have stopped on the landing below. The boots clump toward them and keep going. No one even tries the door.

"That was weird," Tribal whispers.

But Jimmy gasps when he tries to answer. It takes him several long minutes to re-establish control, eyes closed and pursuing some sort of stoner's mantra. When his breath returns to the simple wheezing of before, he opens his eyes and brushes the bolt with his fingertips as if reading braille.

"This door must always be locked," he says. "Why else wouldn't they try it?"

Tribal looks at the bolt again. "Why the fuck was it open just a few minutes ago, then, eh?"

"Because," says a voice that sounds of rust, drifting up from the blackness of the descending stairwell, "I opened it fer ya!"

The four of them spin to face him as he climbs out of the blackness on stiff legs. "Cottonmouth!" Tribal and Jimmy spit out simultaneously.

The old man contemplates them both in return with dim, complicated eyes. Then he leers at Tribal. "Reckonin', boy! I told ya. She ain't ever wrong. *Ever.*"

Tribal's eyes harden and his grip tightens on the knife's handle. Jimmy, though—he looks at the wild old man as if for the first time. Without breaking eye contact with Cottonmouth, Jimmy lays a calming hand on Tribal's shoulder.

Simon and Alise, closest to this ragged apparition, stay stock-still. But Jimmy knows Alise well enough—if she feels threatened by proximity, she'll react. And beneath that aura Simon wraps himself in, Ten-Bones still lurks. Jimmy breaks the silence.

"You said you opened the door for us. Why?"

Cottonmouth glares up at Jimmy, a fierce and challenging gaze—but Jimmy meets it, unblinking. After a dozen heartbeats, the ancient shoulders sink and the rheumy eyes soften. "Need ya," he says softly.

"For what?" Alise asks. The jagged point of the rebar sinks, coming to a rest beside one of her oxblood eight-holes.

"Tuh help with the boy," the old man replies.

"'The boy'?" Simon repeats. "Do you know where Scotty is?"

But Cottonmouth just turns and begins his stiff descent into the blackness.

"Follow," he says.

The haggard old man has a dim flashlight. It isn't much, but it's better than the otherwise impenetrable blackness of the abandoned building's bowels. He leads the four of them along a narrow corridor choked with debris; tattered wisps of rope hang like the ghosts of gallows' nooses from the rusted-out pipes above them. The air is still and cold and thick with the septic soup of pollutants that have claimed this realm as their own. Diesel, corroded iron, mold, decay—the air they breathe is wet with it all. And heavy with the knowledge that, above them, sits a hundred thousand tons of condemned building.

"Where we going?" Tribal asks.

"Told ya. Tuh the boy. Not far now." Cottonmouth gestures vaguely ahead with the dim light.

The corridor turns to the left, away from a gaping darkness reeking of mildew and something dead—angry squeaks of rats fighting over it fill the invisible chasm. The pale beam of the flashlight briefly catches the crumpled edge of a greyish-white surface within, but that is all.

Alise hisses sharply and swats at the frayed tangle of wires she just walked into. "Shit! Jimmy, Tribal—use your lighters or something! That flashlight's about as useful as a tit on a fish."

"Almost there," Jimmy says.

"How the fuck d'you know that?" Alise snaps.

Jimmy's silhouette shrugs. "Just feel it, I guess."

And he's right: Cottonmouth guides them around a corner to the right and then stops at a rusty sliding door, half open and corroded permanently in place. Beyond the opening is a cavernous room, lit vaguely by the warm light of an old kerosene lantern set on a metal oil drum between two chairs. On one chair rests a stack of folded newspapers; on the other, wrapped up in a filthy quilt and shivering noticeably, is Scotty.

"Fuck me," Alise mutters as she pushes her way through, descending the five corrugated steel steps that lead to the concrete floor. She weaves through the clutter—fallen pipes, broken cement blocks, decades of trash that somehow ended up here—until she reaches him. Simon picks his way across the cavern in her wake. Beyond the small group now gathered around the lantern looms the dead machinery of the past.

"Like some sort of fossilized alien shipwreck," Jimmy muses.

Tribal ignores Jimmy and turns on Cottonmouth. "What happened to him? To Scotty, I mean?"

Cottonmouth's craggy face looks so ancient in the lantern light that Tribal imagines that pallid flesh suddenly crumbling away like dried mud. The old man's eyes, too—feared by so many, like his words. But now.

But now.

"Found him," that wreckage of a mouth says simply. "Fished him up from the sump hole. He fell in." Then his gnarled hands begin to worry themselves and he turns to face Tribal. "Help him—you got tuh. Help him get what he come fer." And then he, too, hobbles stiffly down the stairs.

Tribal and Jimmy join Alise and Simon. Cottonmouth shuffles away into the shadows about seven or eight metres to their left, a peripheral ghost for the present.

"We gotta get him the fuck outa here," Alise says. Tribal nods in agreement, reaching for one of Scotty's bony arms still buried in the tattered old patchwork blanket.

"No." This from Simon, who stays Tribal's hand with his own. "Scotty needs to go home first."

Tribal glares at Simon. "Are you fucking *kidding* me?"

Jimmy, closest to the other chair, picks up one of the newspapers and holds it up to the lantern. *Child's Remains Incomplete*, it proclaims. Just like every other paper in the pile.

"Simon's right," Jimmy says softly. "We aren't here by chance. Scotty needs to find something up there. I'm right, aren't I, Scotty?"

And Scotty, weary-eyed, looks up at Jimmy. Directly.

Yes.

Then Jimmy gives the yellowed newspaper a gentle shake, and out falls a child's drawing on paper brittle with age—a drawing of a smiling boy in a red shirt holding hands with a black silhouette.

27

SHE AIN'T EXACTLY LIGHT on her feet, Tribal appraises, *but she's brave as fuck. I can see why Simon's into her.*

Above him, maybe a half-dozen steps up, Alise pauses to listen before stepping onto the eleventh-floor landing. It's a miracle they've made it this far, and the three of them know it. Scotty follows Tribal, staying just within arm's reach.

"We're good," she whispers, and steps up onto the landing. The steel door, already ajar, opens with a creak as she pulls.

THE DECISION WAS SIMPLE: Jimmy and Simon would stay to learn what they could from the mad old recluse, while Tribal and Alise escorted Scotty to his old apartment. Only Simon objected, but Jimmy handled it.

"Look, brother, Cottonmouth . . . he's got a—a *way* with our kind. Evil juju, you know? But you . . . Man, you're from another world."

Simon had smiled despite himself. "*I'm* from another world? Jimmy, you're—"

"Yeah, yeah, yeah. But he *knows* things. About me, Tribal, all of us. Probably even Alise, but maybe not. Don't matter. He's figured each one of us out and he can . . ." Jimmy paused, his eyes growing distant with something. Memory, maybe. Then he seemed to find the words he wanted. "Hard to explain. He gets inside your head, like his voice is made of earwigs or something. They crawl around, poisoning whatever they touch."

"He hasn't said anything much since he found us," Simon pointed out.

Jimmy's face grew troubled. "I know—but he *can*. He doesn't know you. And there's a more important piece to this."

"What's that?"

"You know *him*. You know about his past."

Simon shrugged. "So? And how the hell do you know that I found that stuff out?"

"Alise told me you found it in a box—his name and things. Ten-Bones, that shit's fucking *totemic*! You gotta stay here with me. I *need* you."

And that was the end of it. Jimmy gave Alise and Tribal an unnecessary word of caution before they left the furnace room, though.

"Not a sound—we stirred up that nest of vipers right proper."

"More like a nest of wasps," Alise had said with a humourless smile.

Jimmy smiled, too, nodding.

"Don't let them find you. Hide if you have to—don't fight. Tribal, you listening?"

But Tribal was already heading toward the exit, Scotty in tow.

Tribal and Alise led Scotty back up the stairwell to the ground floor, leaving the heavy steel door unlocked. A calculated risk; pragmatic, though—if no one checked it in the heat of that chase, the denizens of this building must know that it is always bolted. Just another piece of wall, as far as they're concerned. The short jaunt to the main lobby was easy enough, the three of them moving like shadows, and then to the stairs that accessed every floor above.

The eleventh floor is a sagging disaster. To the left, the corridor has collapsed into the floor below, leaving apartment doors suspended above the wreckage. Without a ladder or serious acrobatics, those doors will remain closed.

"What number did Simon give us?" Tribal asks.

"Eleven twenty-six," Alise whispers. "It's to the right, I think."

"Well, that'll help, eh? I ain't a fuckin' mountain climber."

Scotty has grown anxious behind them, craning his neck to see down the shadowy hallway. A few doors are open or missing, letting in dim glimmers of daylight from the apartment windows beyond. Alise reaches back to brush his scraggly hair from his face.

"It's okay, Scotty—we're almost there."

Scotty freezes at her touch, but he doesn't get that look of disappearance or detachment; instead, he pushes forward and pads down the mold-blackened carpet and into the shadows.

"Guess he's leading," Tribal says.

Scotty takes them down the hall and then turns left at the intersection where the elevators are. The left elevator door is closed; the right one, however, is jammed open. Tribal leans over the yawning pit, looking down the shaft, but he staggers back almost immediately due to the intense stench.

"You alright?" Alise asks, glancing back at him.

"Holy fuck—you think this building stinks, try that elevator shaft."

"Cheers, I'm good. C'mon—Scotty's stopped at a door up there."

1126. HOME.

The door is closed. There is a large black letter spray-painted onto its surface, a "Y." Other letters are on the wall to the left of his door, along with an arrow pointing farther down the hall. A message. Scotty doesn't care.

Home.

The word floats aimlessly, unmoored. He tries it again.

Home. I lived here.

Better—the word takes on substance, weight. It sinks until it is within reach. Scotty touches the doorknob tentatively, exploring its surface. He lays his other hand against the door itself. Then he grasps the knob and turns.

"Scotty, wait!" Alise runs toward him, Tribal just behind her. Too late—he's already inside, door closing behind him. Click.

Behind Scotty, the door shakes in its frame. Alise pleads and Tribal curses, but it doesn't matter. Some things cannot be shared. He scans his dismal surroundings—nothing is the same. It has the look of tragedy, but of someone else's: unrecognizable furniture, trash bags bloated with a million unsolvable mysteries, kitchen cabinets thrown open to reveal a few grungy plastic cups and broken plates, a rotting mattress in the middle of the living room. Beside it are the stubs of candles, cold wax congealed on the few remaining sticks of the cheap parquet floor. Behind the candles is a cracked fishbowl half filled with strange palm-sized cubes.

Someone else lived here after us. Maybe a lot of someones.

Then he notices the couch jutting out of the pile of garbage bags—the same one that was there when they first moved in. It has decayed down to its skeleton, but the ragged remains of plaid upholstery still cling stubbornly to its corners like desiccated flesh. For years, Scotty stared at that ugly pattern. His little cot sat behind it.

One of the garbage bags squirms. Too much for maggots, Scotty can tell even from where he stands by the stained ruin of a mattress. And there isn't that tell-tale stench of decaying food—just the cloying funk of unwashed clothes and cigarette smoke.

Rats' nest, he knows, and shudders. He needs to get back there, behind the couch. *But maybe I could look around first. Everything is . . . is so . . .*

So utterly unsalvageable, so irreparably ruined, so unrecognizable that Scotty can't help it: the tears slide down his wan cheeks like they did outside on the sidewalk an hour or two ago when he first faced this monstrous carcass of a building. And now here, in what might be (had he the words) an antechamber of sorts to an immense and complex tomb, he weeps for that lost little boy trapped forever in silence—a child left to squat on bony haunches in the neglect and filth of a tiny kitchen, to play listlessly with a broken toy truck he scavenged from the weeds in the park, a child left at night behind a wall of sour-smelling plaid, curled up on a mildewed old cot and watching the fluctuating shadows creep and recede across the ceiling. For that child, sleep was accompanied by the muffled laugh tracks and alien voices of the blasting television in the apartment above—it was on day and night, a mysterious litany of unrecognizable sounds until the final high-pitched hum of the test pattern. Then the boy could sleep.

Scotty weeps as he walks, shuffling into the narrow space that separates the galley kitchen from the tiny washroom. In the kitchen, the appliances are gone, as is the sink. A grimy and battered light blue cooler occupies the space where the fridge once was, like a sad and stubborn joke. Its lid is scarred with blackened burns where cigarettes have been butted out, and the entire peeling linoleum floor is covered with rat droppings, empty tin cans, used syringes, and deteriorating plastic bags.

He turns to peer into the shadows that cloak the washroom. Melted candle wax hangs like stalactites from every possible surface: from the top of the rusting medicine cabinet and down the smashed remains of the mirror; along the rim of the tiny vanity and into the sink; across the top of the toilet tank, although the bowl itself is nothing but porcelain rubble; and along the length of the bathtub, where wax has pooled along the edge and the floor like caulking, and down the inside wall as well. A frozen river of waxy white and red stretches from a dozen points, like tributaries, to form a single marbled road of wax to the tub's drain. Most of the fake tile board that once covered the walls of the tiny room has either fallen off or been torn down. The ceiling above the toilet bulges downward like a mold-covered tumour.

One door left. It is closed, strangely intact, at the end of the six-foot-long hall between kitchen and washroom. His mother's bedroom.

Behind him, the front door explodes inward. He spins in alarm, but it's Tribal.

"The *fuck*, Scotty!" he barks. "This ain't the time or place to get all touchy about privacy!"

"Jesus, Tribal," Alise hisses as she follows him in, "keep it *down*. That kick was loud as shit! You don't gotta yell on top of it!"

Tribal is furious, though. *And scared*, Scotty notes. He can see it in his bravado strutting, his clenched fists. Then it hits him.

He's scared for me! He looks again at the two of them as they take stock of their surroundings. *For me, not for himself!* He pulls the back of a hand over each wet eye and turns to face the closed bedroom door.

"If you got something to do," Tribal says in a tight voice, "now's the time."

"Yeah," Alise agrees. "We gotta get outa here."

I know. Scotty turns his back on the closed door and heads over to the couch. He can avoid touching any of it—the rotting upholstery, the garbage bags—if he moves a bent and battered heap of TV tables out of the way first. Alise seems to anticipate his intentions and moves to help, but then that garbage bag squirms again. She leaps backward.

"Goddamnit!"

"What?" Tribal demands, knife now back in hand.

Alise waves him off, though. "Nothing! Just—rats, I guess. Nesting in whatever's in or under the bags on the couch, eh?"

"Oh," he says. But he moves back toward the front door. Tribal hates rats. Instead, he looks down at the mattress and the fishbowl of cubes. One curious boot tips the bowl over to spill the contents across the floor. He steps on one of the grey blocks, and it gives. Sponge. A full sponge, the sort used to wash cars, is half concealed by cobwebs and dust close by. Tribal sneers in disgust.

Cautiously, Alise clutches one of the tarnished brassy legs of the tangled pile of TV tables and gives it a tentative tug. It shifts toward her, too intertwined to move as anything other than a single mass. She gives it another tug. It's light, but she'd rather not aggravate the nest with sudden movement in its immediate vicinity. Small miracle Tribal's stunt with the door didn't trigger them.

"Hey, Alise."

"Busy, Tribal—what do you want?"

"You, uh, need some makeshift birth control? Lil' STD protection?" He kicks a cube of sponge in her direction.

She glances over and then shakes her head. "You're a real sensitive prick, you know that? Like your brother."

The contorted pile of bent metal is out far enough—Scotty slips in behind the couch and squats next to the mold-black wall where his cot once stood. He pries at a rusty vent almost lost in the shadows that collect there like the other dust and rubbish.

And then they hear it: voices down the corridor.

"Shit," Tribal growls. He glances around, picks up a wooden table leg, and moves behind the kicked-in door.

Alise crouches low, but Scotty still works at the vent. "Hold up!" she whispers at him.

He can't. It's loose, almost free—he pulls at it as quietly as he can, and then it gives with a scraping squeak. Nothing too audible, and certainly not from the hallway, but Alise cringes anyway. Scotty reaches into the blackness and gropes around. Then he finds it—he gasps, a quick intake accompanied by widened eyes.

There you are! He withdraws his arm, something concealed in his soot-covered fist.

The voices are closer now—slurred and deep. At least three, but drunk. Behind the door, Tribal readies himself; Alise clutches the rebar like a spear and hardens herself as well. Scotty, as far as Alise can tell, has slipped into some part of himself, mesmerized by his find.

"In here," one of the voices says, and in he staggers. Heavy-set, shaved head, wearing a bomber jacket and white laced fourteen-hole Doc Martens, he holds a mickey of whiskey in one hand and what appears to be a rusty machete in the other. A skinny punk with a swastika on the back of his leather jacket stumbles in behind him. Skinny neon green spikes cover his head like protrusions on a sea mine.

"No one in here since that fuckin' whore OD'd, like, last month, eh?" the punk says.

"Then why the fuckin' door kicked open, retard?" the bigger one says. "Where's Paul?"

If the punk has an answer, it's lost in the moment: Tribal pivots around the door swinging the table leg hard at the skinhead's meaty face, but he ducks and the wood clips the top of his skull, peeling back a heavy flap of scalp—boxer's instinct saves him from the full collision. Blood wells up immediately, though, pouring in a torrent down his face.

Startled, the Nazi punk stumbles backward, tripping over the rotting remains of the mattress and landing backward onto the glass fishbowl, the dull crunch followed immediately by a howl of pain. Alise bursts out from behind the couch and brings the rebar down in a blurring arc onto one of the punk's skinny shins, snapping the bone. He screams.

Blood-blind, the skin snarls and swings back at Tribal, but the rusty blade ricochets off the edge of the broken door. The skin's no quitter—Tribal sees that clearly. Dodging to the skin's left, Tribal swings again, this time connecting with the outside of his knee. The table leg shivers with the impact as the skin's leg buckles under him and he crashes to the floor with a grunt.

"What the fuck's going on in—" Paul, they presume, stops mid-sentence as he surveys from the doorway. About Tribal's size, the white power skin struggles between two finite choices. Alise, however, makes the choice for all of them: she drops the steel bar, grabs the squirming garbage bag with both hands, and hurls it at the newcomer. He leaps back out of instinct, but the bag tears open as it arcs across the room and a shower of brown rats hits him anyway.

Tribal, wild-eyed, jumps over the prone skinhead toward the newcomer, but he crashes heavily to the floor—*No quitter*, Tribal thinks; the skin has his ankle. He kicks viciously with his held leg, hoping to loosen the grip. Which probably saves him from most of the machete: it arcs down on Tribal's already moving leg and glances off his calf. Tribal barks out in pain.

Alise watches the one named Paul recover from the rats and weigh in. He pulls out a switchblade, reckless fury barely in check because Alise has recovered the rebar.

Tribal kicks free, spoiling the second machete swing—rolling to his left, he brings the wood down heavily on the prone skin's elbow. He grunts as the machete clatters to the floor.

Paul steps toward Tribal, but Alise stalks forward, steel bar back for the swing.

Tribal gets to his feet, narrowed eyes watching Paul's. *Worth a try*, he thinks, and shouts over his shoulder at the closed door behind him.

"John! Pete! Get out here and kill this fuck!"

Which does it for Paul. He turns and bolts.

"Fuck! Now what?" Alise yells.

"Go!" Tribal barks. "Before he gets to the stairs!"

Alise clears the room in a heartbeat, Docs pounding on the sagging underlayment.

SCOTTY HAS FORGOTTEN.

To hold his breath, that is: instead, he sees it playfully weaving across the garbage bag hill, along the counter top, behind ruined walls. It laughs its shadowy laugh as it capers.

Come here, Scotty says firmly.

NO! CATCH ME.

I can't. Not here.

ARE THOSE YOUR FRIENDS?

Scotty hesitates, unsure of what to say.

IF THEY ARE, YOU SHOULD HELP THEM.

I'm helping you, he says. *Can . . . can you help?*

Laughter, cobweb quiet—no louder than a spider's footfall.

Then, *YES.*

Scotty's breath slips out the door, following Alise down the hall.

"I FUCKIN' SEEN YOU, you fuckin' skid piece-of-shit!" The white power skin, now cradling his elbow in a meaty fist, glares through the blood at Tribal from the ground. "We're gonna hunt you!"

"Yeah," Tribal says. Casually, though, as if agreeing on the weather. He uses the table leg for support now. The wound is shallow, but it throbs and blood has already seeped into his boot. The machete lies forgotten amongst the rubbish.

The Nazi punk isn't handling the pain well, nearly unconscious. The surge of adrenaline might have distributed whatever chemical cocktail he's on at an accelerated pace, though. This is a possibility. Tribal turns instead to Scotty and gestures.

"C'mon—we gotta go."

Scotty, eyes caught in the refuse at his feet, shuffles forward. He looks back, though, at the closed door at the end of the short hall and hesitates.

"Seriously, man—*now!*" Tribal grabs his arm and pulls.

Stay closed then, a part of him intones.

Stay closed. Goodbye, mama.

TRIBAL AND SCOTTY SEE Alise's dim silhouette at the end of the corridor, standing just inside the open space where the elevators are. Her mohawk is more of a dark purple than pink in this light, and her shoulders heave with exertion. Tribal closes the distance as fast as his leg will let him.

"You catch that fuckin' guy?" Tribal asks.

Alise doesn't answer. She just points at the yawning hole of the right-hand elevator shaft, then down to the floor in front of her. Part of the blackish-red carpet, rotten and slimy, has torn loose—a long strip of it, in fact, that ends in a bunched-up mound in front of the shaft's threshold.

"He slid," she says finally. "He got to here and tried to cut the corner, but he slid. Right into the shaft."

Tribal stares at the blackness of the opening. "Holy fuck," he says.

Scotty, too—he watches the shadows inside that gaping darkness and feels a part of it watching him back.

Did you do this? Did you?

But the darkness says nothing.

"C'mon," Tribal says. "Gotta get back to Simon and Jimmy." He limps heavily down the corridor toward the stairs.

"Shit, Tribal—you're bleeding!"

"Yeah, Alise, I know. Hurts like fuck, too, so let's get going, eh?"

But Alise looks back at the elevators.

"Not your fuckin' fault," Tribal says. "Like you said, he slipped. Shit luck. For him, not us. Now, if it's not too much trouble . . ." And he gestures down the hall toward the steel door to the stairs.

28

ALMOST FORTY METRES BELOW, Simon surveys the wreckage in the cata-
comb-like sub-basement, this undercroft for the interred machinery of a
dead building. Its sprawling skeletal remains rust away quietly, the silence
interrupted only by the incessant plopping of invisible drops of water or
the squeaks of indigent rats.

Jimmy, stone-still and brow-furrowed, stands beside one of the antiquated oil drums. He seems to be contemplating the ooze that leaks from
its compromised seams, but it is hard to tell in the dim lantern light. *And,*
Simon thinks, *where the hell is our goddamn host, Norman?*

Then, as if summoned, Cottonmouth shuffles into the weak glow. He
looks at them with a queer expression—perplexed, or maybe with eyes that
see something else altogether. A different time, or a different pair of people
in front of him. He wheezes as he breathes, inhaling in unsteady gasps and
exhaling until a hideous rattle echoes in his sinewy chest. *Like he's made of
hollow wood,* Simon thinks.

"Help me," he finally says in that ancient rusty voice. "Help me with the
boy."

Simon looks at Jimmy in confusion, but some terrible understanding
begins to bloom in his companion's strange eyes. Neither Simon nor Jimmy
move.

"Scotty's gone upstairs," Simon finally offers. "Only us here."

Cottonmouth turns his haunting gaze on Simon, eyes that seem to pierce through to the core of memory itself. He points back toward the shadowy corner he emerged from.

"We ain't alone. Come help with the boy."

Simon looks over Cottonmouth's shoulder at the inky blackness, and then at Jimmy. But Simon's enigmatic companion—eyes closed tightly— shakes his head slowly, sadly. His narrow shoulders slope as if under a burden; one long-fingered hand rests on the rusty surface of a barrel. "Of course," he whispers. "Of course."

Simon sees it then, the similarity. Not of blood, but of fellowship—as if the rag-and-bone scarecrow still half concealed in shadow were the Ghost of Jimmy Future. *As if they share some kind of subterranean worldview, or see the same kind of visions*, he thinks. Clarity, sudden and sharp, stabs at Simon—he knows that Jimmy sees it, too: his own dark destiny of dust and rust and other dreamscapes; of reading signs and sigils for a handful of coins; of clawing his way blindly through the blackness between Visions.

A forlorn and forgotten traveller without a destination.

Simon crosses the short distance to where the old man waits. "What boy?" he asks softly.

But Cottonmouth's thin lips press together until there is nothing but a tight line in his leathery face, his cloudy eyes challenging Simon's fiercely. They are hard to hold, those eyes—rheumy and milky and ancient, partly concealed behind the loose and leathery skin of his eyelids, like half-de-flated sacks. Below his eyes are heavy bloated blue-grey bags, veiny and grime-coated.

But Simon doesn't flinch. "Norman," he says gently, "what boy?"

Cottonmouth breathes in sharply, a sudden gasp, and staggers. Now tears well up in those wild eyes, slipping silently down his ruin of a face and leaving runnels in the filth. "Help me," he pleads, pointing back at the darkness with a trembling hand. "The boy, he's—"

But a distant wailing scream followed by a thunderous crash makes them all jump in terror.

ALL THE WAY DOWN the gloomy descent from the eleventh floor, Scotty watches the shadows.

The darkest ones, that is, the places he'd be most comfortable. He dances and somersaults, capering alongside Scotty, who now brings up the rear. Alise walks ahead of him, but she has folded inward on herself—Scotty knows this by body language alone, reading it as clearly as others might a headline.

You didn't do anything, he says to her back. *It was me—I asked him to help.* And then to the shadow, *You did it, didn't you? It was you.*

The darkness hesitates momentarily in its playfulness. A coy shrug, maybe. Something else. Chagrin. Then it dances along merrily once more.

Scotty smiles in spite of his misgivings. He looks again at Alise's back, then lets out a sigh. *Nothing to be done about it now.*

NO, the shadows confirm.

And now what? I found it. Scotty shows his closed fist to the darkness. *But I don't want you to go away forever!*

WE'RE TOGETHER NOW. WE'LL GO TO THE FURNACE ROOM TOGETHER. ONE MORE TIME.

"What the hell was that noise?" Simon demands as soon as the three of them enter the furnace room.

Tribal shrugs. "Which one?"

"The scream and the crash—sounded like a goddamn car wreck!"

"Oh," Tribal says. "*That* noise. That was Paul. Paul fell down the elevator shaft."

"He *what*?"

"Relax, Simon! He slipped—we didn't do it."

"Is he *dead*? How the fuck did it happen?!"

Jimmy emerges from the shadows to the left. "Did he belong to that nest we stirred up?"

Tribal nods.

"Then they'll be a little more aggressive in their search. You locked the door behind you, I assume?"

"Yeah," Alise says, haunted and hollow, "I did." She refuses to make eye contact with any of them.

At the sight of her, Simon bites down hard on the storm of words that swarm in his mouth like locusts, swallowing them back; instead, he takes stock of Alise and then Scotty as best he can in the unreliable lantern glow of this place.

Alise moves woodenly, looking ahead and downward blankly. Shock, Simon figures, but not severe. He takes a step toward her but stops himself almost immediately. Right now, she needs some breathing room—whatever happened up there will have to wait.

Scotty, though. He stands at the top of the rusty metal landing, one hand wrapped tightly around the decayed and pitted railing like a wayward sailor clinging to the gunnel to steady himself against a tempestuous sea. His eyes, alive in the lamplight, consume everything in this cavernous wasteland—machinery and mortar, darkness and decay.

Cottonmouth looks up at Scotty.

"You find it?" the old man asks, voice shaking.

Scotty holds up the closed fist of his other hand. And opens it.

Even in the murky half-light of this grotto, they can make out the small coal-blackened shape of the little bone.

Cottonmouth lets out a sob of laughter through his ruined smile. "Bring it," he whispers. "Bring it to Tommy. I got all the rest." Then he turns and shuffles into the gloom.

Scotty descends and follows, his face a serene mask except for the wide eyes. The others watch him pass before falling in, pulled along as if by a current. Or an undertow Jimmy follows last.

Dusty cobwebs still clog the corners of this place, but it seems that Cottonmouth's comings and goings have long since swept them away from the narrow path they now walk.

Concealed in the blackness are several more old oil drums, their toxic contents leaking slowly everywhere. Jimmy suppresses a coughing fit as they enter the thick of the fumes; the entire sub-basement reeks of it, but here against the masonry of the foundation the stench seems to hang like an evil fog.

The light of the lantern far behind them is weak; their eyes slowly adjust, though, and the amorphous shadows become shapes: a trio of pipes still bolted by brackets to the masonry; the remains of several broken chairs, heaped up like the empty exoskeleton of some monstrous beetle; rotten mounds of trash bags stuffed with oily rags; tattered remains of old insulation. Eventually, they face a deeper blackness—a gaping hole in the wall. Smashed blocks and mortar lie in a heap to the hole's right like a concrete cairn. Cottonmouth stops beside the opening and fumbles momentarily with something in his hand.

It is the same dim flashlight with which he led them from the stairwell through the pitch-black corridors to this furnace room. Its beam, a faltering and sickly yellow, falls in shaky fits upon the jagged edges of the hole before resting upon the sooty alcove beyond.

There is still coal in the old grotto, settled now into an undulating bed of black facets that catch the dull light. Upon the coal's surface is a small, ancient grey woolen blanket, spread out carefully and lined with a few simple toys—a cork gun, a yo-yo, an old metal army truck, a moth-eaten Raggedy Andy. A broken model airplane. A toy six-shooter in its toy holster. A few pieces of train track and a boxcar. All toys of a bygone age.

Surrounding the blanket is the wreckage of eight wire fish sculptures, each one opened up and missing the smaller fetal figure inside. But they, too, are here—lying beside the hollow fish, each of the eight figures, headless.

And in the middle of the blanket is a heap of coal-black bones, little skull resting on top.

Tommy.

Eight small pieces are in front of the bone heap, reclaimed at last from their strange vessels where they were quietly placed by quiet hands, and then taken out into an indifferent city to watch over the wretched, the defenceless.

Cottonmouth pulls out the ninth piece—the vertebra in its tissue paper pall—from his pocket. The paper is still soggy, emerging from Scotty's own pocket and handed over after he was rescued from the invisible water. Payment in kind. With a withered hand, he places it with the others.

Jimmy, voice strangely distant, turns to the old man.

"Now what? Now that you have him—have Tommy—what will you do?"

"A boy needs his pa," the old man says.

Scotty feels the weight of the darkness gather around him. He looks down at the small black bone in his hand, the tenth, his last link to his oldest friend.

He found you, even the pieces that the men took away.

A GAME. HE FOUND ME. PIECE BY PIECE.

Where did they hide you?

IN A DIFFERENT PLACE. IN A COLD WHITE BASEMENT. HE TOOK ME AWAY ONE NIGHT.

I . . . I didn't know. That he was looking. I gave you to sad people, the ones who needed you the most.

I KNOW. I PLAYED WITH THEM. SOMETIMES.

Scotty worries the little piece of bone with his fingers, afraid of his next question. For so long, he has hidden the Furnace Boy away in his thin lungs—a playful shadow trapped again and again in the narrow cage within him. His only true companion. Still, he must know.

Will you go away now? Will you leave me?

I WILL SLEEP.

But—but will I see you again?

NO.

I'll be alone!

NO. YOU WILL NOT BE ALONE.

But—

FAITH. HAVE FAITH.

Scotty takes a deep breath. He reaches in, carefully placing the last piece with the others. Withdrawing his pale hand, he releases the breath slowly.

Goodbye.

GOODBYE.

Cottonmouth retrieves a tattered black plastic bag from behind one of the oil barrels and gently places it in Scotty's oblivious hands.

"Take this," Cottonmouth says softly, handing the weak flashlight to Jimmy. "This, too," handing over an old brown key. "Lead 'em out."

Jimmy hesitates, but he takes the proffered gifts and, head bowed, retraces his steps back toward the entrance to the furnace room. Tribal, profoundly quiet, follows.

Scotty stands there in the gloom, too sad to even weep. Alise gently takes his thin arm and falls in behind Tribal. Only Simon remains, standing vigil beside the old man for a moment longer. He places his strong young hand on the ancient bony shoulder for a heartbeat. Then he turns and leaves as well.

They walk in silence, not questioning Jimmy when he pauses momentarily at a juncture and then turns down a black corridor they didn't take to get here. Above them, the heavy thump of boots occasionally echoes like distant war drums. Still they walk on.

Cobwebs hang like tattered drapery, and the detritus of decades of neglect hampers their footfalls. They pass by lightless openings, inky voids to hidden places, where the cold and heavy fug of mildew reaches out for them in the narrow darkness, damp and cloying. Jimmy suppresses a cough.

Another. Still he leads them by weak light through a shadowy world haunted by the angry drums of somewhere above.

Eventually, a rusty metal door. Jimmy works at the heavy lock with the key, coaxing it while Tribal holds the dying light. He unlocks it with an audible click and pulls it slowly open.

It is raining—just a light, late afternoon drizzle as they emerge into the humid air on the south side of the building, squinting painfully in the sudden flood of daylight of late afternoon. The weeds are so tall that they cannot, at first, even tell where they are. Five crumbling concrete steps lead from the forgotten door up to ground level; for now, they crowd the narrow space between the concrete retaining walls on each side of the stairs—Jimmy is on the top step, craning his neck to see over the wild grass and golden rod.

"Let's fuckin' go!" Tribal says. "What's the hold up?"

"Better to leave unobserved," Jimmy answers. "And we should shut that door, too."

Tribal sneers. "Why bother?"

But something behind them has changed—as if the oily smell of the furnace room has followed them like a restless spirit. Or that the building can suddenly breathe. Then a trickle of black smoke creeps out under the top of the steel door frame, the vanguard for the billowing madness that follows.

"For that," Jimmy says, pointing at the smoke, "if nothing else."

Simon spins around, nearly knocking Scotty over. "Shit! What about Norman?"

But Jimmy has already found the remnants of a path hidden by the weeds. "Who do you think lit that fire?" he says. Then he slips into the tangled grass.

It doesn't take long. Heavy smoke leaks out of the condemned building, first as tendrils and then as immense and terrifying columns. Flames soon follow. They lick at the outside walls above the frames of smashed in windows, as if tasting the wet bricks that sheath the building. Then they combine, climbing up from one floor to the next, fierce dry heat accompanied by sharp crackling and a profound roaring hiss.

The far side of the building burns the fastest, although fire finds its way across the structure and toys now with the side they're on. Despite the danger, Jimmy cautions them to keep low and move slowly. They cross the narrow stretch of tall weeds and enter an equally weed-choked automotive graveyard.

Sirens, still distant, fill the late afternoon air; the street itself is still eerily quiet.

"Let's split up," Jimmy suggests. "And maybe lay low for a bit." Then he and Tribal slide between the rusted-out hull of a pickup truck and something that might once have been a Cadillac and disappear.

Simon looks at Alise, and she gives him a sad and weary smile. Between them, they guide Scotty carefully toward Melvin Avenue. He cooperates, walking along between them, but they must physically move him out of the path of things—as if he were also blind.

By the time they reach Simon's car, Faulman Glen Road has been consumed by madness. Sirens, lights, choking smoke, police barricades, onlookers. It was a circuitous route, though: east on Melvin and then north on the next through street to reach Barton. They deposit Scotty in the back seat.

"You okay?" Simon asks Alise as they edge out into traffic.

"Tired," she says. "You?"

"Don't know—can't think about it yet."

They drive in silence for a while, weaving through the grid toward downtown. After a while, Alise laughs, a short and constrained laughter punctuated by nervous exhaustion.

"What?" Simon asks.

"Your day job sucks," she says. "Next 'Bring All Your Friends to Work Day,' count me out, eh?"

Simon smiles, too spent to laugh, and puts a grateful hand on her thigh. "Probably sleep pretty good tonight, though, eh?"

Alise closes her weary eyes. "You kidding? It's Saturday. I got a *gig* tonight, Nine-To-Five."

29

THEIR CLANDESTINE SOJOURN MAKES the front page of Sunday's paper. Or, at least, the consequences do. According to the journalist who authored the article, the fire ranks as one of the most sensational in the city's history. It is duly added to the list:

The MacInnes Warehouse fire at Main Street East and John, 1878, which killed three men and sent flaming shingles swirling over downtown like a swarm of vengeful djinn.

The Lister Block fire on James Street North, 1923, which consumed the sprawling and ornate four-storey structure in the early hours of a February morning so cold that water froze as it was sprayed on the conflagration. All that remained of the building in the weak light of dawn was an ice-coated shell.

The Moose Hall Dance fire of 1944, which killed ten, injured forty-seven, and left twelve children orphaned. An arsonist set the city's deadliest fire to date under the only set of stairs in the modest two-storey lodge building, forcing the seventy survivors to leap from the upper windows to the pavement below.

The Wentworth Arms Hotel on Main East and Hughson, Christmas day of 1976, started by a madman who threw a lit match into a Christmas tree—the fire raged through the hotel, sending its one hundred occupants fleeing. Six weren't fast enough.

And the fire that utterly consumed a condemned building on Faulman Glen Road, formerly known as the Fischer Heights Apartments. August 22, 1987.

Cause: undetermined.

Casualties: undetermined.

For the time being, at least.

"Our investigation," the fire marshal told the paper, "is already underway. We'll get to the bottom of this. There's no point in offering speculation at this juncture."

The article also reports that witnesses caught glimpses of small groups or individuals fleeing the site, but they were the types of people who slipped quickly into the circuitry. The types of people who would rather not be found. And, to be fair, these reports were gleaned from the types of witnesses who were close-mouthed by nature anyway, barely on the radar themselves.

AT AN EARLY MORNING diner, Alise works through a second mug of coffee. She sits in the booth by herself, numb to the dawn. She cannot eat—not yet, anyway. The toast she ate last night before the gig didn't stay down, and her performance on stage was wooden. Detached. Only Joanie, the guitarist, was openly angry about it. Alise knows the others were disappointed, too, though.

"They'll blame it on Simon," she mumbles to herself. "Say I'm losing focus."

But in a way it is true.

She leaves a handful of coins on the table, including one of the new gold-coloured loonies. She doesn't like them—replacing every paper dollar bill in circulation with an oversized quarter threatens her perspective on value. Paper, after all, has importance. Substance. Change just collects in jars and in the bottom of gig bags, or in the couch. Hers is a world in which a few dollars still mean something—they are hard-won. And there's a dignity to them that can't be replicated by a small clumsy heap of coins dumped on a counter, to be sorted meticulously in front of vendors and waitresses and cashiers. It's infantile.

But Alise recognizes this reverie for what it is: a pointless and shallow escape.

"Enough," she says fiercely, under her breath. "You were there, that's all. You didn't do anything wrong. None of us did."

An older man in a nearby booth overhears the sound but not the substance. To him, it seems that the pink-haired girl in studs and leather and shredded up denim is angry at the serviette dispenser on the table. Or maybe at the sugar. Intimidated, he looks away before she catches him staring.

Alise closes her eyes for a moment, breathes deeply, and exhales. Then, with that stony-eyed and defiant stare of her generation, she sets out into the cool dawn air.

"HEY! ABOUT TIME YOU got up. It's almost noon."

Simon's mother is about six dozen cookies into her contribution to some event or other; often, all that remains of these baking marathons is the lingering smell of the sugar and vanilla and chocolate he never sees. Or not often, anyway. He reaches absently for a cookie.

"You're gonna throw my count off!"

"I'm sure the bake sale can manage without this," he says. Thankfully, there's still some coffee in the pot.

"Your shoes stink of gas or something. I threw them out on the porch."

"Oh," Simon nods, sitting down at the small table. "Sorry. Hey, have you seen my necklace?" He noticed it was missing when he woke up. So far, he's fended off the fear that it is not just lost but Lost, but there are only so many possibilities.

"No, I haven't. Just retrace your steps," she says, and Simon smiles bitterly to himself. "Or maybe you lost it when you were sleeping."

"That must be it."

She worries over the arrangement of cookies on the metal cooling rack. Then she checks on the next batch, scrutinizing it through the small window. Frowning, she opens the oven door a crack for about twenty seconds, then closes it again.

"This damned oven," she mumbles.

"Just turn it down if it's too hot."

"No way! Gotta run it hot and regulate like this or nothing bakes even."

Simon looks at the ancient electric oven. Its burners sit on rings of rust and the dials are mismatched, a hand-me-down relic from an old aunt.

"Sure could use a new one," he says absently.

"Yeah. I'm sure that reparation cheque will be coming soon, though."

"Gotta be," he adds. "Only been, what, two hundred years since the first land theft?"

"Two hundred years exact this past February. More like a mugging."

It's a weary game, but dry and humourless cynicism is sometimes better than dwelling on the twin mountains of frustration and rage that cast their six-mile-long shadows over everything. Especially, Simon's mother maintains, when baking.

"You gonna tell me what's wrong?" she says suddenly.

Simon looks back at the oven. "No," he says. "It's nothing anyone can really help me with."

She waits, arms crossed, watching him with those intense dark eyes. He reads the concern and the love and the loss that smoulder in their depths—a mother's look in a place where mothers are the keepers of so much.

Simon sighs and relents. Partially, anyway—about yesterday he can say nothing. "You know that client of mine, the mute one?" he begins.

"Yeah—the older one who's twenty."

"That's him. Scotty. He's probably got until October, maybe November if I really drag my feet. Then he's homeless. He doesn't even know."

His mother nods solemnly. "Thought it was about a girl."

"That's a whole other issue. Two years, Ma. Two years and I'm drowning already at this job. I can't save him."

"Is it your job to save him?" she asks.

"Dunno. I'm not sure *what* my job is anymore."

She slips an oven mitt on and opens the door to retrieve the sheet of cookies. They're perfect, like everything else she bakes.

HE HAS NOT SLEPT. His weary eyes, age-old and haggard in that young face, drift across the park. Practiced eyes—wise gaze honed by a thousand nights under streetlamps, watching.

The sun is right. Or right enough, it is hard to be certain. He has seen this done, but only from a distance as a casual observer. Quickly, he makes his way to the statue of Queen Victoria.

It is harder than he thought it would be, matching shadow to shadow, but there is the latent gift of street prophecy buried in the very skull he frets and fidgets with until it is matched to that of the imperious figure above him. Head's shadow concealed within hers.

He listens, concentrating.

Nothing.

He frowns, disconcerted, but not for long. It is just a matter of time. Everything is. Instead, he steps back, reaches under his weatherworn poncho, and retrieves the old flashlight that was handed to him yesterday.

Reverently, he places it down in the shadow of the statue's head.

Then he walks away without looking back.

"WHAT THE FUCK, TRIBAL—YOU kick the shit out of a gas pump yesterday? Your Docs are fuckin' ripe!"

Sirius delivers this astute observation from the street-salvaged wreckage that serves as a couch in their tiny attic apartment, an illegal fourth-storey walk-up above a vintage clothing shop and a couple floors of sketchy low-rent rooms.

"Where were you, anyways?" he adds.

"Just out with Jimmy," Tribal says.

"Doin' fuckin' what?"

"Nothing much. Now, you gonna help me steal cable from the asshole downstairs, or just sit there and ask stupid questions?"

"We don't got a TV, brother."

"We don't got a TV *yet*."

Sirius gets up. "Oh yeah. Good point. What you got in mind?"

Tribal gives him a toothy grin.

How did I get here?

Scotty can't remember, sitting up suddenly in his dirty little bedroom, fully clothed. Even his shoes are still on his feet. It is dark, but that is to be expected: there is no window and the door is closed. A crack of light seeps in under the door, though, allowing him to make out familiar shapes—a mound of dirty laundry, a lopsided old dresser he's never really used.

His nose wrinkles. *That smell! What is it?*

It lingers, a vapourous presence that hovers above and around the familiar stale fug of unwashed clothing and old sweat—smells he associates with safety, with security.

His shoes, he realizes. The canvas has soaked up something evil-smelling, like paint thinner but heavier, dragging it in here like another ghost. Scotty takes his shoes off and carries them out toward the slider. But he's never really opened it before, and he doesn't feel like it now, either. Instead, he drops them by the balcony door and goes into his little kitchen.

Spider waits in his tiny bowl patiently, passively, indifferent it seems to everything. Scotty looks at the clock—it is a touch after noon, which surprises him because he never sleeps late.

And then yesterday rushes back upon him, a crushing black wave, and his legs give way. Wide eyed and ragged limbed, he slides down the door jamb onto the peeling linoleum, hitting the floor with a muffled thump. Scotty looks around desperately—into the thin shadows of his gloomy apartment kitchen, down the short corridor into the thicker darkness of his bedroom—and fights for breath in sharp rapid gasps.

Where are you? Where? But there is nothing but silence from the empty apartment. He is utterly alone. Numbers elude him; there will be no counting to catch his breath this time. His breathing becomes ragged, shallow.

I need—I need you! Where? Where? Where— Wh—

A burst of bright lights flash across his dimming vision. His ears roar.

He slips into darkness.

Scotty dreams.

He dreams that he is under warm water, submerged completely. Beside him floats Spider. They are friends—they play tag, and they laugh fishlaughs together. Spider swims off to hide, another game, but Scotty can't find him. The more he looks, the harder it is to float; the deeper he sinks, the lonelier he feels. It is a sad dream now.

When his eyes flutter open, they are blurry with tears. He blinks the moisture away, focusing on the plethora of crumbs and dust and webs that have collected along the bottom of the kitchen cabinets. His cheek is stuck to the grungy linoleum; as he lifts his head, the floor releases his skin reluctantly.

Scotty struggles out of his curled-up position on the floor, rising unsteadily. The clock says it is after four; panic seizes him and he turns quickly to check on Spider, but the fish still floats indifferently in his bowl, seemingly unconcerned that Scotty hasn't fed him yet. Scotty drops the designated number of pellets into the water and watches as Spider casually gobbles them up, one at a time.

Then, an idea.

He looks over at the roll of light gauge chicken wire. *I have enough*, he decides. *One more. Just one more thing to make.*

A KNOCK—ALISE'S. SHE OPENS the door herself before Scotty can get up from his table, though, remembering that they hadn't locked it yesterday. She's carrying a pizza box, and within seconds the pleasant aroma of hot cardboard and cheese fills the room.

"It's after seven, and I'll bet you haven't eaten a thing today," she says.

And she's right, Scotty suddenly realizing just how hungry he is. Alise puts the pizza down on the work table, balancing it carefully on top of the sharp scraps of wire, pliers, paper, jars, and cans that perpetually live there. Then she walks over to the slider.

Scotty falls to without ceremony—the pizza is still hot, a rarity in his small world of leftovers and visitors' scrap ends, and it is whole. She bought it just for him, he realizes. By his fifth slice, however, frugality resurfaces. Saving the rest would be wise.

"Your shoes, too," Alise says from the far side of the room. "All that old fuel down there. Hey, do you have another pair of shoes?" Not that she's expecting a response, but he can't wear canvas sneakers that reek of heating oil—at least, not to where she means to take him.

Alise watches dusk's slow descent through the window. Behind her, she hears Scotty working at cramming the pizza box into the undersized fridge, and she smiles.

"Hold up," she says, joining him. "You don't need the whole box in there." She throws the remaining pieces on the only plate Scotty owns and slides it on a shelf. Then she puts the box on the narrow counter that divides the kitchenette from the living room. "Hey," she says, looking around. "Where's your beta?"

Scotty looks in the direction of his bedroom, and then down at the floor.

"Oh, you moved it." Then she looks up at the clock, considers the walk ahead of them, and frowns. "No other shoes, eh?"

Scotty spots a tiny brown ant weaving its way across the linoleum. *No.*

"Look, we gotta head out, you and me. Remember when I said I could sneak you into the AGH? The Art Gallery? That's happening tonight."

He hesitates, as if thinking about it. Then he disappears into the darkness of his bedroom, only to re-emerge a moment later with an old, threadbare backpack slung over his shoulder.

Alise smiles. "Shouldn't take more than fifteen minutes to walk there. We'll stop at my place first, though—I got some shoes that'll fit you. Let's go."

The shoes that Alise scrounged up for him feel strange on his feet. Why she would have a used pair of men's high tops in her apartment eludes Scotty altogether, and he feels the awkward weight of the mystery wrapped strangely around each ankle.

Like I'm walking as someone else, he muses, *and I can't remember where I've been*. As if memories collect like dead leaves below old trees and he now walks through an unfamiliar forest, having never witnessed the fall. *But at least she's here to show me where to go.* It's a small comfort.

It is a warm and dry Sunday night, and Scotty notices that the air smells almost clean. Gone is the redolent stench of exhaust, the clashing scents of different foods as they waft out of storefronts or dance about the occasional street vendor's cart. Only once on their walk down King Street do the clingy, fierce tendrils of a summer dumpster reach out for them, but they pass by at a brisk pace. Alise walks with purpose; Scotty walks just to keep up.

Before long, Alise cuts across King's five lanes of one-way traffic, and Scotty must follow. The street is all but deserted: there are a few cars behind them, but they are blocks away still. They reach the south side of the street and then slow down, walking now at a more casual pace.

She stops at the corner of Summers Lane, a dark and narrow alley that runs between the Hamilton Convention Centre and the AGH. After a momentary pause, they slip into the darkness and walk another five or six metres before stopping again. Halfway down the lane is the entrance to the underground parking garage, but they don't approach it on foot. Instead, Alise leans indolently against the brick wall, gesturing for Scotty to do the same.

A moment later, a dark box van rounds the corner. It slows down to a crawl as it passes them; Alise reaches out, pulls the latch on the side door to the cargo bay, and ushers Scotty inside. She jumps in behind him and pulls the door shut.

"You sure about this?" Alise says to the back of the driver's head. It is blunt and cropped and set upon heavy shoulders.

"You paid me to get you in. I'll get you in," he says in a gruff, slow voice.

"And *out* again, remember?" Alise says.

The head nods slowly. "I know."

Scotty leans up against the metal wall of the van, which is as uncomfortable as the ridged floor. It smells of old rubber and stale potato chips and something else. *Vinegar*, he ventures, but that isn't it. *Sweaty clothes*—that's another smell. There's a gym bag near the back doors.

The van passes through the gate and begins its descent, a slow circular drop into the city's bowels. The driver stops in front of a pair of empty squad cars. There are more of the same parked farther down this dim level.

"Are you fucking *kidding* me?" Alise snarls. "Are we below the goddamn cop-shop or something?"

"It's safe," the driver says. "Empty, I mean. This is sub-level three. It's where the RCMP and cops park their cars."

"Are there cameras?" she asks.

"No. Well, yeah, but they ain't manned right now."

"How do you know that?"

The bull-headed driver shrugs his bulky shoulders. "Budget cuts. They only stick someone in the monitor room half the time." Then he points to an elevator. "That's the service elevator to the AGH. Take it up to ground level. I'll use my key so you can get in."

"I'm staying here," Alise says. "I wanna make sure Scotty gets out the same way he got in."

The driver shrugs again. "Whatever you want. You got a four-hour window. After that, I gotta leave." Then he turns around to look at Alise meaningfully. "With or without the kid."

"Four hours. You hear that, Scotty?"

But Scotty is already opening the door of the van, slinging his bulky pack onto his shoulder. Alise jumps out with him.

"Look for an art show that isn't finished yet. Lots of stuff everywhere. There's a big wooden crate—it's skinny and vertical. Standing up tall, you know? Your cardboard is in there."

Scotty stops in front of the elevator door and stares at the wall just in front of his feet.

"Four hours, Scotty—then get back here."

Scotty slips through the shadowy spaces of the museum, drifting from giant room to giant room like a phantom. He finds the gallery with the half-finished installation, boxes and packing material and crates everywhere. Only one crate stands up the way Alise described, tall enough for Scotty to walk into without ducking. In the back, tucked in behind large painted canvas panels, are his cardboard signs.

He doesn't know how or why they are here, but these things are irrelevant. Alise said they would be there, and that's enough for him.

The floor space is immense, even with the packing materials and half-finished art of others cluttering up the space. *I'll do it right here*, he decides. *I only have a night to do this.*

Alone, Scotty works at a frenetic pace, as if unsure of how long a night actually is. As if "night" means something different, depending upon where you are. Or on who you are.

First, the cardboard. He spreads out the myriad signs harvested from a hundred desperate corners, a hundred lonely islands. There is no real order to how he arranges them on the floor of the gallery—he lets Chance govern most of his choices, and aesthetics guide the rest.

The signs range from small pieces the size of a shoebox lid to jagged-edged placards. They are mostly made of corrugated cardboard, but some signs are on poster board; a couple are on paper.

Some signs beg for change. Some ask for prayers. Many cry out for work. Or for work and food.

Some few are honest: *I just need a drink*, one claims. Another asks for the same, but adds, *Why lie?*

Others do just that—lie. *Homeless mother of three anything helps*, taken from a girl little more than a child herself who lives in a halfway house. *Just need enough to buy a ticket to Toronto*, says another. Or to Ottawa. Or to wherever. Bus station vagrants, all of them.

Some are simple. *Help me*, says one. *Please*, says another.

Most invoke a deity—there are few, if any, atheists among that tribe. Officially, anyway. *God bless*, they say, a contemporary manifestation of the most ancient and sacred of invocations, for to the gods of older worlds, beggars and wanderers were sacred. But it is more of a threat than anything else: a more fortunate man's chance to give a few coins or a bit of bread to ward off the Evil Eye.

Scotty arranges them all into ragged rows, a mosaic that almost fills the open space of the gallery floor—

Will work 4 food
escaped domestic violence need help
please ANYTHING helps
Give
Hungry Childern we Live on this cornr!
Even a smile helps
i am not invisible. why do you act like i am?
Help me stop doing this
Be Blessed
Ill bet you 1$ youread this sign
Homeless Grateful for any Help
No Home No Food No Hope
Clean and Sobre. Just need food or work
its not 4 me its 4 my dog
lost apartment in a fire We have nothing!
Please Please Please Need Diapers For My Baby
Hate to walk in the rain? Try sleeping in it
I surrendered my kids to save them from
homelessness
I'm a person like you! Help me
Down on my luck any help is Welcome
No family. Mental illness. Please help
Stranded! Need $$$ for ticket Home!

Please help me I have nothing Pray for me
dying of hunger, God bless
All I got is faith. You can't eat faith
We live in a car Please help us
Homeless and a shamed
adicted no famly suport plese help me
1 day it could b u
This wasn't what I wanted to be when I grew up

Among many others, all bleak. Variations of desperation, loss, despair.

When everything is finally arranged, Scotty pads carefully to the centre with a tattered black plastic bag. The same bag that the old man placed in his hands yesterday, although it seems so long ago, that dreamlike under-world of loss.

And redemption.

Gently, he unwraps the object within—a child's picture, weathered and old, secured to a piece of cardboard. The twine Cottonmouth used to hang it around his neck is now gone; Scotty picked away at the stubborn knots in the van.

He places it carefully on the floor at the centre of the collage, worrying at the edges until satisfied with its position. Then he returns to the edge of the assemblage to retrieve his frayed backpack.

Scotty only has a dozen wire figures left, small fetal people with their strange cargoes, small black objects enclosed by metal tendrils: an acorn or a drawer knob or a stone. Or a cassette wheel. Or a marble. He has well over a hundred found objects, though, every one of them painted as black as shadow. There are the fifteen or twenty walnuts Alise brought him upon her return, the same day she gave him Spider; a handful of glass marbles, their scintillating cores concealed below the blackness; several nuts wrested loose from stubborn bolts, a mystery to confound his apartment's maintenance man. Then there are fragments of asphalt and shards of glass; cherry pits and hard candies; a robin's egg; a squirrel's skull. Dozens of discarded and worthless objects, every one of them meticulously painted black.

Scotty places a single item on each cardboard sign, working his way inward despite the difficulty he will have navigating his way out. As each object is placed, he wraps it loosely in cassette tape, unspooling the roll until he reaches the next sign's small anchor, retrieving the next roll when he runs out. One tiny orbit and on to the next one. There is now a pattern, a purpose. He works his meticulous way around the collage in a spiral—a gyre that draws everything toward the centre.

When the small black items are all in place and connected by a continuous thin black line, he moves carefully to the middle of this hermetically abstruse totem. And there, on the nine signs that flank the central picture, he places nine of the wire figures. The remaining three he arranges on the picture itself.

One for the little boy in the red shirt with the crayon smile.

One for the black figure that holds the little boy's hand.

And one for the tall man, gaunt and grey, that Scotty carefully drew on the paper last night. The old man leans down to hold the coal black hand of the child taken from him so many years ago.

And he smiles.

30

CARL ISN'T A BAD guy, just ignorant. Like most of them.

Simon isn't making excuses for Carl, or for any of the others. But it really was the final straw—the last cheap glass bead ever offered, and the first he truly rejected in an official capacity. Fully and completely. But he knows how his mom will react when he tells her: she will take his face in her tired hands and look at him with her tired eyes. And she will smile.

None of this was planned or intentional. But sometimes things just unfold in unexpected ways. "Cosmic clarity," Jimmy would say if he were here right now, sitting with Simon in his car as he drives away from the CAS building on a Monday afternoon.

Maybe, Simon thinks.

Because:

Carl walked up to Simon's desk carrying a pizza box with three files stacked on top of it. "Top one's yours," he said.

"Thanks." Simon took the top folder, looked at the name, and winced.

"Rough one?" Carl asked, not unsympathetically.

Simon nodded. "Same thing over and over with this kid."

"It happens—can't save 'em all, eh?"

Carl had seven or eight years on Simon, and burn-out was setting in. That was Frank's confidential opinion, anyway. Carl set the pizza box down on the cluttered table of paperwork behind Simon's desk. Simon sighed; this would lead to the same tired conversation Carl had been initiating ever since Simon arrived.

"You want a slice?" Carl asked.

"Maybe in a bit, thanks."

But Carl was already drifting through the bulletin board clippings Simon had pinned above his desk, a collection of articles on First Nations land claim politics, from dull legal documents to sensationalist journalism. He pointed to a long, horizontal picture at the top of the cork board depicting a tree shape flanked on each side by a rectangle and then a square.

"That's your tattoo!" he said.

"Yeah."

"What is it?" Carl asked.

"Symbol of the five nations of the original Confederacy—the Haudenosaunee."

Carl nodded, as if sagely agreeing with its meaning. Then he changed topics—or so Simon thought, at first.

"Sorry to hear about your mute—whatshisname?"

"Scotty."

"Right. Heard he's not gonna make the next cut for extension." Carl looked again at the bulletin board. "Is he, you know, one of your people or something?"

Simon tensed, an all-too-familiar feeling. "You mean is he Indigenous?"

"Yeah." Then he laughed, embarrassed. "I never know what to say—Indian or Native Americans or First Nations or whatever."

"Must be real tough."

"Well," Carl said with a familiar pat on Simon's shoulder, "you people don't exactly make it easy! I figured that's why you've spent so much time on this guy." Then he looked closely at a pair of maps pinned below the picture. One depicted the original territory given to the Six Nations—close to a million acres. The second one depicted the 46,000 acres that remained. "Can I ask you a question?"

"Can't wait."

"Way I see it, you guys got it pretty good—tax breaks and all. Why all the fuss and bother over land claims? There aren't that many of you, ya know?

You guys seem to want half of Ontario!" Then Carl laughs. "Not really, but *you* know what I mean."

"Can't say I do."

"Oh, *c'mon*, Johnson! You read this morning's paper? See that latest attempt to squeeze money out of the Province? Millions and millions and *millions* of dollars for a chunk of Caledonia or something. It's ancient history. Gotta move on."

Frank's voice suddenly penetrated the general noise of the office. "Carl! You here?"

"Damn it. Hung around too long!" Carl said. "Watch my pizza, will ya, chief?" He winked at Simon and headed off to Frank's office.

He doesn't mean any harm, Simon thought. But inside, something rattled on the cage and sang in the old fierce rhythm of blood. *Chief, chief, chief*, it chanted. Then laughed. Then rattled some more.

Until something shook loose. "Fuck him," Simon muttered. He rose, picked up the pizza, and headed downstairs.

Fifteen minutes later.

"Hey, buddy. Uh, where'd my pizza go?" Carl smirked, prepared for the punchline. Just a hint of annoyance gathered in the corners, though. Eyes and mouth.

Simon was busy taking down the Haudenosaunee picture. A number of the other articles were already stacked on the desk. He looked up innocently. "Huh?"

"My pizza, chief. Where is it?"

"Oh, that. I sold it for you. To the guys downstairs."

Carl cocked his head, looking at Simon like he was barking mad. "Sorry. You did *what*?"

"Sold it. By the slice. I'm gonna keep the money for you, though—you know, in case you're irresponsible with it. Saved you a piece, though!" Simon opened his desk drawer and removed a small triangle just large enough to hold a single circle of pepperoni. He tossed it onto the desk.

Carl's face flushed and went through some curious acrobatics. "Lemme get this straight," he said tightly. "You *sold* my pizza. *And* you're keeping the money."

"Yeah. I mean, it's your money, man. I'm just holding it for you. Hey—eat your pizza before it gets cold."

Carl picked up the pathetic fragment, stood for a moment more, then stormed out. He returned with Frank in tow a minute later.

"What's going on?" Frank asked, clearly perplexed.

Simon stacked the last of his articles, maps on top. Then he looked at Frank.

"Carl here had a question about my 'people' and our land claims. I answered it as best I could."

"How is giving my pizza away answering a question?" Carl barked.

"Calm down," Frank said. "I'm sure it's just a misunderstanding."

Simon neatened the stack, noting Frank's growing expression of concern as he took in the blank bulletin board.

"Here's how it works," Simon explained. "That pizza *was* yours, but you offered it to me."

"*One slice!*"

"Well, sure—but I figured that was open to interpretation. The point is, I sold the slices for you. Got the money right here." Simon pats his back pocket.

"Hand it over!" Carl snapped.

"Not so fast—I gotta spend some time thinking about how to get this money to you. I mean, I saved you a piece. You should be grateful."

Carl began to sputter. Frank intervened as smoothly as circumstances allowed.

"Simon, I'm not sure what this is all about, but maybe this joke has gone on long enough. Okay?"

"Yeah . . ." Simon sighed. "You're right there. This joke *has* gone on long enough."

"I don't understand," Frank said.

"If Carl were Indigenous and that pizza of his was, like, a million acres large, *he'd* get it. I let him keep a bit."

"This is fucking ridiculous!" Carl shouted.

"Correct," Simon agreed. "Welcome to the three-ring shit show that is the world of Indian personal land claim settlements." Then he looked hard at the two white men. "I mean, just look how pissed off Carl is—and it's just a fucking *pizza*."

Frank watched as Simon picked up the stack of clippings. "Simon, look—"

"You've been a great mentor, Frank. I appreciate everything you've taught me. But it's time I started giving back to my own community."

"But—"

"Frank, I quit." Simon smiled fondly at the older man. "There's an opening in our own Child and Family Services. It's time." And then he began the trek toward the stairs.

"What about my *money*?" Carl yelled after him.

"Don't worry, asshole," Simon shouted back amicably over his shoulder. "I'll send it to you. Honest Injun!"

He pulls into his mother's driveway and turns off the ignition. *Cosmic clarity*, he thinks again, smiling sadly. Hurting Frank didn't feel right, but what's done is done. He gets out of the car and passes the ramshackle shed—weathered plywood with a roof of rotten planks held together mostly by tar paper and heavy plastic staple gunned in place. He peers inside.

His father's old motorcycle is there, carefully tarped, as are other remnants of that lost life: a pile of sagging boards that was going to be a fence for the garden; an ancient Davis Commando lawn mower missing its blade; mason jars filled with a plethora of rusting nails, nuts, screws, bolts, and washers of every size and description. Junk, really. Except for maybe the bike. Simon's mother has no use for any of it; Simon himself stands in the crooked opening once in a while to take in the cloying smells of rotten wood and rust, damp dirt and old oil. Mice have built nests in the corners and an owl lived in there for two years. Then a stray farm cat. This slowly collapsing structure is all Simon has left of his father, and it calms him to stand in its presence.

After a while, he climbs the three old steps to their front door. The ranch-style home is humble, but as well-kept and clean as the shed is neglected. The front garden that runs the length of the house bursts with peas and potato plants. Simon thinks of the commune gardens under the Skyway and smiles.

And then he stops, hand suddenly frozen in the space between him and the door knob—an idea takes root, a possible solution to a problem. *Maybe*, Simon thinks. *Worth a try—it's all I got.* Then he puts the thought aside for now, and goes inside.

Simon's mother sits at the small kitchen table cutting fabric into triangles. Piles organized by colour occupy much of the table's surface, while the scraps gather quietly at her feet. A quilt pattern hangs on the door of the ancient fridge, held in place by two magnets. She looks up at her son and smiles.

"Wasn't expecting you home until later. It's only 2:30 p.m.! Got nothing made to eat yet." Then, weary eyes still sharp, her smile fades. "Simon, what's wrong?"

"Nothing," he says. "And everything. I hurt a good man's feelings today."

"That's not nothing," she says, putting down the scissors. "Tell me."

"It's okay, Ma—it was a necessity." Simon lets out a breath, releasing in him something long held in check. He feels it now, the skeleton dance within. It is not Simon Ten-Bones, a white man's frivolous invention, but something older. Much, much older. Simon's long straight hair is a black echo of his mother's own long straight hair—greying in the powerful shades of iron, of storm scud. He catches the dark eyes of the woman before him. She is beautiful in her solitude; he never realized just how much strength her solitude must require. Necessity.

Simon pulls out the second of three chairs and sits down in front of her. "I quit today. I'm gonna apply for that opening here at home."

His mother watches him, holding his gaze for a long time. Then she reaches across the table to take his face in her hands. She smiles. Her joy is contained deep in those wise, tired eyes, her own skeleton dancing far within. Happily—fully and completely.

"It's about time," she says.

SIMON REACHES THE REBECCA Street apartment after sunset, weary from a busy afternoon.

Alise paces the lobby—Simon sees her as he approaches the apartment building's glass doors. Already he knows it's something bad, her body language that of a lonely Norn with news. He raps on the window instead of digging his key out of his pocket.

"What's wrong?" he asks as she opens the door.

"I didn't know if you were coming over or not tonight. Couldn't wait upstairs."

"Alise, what happened?"

The elevator opens and an elderly man escorts his wife out and across the lobby. The old man is better than his wife at disguising his disdain for Alise's hair and ink and attire, but not by much. Alise doesn't notice, waiting for them to exit the building.

"Fuckin' cops came around today. They wanna talk to Scotty."

Simon staggers, as if he'd just stepped onto a lurching deck. "What?! Did they say why?"

"Nope. They're cops."

"And where's Scotty? Is he okay?"

Alise gives Simon an evil grin. "He's in my apartment. Been hiding there all day."

"Someone must have seen him on Saturday. Us, too. This ain't good."

The elevator opens again and they both look up a little too quickly. The car is empty, though, so they close the distance and get in.

"No one saw us Saturday. Or no one who cares, anyway."

Simon takes a breath. "Alright—then why the cops' sudden interest in Scotty?"

Alise holds up a finger for silence as the elevator reaches the third floor. Together, they walk to Alise's apartment and go inside. Scotty is nowhere to be seen.

"He's in the bedroom," Alise explains. "Been sitting on the floor for hours."

Simon shakes his head, walking over to the bedroom door. Alise is right: Scotty looks like a bony little scarecrow that fell off his pole and doesn't quite know what to do next.

"Hey," Simon starts. "Don't worry, Scotty—Alise and I will sort this out. Sit tight."

But he might as well be talking to the dresser.

Back out in the living room, Alise waits on the couch with two bottles of beer. Simon sits down beside her.

"How're you doing?" he says. "Sorry for not asking earlier, but you're the toughest of the three of us."

Alise smiles grimly. "Lucky me. I'm fine—I don't faze easy."

"So, wanna start from the beginning?"

"Sure," she says, taking a sip from her bottle. "You might not be totally cool with this, though."

"I still want to know," he says simply.

"Alright. Cops showed up at the AGH this morning because someone kinda broke in last night and left a big installation piece on one of the gallery floors."

"Installation piece?" he asks flatly.

"Lot of cardboard signs and a bunch of wire fish. Some other stuff, too."

Simon takes a swig, shifts on the couch. "So . . . lemme get this straight: Scotty broke into the AGH with a pile of art and went rogue all over the floor?"

"Yeah. Well, approximately."

"Why do I feel that you're leaving out a crucial part of this story?"

"Probably because I kinda made the arrangements?" she offers.

"That's probably it."

Alise gives Simon a suspicious sideways glance. "You're way more calm than I expected you to be, eh?"

Simon shrugs. *None of this will matter tomorrow*, he thinks. Then, "Hey, what did he make?"

"Dunno, didn't see it. There are lots of pictures taken, though. They'll pop up eventually. And some of the artists showing right now don't want it touched at all! They claim it's now part of the show. Others think it's there to ridicule them—one asshole called it 'Vandalism *Chic*' but probably because his own art is utter shite."

"I take it you know some people down there besides Ms. Emily Steiger."

"Well, I—"

"The cops, Alise. Where do they come in?"

"The cops," Alise repeats, as if focusing, and she takes another drink. "So, a friend told me this morning that the cops had already put a couple things together and figured out that the fish and Scotty have been seen together quite a bit this summer. I went upstairs, grabbed Scotty, and brought him down here."

"Wait—I'm confused. Did the cops come to your door? Is that where you talked to them?"

"Fuck, no!" Alise scoffs. "I waited outside Scotty's apartment as if I was looking for him, too. They had the super with them and they made him key the door, no fucking warrant, eh? I told them he was usually down at one of the parks at that time of day. They asked how I knew him and all that shit, but I was pretty vague. The super was cool—he didn't say a thing."

Simon finishes his beer. "That was quick thinking, waiting up there."

"Thanks."

"Let's go."

Alise looks at him. "Go where?"

"Scotty's. Help me pack him up. I'm moving him out of here tonight."

They don't turn on the light, instead using memory and habit to see them through Scotty's minefield of a front room. It doesn't work well, though.

"Ow! Fuck."

"You okay?" Simon asks.

"Walked into the table."

Simon pauses. "He might want some stuff from in here. You don't have a lighter, do you?"

Alise sighs. "No—kinda weird that neither one of us smokes, eh?" Then she turns on the light, stopping Simon before he can object. "He made art, not a bomb threat. Trust me—the Hammer-pigs haven't set up observation posts and bugged the place."

Simon submits to this wisdom and begins to gather Scotty's tools—pliers, wire cutters, a wrench, a collection of screw drivers. But most of what remains on the table are scraps of wire and broken pieces of cassettes. He surveys the rest of the room.

"Where's the fish? The real one, I mean?" he asks.

"In his bedroom, I think. That's where he looked when I asked yesterday."

They each grab an empty garbage bag from the pile of plastic that has begun to accumulate in the corner—the newest obsession—and head toward the bedroom.

Simon pushes the door open and Alise gropes around for the light. In the darkness of the little room, the heavy reek of dirty laundry and unwashed sheets wafts over them like a murky wind.

"Holy shit," Alise gags. "I don't think we're gonna find clean clothes in here, eh?"

"He needs clothes anyway. You find that light?"

"Yeah—got it," she says. The single bare bulb on the ceiling flickers reluctantly into a weak yellowish glow. Clothes lie in stinking piles on the bare floor, or heap up around his all-but-empty lopsided dresser with its missing bottom drawer. *Like pathetic suppliants around a Salvation Army Ark*, Simon thinks. If that Ark were reserved for silverfish and earwigs, that is.

But on top of the dresser is an old cassette tape recorder. It's missing its pause button and the cassette window is scratched up so badly that it is opaque. Sitting on top of the speaker panel is a small neat stack of cassettes.

Curious, Simon takes a closer look. The top cassette has a label: "Jmee." The one below it is labeled "alees." Then "simN." Beside the dresser, almost completely buried by dirty clothes, is a milk crate containing the gutted remains of dozens of cassettes. They lie in disembowelled heaps, cracked open or pried apart, tangles of tape spilling out and downward.

"Hey," Simon calls softly, "look at this."

"This first," she answers.

Alise stands by the narrow bed, blankets pulled down to expose one last creation: a large wire sculpture, crudely man-shaped and curled into a fetal ball. Enclosed within its head is the fishbowl, the beta floating silently within like an unspoken thought. Or a secret. Or a dream. Dangling in the hollow where the heart would be is a wire fish. It is stuffed to bursting with a multitude of tiny black objects.

"I'll get the wire cutters," she says quietly, handing Simon her empty garbage bag, "and save the fish. Grab some clothes for him and let's fuckin' split, eh?"

"Yeah," he says absently.

He pockets the three cassettes and then rummages for salvageable clothes.

Simon shoves the two bags of clothes and the crate of odds and ends in the trunk of his car. He pauses before slamming the trunk closed, though, surveying the meagre collection.

"It's not much for twenty years, is it?"

"Huh?" Alise says.

"His whole life fits in half the trunk of my car."

"Oh," she nods. "Guess it does."

But Alise doesn't seem as moved by the thought; he closes the trunk and heads back across the dark parking lot toward the apartment building.

"Hey," she says, walking up beside him. "You never said where you were taking Scotty."

"I know. But it's better if I don't—it's safe, though, and he'll fit in."

And although he shouldn't, Simon finds it strange that Alise drops it altogether. Instead, she slips her arm into his, her other arm cradling the fishbowl, and they walk back together in silence.

31

WHEN THEY RETURN TO Alise's apartment, Scotty is no longer tucked away in the back room; he sits on the floor in front of the stack stereo, cleaning the tape heads of the double deck with a Q-tip. A bottle of rubbing alcohol is tucked in the hollow made by his crossed legs. He doesn't so much as flinch when they walk in, so intent is he on his task.

His movements are measured, deliberate—just another one of the enigmatic mute's obscure rituals, hunched over and flanked by the two heavy floor speakers. From each metre-high cabinet emanates a serpentine hiss, then the hint of a click and silence, then a hiss. Scotty's thin fingers know this rite well.

Like this, man, Vince's kind and patient voice coming back to him after all this time. Scotty hears it, gentle words slipping out as if by accident from the mouth perpetually between the headphones in an East End makeshift basement studio. Scotty's eyes mist over and even the memory of sugary kitchen smells that lived with them in that little house return to him, Donna's footfalls above the basement keeping a reassuring rhythm as she paced between oven and counter on the days she was home. "Like this," Vince's hands gliding effortlessly over the tape deck. "Rewind and fast-forward for the tape head, play for the pinch roller and capstan. Swab it with even pressure. Now you try."

Scotty alternates between fast-forward and rewind, running the swab evenly over the tape head. Then, with a new Q-tip, he swabs the rollers that flank the little silver mound.

"Get rid of the wrinkles," he said next. "Wrinkles wreck the reel." I remember. Scotty picks up one of Alise's old cassettes that he'd set aside and coaxes out a long loop of tape with a clean Q-tip, inspecting the thin brown-black surface carefully. Satisfied, he rolls the tape back into the cassette with the nubby remains of a dull pencil. Then he punctures the old pieces of scotch tape that cover the tab holes so that it can't be recorded over.

Insert into the deck. Rewind to the beginning. Fast-forward to the end. Rewind to the beginning. Smooth it out by even tension. Press play.

"G'day!" says a distant voice in a thick Australian accent. "Sorry, Alise—didn't much feel up to writing, so I recorded this for you. 'Ope you don't mind, but I couldn't find a blank—recorded over part of this Big Audio Dynamite cassette, for which you are fucking welcome! Now, about this gig the weekend after next . . ."

Scotty presses the stop button.

"I thought that tape was ruined," Alise whispers.

"The drummer?" Simon asks.

Alise nods. Then she leans down and hugs Scotty around his chest from behind, whispering something in his ear. Scotty becomes rigid, alert, as if listening to far-off thunder or for the return of someone long overdue. She releases him and retreats to her bedroom without another word, closing the door behind her.

Simon sighs. "C'mon, Scotty. We have one last trip to make. It's time, man—it's time you had a real home."

But before they leave, Simon quietly places the cassette labelled "alees" on top of the stereo.

ONE LAST RIDE—NOT TO Group, but off the grid altogether.

It is a little after 10:00 p.m. when Simon and Scotty pull up to the gate. There are no streetlights—just whatever reaches this forgotten corner of the city from the Skyway Bridge. But it is also cloudless, and the pavement is like pale parchment in the moonlight.

Beside the gate, Doug waits in the near-dark.

Simon fetches Scotty's things from the trunk and carries them over. "You sure about this?" He asks.

Doug nods. "I talked to the others. We're sure."

"I can't come back to get him."

"You don't need to. Cain takes care of its own."

Simon nods and walks back to the car, opening the passenger door.

"This is it, Scotty," he says, smiling sadly. "I can't help you anymore. They took away everything. But I want you to meet someone—or maybe I'm just reacquainting you with someone you knew a long time ago. Doug. You remember?"

Scotty sits stone-still, old backpack clutched in his thin fists. For all of the tension in that grip, his face is calm, passive. He stares at the glove compartment as if able to discern the contents through clairvoyance.

"Doug," Simon tries again. "He was your first worker. When you were little. He was . . ." But his voice trails off, surrendering to the silence. At this moment, Scotty is as alien to him as he's ever been, drifting in that incomprehensible world of his, a thousand light years from this one.

Simon sighs. His body begins to feel heavy and exhaustion creeps up the back of his neck and into his head, settling behind his eyes. He laughs then—dry and humourless.

"I don't know if I've ever helped you. If not, I'm sorry, man."

Scotty's hands loosen their grip and he looks down at the bag in his lap. Slowly, he unlatches it and pulls it open. The top of his mother's urn emerges briefly, surfacing as if out of black waters before sinking under again. Other things are there as well, but Simon merely hears the sounds they make shifting around as Scotty searches inside.

Finally, his hand re-emerges holding a delicately wrought wire fish sculpture. It is small, no longer than the length of Scotty's forearm, but it is so meticulously rendered that Simon is taken aback by its graceful beauty. Within, hanging from something invisible in the weak light of the car's interior light, is a tiny wire person containing a flat wooden disc.

His lost turtle pendant.

"How—where did—"

But Scotty points slowly, deliberately, to the car's tape deck.

Then he gets out and walks toward Doug.

Simon digs around his back seat until he finds an empty case, and then carefully stows Jimmy's cassette inside. He will give it to him when they cross paths. But he's halfway back to Alise's before he slips the cassette Scotty made for him into the car's tape deck.

At first, there is nothing, just static. And then.

Words.

Scotty's voice? His actual voice? Is it?

He wants it to be, wills it, in fact—but Scotty is an artist of considerable talents; the sentences are spliced together, fragmented shards meticulously arranged. And *familiar*—the speaker's intonation, inflections, tone—Simon hears that haunting closeness even though some of the words are constructed of more than one word.

Then it hits him.

The words are his own—recorded secretly over the span of lonely months to be restructured, reordered, repurposed.

The message is not long:

S | I'M | ON | THANK YOU | FOR | EVER | Y | THING | YOU | V | DONE

| YOU | ARM | I | FRIEND | I TR | EYE | D | TO | HELL| P | YOU | TOO | I

WISH I | WAS | N | T | THIS | WAY | ONE | DAY I | W | LL S | PEAK | I |

W | LL | FIND | YOU A | ND | S | PEAK | I | W | LL | FIND | YOU A | ND |

S | AY | S | I'M | ON | YOU | AR . . .

There is a pause.

Then a voice that is *not* Simon's whispers gently, carefully:

". . . m-my friend."

Acknowledgements

I'LL START WITH SOMETHING (stereo)typically Canadian—some pree-mptive apologies.

First, to Arliss Skye and Kathleen Philpot Lazar, the pair to whom I owe the greatest debt of gratitude and who will likely be, for better or for worse, my strongest critics. Both work in the frustrating and severely under-appreciated world of social services, and both were kind enough to agree to interviews so that I could (I hope) more precisely represent the severe impediments that stand between theory and practice.

I reached out to Arliss Skye on the recommendation of the Elected Council of the Six Nations. As the Social Services Director for the Six Nations of the Grand River Territory, she was the perfect contact for a white author attempting to accurately depict the sort of conflicts—both personal and professional—that Simon, a young Mohawk social worker, might face. And although I had the best of intentions, that doesn't exclude me from making unintentionally insensitive mistakes along the way; any misrepresentations or offences are entirely the fault of the author. That said, I encourage you to visit the Six Nations website and read "A Global Solution;" it's a candid account of a litany of past and present injustices that, for the most part, fall on deaf—or indifferent—ears. Arliss, thank you for guiding me to that document; it was eye-opening, to say the least.

Kathleen is a friend from the old days who became a social worker, fos-tering high-risk youths who were in and out of homes, school, and jail; she also oversaw the creation of Hamilton's very first youth shelter. With Kathleen's guidance, I did my best to create a plausible past and present for

Scotty, a victim of circumstance suffering from both undiagnosed Selective Mutism and a horrific past. If I fell a bit short, I apologize.

On the lighter side, I suppose I should also apologize to all the owners of 826 to 850 Beach Boulevard in Hamilton. I removed your homes, put in a pair of nameless roads, and turned your properties into a hippie compound. Please help yourself to anything in the garden. It's imaginary, of course, but you can't have everything. I did, however, add a fair bit of rainfall to August of 1987; in reality, it was a miserably hot and dry month—I remember, because I spent it working in the yard of a (now extinct) concrete block factory in Burlington.

I also took some liberties with the East End by connecting Melvin Ave to Barton with the fictitious Faulman Glen Road, named after Glen Faulman, a.k.a. the "Hamilton Kid." This means, of course, that a few actual businesses got erased. Take that, East End—I flattened buildings and replaced them with a street named after the Hammer's premier punk! No apologies for you. In fact, you should go down to This Ain't Hollywood on James St. North and thank Glen in person for the honour.

NEXT, SOME ACKNOWLEDGEMENTS.

I've mentioned Kathleen and Arliss already, but again: thank you both. I am grateful to my beautiful wife Darcy for her honest feedback and genuinely amazing ability to manage my various creative neuroses. And to Sandra Kasturi, cruel mistress of editing and the cause of my various creative neuroses. To Drew Forsberg for working so hard to get a passable picture of my ugly mug (and my Crash Landing shirt); to Gabriela Gavala for providing the Romanian dialogue; to Erik Mohr and Made by Emblem for the cover art, Errick Nunnally for layout, and Leigh Teetzel for proofing/copyediting; also, many thanks to those back home who support my efforts—especially Donna Stechey (unofficial publicist); Deborah Serravalle (fellow Hamiltonian author, much classier than Yours Truly); Jamie Tennant (fellow Hamiltonian author, not classier than Yours Truly); Lou Molinaro and Glen "The Hamilton Kid" Faulman (of This Ain't Hollywood fame); Crash and Sue (of Crash Landing Music); Craig, Leah, Rufus, and the punks of Hammer City Records; and—of course—Jay MacDonald (the Hammer's spirit animal, whether you know it or not).

Many thanks also to Liz Hand, Jim Morrow, Lauren B. Davis, and the one-and-only Johnny Blitz who kindly took time out of their busy lives to read this thing and write some (overly) kind words. Liz's Generation Loss transformed how I write, Jim's mentorship is why I write, Lauren's generosity was like a seithkona's blessing from afar, and Johnny . . . well, what can I say? Getting a nod of approval from the drummer of the Dead Boys is, for this aging punk author, beyond words. Also, my deepest gratitude to Johnny's wife, Teresa Blitz: your kind words and selfless support in the final weeks of this process—for a complete stranger, no less—embody everything I love about punk culture. Much love to the five of you.

As for beta readers, I asked all the right people at all the wrong times. A few, however, actually managed to find the time to offer some serious critical feedback. My thanks (again) to Darcy, who caught some early flaws and probably saved Sandra much undue frustration; to poet and former punk band manager Dave Surette for not only offering to beta read in the eleventh hour, but for coming up with one of the better fictitious band names in this book—Fur Hammer; and to Sophia Magri, a brutally honest critic who also happens to be (A) one of my students and (B) the most badass punk girl poet I know under twenty—you want intelligent and meaningful feedback on something you wrote? She's your girl.

I would be remiss if I didn't say a few words about the spring of 2019, when I received one of the greatest honours of my life: The Letdowns, a heavy-hitting punk band, launched an album named after my first novel, What We Salvage.

The launch happened at This Ain't Hollywood, a CBGB-style venue in the heart of Hamilton, Ontario—the steel city, affectionately nicknamed "The Hammer," that the great (and sorely missed) Gord Downie once called the best Canadian city for playing live music. In the humble opinion of Yours Truly, nowhere is this more evident than in the punk scene that congregates in the dark recesses of the Hammer's most iconic rock bar. The Letdowns played on a stage that has seen its fair share of punk greats: Simply Saucer, The Forgotten Rebels, Cockney Rejects, The Strike, the infamous Lydia Lunch of Teenage Jesus and the Jerks, The Dead Kennedys' Jello Biafra, Teenage Head, Glen Matlock of the Sex Pistols, The Dik Van Dykes, The BFGs, Richie Ramone, Pantychrist . . . to name just a few.

Seriously, the album launch was the highlight of my year. As a former guitarist in a hard-working but long-forgotten punk band myself, what greater compliment could I possibly get? The Letdowns are true sons of the Hammer, and this boot culture refugee is forever grateful. Love you guys.

Finally, I suppose I should thank my mom, Donna Baillie, for providing me with a useful childhood nightmare—the Furnace Boy. That's right, folks: my own mother invented a terrifying spirit and then set it loose on her children. In her defence, she was a young mother of four little boys with hardly any help on the parenting front because our father's work schedule was ridiculous. Running that three-ring shit show from inside the monkey cage required help, and the Furnace Boy was there to make sure we left the basement playroom when we were told, rattling away in the air ducts or slinking stealthily through the shadows to steal the toys we didn't put away. . . . Necessity—the Mother of Invention.

Or, in this case, Mother—the inventor of necessity.

About the author

DAVID BAILLIE WAS BORN, raised, and educated in Hamilton, Ontario. He played in a couple of hardworking but (alas) long-forgotten punk bands before immigrating to the States to teach modern and postmodern literature at a down-to-earth, urban New England college prep school. He also sneaks in as much punk history as he can into anything he teaches. His first novel, *What We Salvage*, was a Hamilton Literary Awards finalist; like *Little Bones*, it draws upon Baillie's own experiences in the boot-culture scene of the late '80s. He currently lives in central Massachusetts with his artist/educator wife, Darcy, and a menagerie of children, dogs, and other assorted pets.